'A finely honed story which proves the thriller genre is alive . . . Can't wait for the next one'

Sunday Times

'Great action'

Amazon reader

'Phelan gets the balance absolutely right . . . An absolute must-read for fans of Clancy, Ludlum et al.'

Bookseller & Publisher

'Like all good thrillers . . . Phelan keeps the reader guessing right up to the last page'

The Age

'Phelan's techno-thriller is in the same league as Clive Cussler and Tom Clancy'

Sun-Herald

'A good and enthralling read'

Amazon reader

ALSO BY JAMES PHELAN

The Jed Walker books

The Spy

The Hunted

Kill Switch

Dark Heart

The Lachlan Fox books

Fox Hunt

Patriot Act

Blood Oil

Liquid Gold

Red Ice

The Alone series

Chasers

Survivor

Quarantine

JAMES PHELAN

THE AGENCY

CONSTABLE

CONSTABLE

First published in Australia and New Zealand in 2018 by Hachette Australia,
an imprint of Hachette Australia Pty Limited

First published in Great Britain in 2018 by Constable

This paperback edition published in 2018 by Constable

1 3 5 7 9 10 8 6 4 2

A CIP catalogue record for this book
is available from the British Library.

ISBN: 978-1-47212-723-5

Typeset in Simoncini Garamond by Bookhouse, Sydney
Printed and bound in Great Britain by CPI Group (UK), Croydon CRO 4YY

Papers used by Constable are from well-managed forests
and other responsible sources.

Constable
An imprint of
Little, Brown Book Group
Carmelite House
50 Victoria Embankment
London EC4Y 0DZ

An Hachette UK Company
www.hachette.co.uk

www.littlebrown.co.uk

For Nicole Wallace, for joining me in looking outward, together, in the same direction.

THE AGENCY

PROLOGUE

'You make a mistake, you will die.'

Walker didn't take it personally.

'You miss your target, you will die.'

The instructor was just doing her job.

'You get a jam, you will die.'

Three weeks together and he could tell she was good at her job.

'You get distracted, you will die.'

And she was quite attractive.

'You listening, Walker?'

'Yes, ma'am,' he replied.

'Good,' she said, then looked up and down the line of seven recruits. 'Because you've been trying to finish first and only first, for three weeks – you think I didn't notice? You're the only Air Force out here, with these Army and Navy and Marine vets, the best they had to offer. Me included. And you know what they say about Air Force?'

'No, ma'am,' Walker replied.

'Me either. No-one gives a damn about the Air Force, so why talk about them?'

The six other recruits sniggered.

'Run the op again,' she said, looking to the staffers to confirm the training scenario had been reset. 'This time I want that building

cleared and the objectives completed in under two minutes. *Two minutes.* You hear me, recruits?'

'Ma'am, yes, ma'am!' the seven replied as one.

She gave a signal to the kill-house training officer, and he blew a whistle. They had a minute to prep.

Welcome to The Point, Walker thought. It was the CIA's hands-on training facility, formally known as Harvey Point Defense Testing Activity Facility, a sprawling North Carolina campus owned by the Department of Defense. It was where the country's top front-line operators from all branches of the military and intelligence agencies were sent to hone their field skills. The place was meant to test and train the best of the best: Top Gun for door-kickers.

He rushed the house. They had already assaulted it twice, and had failed miserably both times. Seven going into a double-storey building up against an unknown number of hostiles to subdue, an unknown number of friendlies to protect and get out, and three marked objects to retrieve – last time it had been a briefcase, a laptop and a thumb-drive, the latter hidden in a stitched-in seam inside a bad guy's jacket, which they had failed to find. Six men and one woman going in and, like Walker, all were military. All practised at this kind of thing. All well trained. But this was different. This was designed to break recruits, to be near-on impossible, so that things in the field paled in comparison. Classic special-operations training.

However, this was even beyond special operations, at least as the DoD knew it; these new recruits had already been through the best the nation had out in the field: two Navy SEALs, two from Delta, a Force Recon Marine, an Army Ranger – and in Walker's case, an officer from the 24th Tactical Squadron, the Air Force's boots on the ground to Joint Special Operations Command.

Walker shadowed an ex-Army Delta Force guy named Clive Gowan, moving quickly to the rear of the complex. The other five were breaching the front doors and windows. They had their choice of silenced 9-millimetre weapons, and most, including Walker, were using

an MP5 sub-machine gun. Good and accurate in close quarters. His secondary was a hip-holstered H&K USP 9-millimetre. The weapons fired blanks, and all wore laser tags. The flash-bang grenades and door-breaching charges were real, albeit dialled down. The people in the building were real too. Playing roles. Like the seven assaulters, they wore protective eye and ear coverings. Like the assaulting force, they didn't want to lose.

The whistle blew, twice. Go time. Two minutes on the clock.

Clive tried the handle of the rear door – nothing made an operator feel more stupid than kicking in a door that wasn't even locked.

Click.

It was unlocked. He opened it a thin crack, then used the back of his combat knife to slide from the ground up in that slim opening. Gently. He paused, about a foot from the ground, and shook his head. Walker closed the door. There was a trip wire, which in a real-life scenario might be connected to an explosive charge. In this case a smoke grenade, to signify an explosive charge.

Walker pointed to the window. Clive nodded, tried it, and it slid open. Safety glass, in case it smashed. Gym mats were positioned below each window, on the off chance someone fell through. The course was designed to break recruits, not maim them. Walker covered the Delta guy as he shimmied through, then saw the all-clear signal, and it was his turn. Clive was typical Delta: small and wiry, 180 pounds wet. Walker was taller and heavier, and didn't land with the same kind of grace as his fellow recruit.

A figure emerged in front of them, coming around the doorway to what was set up as a small kitchen. Clive shot him with his silenced MP5. And got shot in the process. Exact timing, couldn't do it again. Both were out of the game, and sat on the floor. Clive looked pissed. The instructor looked pleased, which told Walker that he'd done his job, and that meant that there were at least six hostiles still in here, each of whom had been tasked to take out a recruit.

He stepped around the instructor, then paused. He bent down, saw the lit-up area on the guy's shoulder where Clive had zapped him twice.

Walker whispered, 'That kill you straightaway?'

'Huh?' the instructor said.

'I guess not,' Walker replied, and he ditched his MP5, pulled his sidearm and then hefted the instructor to his feet. He pressed the end of his pistol's suppressor under the guy's chin, pinning him against the wall. 'Ever had a blank fired close-up against your skin?'

'You're mad.' The guy was an old Army sergeant. Green Beret. Walker liked him, and wouldn't shoot, but he wanted the intel, and he kept the pressure on the pistol.

'We fail this run, we're out,' Walker said. 'How bad do you think I want this?'

The instructor was silent.

'Imagine I'm now doing something especially nasty to you, to get the intel,' Walker said. 'Play along. Use your imagination.'

The instructor's eyes searched Walker's. He sensed something harder, and said, 'Upstairs, south-east room. Two captives. Three pieces of intel, all on the person in charge.'

'Number of hostiles?'

'You're on the clock,' the instructor said. 'Tick-tock.'

Walker lowered his silenced pistol, took a pace out the door.

'Asshole,' the instructor said.

Walker shot him in the torso, twice. The guy was lit up all over. Clive's laugh was drowned out by the loud boom as the front door was breached.

Twenty-one seconds down.

Walker was already moving up the stairs, and motioned for the two SEALs to follow him, and for two other recruits to clear the downstairs rooms while the remaining operator took up a cover position. As he ascended he led with his pistol in a two-handed grip.

He sighted and double-tapped the first two targets that emerged at the top of the stairs. Imprudent move on their part – they should have waited for someone to rush up. But they probably figured the boom from downstairs was the first entry into the house and they would be in position faster than the attackers. Fine by Walker.

Three targets down. At least three remaining. Thirty-six seconds in.

Walker paused at the hallway and provided cover, motioning to his colleagues to head onwards. He felt a pat on his shoulder, and watched as the two SEALs went past. They were competent operators, Walker thought, as they moved warily but quickly towards the northern end of the house, where four rooms branched off the hallway.

At the top of the stairs, Walker turned right, heading to the southern end. He didn't bother to check the south-west door. Instead he kicked in the door to the south-east room and rolled through the open doorway. Immediately he saw two captives seated on a bed, and a guy with a gun covering them. Walker sprang up and forward, rushed him, and as the trainer brought the gun to bear, Walker crash-tackled him, hard.

His college football coach would have been proud of the impact. He hit with his right shoulder, just under his opponent's ribs, and kept his force going onwards and up. He hefted the instructor off his feet, and kept going until they smashed out the window, the safety glass shattering into a million little pieces. The drop was twelve feet. Walker didn't want to get busted out for maiming a trainer, so he twisted as they fell, breaking the guy's fall with his own body as they landed on the gym mat. The downside was, 200 pounds of man crashed onto him, and Walker was winded and sore – but not regretful.

'Prick,' the trainer said, getting to his feet.

Walker stayed on his back and shot him, three times.

Forty-six seconds in.

Ten seconds later, the whistle blew.

Under a minute. A new record.

Walker stayed on his back. The other six recruits shuffled over. The SEALs had extracted the two captives.

'He's got the intel on him,' Walker called out, pointing to the instructor he'd taken out the window. His cohort patted the guy down and quickly found it all – documents, a thumb-drive, photos.

The chief instructor stood over Walker, smiled, then held out her hand and helped him to his feet.

'Welcome,' she said, 'to the CIA.'

FRIDAY 26 AUGUST

1

Three weeks later, Walker was one of five who completed the training.

Clive, from Delta.

Jim and Hank, the SEALs.

Sally, the Marine.

Two Army guys flunked out. Scott suffered a broken back after slipping in a helo insertion in the first week and was in Walter Reed learning to walk again. The other, Brad, was booted for disciplinary reasons following an enhanced-interrogation simulation after the final clearance op. Brad had been the interrogator. Walker had been on the receiving end and had almost been drowned by excessive waterboarding before the exercise was called off. When freed of his shackles, Walker laid Brad out on the floor. The last they saw of him he was being stretchered back to base, and later that day, all his stuff was gone. Walker wondered if the Army would take a guy like that back. Probably. With the wars in Iraq and Afghanistan at full tilt, they needed all the hardened nutcases they could get. They'd probably give the guy a promotion.

Now, the five freshest graduates of the CIA's Special Activities Division sat in a bar. It was more a wind-down than a celebration. They'd been at such a high operational tempo that just sitting around and talking shit over a few drinks was the good medicine they needed. There wasn't much choice, and the place they settled on was a long

cinder-block rectangle with a corrugated-iron roof and no windows. Agricultural looking, but more likely repurposed from some kind of auto-repair workshop due to its proximity to Route 17, which carved through this part of North Carolina. Plenty of military types around, because it was that kind of bar, and it was just enough miles from Harvey Point and Norfolk Naval Shipyard for patrons not to worry about muscle-bound MPs crashing the party.

Walker and his cohort sat on battered timber stools that creaked and moaned with every movement, a table between them. No doubt the proprietor had learned the hard way that sturdy bar furniture made from steel tubing made all the better for bar fights. An ice-filled bucket of Bud Lights condensed between them, along with a heaped pile of buffalo wing bones devoured by the two SEALs. It was like genocide for chickens, Clive had quipped. Cheeseburgers did the rounds at the three- and six-hour marks. A recycled five-gallon oil can full of peanuts was half-gone, the shells by their feet. Good times.

They had been there since noon, residing in quiet reflection and simple banter. Taking stock. They had been through a tough grind, and they needed the change of pace. Classic rock played from a CD-stacker jukebox. Laughter and arguments came and went from the far reaches of the bar. They made small talk and watched via a television above the bar the White Sox win 5–3 over the Mariners. Walker had made ten bucks from one of the SEALs on the result. Around six pm the place started to fill up and conversation became hard to hear, the bare concrete floor and walls bouncing the sound around, but that was fine with Walker. They'd taken it in turns to flick through *USA Today* and the *New York Times*. They watched exhibition football, where Cincinnati Bengals did a good job of dismantling the Washington Redskins, and at half-time they had the barman switch it over to CNN's rolling updates on the war in Iraq. The ticker reported that the Iraqis were protesting as a new US fire base had flattened an area of historic significance from Mesopotamian times.

'Ungrateful is what them Iraqis are,' Jim said. 'They better pay us back in oil contracts for liberating them.'

'Reckon we'll ever find the supposed WMDs?' Sally asked.

'Who cares,' Hank said. 'They've got oil. We own it now.'

'WMDs are there,' Jim said, looking over his beer to Sally. 'Saddam had chemical and biological, that's a fact.'

'A known known,' Clive said with a grin.

'Probably buried in a sand dune someplace,' Jim said, sweeping a pile of empty peanut shells to the floor.

Sally said, 'I heard Saddam moved all his WMDs to Syria.'

'Then we should roll on into Syria next,' Hank said.

'You don't think we've got enough to deal with?' Sally suggested.

'Maybe the lady's right,' Jim said. 'Maybe we should pack up and move home. Mid East be damned. Leave them to fight it out on their own.'

'*Lady*?' Sally said. 'Want me to break off your arms and shove them up your boyfriend's hot wing–tinged butthole?'

Jim grinned and hoisted his half-drunk beer as a kind of capitulation and apology. Sally clinked it with her bottle.

'Respect,' Jim said.

Clive shrugged and drained his beer, then went back to the bar to reload their bucket of Buds.

'What say you, Air Force?' Jim asked Walker.

Walker was silent. The news ticker said something about a storm warning for Florida and Louisiana. He thought back to his friends who were serving. The fact was, he'd had little choice but to move across to the CIA, in order to remain in the fight. The Air Force had just made him a Lieutenant Colonel, and they wanted him back home, at a desk, to help drive things. But that wasn't Walker's style. Not now, with two wars in full swing. Not ever.

'Right,' Jim said, looking back around the bar. 'Man, I need to get laid.'

Sally said, 'You couldn't get laid if it was the end of the world and you looked like Brad Pitt, and Hank looked like Angelina.'

'Hardy-ha,' Jim said.

Clive returned. 'Get them while they're fresh.'

'As fresh as Bud Lights can get,' Sally said, flicking the top off a bottle and necking it.

'Five-oh,' Jim said, motioning to the entry of the bar.

Walker turned and saw a couple of uniformed MPs on the scene. Army. A sergeant and a major. Not there for a friendly drink. Senior men doing serious business. They were scanning the room. Only a couple of groups of patrons were in uniform – a gang of Army Rangers playing pool, and a bunch of Navy enlisted celebrating a bachelor party. The sergeant's eyes settled on Walker, then he spoke to the major, who looked Walker's way, and then they headed over.

'I think they've got a hard-on for you, Walker,' Clive said.

'Maybe *he's* gonna get laid tonight,' Jim added.

'Spit-roast for Air Force,' Sally said.

The four of them laughed. Technically they were all still in the military, for insurance and legal purposes, until mustered out of training at The Point and sworn in as CIA operatives. And that meant Walker was the senior officer. But the respect that came with rank had meant little at Harvey Point, and even less in this bar.

'Lieutenant Colonel Walker,' the major said, and snapped off a crisp salute as he and the sergeant took position a couple of paces away.

'At ease,' Walker said.

'Message, sir, outside please,' the major said.

Walker finished his beer, left a few twenties on the table for his colleagues – he was the ranking officer among them, and some things never changed.

'And here,' he said, passing ten bucks to Hank. 'You need Jim's money more than I do. It should be enough to get you a blow job from one of those Navy guys.'

He left the four to drink and laugh as he followed the MPs out. It was good to be outside, in the fresh air and away from the din.

There was a Crown Vic sedan parked on the kerb, unmarked but with the MP radio whip antennas on the boot and domed light on the dash that signalled it as a police car.

'What's the message, Major?' Walker asked.

The two MPs turned around, and the major pointed to the car park over Walker's left shoulder.

There were around forty cars and trucks in the parking lot between the dark bar and a brightly lit Chili's and Cracker Barrel further down that fed off the highway. Four tall lamps threw down shafts of yellow vapour light. Lots of shadows, no movement. It took a moment for Walker's eyes to find him. A man in a dark suit and shirt leaning against a dull black pick-up. His arms crossed. A bright orange flare of a cigarette at his lips. Waiting.

2

Walker slowed as he neared the man in the suit. *The smoking man*, they'd called him at training. He would show up each week, always standing at a distance, observing, often with a smoke in his mouth. Sally had joked he was working for the FBI's X-Files. Up close, Walker could see he was the other side of fifty. A well-worn face, like he'd spent decades working outdoors in a sun-drenched environment, and the lines had created permanent crags in his skin, like a topographical map of the Grand Canyon. His dark hair was a couple of inches longer than military regulation, thinned with age and worry. His posture was slightly stooped, like the weight of the world beat him down year on year. Slight and compact, maybe five-seven or five-eight to Walker's six-three, 170 pounds to Walker's 240. Despite the appearance, there was a restless energy about him – his eyes were jittery with ideas and things that needed to be done. Dressed in a suit that looked a size too big for him. A black or charcoal shirt under that, crinkled with wear, unbuttoned at the neck. The same or similar outfit Walker had seen him in seven times now.

'Walker,' the smoking man said, standing free of his car and extending a hand. 'Rob Richter.'

His handshake was firm, his hand hard and calloused. Richter was clearly no office man.

'I get the feeling you know all about me,' Walker said.

'Yep,' Richter replied. 'You've heard my name before?'

'No.'

He nodded. 'That means I'm good at my job – and others are good at theirs.'

To Walker's ear, Richter's accent was Arkansas. A southern boy doing good by his nation.

'That's the CIA for you, right?' Walker said.

'Yeah, well . . .' Richter looked around and tossed his cigarette butt, then immediately reached into his inside jacket pocket and shook another Camel free from a soft pack. He lit up, and as he pocketed the fancy Zippo lighter, Walker saw the butt of a polymer automatic in a concealed shoulder holster. Walker knew that the CIA didn't arm their staff on US soil, but maybe the smoking man was openly carrying a weapon across all states in some kind of second-amendment middle finger to rules imposed on his government agency. Or it could have been out of paranoia. Maybe the spook had been on one too many ops overseas, and thought the Russians were still on his case. Walker didn't blame him. Far from it. He knew from experience that special-ops forces the world over opted to always have a good weapon at hand, even at home. They slept better, lived better. And longer.

'Let's go for a drive,' Richter said.

Walker checked over his shoulder – the MPs were in their car and drove off with a spin of the back tyres on the blacktop. Not their tyres – the DoD probably had a schedule to change them out every year, worn out or not, every set on every MP vehicle, so why not drive it like you stole it. He glanced at the bar and figured his Point cohorts wouldn't be getting a cab back to base until the early hours of the morning. Tomorrow was a day off, then they were all scheduled to fly home on Sunday and await further orders from Langley, which could take up to two weeks. Walker had put in a preference for assignments in the Mid East, Afghanistan and Europe, in that order. He'd seen plenty enough of the Mid East, but he didn't much expect to be assigned any place else for the foreseeable future. *Welcome to the age of the War on Terror. Us and them.*

'Where we headed?' Walker asked.

'That depends on how our next conversation goes.' Richter climbed into his side of the truck and Walker headed around the hood and slid onto the passenger seat. The windows were open. August in North Carolina, a clear but humid night. Walker wore a T-shirt, a plain grey undershirt that came with his mountain camouflage fatigues for Afghanistan, with black jeans and pull-on boots. The relentless PT sessions over the past six weeks had made it hard for him to tie laces because of the ache and lactic acid in his bulging muscles, which had gained ten pounds of bulk. He couldn't have either of the SEALs beat him in the bench press or bicep curls. Inside the truck smelled new, and as Richter started the engine, a big V8 thrum, Walker noticed the rental tag on the key fob.

Richter was an Agency man, probably from Langley, Walker guessed. He would have rented the vehicle from the airport at Chesapeake, or he might have driven straight down – a four-hour trip. Walker wasn't surprised that the CIA didn't have a fleet of cars waiting for their staff in every major city – this was no longer the military life, far from it, and he would have to learn to make do with the limited resources that came with the change. The Agency threw big money at overseas resources and assets, literally bags containing millions of dollars to foreign agents and foreign government officials, but Walker had learned that for the intel officers who were out there recruiting and putting their lives on the line, it was a tight ship. Gone for Walker were the Pentagon's billions of dollars worth of toys and equipment.

'So . . .' Richter said as he drove, hanging onto the 'o' for quite a while. 'You did well at The Point.'

'Where'd you hear that?'

'Birdie. Little one. Told me so.'

'I thought they said from the get-go that they weren't marking us.'

'They don't,' Richter said. 'But they do write reports, like you wouldn't believe. They watch and listen to you at every turn, from the sleeping quarters to the mess hall. Not just your tests and training,

but your interaction with others. You know they've even got cameras in the bathrooms?'

'Spies, right?'

They drove in silence for four miles north-east along Route 17, *away* from Harvey Point. Trucks laboured on the road. Cars and vans rattled along. No urgency. No bombs going off, no snipers on high, no hidden IEDs. America, but not as Walker had seen it for close on seven years of continuous overseas deployment.

'What kind of intelligence officer do you see yourself as?' Richter said eventually.

'One who gets to live on at the end of the day, while making some kind of difference, would be a nice concept,' Walker said. 'That still a thing?'

'Show me that person, and I'll believe you. They've gone the way of the dinosaurs, those fine men. And they were mainly men, coming home from fighting Nazis. Don't build 'em like that anymore.' Silence fell for a few moments before Richter continued. 'You and the others who just graduated? It'll be the Directorate of Operations; or the Special Activities Division. But it's not so special. But then you know that, right? The chances are you'll be back out there, with the spec-ops teams, kicking down doors in Baghdad, just like you've been doing for the past seven-odd years.'

'I know that.'

'Well, I represent another element of intelligence officers. A far smaller group. Extra-selective. Interested?'

Walker looked across at him. 'And what would that be?'

'Agent provocateur.'

'Sounds like women's undergarments.'

'Do your job well, you'll get to take plenty of those off. I'm not saying that chicks go wild for spies, because no-one's going to know what you really do. But seduction of assets is a tool at your disposal, and you're going to have to use it.'

'Use my tool, got it.'

'Hmph. Funny guy, Walker.' Richter glanced across at him. 'How much have you had to drink?'

'Too much for this recruitment spiel,' Walker replied, looking ahead.

'You let your guard down, even for a second, you can get killed out there.'

'I know that.'

'Yet you drank all afternoon.'

Walker was silent.

'What are you thinking over there, Walker?' Richter glanced across at him.

'Your comment about using the tools at my disposal,' Walker replied. 'I'm married, so I guess I'll figure another way to get information out of foreign targets.'

'Right. Married. To Eve, back in Texas,' Richter took a long drag on his cigarette, blew the smoke out a crack in the window and the airconditioning chased it out. 'The two of you have been separated – what'd she say, going on two years now?'

Walker looked across at Richter. It was a statement, not a question. No-one knew that they were separated. No-one but he and Eve. *Had Richter spoken to her personally? Or had it come up via a higher security clearance coming his way?*

'I'm gonna tell you what a guy told me when I was a newbie like you,' Richter said. 'You want to stay alive out there, what matters most is how well you walk through the fire. You think you can walk through fire, Walker?'

'I can try.'

'Damned well you'll try. You'll get your turn, hot shot. Take a look in that bag, Walker,' Richter said, motioning to the small black duffel in the footwell between them. 'Go on. It's your future. And it starts tonight.'

3

Inside the bag were two sets of clothes, all black and grey and dark blue. Not new, worn in. All looked like they'd been taken from someone's closet, or were good finds in the 99-cent store. Inconspicuous in any crowd. A plastic bag with basic toiletries, all name brands you could purchase anywhere in the world. A well-creased black leather wallet.

'Take a look inside,' Richter said, keeping his eyes on the road ahead. No cars coming their way on the highway. The glow of Norfolk, Chesapeake, Virginia Beach ahead. Wisps of clouds in the night sky, illuminated by distant street lights.

Walker opened the wallet. Inside was a few grand in used bills. Four cards: Social Security, Texas licence, Bank of America credit card, firearm licence. The date of birth on all made the ID exactly a month older than Walker's true age. For ease of remembering. Same thing with the Texas licence, as Walker had spent some of his youth there, where his family went back generations.

The cards were in the name of Tom Archer, and the image on the licence was from Walker's own legitimate licence.

'What's this for?' Walker asked.

'Your first op.'

'Is this a live op, or a final test?' Walker asked.

'Does it matter?' Richter looked at him. 'Working for the CIA, no-one knows what you're doing. Not your friends, not your co-workers

if you're undercover, not your loved ones. Sometimes not even you know what you're really doing. It's a lonely life, but you get used to it.'

'Guess it doesn't matter then, if it's a real op or a test,' Walker said. 'But it'd be handy to know, if an issue comes up and the use of force is required.'

'It is what it is, and you should assume that what we tell you to do must be done at all costs, any which way it plays out,' Richter said, looking back out to the road ahead. 'Look, either way, Walker, your future at the Agency depends on your success. You fail this first op, you're out. You pass this one but fail the next one, you're out. And so on. Got it?'

'Got it.'

Richter shifted upright in his seat, looking around the dark night. 'The CIA doesn't take to failure these days. Too much heat on us. Everyone everywhere in intel and all those in between are responsible nowadays, got it?'

'What was it like before?'

'Pretty much like any other government department,' Richter said. 'Only we got to overthrow governments and kill people. Publicly pinning the decision to go into Iraq on us? That, Walker, has changed *everything*.'

'Find those WMDs in Iraq and all will be rosy though, right?'

'It'll take a hell of a lot more than that,' Richter said. 'Waterboarding. Rendition. Torture. Gitmo. Things will get worse with all the backlash coming our way before they get better for us. But let's talk about you. Your cover ID for Tom Archer? Make up your own legend. Whatever you like, it doesn't matter. What matters is succeeding in your objective.'

'Which is?' Walker asked, holding the wallet in his hands, turning it over and over, feeling the edges and seams, learning it.

Richter shifted in his seat, sat a little straighter. 'What do you know about power?'

'The ability to do something or act in a particular way?' Walker said. 'Power of free speech? What's the context?'

Silence.

'Political power?' Walker said, looking across at Richter. 'The ability to direct or influence the behaviour of others or the course of events?'

'All that and more,' Richter replied. 'You're to head to New Orleans. There you will receive your further instructions. Got it?'

'Yes.'

'Do not blow your cover, not for *any* reason. All your stuff back at The Point, and your ID and phone on your person now, will be bagged and waiting for you on the other side of this mission.'

New Orleans? Hardly the gateway to the Mid East. It smelled like a final test, rather than a live op. *Something on US soil. Maybe heading out of the Gulf to Central America.* Walker went along with it. He nodded. Richter kept his eyes on the road ahead, took the turn-off to the airport.

'Am I working alone?' Walker asked.

'You're always alone, even if you think otherwise,' Richter said.

'Duration of the op?'

'Days, not weeks.'

They drove in silence for a minute, then Richter said, 'I saw in your files that your old man is a friend of Marty Bloom.'

'Yeah,' Walker said, looking across at Richter, seeing nothing telling in the man's expression. 'And?'

'And nothing. I just saw it. Thought it was interesting.'

When Richter didn't continue, Walker said, 'Marty and my dad go back to college days. He's like an uncle to me.'

'You know what he does?'

'I know he works for The Agency,' Walker said, and Richter nodded.

In the new silence that lasted for five miles as they headed north-east, Walker wanted to ask all kinds of questions. *What's this about? What's the end game? What are my rules of engagement? Are there*

adversaries present? What are the stakes? What if I need help? He felt almost inebriated enough to voice all his questions, but he could tell that Richter would stonewall. He'd told Walker where to go, and to succeed.

'You're going to be on your own from here, Walker,' Richter said as he pulled up to the airport drop-off line.

'How do I know when I'm done?'

'You'll know.'

Walker looked at the bag.

'Give me your wallet, phone, watch, anything else you have on you,' Richter said, his hand out. 'Get yourself a hotel. Make contact. Follow the mission through.'

Walker passed them over.

'This location, memorise it,' Richter said, dumping Walker's stuff in an envelope and then passing over a scrap of paper. 'Grab a seat at the bar, and at midnight tonight a man will ask you about the weather. You need to reply that it seems good for this time of year, but that you heard a storm is coming. He'll then say, *The Gulf is clear*. Got it?'

'Weather's good for this time of year, but a storm's coming. Gulf of Mex is clear.'

'*The Gulf is clear.* Simple. A four-word sentence. Got it?'

'Got it,' Walker said as he memorised the bar's name and address. 'Who's the guy?'

'He's the guy who'll tell you what you need to do. And you'll do it, no question, no hesitation. Got that?'

Walker paused, then said, 'Got it.'

Richter took the scrap of paper and shoved the bag across the bench seat. Walker took it, hefted it over his shoulder as he got out of the truck, and then bent down to the car's level, eyeing the senior CIA man.

'You won't see me again,' Richter said, looking ahead, not at Walker. 'Do not fail.'

Walker stood back as the truck tore off. Watching the tail-lights of Richter's pick-up disappear on the north-bound highway, Walker headed into the terminal. He checked his boarding pass. American, economy to New Orleans. Departing in a little over an hour. No time to reconsider. He wondered if Richter had left time to organise a back-up option should Walker have refused the mission. Would he have gone back and picked up one of the other recruits? As he put his bag onto the belt in the security line, there were two people ahead of him. No-one behind. The end of the night shift, the last flights out of the small airport. The beginning of his life in the CIA.

4

Walker slept on the flight. The military had taught him that: sleep when and where you can. Three solid hours, from wheels up to touchdown. It was a small Embraer jet, an aisle separating two seats on one side of the fuselage and a single seat on the other. He was in the latter, a few rows back, over the wing. He would have selected the front, the very first seat, with more leg room right by the door. But sitting there might invite discussion with the cabin-crew member sitting diagonally opposite, or those entering the plane might bump him or step on his toes, which would make for eye contact or small talk. Contact that might be memorable. Walker knew that in the life he was heading into, he needed to be forgettable.

As he walked through the terminal at New Orleans, the small carry-on duffel over his shoulder, he thought of the first time he'd been to New Orleans, with his parents, on a road trip. He was eleven years old, and Hurricane Hugo had chased them from Florida. Then he'd visited again, in what was his favourite time here, with Eve, between his first tours of Iraq. *Find what you love and let it kill you*, his mother used to tell him, when he was a teenager. *Your job is going to kill us, you know that*, Eve had told him on that trip. They'd fought about his work, but they'd made love more than they'd fought, and their relationship had been like that for a few years afterwards.

Outside, Walker checked his new watch, a generic Casio G-Shock. Just over two hours to the meet. He took a cab to the edge of the French Quarter, the drive sticky and uncomfortable, even with the window down and the dilapidated aircon blowing on full. The Gulf was hot this time of the year, and the weather helped turn Louisiana into an open-air lunatic asylum.

What do you know about power?

Not a hotel near the airport. They were full of overnighters, businesspeople there for a night or two or more, the location and cheap hotel bar a convenience. But those places were full of conversation at the bar and over breakfast. Walker walked from the hotel the driver had dropped him at and headed into the next one. It seemed like a dive, but that was fine. He used his Tom Archer ID and credit card to book four nights; he figured he would move tomorrow and keep this as a secondary place. It wasn't his money.

His room smelled like stale smoke, and he opened the windows and turned the airconditioner on. He kept the room dark as he searched for the best hiding place; eventually he settled for the gap between the airconditioning unit and the wall. He took the cash from his wallet, which he pocketed, and then slid the wallet down that gap. It was a snug fit, and even when he turned the overhead light on, he couldn't see it for the shadows down there. You would need a coat hanger to dig it out, and even then you'd have to know where it was by feel alone.

He had over an hour to the meet, and figured it was a ten-minute cab ride this time of night, so he went to the bathroom and splashed cold water on his face, then drank as much water from the faucet as he felt he could take in. That done, he locked up his room, headed outside and hailed a cab.

Grab a seat at the bar, and at midnight tonight a man will ask you about the weather. You need to reply that it seems good for this time of year, but that you heard a storm is coming. He'll then say, The Gulf is clear. *Got it?*

Got it.

Walker had no idea what he was getting into.

•

Richter sat at home in McLean, Virginia, and poured himself a whiskey. Generic brand, for the effect rather than the flavour. He paced his kitchen. Looked at the phones on the granite countertop. Ran a hand through his hair. Drained the liquor and poured another.

Finally, the phone rang. Not his government-supplied secure cell. The burner phone. Pre-paid. Mission specific. No number was displayed.

He drank the whiskey and then put the empty tumbler down as he picked up the phone. 'Yeah?'

The voice said, 'Is it done?'

'Yes,' Richter replied. 'He's on his way.'

The line went dead.

5

Gotta love a town with twenty-four-hour bars, Walker thought as he was dropped off outside The Harbor Grill with less than an hour to his meet. Though why they bothered to put locks on the doors of places that never closed was a question for another day. The place was doing a busy trade. Plenty of people milling about outside smoking, eating and drinking, enjoying the music.

Inside, Walker took a seat at the bar, third from the end. He ordered a large Coke and looked around. It was dimly lit, and sparsely decorated. The main light source was a few lamps above the shelves of bottles to light the work area for the bar staff. There were three people behind the bar, a man and two women. The patron area could fit maybe a hundred people standing and close-in dancing. Right now it was half-full, on a hot August night, in New Orleans. They didn't much look like tourists to Walker, but then he'd spent less time in American bars than overseas ones for the past seven years of military postings. No challenge coin games for him.

He gave a moment's thought to what would have been had he stayed in the Air Force. Best case, he'd have done a brief stint at CENTCOM in the Mid East on the way home. After that he'd have been stuck in the Pentagon, maybe with a posting in Colorado on the way through until he made full Colonel, then, *the desk*. Walker was not one for sitting around shuffling papers or looking at a computer

all day. If not for the CIA, he'd have gone back to Texas and figured out something to successfully ranch on the family farm, which for three generations had been agisted out to neighbours to run livestock. At least back on the farm it was only the rattlesnakes that could kill him. It would make his mother happier, who was the place's sole full-time resident.

'*The secret to a long and happy marriage*,' she'd told him when he announced he was engaged to Eve. '*Living in different states*.' It had been a joke, but there was truth to it, Walker saw that in his mother's eyes.

Walker drank his Coke, listened to the rock music, and felt that there was something quintessentially American about the experience that somehow drew him to the centre of what made the country great. A reminder of what he was fighting for. He should have done more of it. He should have been there more for Eve.

Walker leaned back on his bar stool. Here he was, out of uniform, in a crowded room, and the good guys and the bad guys all looked the same. Walker had trained in this at The Point, but it didn't go far enough. Be aware of people following you – use actions and movement to create angles to see behind you. Look out for anyone who might be on a phone, talking to another follower, watching you, leapfrogging and swapping out. See the same person twice, shame on them. See them three times, shame on you.

Between the music and hubbub the bar was loud. Too loud to properly hear a conversation, unless the person was up close. Walker was onto his second Coke, the biggest glass they had. He felt his body sweating out the beers he'd consumed earlier. The tequila shots had been a bad idea, but then he'd been thinking today was a day of celebration and letting loose after six weeks of hard slog.

A woman bumped into his left elbow, leaned across the bar and shouted an order. She had pale skin visible below and above a short tartan skirt that looked like a kilt, and a loose top that was tied above the waist and showed the curvature of her hips. Walker figured that

she worked here, bussing drinks and jello shots around to customers who preferred to sit and drink and tip a waitress rather than have to use their own steam to get to the bar and order. The barman put a drink on the counter, something resembling a grown-up version of a Shirley Temple, and she passed over ten bucks and waved away the change. She turned to Walker, sipping at the straw. So, not bar staff. She was looking right at him, her big eyes lined with make-up, and he looked away.

She leaned in close, and he could smell her perfume. Familiar. Floral, citrus, sunshine on linen.

'Excuse me,' she said into his ear. 'Mind if I sit here?'

'Free country,' Walker replied, looking forward. He went back to his drink. Glanced at his watch: fifteen minutes. The music changed. Springsteen. The Johnny Cash cover. Somewhere deep in the bar a patron gave a woot. Somewhere else a couple sang along. Walker heard knife and dull and valley and skull. American poetry.

She sat and leaned towards him again. 'Here for work?'

Walker nodded. He had his legend prepared, and figured this would be a good test to hone it, iron out any bugs.

'Drilling,' he replied. 'Health-and-safety inspector. Doing the rounds.'

'Nice,' she replied. 'Travel much?'

Walker tried to place her accent. Nowhere America. Maybe west coast. Generic. He was usually good at placing accents to their respective states. This woman was a cipher.

'Yeah,' he said. 'Too much. You?'

She looked down at her glass, the beads of perspiration running down the sides. Her top lip was wet with it too. The dull light of the bar gave a halo effect to the side profile of her face and neck, as though an artist had drawn an elegant curved line from the top of her head down her nose and chin and along her long neck. Late twenties. Long eyelashes. Thick dark hair; maybe an auburn tint in the right light. No make-up but for her eyes and lips. Her lips made

a pout. She looked across at him. Green eyes. Faint freckles on her nose and cheeks. Naturally blushed.

'Yes. Lots. Sometimes too much.' She glanced behind her.

Walker sipped his Coke. He had a sight line through the bottles behind the bar to a mirror. Not much to see for the dim light, but he would clock anyone close behind him.

'I'm Steph,' she said, putting out a hand.

Walker took the hand in his. It was maybe half the size, but the grip was strong.

'Tom.'

A guy bumped in behind Steph, to the other side, a twenty in his hand. New arrival. Walker saw his eyes in the mirror.

Steph finished her drink and stood, in the space between their two bar stools. She leaned in again, her lips close to Walker's ear. When she spoke her breath was hot. And her accent was changed. Slightly. The inflections, the way the vowels sharpened.

'Restroom, second stall, in the cistern,' she said. 'Something to help you. If you get out of this alive, I'll find you.'

Walker watched her, and the guy, in the reflection of the bar's splashback, and she whispered again with hot breath into Walker's ear: 'He's not who you think he is. He's here to kill you.'

6

Walker watched over his shoulder as Steph headed out of the bar. She wasn't much over five feet tall, and she moved in quick, deliberate, balletic movements to weave out through the crowd. Gone in five seconds.

The guy took Steph's vacant seat. He ordered a beer. As he drank from the bottle, his eyes found Walker's again in the mirror. He turned, said, 'How about this weather?'

Walker took his time. The guy was early thirties, six-four, big shoulders and back, military haircut, dressed in khaki pants and a short-sleeved shirt that seemed to have split around his biceps. Serious side of beef, and not USDA approved – this guy was juiced up on steroids. Walker looked around. Nothing doing other than people having a good time, checking out of their daily grind, getting their Friday night drink on, having a laugh.

'Excuse me?' Walker said, leaning in a little to the guy. Thought back to Richter. *You need to reply that it seems good for this time of year, but that you heard a storm is coming. He'll then say,* The Gulf is clear. *Got it?* He took a measure of the way the guy's weight was distributed on the bar stool, and at the point where his triceps rested on the bar. Wondered about the math and angles if he kicked that stool out, figured that the guy would be on his feet and ready to respond as quickly as Walker.

'The weather,' the guy said, leaning in. 'Pretty good, right?'

Walker nodded, watching the man in the reflection. His eyes were a little edgy; something beyond adrenaline.

'Who's the guy?'

'He's the guy who'll tell you what you need to do. And you'll do it, no question, no hesitation. Got that?'

'Yeah, seems good, for this time of year,' Walker said. He'd seen that look plenty of times before. Calculation. Anticipation. And a substance. Probably modafinil. Plenty of soldiers back in Iraq and Afghanistan were on it, keeping them jacked to maintain the gruelling operational tempo. Especially since most of the hunting went on at night, and the soldiers reversed their body-clocks to live by night and sleep by day. 'I heard a storm's coming, though.'

He'll then say, The Gulf is clear.

The guy nodded, drank his beer and looked around. 'Let's get out of here,' he said a moment later. 'Back door.'

Shit. Walker nodded as he stood. Imagined this guy killing his legitimate contact – a contact who had given up the code under duress but had the wherewithal to help out a fellow operative by not giving the correct coded sign. Another star destined for the wall at Langley.

The guy was jittery, hustling to get out, looking all over the place – at Walker, at the bar, over his shoulder. Eager to get a job done, on the clock. Working the tension out of his neck and shoulders as he stood, an inch taller and thirty pounds heavier than Walker.

He's here to kill you.

Walker stood and headed for the rear of the bar. A neon sign flared 'Restrooms' with an arrow. The slab of beef followed close. Walker felt his presence, caught reflections of him on the way. Beyond the bar was a door marked 'Exit'. Another marked 'Staff only'. And two restrooms, each with the universal symbol for male and female. Walker made a beeline for the little standing man.

'Hey!' the side of beef said.

Walker held up a hand to gesture to the bathrooms, and the guy let out a noise that might have been a grunt and then tapped his watch.

Inside the restroom, the door shut behind him, the din of the bar mostly closed out for the rabbit warren of corridors they had taken to get here. There was a mirrored wall, two ceramic basins. A stainless-steel urinal along a wall. Two cubicles. He went to the farthest and closed the door behind him. The cistern lid was ceramic, and loose. Inside – nothing but water. He was going to check the other toilet, then paused, and felt the weight of the lid in his hand, then turned it over. A compact Glock pistol in a zip-lock plastic bag was duct-taped inside the cavity.

The door to the restroom opened, and a single figure entered. Rubber soles on the tiled floor. The dim sounds of the bar followed, then were shut out again.

Walker took the Glock from the zip-lock bag and checked the slide – a 9-millimetre round was chambered. Triple-stage trigger, no safety. Point and shoot. He tossed the bag back into the cistern, replaced the lid, went to flush the toilet and stopped.

The figure in the restroom was still. Quiet. Not taking a leak. Not washing his hands. Walker closed his eyes. Listened.

His hearing had always been sharp, and it had saved his life several times in Afghanistan, in the dead of night, in mountains and in caves and tunnels filled with waiting Taliban fighters. The black echo, soldiers had called it in Vietnam, and it endured into today's military parlance. Where even the sound of your own breath could give you away. Walker focused, relaxed his breathing and heartbeat, finding a stillness, and he used sound to place the exact location of the threat.

Walker pushed out the faint hubbub of background bar noise. The whir of the dust-clogged ceiling fan. He heard the movement of the guy. Near-silent footfalls as he checked the room, hunting. Then, sounds that Walker had heard countless times on countless raids at zero dark thirty, that dead-of-night time in which the special-ops forces hunted: a weapon being readied. In this case, a pistol being drawn

from a polymer-weave holster, then the slow twist of a suppressor being fitted into place.

Walker didn't wait for the sound that would come next.

He turned, aimed and fired. He opened the door. The 9-millimetre bullet from the Glock had hit his contact from the bar in the forehead, and Walker didn't bother to follow up with a double-tap – and not just because he was wary of the sound of another gunshot going off in the confines of the tiled room.

The back of the guy's head had been blown out by the explosive force of the bullet's kinetic energy. The wall behind him, above the stainless-steel urinal, was splattered like a Jackson Pollock–inspired rendering of the American flag, bright reds against the white-painted wall, muted grey matter stripes and skull chips for stars. Walker checked the guy over. The gun on him was a .45 H&K SOCOM, with a 9-inch silencer; a state-of-the-art close-range killing weapon developed for the US military's Special Operations Command. It was a match-grade pistol capable of making a two-inch group at around thirty yards. On his person he had a set of car keys, a hotel room key, and about three hundred bucks in cash. Walker took it all, and left the bathroom before someone responded to the sound of the gunshot.

He took the rear fire escape, which was alarmed, but he didn't care – he wanted distance, fast.

Instead, he met a woman.

SATURDAY 27 AUGUST

7

'Come with me,' Steph said. She was sitting on a scooter, the engine idling. No helmet. No more American accent, either. British.

Walker looked up and down the alley. Cars were parked on one side; trash cans and dumpsters lined the other. A drunk couple more than making out on a dark stoop. The alarm of the bar's rear door would draw the security out at any moment. A police siren wailed in the distance, possibly responding to a 911 call about the gunshot.

'Well?' Steph said, giving the engine a rev.

Walker climbed on the scooter behind her, and adjusted the two pistols tucked into the back of his belt as she took off.

The police siren was growing urgent. Steph turned towards it and then wound out the little engine, the speed creating a cool breeze in the hot, sticky night air. She was good on the bike. Confident in the corners. Knew the brakes and gears well. Never lost much speed, despite the overload from Walker's bulk.

Walker's hands were on her waist, just above her hips. Her skirt was thin to the touch. Cotton, or linen. The line of her underwear a faint seam. No room for a concealed weapon.

The streets were half-busy, emptying out and filling again. Partygoers visiting, letting loose. Not an exodus, but an exfiltration. And an infiltration. Moving out, moving in, for a purpose. Gone were those who'd had enough, in came those who needed more. And

for those who weren't going anywhere, who never have enough, this was their town, for now.

Steph buzzed through Lakeview, then down through City Park, taking side streets and parallel blocks headed south, as if she were shaking a tail or she knew exactly where she was going via a series of favoured shortcuts. And she did, because soon the rows of offices of Mid-City gave way to the residential neighbourhoods of Broadmoor and then Touro and she pulled the scooter to a stop at Domilise's Po-Boy and Bar. Their destination.

Walker got off and watched as Steph leaned the scooter on its tiny stand.

'Come on,' she said, heading inside. 'Eat when you can, my grandmother always told me. But then, she lived through the war.'

He followed her in, hands behind his back as he went, unscrewing the silencer and pocketing it so that the SOCOM pistol could be hidden away under his shirt next to the Glock.

Two minutes later they had ordered and were back outside. It was dark out but lighter than the bar had been, with yellowed incandescent lightbulbs strung up above the outdoor seating area to form a canopy of dull illumination. Jazz on a tinny speaker system. They dined alfresco, sitting on a low cinder-block wall separating them from the next-door lot.

'My ma always told me not to eat anything bigger than my head,' Walker said to Steph as she settled a styrofoam plate on her lap, a hulking muffaletta sandwich full of meat and cheese and olive and tomato tapenade weighing a good couple of pounds.

'Clearly she's never been to Domilise's.'

'Nope. How many times have you been here?'

'Enough.'

Walker nodded, then sat back and gave her the room to speak first. To reveal her agenda.

'So . . .' Steph said, looking at the street, then taking another bite. 'That guy at the bar?'

'Yeah?' Walker said. He was yet to eat. He drank from a tall iced tea. His po-boy was battered shrimp, roast-beef gravy, melted Swiss cheese and shredded lettuce.

'What happened?'

'He died.'

'I heard the shot.'

'Lucky for me that you were there.' Walker could see that Steph was confident. She knew he was armed. He knew she wasn't. Unless she had a small piece strapped to the inside of her thigh. Or something concealed here, or someone watching their meeting, at a place she'd been to *enough*. 'Can you tell me who he was?'

'I was hoping you could do that,' Steph replied through a mouthful.

Walker took another drink. 'Like you said, he wasn't who I was expecting. I found the Glock. Thank you. He drew down on me, and I had to take the shot.'

'Him or you.'

'Yep.'

'Was he carrying ID?'

'Nothing. Got a hotel key, though.'

Steph nodded as she ate her sandwich.

'Who are you?' Walker asked.

'Eat your sandwich,' she said.

'Afraid I'll waste away?' Walker replied, starting in. It was good, and he could see why Steph was a return customer.

'No,' Steph said. 'But you smell like booze. And I need you sober. As long as you're around, you've got to bring your A-game. Think you can do that?'

'As long as I'm around? What's that mean?'

'It means,' she said, wrapping up the unfinished half of her sandwich and drinking from her bottle of water, 'as long as I find you useful, I'll keep you around. As soon as you're not, you're on your own. But be careful, *Walker*. Someone in New Orleans wants you dead.'

He paused, watching her.

'Yes, I know your name.' Steph's expression and poise changed a little. Like she was letting her guard down. 'And I need your help.'

8

'I arrived a week ago, via Miami,' Steph said. Her palms rested on the low block wall where they sat. She watched him as she spoke. 'Tracking a buyer.'

'A buyer for what?' Walker asked.

'I don't know.'

'Who are you tracking him for?'

'The good guys.'

'As in . . .'

Steph drank some more of her water and looked around in silence.

'What's a Brit doing here tracking a buyer of something unknown?'

She smiled. 'A girl's got to work.'

'Freelance?' He was thinking not so much private-detective types, but *private spies*, who had proliferated since 9/11, with all kinds of outfits across the globe recruiting ex-government spies and selling their services back to those very governments, often with little oversight or constraint.

'No.' She shifted on the cinder-block wall, her skirt catching on a torn piece of concrete. 'Why don't you tell me about your employer?' she said as she picked at the pull in the fabric.

'Not much to tell.' Walker wondered what kind of work a British operative could be doing on US soil. Did she know he was CIA? 'What happened to my contact?'

'Nothing good.'

'Dead?'

'Yes.'

'By that guy from the bar?'

'Yes.'

'Then I'm glad I did what I did.'

'So am I. See. We are birds of a feather, you and me.'

'In what way?'

Silence from Steph as a group of late-night diners crowded by.

'What can you tell me about my contact?' Walker asked. 'And the guy at the bar – how'd you know he was going to kill me?'

'Right.' Steph settled in for her story, tucking loose hair behind her ear. 'Since I got here, I've had a tail. One lonely guy, and he was good at it. So, I set up counter-surveillance, but my man lost him – for a while. We found him in his hotel. Dead. That was your contact, not that I knew it then. I managed to pull CCTV from the scene, the hotel cameras – but they'd been scrubbed, the hard-drive bleached.'

'Professional job.'

'Yes. But this guy – the one who'd been tailing me, your original contact? He had set up a camera of his own, for security, hidden in a smoke detector in his room. Little digital thing. It captured the kill. And that guy from the bar tonight was our culprit.'

'How'd you connect it to me?'

'It was clear from the footage that they knew each other. There was no audio, but the deceased let the other guy into his room. They shook hands. Sat and talked for ten minutes. The visitor was leaving, but then he turned and choked out the guy. I then put eyes out for him—'

'Eyes? Like what? Cops?'

'In a city like this, manpower is cheap. A few thousand dollars recruited me twelve amateur surveillance assets for the week. And this killer wasn't going out of his way to hide. Why would he? No-one was looking for him, at least in his mind, because he'd covered his tracks.

He popped up in a diner in the Ninth, ran a few errands, including picking up an H&K pistol with suppressor from a disreputable gun shop, and then went to that bar to meet you. He was there three hours before you, checking exits and vantage points, then watching from across the road. While he was watching from the front, I slipped in the back and planted the gun. Just in case.'

'So, he killed my contact and assumed the role – he then went to meet me.'

'Yes.'

Walker paused. 'How'd you know he was going to meet me?'

Steph tilted her head slightly. 'Sorry?'

'You came up to me first. You knew I was the contact – in this case, the target. How?'

'I saw a photo of you; he picked it up from the original contact's room. I had a tech guy here zoom in on the shot and clean it up. It was a picture, and a name. Your alias. I then put your image into the system back home and got some information back on you.'

'I don't buy that.'

'You don't have to, but that's how it happened.'

Walker asked, 'Why'd you give me the heads-up?'

'Because,' Steph replied, 'you're the enemy of my enemy.'

'Is that what you are to me? A friend?'

She smiled. 'I know myself, Walker, my motive. It's you I need to know more about. You owe me – I practically saved your life. So, tell me: what are you doing here?'

Walker looked around. 'I don't know.'

A car was coming. Sedan. Dark. Large. Crown Vic. Unmarked. Whip antennas on the trunk. Spotlight clamped to the A-pillar. Blue plastic dome light resting on the dash. Two guys inside. The passenger eyeballed Walker as they cruised past.

'Second pass of that car,' Walker said. 'We should go.'

9

Steph's hotel was at the western edge of the French Quarter, near where Routes 90 and 10 converge. A good locale for bugging out of town in a hurry. It was a Greek Revival style with deep balconies. They took the stairs to her room on the second floor. Inside, a lamp was on, the bedsheets turned down, the room otherwise made up. There were no bags or clothes or personal items.

'Clean room,' Steph said by way of explanation.

Walker knew what she meant: no-one had ever seen her there. It had been booked on her behalf, and the key had been handled by a third party to get its way to her. It was an off-the grid hotel in terms of security cameras and staff overlooking a lobby. Smart operational security. MI6, Walker presumed, Britain's foreign intelligence service, their equivalent of the CIA. He followed her inside then closed and locked the door.

Steph put on the television, cable news, for background noise. She flicked on the overhead ceiling fan, kicked off her sandals and sat on the bed.

'What's next?' Walker asked.

'I'd say you need to make contact with your superiors, since you're now in position and aimless.'

Walker sensed she was holding something back. 'But?'

'But, can it wait until morning?' Her eyes searched his. 'As soon as they learn they've lost a field operative in your dead contact, they'll likely send more people. That might spook my thing. Which is probably your thing too. So, you need to be calculated about what information you pass up the chain, and when.'

'Can I mention you?'

'Sure. What little you know.'

Walker nodded. He'd already decided to wait until the morning to get word to Richter. As far as he knew, there were still a few days for the clock on this op to run down, and he figured it was better to be in contact with his superior armed with every bit of information he could obtain. And that meant getting more out of Steph. He sat on the edge of the bed and kicked off his boots.

'I'm not going to sleep with you, if that's what you're thinking,' Steph said.

Walker almost laughed. He turned to face her. 'Relax. You're not my type.' It was a lie, but he thought he sold it.

'Maybe in another life,' she said, opening the remains of her muffaletta sandwich. 'Under far different circumstances. Agreed?'

'Jesus, why don't you just say what you think.'

'I'm joking around with you. Lighten up, America.'

'How about you fill me in some more?' Walker crossed his arms over his chest, his back now against the brass pipe headboard. 'You want my help, right?'

'With sex?'

'With the op that you're running, the buyer you're tracking? Your thing that might well be my thing.'

'My thing, your thing, *now* who's being dirty . . .' Steph nodded and smiled after taking another bite.

Walker just gave her a look.

'Okay, okay . . .' Steph replied. 'Helping me get near this buyer would be a good start.'

'Because the British government needs American help? On something going down on our own soil?'

'I'd call it Her Majesty's Government, but yes.' Steph absently picked at her food. 'It's a big deal, we know that much. And when you do check in with whoever is handling you and confirm your next step, twenty quid says we're here for the same thing.'

'You sure about that?'

'Of course. I mean, why else would the CIA be sending intelligence officers out on missions in their own country?'

'How'd you know I was CIA?'

She smiled. 'Haven't we already covered this?'

Walker was silent. He would expect her to be able to readily have him identified as Air Force, but it surprised him that his new employment in the CIA was available to view, even for his nation's staunchest ally.

'Your original contact was identified as CIA,' Steph said. 'This in turn helped to ID you, okay? You're green, I get that. This is your first op?'

Walker remained silent.

'Oh, dear,' Steph said. 'Don't feel bad, Jed Walker. Allies share info. We're chums, after all.'

'How about you share with me?' he said, looking across at her. He didn't let his stare waver. Hers eventually did.

'Sod it,' Steph said. 'You're sitting down, so you can handle it, I suppose.'

'You sure you don't need me to lay down, just in case I faint?'

'Might be the smart move.'

Walker waited.

'Right,' Steph said, setting the remains of her sandwich aside. When she spoke, she looked absently at the television screen. 'What do you know about power?'

10

'We got SIGINT chatter out of . . .' Steph smiled. 'SIGINT is intel jargon, for Signal Intelligence, like intercepting phone calls and emails—'

'I'm not *that* green.'

'Right. SIGINT intercepts in and out of Grozny, about a Chechen group – and I use that term loosely; they're Russians, through and through,' Steph said. 'The Chechen cover is just a way for the Russian regime to keep officially arm's length from this little op, but it's being run directly out of the Kremlin.'

'Arm's length from what?' Walker asked.

'They're making a big money play.' Walker felt Steph watching closely for his reaction. 'For something they want to buy.'

'A weapons system?'

'Maybe. I've been on this for several weeks, and it's not that clear-cut. Our translations kept referencing something they refer to as *power*. That led to speculation that it could be everything from an EMP device to a code that can hack an energy grid or nuclear power plant.'

'Could be anything though, right?' Walker said. 'Power as *influence*. Could be a political thing. A psy-ops thing. A long game. Like hacking the next election. Make the hanging chads seem like child's play.'

Steph nodded. 'And anything between, granted. But this is a lot of coin for influence, even political, so I'm leaning towards military hardware.'

'How much money are we talking?'

'The exact amount is unknown. We doubt it's cash – it's too big. Not tens of millions.'

'Hundreds of millions?'

'Yes. The signs point that way. But we're talking shell companies and dodgy lawyers in tax havens, and the ballpark we've put together is between three-hundred and five-hundred million.'

'What military hardware's worth that kind of money?' Walker said, getting up and checking out the blinds. The street was busy. Groups of revellers, solo pedestrians, couples holding hands. Nothing untoward, but you could watch all night and see something new with every passer-by. 'You could buy a navy destroyer for that. Not much use in Chechnya, though. But then, you said they're just intermediaries, for the Russians.' Walker looked back at Steph. 'Who's the buyer?'

'Garden-variety oligarch, worth a few billion. Known Russian SVR agent, tied to Russia's puppet regime in Chechnya. Made his money by carving up state assets like the rest of them. He's personally not here, but his representatives are.'

'They were in Miami?'

Steph nodded. 'And now they're here. With quite the entourage.'

'And Homeland and TSA just let them all in?'

'They're legitimate businessmen, if you asked them,' she replied. 'And they came via super-yacht, all the way across the Atlantic from St Tropez, and via Cuba. You should see this boat, it's really something. Jet skis. Swimming pool. The tender craft puts most cabin cruisers to shame. And a roll call of obligatory Eastern European women.'

Walker asked, 'When did they get to New Orleans?'

'Four days ago.' Steph paused. 'You're wondering if your operational orders could predate their moves?'

Walker nodded and sat back down on the bed.

'I'd hope so,' Steph said. 'I'd hope that the CIA and NSA and FBI and Homeland are across this, at least as much as we are. Surely. Surely you guys have learned from Iraq, and the vial of anthrax, right? And 9/11? You've redoubled your efforts and are really across things now, right?'

'So, you're MI6, and you're infallible?'

'Six. Five. GCHQ. We've got the full family at work on this.'

'And where do you fit into that family tree?'

Steph shifted position and rolled onto her stomach, rested her chin on her hands and looked up at Walker. 'I'm the cousin that everyone loves to invite because she's the life of the party.'

Walker shook his head. 'You're incorrigible, is what you are.'

'It's a gift,' Steph said with a grin.

'And you're MI6,' Walker added. 'And this is yours,' he said, taking the Glock pistol from the back of his waistband. 'Thanks.'

'Some say I'm a firecracker,' she replied, checking the Glock over, ejecting the clip and the chambered round. 'Incendiary, for sure. But make no mistake – I'm good at what I do. Very good. A star in the making, I've heard those on high say.'

'Is Steph your real name?'

'Sure. Is Jed Walker yours? I know it's not Tom.'

He nodded. 'You got a surname?'

'I do, funnily enough.'

Walker was silent.

'Sure, you'll get it sooner or later I suppose. Mensch.'

'So, rising star Steph Mensch, what's your next step?'

She spun the unloaded Glock on her finger. 'You want to skip all this foreplay?'

'I mean with your boatload of Russians.'

'Keep tracking them. Find who they're meeting. Make *that* group. Uncover what it is that's trading hands. Then we can talk shop on how best to deal with it all. I for one would love to wait until the deal is

done and the Russians are back out in international waters then have a Trafalgar class torpedo their arses out of the water.'

Walker liked the sound of that, however implausible it seemed to have a UK nuclear-powered submarine in the Gulf of Mexico. 'I should get back to my hotel, get things moving. We rest, then first thing in the morning we try to get ahead of the next play while we have a small victory in our pocket. Do you have the footage of the murder of my contact?'

'Not on me, but it's somewhere safe.' Steph paused, looking at him. 'I can get it in the morning.'

'Thanks, I'll need it.' Walker handled the SOCOM pistol and matching suppressor. 'Specifically made by Heckler & Koch for our Special Operations Command. Hard to come by this model, even at unscrupulous gun stores.'

'You think it was blue on blue? A sanctioned hit by your own side?'

'Maybe. That guy at the bar wasn't Russian. He was Mid-West born and bred, I'd say. Ohio, or Indiana. Kentucky maybe.'

'Plenty of Russian agents are American. From Ohio. Or Indiana. Kentucky maybe.'

'Provenance of this pistol doesn't prove him to be a government agent, nor serving military,' Walker said, the SOCOM in his palm. 'This could just be a black-market weapon, and the guy picked it out because it was the best pistol in the store. Making him anyone. A lone wolf, maybe. A disgruntled agent my contact was running. An underworld contact he was using for surveillance or to get weapons. Totally unrelated to your thing.'

'Maybe, maybe not, but now you're thinking and I like it,' Steph was smiling again. 'I think you'll become good at this, old sport.'

'It's a gift,' Walker replied. 'Some say I'm a star in the making.'

'Well, we know for sure your contact was killed by a man he knew. And then he went after you, armed with a specialised US military firearm. So, someone was planning to take two CIA pieces off the board. Why? Who or what is the beneficiary?'

'Either your op, or mine.'

'I'm telling you, America, it's one and the same.'

'Twenty bucks?'

'I said quid. British pounds. Worth more than your silly US pesos.'

'Okay. What else can you tell me about your op?'

'Nothing, not until I see more of you and yours.'

'How is it that almost everything you say comes out dirty?'

Her eyes twinkled. 'It's a gift.'

Walker stood, pocketed the silencer, tucked the SOCOM pistol into the back of his jeans.

'I'll meet you for breakfast,' he said. 'The place we passed a block to the north – La Salle? Oh-seven-hundred. Bring the camera with the footage.'

'Where are you going?'

'Back to my hotel.'

'Scared of the sex if you stay here?'

Walker smirked and shook his head as he made to leave.

Steph called out, 'And, Walker?'

'I know,' he said at the door. 'Be careful. Don't get followed. Don't give up our position.'

'I was going to say, you talk a lot, for a spy. But that's okay. I dig the accent.'

'I don't have an accent,' he said on the way out. 'You do.'

11

Walker headed back to his hotel on foot. He needed the air, and the thinking time. It took over an hour. He stopped once to drink from a garden hose, and by the time he got to the corner of his block, he felt clear and sober and free of cobwebs. It was the dead of night, just after 3am. Quiet in this neighbourhood. Sunrise was around three hours off. He wasn't hunting right now, but he needed to make sure he was not the prey.

He stood on the street corner, in the shadows, away from the weary old overhead vapour lights, and waited. Coming back here was dangerous but it was his contact back to Richter and Langley. Richter had the name he used for the booking, therefore he knew where he'd be staying. But if the op was compromised, his alias could be blown. There could be another guy like the one from the bar. Waiting in the shadows, like him. Watching.

Walker did the block. Nothing doing. He strolled by a closed diner, an open convenience store, a dry cleaners, a father-and-son electronics store, a row of offices. Kept going until he'd covered the rear of his hotel and was back around the front, now at the other corner. Nothing out of the ordinary. No nondescript men sitting in cars, watching. No obvious loiterers. No heads on rooftops with telescopic lenses casing his moves. Nothing he could see.

Which didn't mean there was no surveillance. He took his room key in one hand and the SOCOM in the other and went to his door. In the jamb, exactly a hand-span from the floor, the tiny scrap of paper was still in place. He slipped into the room and chained the door behind him, then sat on the edge of the bed in the dark, the dull street light spilling in through the lace curtain just enough to see by.

He emptied his pockets. The hotel room key from the dead guy: the Marriott, no room number. Worth looking into, and Walker was glad he didn't share the details with Steph.

A sound made him jump.

The cell phone, next to the bed, gave an offensive whine. No caller ID. He got it on the second ring.

'Yeah?'

'What happened?' the voice said. Richter.

'Contact was made,' Walker replied. 'But it was an imposter. Another guy showed. He had a partial on the code-word greeting. He tried to take me down, and I had no choice but to act first.'

'I know about the dead guy,' Richter said. 'It's on the news. Nothing to be done about it now. Your face is with the police, too, but we've managed to keep that from going to air. You're wanted by New Orleans PD for questioning. I think it's time to come home.'

'Who was he?'

'You need to pack up.'

'There's something here.'

'You're not listening,' Richter said. 'You're cooked. You can't just do what you did and have it slide like nothing happened. Jesus. It's a cluster fuck. You clean up after, however big and messy that has to be, to cover your tracks, you got that? You should know that.'

'Know that?' Walker echod. 'I was caught out. No choice. I took the shot. Clean up? It was busy in the bar and the gunshot brought—'

'Welcome to the majors, son. It's going to happen time after time, shit going sideways then south. It's what you do next, in the immediate aftermath, that shows how good you are, that proves what kind of

longevity you're going to have. And so far I'm not seeing anything to convince me you're as good as people say you are. Tell me where you're at right now, and I'll have a couple of local guys pick you up.'

'Look . . .' Walker leaned forward and pinched his eyes closed. 'I've made a contact here. Someone who has intel on the guy from the bar, who killed our guy. Let me chase that.'

Richter paused. 'What kind of intel?'

'I'll find out in the morning, early,' Walker said.

'Who's the contact?'

'A witness, of sorts.'

'Shit – to what you did in that bar?'

'No – not really. I'll know more in the morning.'

Richter was silent.

'What was my contact meant to point me towards?' Walker asked.

Richter replied, 'Doesn't matter now.'

'Was it something about a group of Russians with Chechen muscle on a big boat?' Walker asked.

Silence, then, 'Where'd you hear that?'

'I heard about a boat here. Big one. Super-yacht. It was hard to miss. Russian babes and the beefy entourage and all that.'

Richter was silent, but his exhaled breath was audible over the line.

'Let me follow this lead, see what's what, report back in the morning,' Walker said. 'If the heat's died down a little by then, maybe I can still do your thing.'

'Take down this number, and you call in once you find out what you can,' Richter said, relaying a cell number. 'And Walker? This witness?'

'She's not a witness.'

'I want to know everything about her.'

Walker said, 'It's complicated.'

'How? Did she know our guy on the ground?'

'No,' Walker said. 'It was a happenstance thing.'

'It doesn't smell right,' Richter replied. 'Get me details on her.'

'Okay.'

'Call in as soon as you know more,' Richter ordered. 'And keep tabs on her, in case she leads to something.'

The line went dead. Walker put the phone back on the bedside table, kicked off his boots and lay on the bed. As he closed his eyes he felt the bed springs, soft and uneven from years of hard use. His mind shifted to what it, and the room, must look like under a CSI black light, all the bodily fluids and whatnot. He shook off the thought. He was asleep inside of a minute or two. The military trained him how to do that. And it also trained him to sleep lightly.

12

The sound that woke Walker was infinitesimal, but it was there. He sat upright, fast. It was just after five am. He was still dressed, sans boots. The SOCOM pistol was in his hands, in a double-handed grip and pointed at the door to his room. The sound wasn't a key in the lock – it was a lock-pick. Wire or metal working at the tumbler to get access to his room. Not housekeeping, nor management, nor another guest who'd been given the wrong key.

A threat.

Walker swung around from the bed, and went silently to the window. The street lights gave just enough illumination to see a figure at his door, hunched at the lock. Small, not big. Moving with purpose. Getting frustrated with the task. The figure stood, and was caught in more light.

Steph.

Walker went to the door and pulled it open.

She moved back, startled, and swept some hair out of her face and behind her ear. She had bent hairpins in each hand. She was dressed in jeans and a tight T-shirt.

'I really should have come better prepared,' she said, pushing past him. She took off a small backpack and withdrew a laptop computer.

Walker said, 'You followed me?'

'Yes,' she replied. 'Did you really think I wouldn't?'

Walker didn't bother to hide his displeasure. Not at her, but himself. 'I didn't see you.'

'I'm actually very good at some things . . .' Steph said. She opened the computer and typed in a password. 'I followed you here. Saw you being cautious about a tail, and potential eyes on this place. You did well. And you'll do better. Then I got a cab to another hotel, had a nap, and picked up this.'

She turned the computer around. It was a movie file, paused and ready to start. The image was grainy and obscured top and bottom, because the tiny lens had been hidden inside the smoke alarm set into the ceiling.

'Couldn't this wait until oh-seven-hundred?' Walker took the laptop.

'I was never in the military, describing the time like that means nothing to me,' Steph replied with a cheeky smile. She sat on the bed and bounced a few times. 'I'm betting that this bed is original French colonial. Really, the Agency can surely spring for better digs than these.'

Walker glanced at her. 'What were you going to do once you broke into my room?'

'The thought had crossed my mind to shave off one of your eyebrows.'

'You'd really do that?'

Steph bit her lip, acted mock aghast. 'Oh, so I take it you wouldn't see the humour in it?'

'What if my reaction was to start shooting?'

'You're a white American male, and you've been to university, right? So, one can only assume that you've had far worse done to you than having an eyebrow shaved off when passed out drunk around your friends.'

'What's that have to do with anything?'

'I'd always heard guys like you do pranks like that. Some weird ritual of the white American male. A little light hazing, just for

the joke. A carrot up the bum, that sort of thing. All in good fun, of course.'

'You're nuts . . . Please don't try breaking into my place again, it might not end well.'

'Sounds like you might be leaning towards liking it rough. Which in itself isn't a bad thing. Ooh, do you have a safe word? Good to know such things early on, right?'

Walker shook his head, switched his attention to the computer and pressed play. The screen showed a hotel room, and within it moved a man Walker assumed was his CIA contact. Average height and weight, mid-forties, thick grey hair. There were muffled sounds, too indistinct to make out even with the volume up to full. The contact came back into view, this time with another figure – the guy from the bar. They spoke for near on ten minutes. The contact was seated on the edge of the hotel bed. The killer sat in a chair next to a small desk. Three feet between them. Conspiratorial. A pow-wow. Planning. Conniving. After their conversation, they stood, shook hands, and the contact moved for the door – and then it happened. From behind. A choke hold. Like what police do, but for keeps, no hand on the back to control the pressure on the wind pipe. It took but moments. The guy from the bar then sanitised the room, taking a backpack with all the contact's belongings, and left.

Walker looked to Steph.

'That's it,' she said. 'All she wrote. And the footage is the only thing of note that your contact left behind. I went through the room and then called it in to 911.'

'I'm sure the Agency will love you for that.'

'They *should* squirm – they are responsible here. At least in part, if it came down to your compatriot being taken down by a trusted contact. Either he was inept, or he was double-crossed. He probably leaves behind a family, and they have the right to feel angry. I hope New Orleans PD gives the Agency some hell over this.'

'It'll amount to nothing,' Walker said. 'Nine-eleven changed everything. Right now, Homeland Security trumps all other local agencies. And cops nationwide have always been overworked and understaffed. They'll be glad to hand the case and crime scene over to some federal suits.'

Steph was silent, and she got to her feet.

'What's next?' Walker asked, passing the laptop back.

'That's why I'm here,' Steph said, shouldering her backpack. 'When I was taking my nap, I was woken by a call. I got word, from one of my paid watchers, hence I didn't wait until *oh-seven-hundred* to bring you up to speed.'

'Word of what?'

'Our super-yacht moved out of the harbour, about an hour ago – oh-four-hundred, I think you'd call it. Which puts us in a pickle, America.'

13

To Walker's mind, there was only one good option: coffee. Lots of it. He had it black, a whole pot of local New Orleans dark roast. Steph added cream and a sugar. They were in Morning Call, a 24/7 cafe in City Park under a huge verandah where they sat and looked out at the massive old oaks as the sun was rising. Too early for tourists. Change-of-shift types. Some on their way home, getting a bite to eat and decompressing after a busy night of dealing with scumbags hell bent on nothing but a good time. Then there were those about to start their day, reading papers and drinking coffee and eating sugar-dusted beignets or waffles or eggs or all of it, prepping for a day of manual labour, catering to the good-timers blowing through the Big Easy.

'You're sure it's *our* super-yacht, not just yours?' Walker said. 'My thing might not be your thing.'

'Let's just assume it is, until proven otherwise,' Steph said.

Walker looked at the sky. Cirrus clouds shimmered and rippled up high. A frontal system for something bigger on the way. 'Any way of tracking this yacht?'

Steph gave a noncommittal shrug as she sipped her coffee. 'Track, not so much. But a boat like that's hard to hide anywhere they might come ashore. It'll pop up. But it's the timing that bothers me.'

'You think your guy got spooked?' Walker poured more coffee. 'By what?'

'The thought did occur to me,' Steph said. 'They may have made one of my surveillance assets.'

'You checked that your assets are all still on the board?'

'Sure, right in between saving you and furthering your op, I've checked in on all the surveillance assets I'm running around town to make sure they're all tucked in tight. Even found the time to read them a nice bedtime story. *Peter Rabbit*, in Latin.'

Walker looked at her. 'Why Latin?'

'Beatrix Potter's rabbits were descendants of those brought over by Hadrian's legions, so technically they were Latin in origin. But then you know I'm being facetious right now, right? One does not simply check in with so many people to make sure they're all A-okay. Some are homeless. Many are criminals. I didn't hand out cell phones to all and sundry. But I hid burners in neighbourhoods for them to use.'

Walker looked at her. 'Well, checking on your people could be a good next move. Find someone missing, work that.'

Steph sipped her coffee. 'Sounds like you have experience, despite being so green to the intelligence world. I'm not saying you're not intelligent, of course.'

'Tours in Iraq and Afghanistan taught me a bit about running local networks. Particularly the need to keep them safe.'

'Don't worry too much, they'll be fine. The Russians probably just moved their yacht for a different reason.'

'Don't underestimate how important they are to you – or how important you are to them.'

'I must say, you sound like such a pro in the morning.'

'I'm just saying, that's what I'd do.'

'Well, lucky you're not me, because then I'd be you, and then I'd know what true disappointment and failure must feel like.'

Walker shook his head. 'Why are you like this?'

'Vexing? Funny? Just a little bit naughty?'

'Petulant. Scattered. Just a little bit annoying.'

'Damn, I was going for all-out. It's who I am.' She sat forward, elbows on the table, coffee cup cradled in her hands. 'Look, Walker, my assets? They're in the field, and most of them are transient. Bums, you call them, right? Odd word choice. Anyway, they're hard to find and pin down, let alone reach out and contact in a hurry, unless we start checking abandoned houses and shelters and whatnots.'

'Whatnots?'

'Technical term.'

Walker sipped his coffee. Imagined Steph going to Walmarts and RadioShacks all over town and purchasing bags full of cheap cell phones to charge up and squirrel away in hidey-holes for her makeshift surveillance team to use. Then he thought about all the upkeep that came with that – making sure the phones remained charged, replacing those that got broken or stolen. A big job. And he'd not noticed her taking calls on some kind of grapevine hotline.

'Who's taking all the calls?' he asked. 'Who's maintaining all the phone calls that come in from the field? And charging them up and swapping them out? It's more than a one-person op.'

'Darling, *please*,' she said, adding more coffee and then sugar and cream to her cup, tapping her teaspoon on the porcelain edge. 'You seriously think I'm going to sit around taking calls all day? I've outsourced that, too. It's all about delegation, this business we're in.'

'Like outsourcing keeping eyes on your target,' Walker said. 'How'd that work out?'

Silence. Then, 'Yeah, you know what, I should have outsourced that warning through to you, right? And planting the Glock.'

'Fair enough, I'll give you props for that,' Walker said. He drained his coffee and looked out at City Park. The cacophony of morning birdsong was a New Orleans jazz ballad all of its own. Blue jays and wrens and finches danced in the lightening sky to welcome the brand new day. 'You know where the Marriott is in town?'

'Yes, why?'

He leaned back in his chair, fished into his jeans pocket and pulled out the hotel key card. 'The guy from the bar.'

'Holding out on me,' Steph said, smiling. 'We'll make a spy of you yet, Jed Walker.'

14

The Marriott was exactly the kind of hotel that Walker liked to avoid. Typical of every other business-class hotel in the world: the rooms the same, the food the same, the drinks the same. Could even be the same staff, in the same uniforms, who went around to different properties as some kind of grand joke.

'How are we doing this?' Walker asked. They were across the road, watching the scene. A hotel shuttle pulled up in the driveway, and merry tourists piled out. Staff went about unloading huge suitcases.

'How would *you* do it?' Steph countered.

'You could run a distraction, get the driveway staff to move away,' Walker said, 'while I use the bell desk's computer to scan the card and get a room number.'

'That *could* work,' Steph said. 'But there're cameras. And a glass wall through to reception. And people all over the place.'

'I'd feign something benign, like I was using the computer to check the weather.'

'Oh, I've no doubt you could be a convincing idiot.'

'Is this mood because you haven't slept properly?'

'I just think you're taking unnecessary risks when you could be smarter about it. What other options are there?'

Walker looked around. He couldn't just take the card to reception and say he had a big night and forgot his room number, because he

didn't know the name that corresponded with the room key. And he couldn't bribe the bell boy, not even a hundred bucks at a fancy place like this, because he'd cherish his job more than the tip. He could try using brute force, flash his wallet and threaten all kinds of federal crimes unless the employee complied and gave over the room number. But, again, in a flashy hotel like this where everything was above board, the staff wouldn't be as easily swayed as those in some cheap hotel where they were getting cash payments off the books to avoid taxes and immigration issues.

'Door to door?' Walker suggested. 'I could take the room card and try all the locks until one pops open.'

Steph looked at him. 'And how long would that take?'

Walker looked up at the building. Sixteen storeys. Maybe thirty rooms per floor. Maybe more. Start at the top and work down, taking the fire stairs. Maybe ten minutes per floor. All kinds of people coming and going as they started their day. How many times would he have to apologise and say he'd got the wrong door? Too long.

'There'll be cameras in the halls, too,' Steph said. 'Security will see exactly what you're doing. It's a dumb idea.'

'There are no dumb ideas,' Walker said. 'Just ideas that don't quite work out as planned.'

'Well, I guess that explains the Iraq War.'

'Touché.'

'Okay, have you given up?' Steph watched him. 'Can't see your best option, despite it staring you right in your stupid American face?'

Walker stared at her, silent.

'Card,' Steph said, holding out a hand.

Walker passed it to her.

'Now, watch,' she said. 'But not too closely. We don't know each other. I'll meet you in the lift lobby in two minutes.' Steph messed her hair and went across the road. She walked like she'd had a night to forget. Not a walk of shame, nor a stride of pride, but somewhere in between. A happy air about her. Walker took a diagonal path across

the road towards the hotel, on a different track. He watched her out of his peripheral vision as she approached the bell desk, where a liveried young man was putting paper tags on a set of luggage. She leaned close into him, a hand on his arm, a feigned need for support, the flash of the card, hesitation on the boy's face – then he took it, and went around to his side of the small bell desk in the hotel driveway.

By the time Walker pressed the lift call button and the doors pinged open, Steph strode by him and stepped in, a grin on her face, her tongue between her teeth in a cheeky pose as she hit the button for the fifth floor.

'It's a gift, and you either have it or you don't,' she said. 'A star in the making, they say.'

'Hubris,' Walker replied, 'will be your undoing, young lady.'

'I'm six months older than you, Walker.'

The lifts pinged open and she walked out.

Walker paused. 'You – wait – you actually read a file on me?'

She turned around and motioned him to follow. 'Come along, my poor American boy. You really are playing catch-up, aren't you?'

15

The patterned carpet, the small desk and chair and lamp, the mid-sized TV and the not-so-comfortable bed, an armchair by a window, an ensuite – just like almost every other such hotel room on the planet.

They started their search in the dead man's bag, which was a worn khaki rucksack on a luggage rack.

'US military issue?'

'Yep,' Walker said. 'Army. But I'm pretty sure the guy used to be a Marine.'

'Still doesn't prove that this was a blue-on-blue attack on your Agency contact.'

Inside were clothes, which they tipped onto the bed and shook out. T-shirts, shirts and a pair of jeans, socks and underpants. Nothing else. Nothing in pockets, nothing hidden in the bag's seams, nothing telling.

'I'll take the bathroom,' Steph said, heading for the small tiled room and emptying the contents of a small nylon zip-up bag into a basin. Walker heard the sound of toiletries and shaving equipment rattling about.

Walker took the wardrobe. A garment bag contained two suits, which he pulled out and laid on the bed. One was navy, the other a black tuxedo. Both were new, and expensive. A pair of dress shoes were polished to a shine that would make any drill sergeant proud.

'Look,' Steph said, showing Walker an orange plastic bottle of pills. She held it with a tissue, as though she were planning to send it off to be dusted for prints – or not wanting to leave her own behind. 'It's prescription, with a name.'

'Phillip Wilcox,' Walker read from the label. 'Might be our guy, might be an alias.'

'When we leave I'll call the hotel, ask to be put through to Wilcox, see if he checked in under that name.'

'He was packed to be here for a while,' Walker said. 'He's got seven changes of socks and underwear, and why pack that if you're staying less than a week?'

'What's that?' Steph pointed at the lapel of the blue suit, on which sat a silver pin, about the size of a nickel.

Walker undid it and brought it up for a closer inspection. It had a bird of prey, an eagle or hawk or raptor, an assault rifle in its talons. A word ran around the top half.

'GreyStone,' Steph said. 'Mean anything?'

'Private military contractors,' Walker said.

'Mercenaries?'

Walker nodded. 'New kids on the block. Like Blackwater, but apparently they're the pickiest of the bunch, only taking the cream of ex special operators.'

'Where are they based?'

'South Carolina,' Walker said. 'They formed about a year back. Their operators do sensitive tasks for DoD and government agencies in our hottest of hot zones.'

'CIA?'

'Probably.' Walker pocketed the pin. 'Let's keep searching.'

'We've done the obvious.'

'Now it's time to tear this place apart. He might have stashed a burner phone, or an ID, or a laptop.'

Walker started with the bed. He tossed the bedding and sheets in a bundle by the door, flipped the mattress and bed base, then

used his folding black anodised combat knife to cut the seams of the mattress apart. Nothing. He did the same with the bedhead, a quilted board bolted to the wall. Nada. There were two pieces of artwork in the room, and he took both off the wall and checked the frames.

Steph worked her way through the bathroom, pulling the toilet apart, and the small vanity unit. Then she moved out to the desk and upturned that and the chair, checking them all over.

'I'll try the armchair,' Walker said, moving to the corner of the room, stepping over the mess they'd created. The armchair was disassembled inside of three minutes and contained nothing but a metal frame and foam wadding and springs in the seat.

Steph cracked the spine of the Bible and shook it. Nothing.

'Pretty sure there's a special place in hell for doing that,' Walker said, moving towards a louvred airconditioning vent. He stood on the desk chair and used his knife to unscrew the panel – the metal shaft contained nothing but dust. He turned and looked around the room. From this new height, about nine feet off the floor, the room looked like a grenade had gone off. Bits of stuffing and material and bedding and clothes and curtains were everywhere.

'Television,' Walker said. It was the only thing left to check. It was flat-panel, about 32 inches, set on the wall on an articulated arm. He pulled it out and turned it all the way towards the wall, revealing the back. There, in a hard plastic pocket set in the back, was a manual for the TV set. And an envelope.

The envelope was C5 size, half an inch thick, and it was heavy. The hotel name was printed on the front. It was sealed.

The sound of the hotel phone ringing suddenly cut through the room.

Walker and Steph looked at it, the red light flashing as it rang.

'Time to go,' Walker said, already moving for the door, envelope in hand.

'It might be the guy from the desk,' Steph said, 'double-checking that I got up here, that I'm not ransacking the joint.'

Walker paused, then nodded.

Steph picked up the phone and listened. Waited. After about twenty seconds, she hung up the handset and said, 'We should go.'

'Who was it?' Walker asked, checking the peep hole, then opening the door, scanning the hallway left and right before moving out.

'No-one,' Steph said, moving fast to keep up with Walker's longer stride. 'But someone.'

'As in . . .'

'I heard breathing. And background noise. Birds. Sea birds.'

'Could be someone near here,' Walker said as he pushed open the fire escape and headed down stairs.

'Right. Our next move?'

'We bug out. Exfil someplace safe. Check the contents of this envelope, and look into the name Phillip Wilcox.'

'See if it matches anything they got from the John Doe from the bar last night.'

'Exactly,' Walker said, descending two stairs at a time. 'And speaking of, let's head back to that bar from last night.'

'Why?'

'I'm holding out on you again, I'm afraid.'

'Ouch,' Steph said, a hand to her abdomen in a mocking gesture of pain. 'I think that was one of my ovaries. You're becoming so good and bad, it's really getting to me.'

•

Jim and Hank, newly minted members of the CIA's Special Activities Division, arrived in New Orleans on the nine am flight and walked out into the humid morning air and into a waiting cab. They had been given the address for Walker's hotel, which had been booked under the alias Tom Archer. Their orders were to get there ASAP.

'And if he's not there?' Jim asked.

'We wait,' Hank replied. 'He'll show. Small town, right? It can't be far away. Besides, Walker's an Air Force man, probably needs a mid-morning nap just to make it through.'

Jim laughed. 'This is going to be easier than invading Iraq.'

16

Back in the neighbourhood of the bar, Walker searched the streets, holding the car keys from the dead man he knew as Wilcox. The key-fob belonged to a GM. It had no rental tag. First he tried the side street to the east, pressing the unlock button, looking for the flashing indicators of a GM sedan or SUV or pick-up. Nothing. At the top of three blocks they turned left, and he tried the lock and unlock function every time he saw a parked GM. Nothing.

They took the next left and headed south, towards the bar. Steph pointed out a Chevy Caprice across the road, and they waited for a gap in the traffic before scooting across. It wasn't their car. They covered the next two blocks without success.

'Maybe there was another person with him,' Steph said. 'With another set of keys and they hightailed it.'

Walker nodded. 'Or it could have been towed.'

'Yeah.'

'Let's try the alley out back.'

'That's a crime scene,' Steph said. 'There'll be cops.'

Walker passed her the key-fob and smiled. 'Then work your magic, shooting star.'

'Star *in the making*.' Steph snatched the key and smiled then backtracked a block north-east towards the bar. While waiting, Walker bought a couple of bottles of water from a street stand. Just

after nine am and the back of his shirt was already soaked through with sweat. He sat on a bus stop bench and waited.

It wasn't long before a GM came from the north, Steph at the wheel. She looked tiny driving it. Tiny because she was diminutive in stature and build, and because of the vehicle. It wasn't a sedan, nor an SUV or pick-up. It was a van. A big one. For moving furniture. Painted black. No windows on the sides, just big sliding doors for cargo.

She pulled up, and Walker opened the passenger door.

'I'm beginning to think that that guy wasn't there to kill you,' Steph said. 'At least, not straightaway.'

'Why's that?' Walker said, climbing in.

Steph thumbed a gesture for him to look behind her.

In the load area of the van was a gym mat, shackles bolted to the floor, and a black canvas hood.

'And this,' Steph said, passing him an object before driving off, merging with the morning traffic.

Walker knew what he was holding. He'd seen them plenty of times before, on the battlefield and in the classroom. The civilian population knew them as epipens, first developed for the military to deliver fast-acting painkillers in the field, straight through a wounded soldier's uniform. This one was unmarked, made from a dull charcoal-coloured plastic. He popped the cap, gave the device a twist and saw clear liquid bead at the top of the spring-loaded needle. He sniffed it. Etorphine. Developed by the CIA to subdue targets for the extraordinary rendition program.

'Maybe he just wanted to get to know you a little better,' Steph said. 'I mean, it's a pretty romantic set-up back there.'

Walker was silent.

'Right,' Steph continued, 'let's get this van somewhere off the radar. I know just the place.'

•

Jim and Hank arrived at Walker's hotel and used a lock-pick to get into Walker's room inside of three seconds. They entered warily. Jim led, with a taser in his hands. He rushed the room, scanning the bedroom, then bathroom, and another three seconds later declared the scene clear.

'We leaving?' Hank asked.

'Soon. First I'm going to take a screamer,' Jim said, a hand on his stomach as he headed for the bathroom. 'Those midnight burritos were a terrible idea.'

'Crack a window, I don't want to pass out,' Hank replied, closing the hotel room door before sitting on Walker's bed and switching the television on.

'Fuck you "crack a window". I'm gonna paint this bowl and leave it for Walker to find, foreshadowing the shitstorm that's headed his way. Fuck with his head.'

'You're a sick man, Jim.'

'It was the burritos and beers and tequila that's making me do it.'

'Well, when you're done laying cable, we'll go take a look around.' Hank flicked through the channels and settled on a rerun of *Hogan's Heroes*. 'I love this town. No sense in sitting in this room all day smelling your mess while waiting for Old Man Walker to show.'

'We might miss him,' Jim called out, then punctuated it with a cracking fart, followed with an exaggerated sigh of relief.

'Walker's Air Force,' Hank said, opening the hotel door again and fanning the room with it. 'Those guys are predictable as shit.'

17

The place that Steph had in mind was a brick-veneer house in the Lower Ninth Ward, on Monticello near North Tonti. The grass out the front was recently mowed, the exact same length and mowing pattern as that of its neighbours on both sides, which meant they either took it in turns to do each other's lawns, or one did all three plots, or they paid the same neighbourhood kid to do them. It had a garage attached, and she pulled the van up and passed Walker a piece of wire to pick the lock. After she drove the van in, he closed the garage, taking one last look up and down the quiet street. The garage was lit inside by a couple of grimy windows facing west. The floor was stained with old spilled motor oil, as if the car usually parked here had a perpetual leak.

'My safe house. Never used it,' Steph said. 'My understanding is the tenants are away for several weeks.'

Walker looked around the garage; workbenches were covered with tools, and an entire wall was stacked with boxes and an accumulated stack of domestic detritus that hinted at a house populated by people for many years. Cheap stuff, and kids' stuff, which put in mind for Walker a family living on the edge of the socio-economic abyss, with at least two children who were now teenagers.

'Okay, the tenants are on a road trip, won't be back for another two weeks,' Steph said, jumping down from the driver's seat. 'One of

my surveillance people was in the process of breaking in when I was driving by. We reached an agreement of sorts, where he now works for me, and he's leaving this place alone.'

'Great,' Walker said. He found a light switch, and two banks of stark white neon tubes came to life overhead. 'Okay, let's see what we've got.'

He started with the front of the van. The glove compartment held registration papers made out to GreyStone, and a Louisiana address, which he passed to Steph and she nodded with raised eyebrows. There was a set of handcuffs, duct tape and a flick knife.

'These guys know how to party, am I right?' Steph said. 'Ooh, look-see.'

She held up a snub-nosed revolver that had been strapped under the driver's seat. 'Colt .357. Well maintained. Loaded with hollow-points.'

'Keep it,' Walker said, headed for the rear of the van.

'We're getting quite the collection of firearms,' Steph said, joining him at the cargo doors.

'You never know when they'll be needed, right?' Walker said, opening the rear doors. 'GreyStone don't stuff around, and if they've got an office in this state, they might send someone out looking for whoever put their buddy Wilcox in the morgue.'

Walker climbed into the van. He checked under the gym mat, and the shackles, and the black canvas hood, but that was all there was to it back there. It was a spartan operation. Walker imagined Wilcox's desired moves: get him in the van, drug him, drag him through to the load area and restrain him, transfer him someplace. For what purpose? Interrogation? To use as a bargaining chip? What would he know, a day into life as a CIA officer? Sure, Walker knew plenty about US and Allied military activity in and around Afghanistan and Iraq, but then so did thousands of other serving and former DoD personnel. He couldn't make sense of it.

He climbed out, went over to a workbench and opened the envelope from Wilcox's hotel room.

'Steph,' he called out.

She came over, stood close by his side. He heard her take in a sharp breath.

'Is that your Russian and Chechen friends?' Walker asked, spreading out a series of 5x8 photos.

'Yes,' she said. She picked up a photo showing a party on the back of the now-missing super-yacht. It was taken by a long lens, zoomed in. A little grainy, but you could use it to positively ID at least six people in full face-on profile. Three men, three women.

'This was in Florida, the final day,' she said. 'This one here – and here,' she picked up another photo, a grainy image, as if it had been blown up from a smaller photograph. 'That's him. My target.'

The photo appeared to show a man in his forties, with a thick neck and shoulders, square head and angular features. A typical Eastern Bloc thug.

'These girls are locals, but Eastern European origin,' she said, moving some of the pictures around. 'Recruited from the clubs. Strippers, most of them. And their friends. They throw money at them, and all the party drugs and French champagne they can ingest. But this woman?' She tapped the picture that she'd first picked up. It showed a woman of maybe twenty-five, dancing with a female friend, their arms in the air. She was strawberry blonde, and she had a natural and wholesome figure that wasn't as sinewy or spray-tanned or surgically enhanced as the others.

'On the last day,' Steph said, 'when the yacht left, I had eyes on it. And there was a commotion, at the jetty. Two women had gone back, but the boat just sped off. I spoke to them, and they were nervous, but I got information, eventually, when I convinced them I wasn't police. This woman?' She tapped the strawberry blonde again. 'They swear that she was on the boat, that the head security man had her captive. And, Walker?'

He looked up from the picture to meet Steph's eyes.

'They only knew her a week, about the same time as the yacht showed up. But the other women liked her. They swore to me they thought she was a cop of some sort, because she was looking out for all of them, and staying clear of the drugs. They thought maybe she was a narc. But I checked it, and neither Miami PD nor Florida State Troopers had anyone on there.'

'What about a Fed? Or Homeland?'

'I got stonewalled, but I was hoping to hear back by now. But this is outside my mission, you understand? My people only care about our target, named Peskov, and what he's buying, not the collateral damage along the way.'

'Okay . . .' Walker looked at the photos, then back to the van. 'Right. We've got a lot to chase up. Let's get out of here and get in contact with our superiors—'

His sentence was cut short by the sound of a car pulling up outside, hard and fast, nothing friendly about it.

18

The garage door was made of thin sheet metal and had no windows set into it, so there was no way of knowing what car had pulled up or who was in it. But the screech of the brakes and the rubber of the tyres sliding on the concrete told him it was nothing good. Either the cops, or the bad guys. Either a hindrance, or a threat.

Walker pointed to the door that led into the house, and Steph tried it as he scooped up the photos and put them in his back pocket. It was locked, and as she pulled out her lock-picks Walker pushed by her then put his shoulder and side of his body against the door. It was a cheap, hollow internal door, basically made of plywood little stronger than cardboard, and he gave it enough pressure to bust out the lock around the handle, and now they were in the house.

It stank.

Walker knew the smell. Death. Not recent. Days had passed, not hours.

He back stepped, took a rag from the workbench and held it to his face – it smelled of kerosene and lawn clippings – and in his other hand he gripped the SOCOM pistol.

Steph was close behind him, and she was gagging at the smell. He ripped the rag in two and passed her half, and she put it to her face and nodded thanks.

Walker entered the first room, the kitchen. The humidity and heat had created a stupefying pong that could quite possibly outlast religion, and the stench matched the mess. It looked like squatters had taken over for an extended period of time. All the cupboards were open. Dirty dishes were stacked everywhere. The fridge was open, its light on, the contents mostly on the floor and in differing states of decay and ruin. The ceiling was beaded with dark stains of perspiration, the whole house a blooming biome full of bacteria and germs. He imagined the family who rented the house had gone away, and vagrants had moved in – and something went badly wrong for them. He hoped that the smell of death would be nothing more depressing than finding an abandoned dog or raccoon that had got stuck inside. But he doubted that.

He didn't have time to search for the culprit, because he first had to assess and respond to the threat out front.

Walker moved fast. He ditched the rag held to his face so that he could grip the SOCOM pistol double-handed. He'd used one before, in training. He preferred a Sig 9-millimetre for its lightness and ease of use, and he knew the .45 had more kick and therefore more of a climb rate as the kinetic energy forced the aim off with every shot. But the H&K SOCOM pistol had awesome stopping power and terrific accuracy when kept on target, plus good endurance, the sum of all that leading to its selection by Special Operations Command as their current sidearm of choice.

He was through the kitchen, past a six-seater dining table covered in the filth of a crackheads' party, and into the front sitting room when he saw them coming. The view, through lace curtains, was of their silhouettes, but it told him what he needed to know, and he got close enough to peer through a gap and get a decent look.

Two men. Dressed in suits, automatic pistols drawn. Their vehicle was a van just like the GM Steph had commandeered, and in that moment Walker knew: the van must have had a GPS tracker in it, and they'd been followed. GreyStone. Bad guys, not cops.

'Hostiles inbound, find cover,' Walker whispered to Steph, and she backtracked out of the kitchen and disappeared behind the view of a breakfast bar.

Walker took a door that led to a hall, the front door to his right, and he kept creeping, to the other side of the house, through an open doorway, into a bedroom—

He found the source of the smell. Human. Two figures. Bloated and covered with flies, surrounded by drug paraphernalia on the bed. He stifled a cough and readied. Crouched on a knee, just inside the door frame, ready to lean out and put four rounds fast and direct through the front doorway. He controlled his breathing and settled his heart rate. He waited, listening to the muffled voices through the door. He imagined the two men conversing, planning how to carry out their assigned tasks – search the garage, hit the house, confirm if the van was randomly stolen by crackheads or by the guy who killed their comrade. The longer they took, the more Walker worried. If they waited for back-up, or went back to their van to get heavier firepower, he and Steph would be in trouble.

Walker moved to the window of the room, a hypodermic crunching underfoot. He had to navigate his way through empty beer bottles and tossed packets of junk food, avoiding them like landmines of noise.

Then noise came in the form of the front door being kicked in. Walker stood, braced in a two-handed firing position, ready to blast a couple of .45 rounds through their centre masses.

But no-one came. No targets. Not even the sound of footfalls on the worn carpet.

Damn.

He moved sideways, towards the window.

A glass bottle shifted and clinked against another, then all hell broke loose.

Gunfire: 9-millimetre and .45, from outside, firing in. The mismatched automatics. The 1911 and M9, in US military parlance.

Both weapons punched their munitions through the fake-brick façade and the sheet-rock internal walls like they were made of paper.

Walker dropped to the floor, the thought of being stuck by a needle preferable to having his head blown off. The shooting lasted five seconds as at least twenty rounds bored holes through the front wall of the house into the bedroom, letting in light, hopefully venting out some of the stink of death.

Walker was on his back, and he moved backwards, so that he was almost concealed from the view of the doorway by the bed. He pulled a filthy comforter over himself, all the while keeping the SOCOM pointed at the sheet-rock wall, a couple of inches to the left of the doorjamb, sure that one or both assailants would soon appear. He waited, thinking the two guys would want to bug out fast to avoid a police presence.

He couldn't see Steph; all he could do was hope she would wait and not blindly rush into the fray.

He heard whispered commands out the front, then the drop of a clip to the front deck, and a reload and the crunch of a slide being pulled back and a round chambered. The Colt, probably. The guy with the Beretta had maybe five shots left in his mag.

Walker waited. Not long now.

He kept his aim to the left of the doorway as he listened to the footfalls in the hall; just left enough to miss the wood structure around the door. The .45 would punch through the sheet-rock as cleanly as the assailants' shots had just done, but hit a two-by-four in the doorjamb and it would ricochet and lose kinetic power.

Walker's wait was over.

The first thing he saw round the doorjamb was the barrel of the silver Colt .45 – at head height, for a shooter about six feet tall. The guy was clearly taken aback by the stench pouring out of the room, bringing a hand to his face as he scanned the scene.

Walker fired, twice. The first shot caught the assailant in the right shoulder, and his own pistol went off, the bullet thudding into one

of the bloated corpses, sending an explosive burst of stewing internal juices into the air, and then Walker's second round hit the GreyStone attacker in the neck, and his head nearly cleaved right off.

Walker was up and moving, keeping low, waiting for shots that didn't happen. He looked out around the doorframe and saw the other suit rushing back to his van. Probably to get a bigger weapon.

He didn't make it.

Walker shot him in the butt. He didn't mean to. He'd aimed for centre mass, but the guy was moving fast, already twenty feet away, and Walker was firing from one knee, on the up, so the .45 round bored its way into the guy's buttock. He went down, yelping and clutching his ass like it was on fire.

'Steph!' Walker called into the house, looking out the front door, checking the scene. 'It's clear.'

She came out of the kitchen, the rag to her nose and mouth, revolver in her hand. She saw the corpse in the hallway, the contents of the guy's head and neck spilled over the carpet, and she started to retch.

'Come on, we have to get out of here,' Walker said.

She peered into the bedroom, saw the two bloated crackheads, then properly emptied her stomach. Walker put an arm around her shoulders, took the Colt revolver and tucked it into the back of his waistband along with the SOCOM and a spare clip from the GreyStone guy's .45, and led her out of the house. They were three blocks away on foot by the time they heard the sirens.

19

Jim and Hank were across the road from Walker's hotel room, sitting in their rental car, a big Chevy Yukon, with the airconditioner running hard and modern country tunes playing on the radio.

'Seriously,' Hank said, 'it's getting cold in here.'

'We didn't all grow up in Tennessee.'

'What's that mean?'

'You can handle the heat and humidity,' Jim said. 'I'm from Montana.'

'I'm from Georgia, dickhead.'

Jim looked across. 'Seriously?'

'Fuck you, seriously. Where'd you get Tennessee from?'

'I thought you said Tennessee. And we're listening to this crappy music. What's the state with the retarded yokels?'

'You're a real prick, you know that?' Hank said, turning the airconditioning down to its lowest fan setting, then he looked out the windscreen and tapped Jim and pointed.

'Any time. Hey, you think Richter will give us our choice of assignments after this?'

'That's what he said.' Hank looked at his comrade. 'You doubt it?'

'Hell, what do I know?' Jim replied. 'It's just he's what – a senior agent? Station Chief at most? That's like a full Commander? Not like they could assign us wherever we wanted.'

'Do I need to remind you we're not in the DoD anymore, bubba?'

'Look-it.' Jim rapped the glass of his window. 'Old Man Walker, strolling back to his digs. And he's not alone.'

'Show time. Get the needle ready.'

'You do it. If Walker sees me with that thing, he'll break my arms.'

'Fine. We'll bring him back to the car and do it here. Away from that woman.'

•

Walker turned on the shower to build up steam. He offered Steph a light-blue cotton shirt, which would be a mid-thigh-length dress on her, and she gladly took it and his belt then went to the bathroom and shut the door. He could imagine her staying in there for a while, soaping and shampooing away the stench of the death house. The air had been so thick and humid with the smell of decayed flesh that it had left a slick greasy film over their skin and hair. Four days, Walker figured. Maybe five. It was hard to tell in those conditions. The flies, their larvae crawling all over. It was too disgusting for the rats to come. He'd seen worse corpses, but the smell was as bad as anything he'd encountered.

There was a knock at the hotel door. Too hard and determined to be housekeeping.

He went to the window, drew the SOCOM from his waistband, and peered out. He saw two familiar figures: Jim and Hank, from spy school. He unlocked the door, eyeballed the pair up and down.

'Old man,' Jim said to Walker, a shit-eating grin on his face.

'Pissant squid,' Walker replied.

'Walker,' Hank said.

'Hank. How's it?'

'Little to the left, as always.'

'What brings you two numbskulls here?' Walker asked.

'Can we come in?' Jim replied.

Walker said, 'I've got company.'

'She looked fine,' Jim said, and the look that Walker gave him made his grin fade, fast. He leaned in towards Walker, sniffed the air. 'Damn. What's that smell?' He looked to Hank. 'You smell that, homie? What do you think that smells like?'

'Shit,' Hank said. 'Smells like shit.'

Jim started to laugh. 'Damn, Walker. You bring a honey back to your room and it smells like *that*? You've long lost any form you ever had.'

'Too old, Air Force,' Hank added.

'Far too old,' Jim said, nodding. 'Hell, tell her we're here; SEALs are always the best in bed.'

'How would we really know though, right?' Hank said. 'It's not like anyone's ever slept with an airman.'

'The only thing old here . . .' Walker said opening the door, so both SEALs could fully see him now. In his T-shirt, the veins on his arms were bulging from the heat and adrenaline. In his hand, hanging by his side, which had been shielded by the hotel door, was the SOCOM pistol. 'Are your lousy jokes.'

'Ah,' Hank said, his eyes on the firearm, then slowly rising to meet Walker's. 'Look, boss, Richter sent us. We've got to talk. New orders from up high. How about you come to our car to talk, in private. Yukon across the road.'

He gestured to a cream-coloured behemoth parked by the kerb, under the shade of a twisted old chestnut tree.

'Right,' Walker said, leaving the pistol on the bed and locking the hotel room door behind him as he stepped outside. 'Lead on.'

He followed Jim and Hank across the road. As Hank got into the driver's seat, Jim made for the rear. Walker took the front passenger seat, twisting around so he could eyeball both men.

'So, what's Richter's latest?' Walker asked Hank, who was the senior of the two former SEALs, and the less annoying in Walker's eyes.

'Jim?' Hank said, gesturing to his colleague in the back.

'Hey? Right . . .' Jim said, looking from Hank to Walker, then vacantly out the windscreen between them. 'Richter. He told us to come out here and . . .'

It was the initial hesitation that warned Walker. Then the overplayed action of looking ahead, trying to draw Walker's attention to follow the gaze, that made Walker react. Jim was still talking, but Walker wasn't listening. Instinct, along with a deep desire for survival, took over. He moved, as the SEALs made their moves. Walker's hands went up to his face as he felt and then saw Jim lean in from behind him, his arms raised level with Walker's neck, and Walker grabbed both wrists as Jim's hands came in to close around him with a length of para-cord meant to choke him into compliance.

Hank leaned in, holding a rendition epipen, close to identical to the one Walker and Steph had found in the van.

Walker jabbed a fist into Hank's Adam's apple, then resumed his grip on Jim's wrists behind him.

The former Navy SEAL had spent a career lifting weights and training and being a hard-ass operator, and his muscles were as thick and developed as any twenty-five-year-old middle-weight pro athlete. Walker used every ounce of grip strength he had. And then some. Fighting for your life did that.

But Jim wasn't having it. Walker squeezed, tighter and tighter, and felt Jim's bones squeeze together, tendons stretching and threatening to tear, bones getting to the point of sheering into splinters, but the SEAL was defiant and intent on his objective to subdue Walker. It became an agonising stalemate, where five seconds felt like five minutes, then ten seconds felt like a week, all the while Hank was regaining his breath and composure and scrambling for his dropped weapon on the front seat.

So, Walker switched to plan B, before Hank could rejoin the party and shut down all available options. Walker bit Jim's arm, as hard as he could. He tasted blood and felt muscle split open, and Jim yelled in pain and immediately relaxed his grip.

Walker let him go.

Hank made his next move – and it changed everything.

He pulled a knife.

Walker pushed towards it, double-handed, all his force out and up, pressing Hank's hands up, then the knife went up and stuck hard into the ceiling of the Yukon, through the felt lining and the padded wadding and at least an inch through the thin sheet metal of the roof, where it stuck and stayed tight against its serrated edge. Hank let go of the weapon and punched Walker in the face, and Walker reciprocated with a right uppercut that bounced Hank's head off the window behind him.

Hank landed a double blow into Walker's side, both fists crashing into his ribs and knocking the air out of him. Walker knew more pain was coming his way and he let it come, his right arm pinned against the dash and his body, Hank raining blows into his side and gut. Walker could have deflected the blows with his left arm, but he didn't – instead, he used it to reach behind his back, where he fingered at the grip of the Colt revolver, and he almost had it pulled when Hank launched another frontal attack, a hard punch right in Walker's solar plexus, winding him. He was bent forward, sucking for air. He'd seen the shot coming, had tensed for it, moved a little into it, but there was little else he could do but take it.

Walker's current state gave brief pause in the attack.

'Get the needle,' Hank said, leaning back and letting Jim move across the centre console. Hank kept Walker pressed hard against the passenger door, while Jim started to look in the footwell.

'I see it,' Jim said, squirming down. 'Slide your right foot right a few inches.'

Hank did as instructed.

'Got it,' Jim said, sitting up and back with the epipen, blood seeping down his forearm from Walker's bite. 'And Walker, you move an inch, and so help me god I'll—'

Jim didn't finish, because the loud boom from the .357 prematurely punctuated his speech.

Hank paused for a moment, wide-eyed, looking back at his colleague, whose chest was a bright red mess from the snub-nosed bullet – then to Walker, who brought the .357 to bear at him. The interior of the car was full of dust and fine particulate from the stuffing of the seat, and the smells of burned gunpowder and coppery blood overpowered the smell of death and decay that Walker carried with him. He wiped blood from his nose. Kept pressure on the short trigger of the dull silver revolver.

'Hank, you've just seen what a .357 hollow-point does at this range,' Walker said. 'So, don't try me.'

Hank nodded.

'Hank, listen to me. *Listen.* That's it. Now, you're going to tell me everything that Richter told you,' Walker said, the Colt held steady. 'You tell me, you tell me now, and you live. You lie to me, you stall, and the last noise you ever hear is this little sucker going off again. Talk.'

Three minutes later Walker stuck the syringe of Etorphine in Hank's thigh and watched as the ex-SEAL's eyes rolled back in his head. Then Walker looked back to Jim, who was bleeding out. He considered reaching back and choking the air out of him, but he figured the guy had maybe a minute to live, and he didn't appear to be feeling pain. Maybe the blast had severed his spinal cord. Maybe his body had dumped a massive load of adrenaline in an attempt to overwhelm the situation. Whatever. Walker left the car and headed across the street. Every movement hurt, and he knew the bottom three or four ribs had popped out of his back. But he had far bigger worries than immediate pain.

20

Inside the hotel room Walker could hear the shower still running. He shut the room's door and watched out the window to the street. He stayed there for a couple of minutes while he stuffed tissues up his bloodied nose. No visible threats. The Yukon didn't move. Jim must be dead by now. Walker had watched and waited for many men to bleed out from gunshot wounds. Some had been traumatic experiences for him, watching as friends died, people he'd tried frantically to save but couldn't. Others had been marauders, killers, rapists, the worst of the enemy combatants, and sometimes the rules of engagement and war were bent and you just had to watch the life snuff out of them as they bled at your feet. It was a trade-off, the good deaths for the bad, a scale somewhere weighed down by the devil's hand.

Like the guy who'd killed one of his childhood friends, a friend who'd joined the Army and become a Special Forces operator, only to be killed by an IED in Afghanistan. *It's okay, Ma*, his friend used to say when calling home. *I'm in the rear with the gear, don't you worry about me.* A NATO forensics unit eventually tracked the IED maker to Kabul. Big kingpin guy, who trained hundreds of others how to turn old Soviet bombs and mines and artillery rounds into camouflaged killing machines to kill NATO soldiers – and plenty of kids who picked up the innocuously disguised objects. Walker had been part

of the raid that went after the bomb maker. They didn't go in that night to take prisoners. That op felt like a win. The scales had tilted their way, and seemed to stay bent in that direction for some time.

Walker moved from the window now, every movement shooting stars of pain behind his eyes. His back was stiff and he was moving like a geriatric, but he knew that he and Steph had to move out of this locale, fast. This room, and his CIA identity supplied by Richter, were dead. As he was, if he remained static. He'd been lucky three times. The fourth time, it would be the CIA or GreyStone or both, en masse, and they would bring the boom. No lonely guy in a bar. No pair of GreyStone operators. No green CIA duo of ex-SEALs armed with a rendition epipen. They would send in a wet-work team. Probably have sniper coverage, armoured vehicles, a couple of squads of guys with fully automatic weapons and body armour. Shaped charges would blow in doors and windows. Flash-bangs to subdue him. The full shebang with all the trimmings.

Not today.

Walker was under no illusion about his limited abilities to fight it out against an overpowering force. He was now the walking wounded. He needed to lie low, recoup, regroup, find out what the hell was going on. Find a weakness, some leverage, and take Richter apart.

Richter wants you taken to GreyStone, Hank had said in the car, at gunpoint. *That's all he told us. That they were dealing, because you're a traitor. Alive, preferably. Dead, if it came to it. That's it. I swear.*

Why?

He didn't say. That's all he said.

Richter?

Yes.

Who at GreyStone? Walker had asked. *Who were you delivering me to?*

We didn't get a name, Hank had said, *just a place. Richter told us to take you to GreyStone's compound at Fort Lee. That's it. Every word of it. I swear on my—*

Then Walker had jabbed the needle into Hank's leg. Lights out.

The information didn't mean much to Walker. The shower stopped running. Walker made his way across the room, each step causing him to grimace. It was all he could do not to lie on the thin carpet covering the concrete floor; he knew that being flat on his back would give him respite from the worst of his current pain, but he doubted his ability to get up again.

'Steph?' he called out when he neared the bathroom.

The door opened, and steam flooded out. Her hair was dripping wet, and she had a towel wrapped around her. The smell of soap and shampoo took over some of the stench that still coated him.

'Jesus,' she said, looking at the bloodied tissues hanging out of his nose. 'What happened to you?'

'You should see the other guys,' Walker replied, moving past her and wiping the steam from the mirror, then gingerly cleaning the blood from his nose and mouth with a face washer doused in cold water. 'We have to get out of here.'

'Why?'

'We've – I've – been made. Get dressed. I'll tell you about it on the way.'

'Okay. You're not going to wash?'

'Not here.'

'It's that urgent?' she asked as she moved out into the main room.

'Yes.'

'Who was it?'

'My people.' He sounded nasal as he kept pressure to his nose. 'A couple of newbie CIA guys like me.'

'Jesus . . .'

'You said that already.'

'Okay, well, where to?'

She appeared back in the bathroom doorway, and Walker had to turn his whole body to look around, for fear of aggravating his dislocated ribs. She wore his blue shirt as a dress, tied at the waist

with his belt. Her sandals were back on, and she was towel-drying her hair. She looked great. Smelled great, too, above the stench of his own body and clothes. In that moment he wanted to just lie down and forget his pain, and have her do all kinds of ungodly things to him to take his mind off his present circumstance. But – real life.

'So, where to next?' she repeated.

Walker said, 'I think we should probably sep—'

'I'm not leaving you, not like this. And not just because you're going to find out that we're here for the same reason. You need help. Look at you.'

'Steph—'

'No.'

'Okay. But we have to go somewhere I've not been seen,' he said, moving for the door. 'How secure is your surveillance person?'

'Very. A beyond-healthy dose of paranoia, I'd say. He's good. Should be, for how much I'm paying him.'

'Let's go there.'

Steph looked Walker up and down. 'He lives on the third floor. No elevator.'

'I'll manage.'

'Are you taking your things?'

'Just the gun,' he said, heading through the bedroom. 'Take it, would you?'

Steph picked up the SOCOM pistol and managed to just squeeze it into her handbag. Then she wrapped her rank clothes with her wet towel, balled all that into a plastic garbage bag from the bathroom and tied it up to take with her. Walker admired her operational security, being cautious about leaving tracks beyond what trace amounts of her DNA might be down the shower drain.

'I'm going to need to find a drugstore along the way,' Walker said once outside. He checked the sight lines, up and down the street. People and cars and buildings. Nothing out of the ordinary.

'For some deodorant, I hope,' Steph said, already stepping off the sidewalk and flagging down a cab.

'Yeah, okay, sure. And pain meds. Serious ones. And something strong to drink.'

'I know just the place.'

21

They stopped at a store in Algiers Point that covered half a block and sold a bit of everything. The cab driver was happy to wait with the meter running. Walker bought a bottle of scotch, a couple of packets of co-codamol and ibuprofen, some topical creams and some strong medical tape. Steph found him jeans and a plain black T-shirt, and a T-shirt, shorts and tennis shoes for herself. He bought a cheap electric trimmer. She found two throw-away cell phones, pre-paid with twenty bucks of credit apiece. Walker paid with the cash he stole from Wilcox, and a minute later they were back in the cab; five minutes after that, Walker shifted himself out with a grunt of pain and they walked another block east to a row of vast brick warehouses.

'My contact is not a fan of the government,' Steph said. 'Consider yourself forewarned.'

Walker nodded as he swallowed a handful of pills with a mouthful of scotch.

The building was a dark-brick structure, three industrial-sized levels with steel windows big enough to drive a bus through, clearly repurposed as the area gentrified and became residential. At the top of front stairs leading up from the street was a panel of buttons with a camera intercom system. Steph leaned in close then pressed and waited. There was no tone, but a moment later the steel gate serving as an entry door clicked open.

Walker followed Steph upstairs, each tread tugging at his ribs. Stretched tendons, he figured, letting his bottom ribs separate from where they were bedded against the spine. He'd had it once before, when he'd been forced to lie prone on a hillside of Afghanistan one night for several hours, completely unmoving as the Taliban were entrenched with superior numbers and heavier weapons. That injury – and that engagement – had earned him two weeks' R and R and intense osteotherapy, as well as a Purple Heart and an Air Force Medal.

The third-floor hallway was made from the same thick raw timber slabs as the stair treads, worn down from a century of use but stout enough to see out another. Steph led Walker to the end of the hall, where they faced two doors either side. There was no spy hole drilled into either door, but a little black plastic dome was attached in the corner of the right-hand one, which Walker figured fed into a screen on the inside. And Steph's contact also had the whole twenty feet of the hallway to see exactly who was approaching. As they neared, the door opened, as if of its own accord, plugged into some kind of remote system.

Steph went straight through the opening, and Walker followed close. The door shut behind him, and Walker turned, again using his whole body as one stiff plank. Behind the door stood a man. A small man. Young. Barely out of his teens, maybe still in them. Dressed like a skater. Big, wide eyes lingered on Walker; there was no nervous energy about him, but there was a cautious look in his eyes.

'Who's your pal?' he said, his hands in the front pockets of his hoodie.

'Luke, this is Jed Walker, a friend of mine.'

'Hey,' Walker said.

Luke said, 'You smell terrible.'

'Sorry,' Walker said. 'Can I use your shower?'

Luke looked at Steph. 'Is he serious?'

'I'll pay you a bonus,' Steph replied.

'I'll need it, to get rid of this smell.' Luke finally looked from Walker to Steph. 'All right. Up the spiral staircase. Through my bedroom. Towels under the basin. Don't touch my shit. I'll know if you have.'

'Right.' Walker looked over to where an ornate wrought-iron staircase punched through a hole in a mezzanine level. *More stairs.* 'Thanks.'

Walker took the bag of fresh clothes from Steph and headed upstairs, taking the treads slowly.

'What's his problem?' he heard Luke ask. 'He's walking like an old man, or he's got a broken ass . . .'

Walker shuffled through the bedroom at the top of the stairs. It was a big open space, enough room to fit several king-size beds. The bed that was in it seemed to be a waterbed. It was unmade. In it was another young guy, naked, a sheet not screening much, snoring softly. Walker found the bathroom, a tight space, all painted and tiled black, with a walk-in shower with four spray nozzles set at different heights and positions. He worked the controls and set them all on, then stripped off with great effort and considerable pain. He used half a bottle of an expensive shampoo to wash himself all over, twice. The drugs began to kick in, and the water pressure felt great on his back.

As he towelled dry, he figured Richter's next step would be to put an alert of some sort out on him, so he spent a couple of minutes with the electric trimmer in front of the mirror. It wasn't a pretty look, but he now had a buzz cut. To give him a distinctive characteristic to stick in people's minds, he used the bare edge of the clippers to shave a forty-five-degree angled cut into the eyebrow above his right eye. The skin was pale underneath, and it looked like it must be a scar from long ago. People would remember that, when describing him. *Tall guy, hunched a bit. Buzz cut. Scar in his eyebrow.* He used the wet towel to clean off his boots, then dressed in new clothes and headed downstairs, the descent easier than the climb had been ten minutes earlier, but the pain in his back wasn't far away.

'You're famous,' Steph said, sitting at a counter with a coffee in hand, and watching a local news channel showing a picture of Walker wanted as a suspect in the bar shooting the night before. She turned around, appraising him. 'Interesting look.'

'You might want to burn these,' Walker said, passing over the plastic bag with his old clothes in it.

'Yeah,' Luke said, taking the bag with pinched fingers and tossing it in his trash can. He passed Walker a coffee. 'Did you really kill that guy?'

'Self-defence,' Walker said.

'Who was he?' Luke asked.

'It's government-related,' Walker said. 'Guys in black suits and black helicopters and all that.'

'Damn. Righteous. Respect, bro.' Luke held out a fist, which Walker bumped.

'Any news from all your eyes out there?' Walker asked Steph.

'Silence, aside from the odd crank angling for a bigger payday,' she replied, and Luke nodded. 'Until my super-yacht shows back up on radar, there's not much we can do.'

'Well, you can start with my back,' Walker said, sipping his coffee then setting the mug on the stone counter and passing her a tube of cream. 'I'll lie on the floor. You need to work my ribs back to where they need to be.'

'Oh, I'm your nurse now?'

'I can call you Nightingale.'

'At least you smell decent now.'

'You two need to work this weird hetero tension out of the air, then move on and be professional,' Luke said, taking his coffee and heading for the stairs leading up to his bedroom. 'I'm gonna leave you to it. Show yourselves out when you're ready, or hang here, up to you. Just don't fuck on my kitchen bench. I'm serious. I'd have to move house.'

Steph looked to Walker, who was manoeuvring his back flat on the floor. He closed his eyes. 'This feels great.'

'I think Luke may be right,' Steph said, taking the belt off her shirt. 'And don't worry, you won't have to move a muscle. Well . . .'

Walker opened his eyes. He felt relieved to be lying on the hard, flat floor, the weight and movement off his back. And the sight was greater still. Steph was in her underpants, and in a moment those too were on the floor. Then she got down and started to undo his jeans.

'Now, don't go getting any crazy ideas,' Steph said, pulling his clothes off. 'Not all British nurses are this naughty.'

22

It was almost noon when Luke trudged downstairs.

Walker was lying back to the floor, and aside from the ache in his back whenever he moved, he couldn't remember feeling better. If he'd had a smoke, he would have smoked it – and he didn't even smoke. Steph's body was nestled into the crook of his arm, her head on his chest, a hand playing with his chest hair. A knitted blanket from the sofa provided them with some modesty. She'd spent the past couple of hours doing the best she could for his back, and his morale. They'd drunk a few drams of the scotch. The television was on mute, but they'd seen his face flash up on the screen a few more times on the twenty-four-hour news channel.

'I hope you kept off my kitchen bench,' Luke said. 'The killer and the English . . . I almost said *lady*.'

'I can promise you that I have not moved from this floor,' Walker said.

'Yeah, well, I'm gonna have my cleaning lady take one of those CSI black-lights to that floor to make sure she cleans it right,' Luke said, heading across the room in an open robe and shorts, taking a diet soda from a double-doored fridge. 'Drink, anyone?'

'We're good,' Steph said. 'Can you check the messages for me?'

'That's why I'm down here,' Luke said, heading past them. One half of the open-plan living zone was set up with several computer

screens and related equipment. Luke took a seat behind his screens and started tapping away.

'I need to get dressed,' Walker said, rolling to his side and using his arms to take the strain off his lower back as he stood.

'I have all the calls and messages go into an automated system. It's much quicker,' Luke called out, keeping his eyes on his screens. 'And I've got keywords to pick up things you're looking for, like government peeps and your Russian or Chechen targets, and their yacht.'

'And?' Steph asked, pulling her underpants up and then putting on her bra as she crossed the room.

'Just the usual case of . . . oh, *helloo* . . .'

'What is it?'

'That little boat that you lost, just popped up and berthed for fuel.'

'Where?'

Luke had brought it up on a map by the time Walker was dressed and standing beside them.

'There,' Luke said. 'Small outpost. Shrimp trawlers, mostly. A few bars and a restaurant, berthing point for boats that don't want to pay the New Orleans city charge. Your yacht doesn't exactly scream understated conservatism.'

'Maybe they just needed to gas up and get supplies,' Walker said. 'How'd you get the hit on it?'

'I hacked into webcams all over the coast and then outsourced, paying some college kids to watch the feeds for me.'

'I told you to keep our business in-house, confidential,' Steph said to Luke.

'Relax,' Luke replied, looking her up and down. 'They're good kids, they know they're doing something on the extreme down-low, and they want to impress me.'

'When was it spotted?' Walker asked.

Luke brought up a file, a still of a webcam at the dock near the gas station. Time-stamped 11.32am.

'We should get a boat,' Walker said to Steph.

'And what?' she said. 'Chase them down and board them?'

'Watch them from a distance. They might not be coming back to New Orleans.'

'This is about GreyStone, isn't it?' Steph smiled. 'You want to find out what the hit on you was all about, rather than see my yacht.'

Walker was silent.

'Wait – what?' Luke said, looking at them both. 'Look, the government is one thing. Those guys are dinosaurs, and they deserve what they get, with their snouts in the trough and their lips on the taxpayer's teat. But GreyStone? They're some bad hombres. They've got no rules. I don't want anything, *anything*, to do—'

'My thing's got nothing to do with what you guys have going on,' Walker said, looking down at Luke. 'You keep working for Steph.'

'But you want to go to GreyStone,' she said. 'To their base on the coast.'

'Crossed my mind,' Walker replied. 'And getting a look at their compound by boat would be a lot easier than by car.'

'You're mad,' Luke said. 'What do you think they'll do to trespassers? They'll have all kinds of surveillance set up. Infra-red, motion detectors, physical. Hell, they've probably mined the beach along their compound.'

'Then I'll be careful,' Walker said, looking at Steph. 'I can go alone.'

'No, we do this together,' Steph said. She passed Walker a burner phone, then they programmed each other's numbers in there, as well as a number to contact Luke.

'Can I use your computer before I leave?' Walker asked.

'Hell no,' Luke replied.

'Just to log into WoW and leave a message.'

Luke paused, then grinned, scooted his wheeled chair across the floor to another console, which he powered up, loaded up the online game of World of Warcraft and then made way for Walker. 'Go for it.'

23

'WoW?' Steph said as they made their way to the harbour. She was dressed in her new T-shirt and shorts. The sun was just over its midway point in the August sky and the day was baking. The clouds looked like cotton balls, the sky beyond the colour of cement. None of it boded well.

'Online game, with players all over the world,' Walker replied. 'I used a forum to reach out to an old friend. He'll get it and contact me.'

Steph nodded, and she linked her arm through his as they crossed a road.

'Look, Walker,' she said. 'What happened before, at Luke's house . . .'

'The sex?'

'The sex. Yeah . . .'

'Don't go all prudish on me now.'

'It was rather nice. I'd be happy to recap sometime soon, make sure it wasn't a fluke. But let's not let it cloud our work, okay? In fact, I hope it'll be the opposite now. Like Luke said. So, the tension can be behind us, and we can concentrate.'

'Fine,' Walker replied. 'Though I'm still not convinced my work thing is in any way related to your thing.'

'The guy at the bar, Walker. He led me to you, remember. That makes it related, your thing and mine.'

'So, by that rationale your thing is also connected to GreyStone.'

'As is your thing. Connected. Ta-da. You're a smart one, America.'

'Okay,' Walker said. They stopped at the water's edge, looking at the marina. 'I don't suppose with all your in-country planning and contacts you've made, you've got a boat on standby? Fully gassed up and equipped for covert surveillance?'

'As a matter of fact . . . no. No, I don't. I never did look into getting a boat. I assumed the Ruskies would do their thing, I'd report back, and job done, fly home to sunny London town and get a pat on the head and a nice cup of tea with the Queen.'

'How's that working out?'

'Not great?' Steph looked around the harbour. 'Ideas?'

'How much cash do you have access to?'

'I can go to an ATM. Log into Gringotts, use her Maj's cash.'

'Better than our silly pesos.'

'What are you thinking?'

'We'll get ourselves a boat, but we'll do it right,' Walker replied. 'Flash enough cash, we'll hire ourselves a beauty.'

•

'Yeah?' Richter said into his non-Agency cell phone.

'Another problem,' the voice said. 'Those two newbies you sent to do a man's job wound up in hospital.'

'How?' Richter asked. 'When?'

'Just now. One's DOA. Gunshot wound. The other is non-responsive, and an expended military-grade injector was found in his leg. I can only imagine what the ME would have found in that.'

'Jesus . . .' Richter fell silent.

'Relax,' the voice said. 'I've got contacts in NOPD. I've managed to reach out to some buddies there, who have picked up your two ex-SEALS and are transporting them here to Fort Lee.'

'They were clean,' Richter said. 'It wouldn't have been traced anywhere, to you or to me – so why take them to your compound? You could have let it be. You've created more risk.'

'I'm containing it my way.' The voice paused, then said, 'They were too green, and probably too friendly to Walker, for this mission. That mistake is on you.'

'They were expendable. I'll send a specialist asset to take care of your Walker problem. A veteran.'

'I'll take care of it from here.'

'Best keep out of it,' Richter said.

'Oh, that's what I need to do, is it? *You* sent Walker here.'

'At your request. Besides, it was your guy who messed up on getting Walker in the first instance.'

'Well, at least he got rid of your troublesome FBI Counter-Intel asset with ease,' the voice said. 'How's that going at your end?'

'The team running him is going ape, as you'd expect,' Richter replied. 'But it's being considered, as it appears from the scene of his hotel room, a suicide. The note was a nice touch.'

'My guy was good.'

'Not as good as Walker, evidently.'

'Walker's a pussy,' the voice replied. 'And he deserves what he's going to get.'

'Right. Well, don't forget *you* wanted Walker there.'

The guy on the other end of the line chuckled. 'Dead or alive will do it.'

24

By mid-afternoon Walker was at the wheel of a boat, motoring out of the Mississippi and into the Gulf. It was a 32-foot cabin cruiser, a tried-and-true craft about as old as he was, and usually rented out with a crew for day-trip fishermen to catch big fish in the Gulf. Two-grand cash and another two-grand deposit and it was theirs for four days, though neither Walker nor Steph thought they would need it that long. Twin Honda outboards out back. Six-foot draught when moving. They had enough gas aboard to cover two hundred miles at fifteen knots. The boat came with a set of detailed laminated maps of the Louisiana coast, along with a one-to-five-hundred scale of the Gulf, all with the best fishing spots marked, along with refuelling stations.

Steph stowed a box of food and drinks below, then joined Walker at the bridge, sitting next to him and passing over more pills and a bottle of water. It was choppy on the Gulf, and sea spray hit the windshield with each rise and fall of the bow. Walker had a marker on the GPS unit, and made his own circular route into the leeward side for approach to Fort Lee.

'What are you thinking in there?' Steph asked him as she reached under his T-shirt and rubbed more analgesic cream into his back.

'Since I've been here, I've been following orders, and then awaiting orders,' Walker said. 'Assuming they were coming. But what if there

never was an objective for me, from that original contact? What if I was sent here purely to be handed to GreyStone?'

'Dead or alive. Don't forget that part.'

'They wanted me there alive, if they could help it. So, there's something I know or can help them with, something they want from me.'

'You really think your boss would do that to you?'

'Richter? I met him on a car ride. A short one. And I'd seen him around training. So, yeah, sure, I believe my classmate who told me it was Richter who ordered they take me to GreyStone.'

'Okay,' Steph said. 'What do you know?'

'What do I know . . .' He put a hand on her bare leg. It was smooth and warm and soft and firm in all the right ways. Steph was the first woman he'd been with since separating from Eve. Eve had been his high-school sweetheart. They'd stayed in contact when he was at the Air Force Academy in Colorado, and she was at Texas State, reconnected and been together since they graduated. Then military life took its toll. He remembered asking his father for advice about getting married, that he'd said to him that it was his belief that every man remembers the girl he thinks he should have married, so don't regret not doing it. That if he didn't act on it, trust his gut, she'd reappear to him in his lonely moments, or he'd see her in the face of a teen girl in the park, reading a book under an oak tree by the baseball diamond, or in the image of strangers that seemed familiar, haunt his dreams. That if he didn't go ahead with it, she'd forever belong to back there, to somebody else, and that thought would sometimes rend his heart in a way that he would never share with anyone else.

'Walker?'

'Yeah . . .' Walker said, rousing from his thoughts. 'I suppose I know a lot of classified military intel, from Afghanistan and Iraq. Too much to figure out what they could want for all the noise, or to make sense of. But there're thousands of soldiers and airmen and sailors in special operations who know what I know. Some of them

would happily give it up for money. GreyStone probably have them on the payroll already. So, I think we can cross off the list that it's got something to do with what's in my head.'

'That doesn't explain why they would go to the trouble to get you here,' Steph said, taking Walker's hand in both of hers. 'With a ruse like that, under the auspices of some kind of mission. They could have kidnapped you anywhere, anytime, and bled you for intel. This seems more like a game, to have you here.'

Walker was silent. He wondered what kind of games spies played against each other. With all kinds of old and modern tradecraft at play, probably a few good ones. But the deaths he'd been around in the past twenty-four hours told him this was no game.

'And remember,' Steph added, taking his water and sipping it, 'they didn't mind if you were brought in dead. So, maybe this isn't about something you know. It's about stopping you from doing something. Continuing something. And they want to know how much you know.'

'From doing what? I'm not working on anything.'

'But maybe you are, and you just can't see it. It's like joining the dots – hard to do from the outset, but looking back it's going to be obvious. Like when I was the solution to getting access to Wilcox's hotel room, and I was staring you right in the face.'

'This about you being a star in the making again?'

The sun was low, and the afternoon was hot, and the boat was rocking just enough to still be pleasurable without busting through his pain meds and lighting up pain receptors in his back. Steph had kicked her shoes off and put her feet up on the dash. Her smooth legs were showing the beginning of a tan. Another time, another scenario, this would be an afternoon to savour.

'Or it could just be about good old-fashioned revenge,' Steph said. 'Someone you pissed off.'

Walker reached into the back pocket of his jeans and pulled out the cell phone. It only had one bar of reception, but there had been no

missed call from the contact he had reached out to on the WoW game platform. He set the phone to vibrate and put it back in his pocket.

'What do you think of that hypothesis?' Steph said. 'You ever piss anyone off?'

'Probably,' Walker said. 'Probably a list as long as your legs.'

'These little pins? I'm rather short. Diminutive. Firecracker. Remember?'

'All in the eye of the beholder,' Walker said. And then, his phone vibrated.

25

'Marty,' Walker said into the phone. He put the engine to idle and let the craft drift so he could hear and concentrate on the call, and left the wheel to Steph as he headed to the starboard side and leaned against the railing.

'You okay?' Marty Bloom asked.

'Yes and no,' Walker replied. He then ran through the previous eighteen or so hours, from meeting Richter in the bar outside The Point, to getting the boat. Not full details, just the Cliff Notes. It took near on five minutes. It felt good, not just to put it all out there, but to share it with a professional of considerable experience, and someone Walker had known most of his life.

Bloom was silent the whole time, then he said, 'Okay, Jed, now you listen to me. This isn't one of those situations where I can send lawyers and guns and money, because from what you say, the shit has already hit the fan, my boy. You're on your own, and your best chance at immediate survival is to stay alone, and get out. Disappear. Got it?'

'I can't just run away.'

'I know that. But I had to say it. Because you're my boy, you know that.'

'I know that, Marty,' Walker said. He looked out at the sun setting on the Gulf, the ochre light melting into the water in a shimmer of

another day's end. 'I appreciate the concern. What do you know of Richter?'

'I've met him a couple of times,' Bloom replied. 'Helluva operator. One of the Agency's best, a legacy of when we actively intervened, specialist in running agents provocateurs. I'm not surprised he was attracted to you, given your service record.'

'Do you think he could have sold me out?'

'No. Not on the face of it. But that's what the ex-SEAL newbie said to you?'

'Yep, and he was telling the truth, at least as he knew it.'

'You got any reason to think otherwise?'

'I've been thinking that over,' Walker said. 'Maybe they didn't get the order directly from Richter. I should have pressed the point at the time.'

'I'll look into it,' Bloom said.

'How?'

'I have to think about that. And I'll need to be careful, with a guy like Richter.' Bloom was silent for a few seconds, then said, 'I'll call you back on this number, inside of twenty-four hours. And meantime, Jed?'

'Yeah, Marty?'

'Keep your head low, you hear me?' Marty said. There was real concern in his voice. 'Your folks would kill me if anything happened to you that I could have helped out with. So, I'm in this now, and in turn that means that you owe it to old Uncle Marty to be smart and safe.'

Walker looked across at Steph, who was sitting in the pilot's chair and looking over the maps of the coastline.

'I hear you, Marty,' Walker said. 'Especially the *old* part.'

Bloom chuckled. 'Keep safe, talk soon.'

Walker made his way back to Steph and plugged the phone into an electrical outlet in the dash by the boat's wheel, and it vibrated to show it was receiving charge.

'News?'

'Nothing yet,' Walker replied. 'But a friend's working on things.'

'What kind of friend?'

'Tell you later.'

'You look relieved.'

'Problem shared, and all that.'

'Right. Well, what's the plan? Still going to storm the GreyStone beaches?'

'We've got maybe an hour's light left. We head west, find the yacht, then we wait till all is dark and quiet and then I swim out and climb aboard, plant the GPS tracker, and we can watch them from afar. Make our move when we need to. Then we can get to GreyStone. They're not going anywhere.'

'Sounds like a plan.' Steph looked at the map Walker had laid out. 'Say we find them close to where we last saw them – which is how far away?'

Walker had already calculated it. 'Forty minutes.'

'Right. So, we eyeball them from afar. Shoot right by. Then wait for night for you to make your move.'

'Correct.'

Steph smiled and pointed to a spot on the map, a couple of miles along the coast from where the yacht was last spotted, deep in the scrubby marshes and bayous, but still within view of the craft via their binoculars.

'So, we have several hours to kill before you can do this.' Steph paused, changed her tone. 'What to do, then? How do we fill that time, do you think?'

Walker laughed. 'I saw they had a tattered old box of Scrabble tucked in the galley.'

'Because you're American, and so fantastic with words?' she said, putting her hands either side of his face and looking up at him. 'You really want *that* to be your night? Being schooled by an Englishwoman in the mother-tongue?'

She kissed him for a long time. Her tongue probed his mouth.

'Okay, well, when you put it like that . . .' Walker said, smiling as he steered the craft towards the sun. 'We'll find a nice little place to moor up for the night, before I go hunting. In the interim, you're the star in the making: I'm sure you can figure out something to keep us busy.'

26

'That's our yacht,' Steph said, looking through her binoculars.

Walker kept their craft ambling along at a leisurely pace. He had two deep-sea rods in holding points on the stern deck. If the Russians were watching them, they'd look like a pleasure craft, out for a twilight fish, the big carnivores running with the currents and chasing the tide fish.

The Russians' yacht was hard to miss, even in the last minutes of daylight. It wasn't the full oligarch super-yacht with a helipad and seaplane and all the trappings, but it was big. At least 180 feet. Its launch craft was about the size of Walker and Steph's vessel. The yacht was docked, taking on supplies and fuel. Judging by the crates stacked on the jetty, Walker figured they were getting enough supplies to make it well beyond Cuba.

Another delivery van arrived on scene. A couple of big guys emerged from the yacht, but instead of helping with the unloading logistics, they went right on by the van and jaunted up the jetty. Their body language was that of a couple of guys in no hurry, headed into town for a last night on land, enjoying all the town had to offer a couple of cashed-up visitors. The waterways around here were busy, with commercial fishermen and pleasure seekers and oil-rig craft, so it made sense that they would wait until first light to head out; better to navigate out to sea in the light of day.

'You ID either of those two?' Walker asked Steph, who was still looking through the binoculars.

'No,' she replied, then put the binoculars down. 'It makes me worry about how many men they've brought.'

'Not our problem,' Walker said. 'Observe and report, you said, right? Call in the Coast Guard when we're sure they've made the transaction.'

Steph nodded. 'But that undercover onboard, captive. I worry about her.'

Walker didn't know what to say about that. He'd been wondering about it himself. Was she still undercover, or had that cover been blown? If so, why would they keep her on the boat as a captive? It would be a massive liability, if their vessel was searched. Even if the crew were travelling under some kind of diplomatic cover, having a US hostage on board would get them cuffed and put into a holding cell. In Walker's experience, it was a liability too big to bear. Better to have dumped her overboard in a weighted bag in the deep waters somewhere between Florida and here.

'You think they're going to stay put at this dock?' Steph asked.

'Looks like it,' Walker replied.

The sun was a magenta orb on the horizon. Fingers of dark grey clouds rippled through the night sky, itself the colour of torn plums. The same in the sky here as he'd seen in the lands of Afghanistan. Same world. Same people. Always bad guys. The remains of the day were being snuffed out. The humidity didn't let up as they motored along, but it was cooler out on the water, where a breeze blew in from way out over the mouth of the Gulf. He headed for the thick scrubby pinnacles and isthmus. Steph sprayed liberal amounts of bug-repellent all over her arms and legs, and soon she smelled of camphor and eucalyptus. Walker slowed right down and circled three laps of the target area, finding a good spot in among the brush oak and invasive brambles to drop anchor and kill the engines.

Silence, but for the bugs and critters calling in the night. School fish were feeding in the shallow waters, eating the bugs. Something bigger occasionally sloshed about, rippling the water and eating the school fish. Same the world over.

Steph set up a couple of candles. They too were of the bug-repellent variety, and threw off a nice ambience.

'Well,' she said. 'I'd say your place or mine, but that's kind of redundant.'

'Above or below deck?'

'That just sounds dirty,' Steph said, and she stepped close enough for Walker to draw her in, then her arms wrapped around his neck and she stood on tiptoe. 'When all this is over, what do you want to do? I mean, we could run away for a week or so . . .'

Walker looked down at her. The day had turned out to be a long one, and the end was nowhere in sight. This moment was the first time he had consciously thought of being with her in any situation other than the present. He didn't mind the thought at all.

SUNDAY 28 AUGUST

27

It was just after midnight but neither Walker nor Steph could sleep more than the quick nap they'd snuck in between rounds, though each was spent. Below decks was a galley kitchen and small bathroom. The living area was taken up by a table that folded away into the floor, and the padded seating that lined each side of the boat and folded out to form two beds. After eating, and drinking, they'd made good use of one of those beds. Then the bathroom, in the tiny shower, where Steph proved that she had twelve years of ballet under her belt. Then came the nap, and then they'd moved to the deck above, with Walker grazing his back on the sandy non-slip coating, a happy pain that lasted until the mosquitoes drove them below decks again where they ended their second night together. Now Steph lay on the bed, and Walker was on his back on the teak floor between the beds. Each covered in sweat, a small fan circulating air around them.

'How's the back?' Steph asked.

'Good, here on the floor, if I don't move.' His head was on a folded towel. His hands linked across his chest. His eyes closed.

'We should get you to a doctor.'

'I know how to treat it.'

'Are fucking and fighting part of that recovery plan?'

'Big part.'

Steph laughed a tired laugh. Moonlight spilled in through the port windows as the boat gently rocked against its moorings. Walker stared up at the low ceiling. It had been a long day. A long ten years. He was tired. Worn out. But nowhere near beaten. Hardly started out, barely broken in, if he stopped to think about how many years he might have in front of him. The thought of it made him more tired. But determined. Hungry for the satisfaction of knowing he'd succeeded in a job well done.

'Tell me about your friend who rang,' Steph said.

Her voice was soft in the night, like she was fighting sleep. Walker closed his eyes. Thought about the question, then the man.

'Marty Bloom,' Walker said. 'Friend of my father, from college. Big guy. A true gourmand. My dad's in academia, but Marty went a different route. He went to Vietnam. Well, Laos actually. He was there for the Agency from '68, or '69. Towards the end, but he'd not have known that. Back then, the CIA was running what they called the Silent War. The US military dropped more bombs on Laos than on Japan and Germany in all of World War Two. More ordnance expended per capita than anything or anywhere in history. And it wasn't just at enemy targets. They wouldn't let planes return to base with any bombs still loaded, so they'd drop them randomly in the jungle or on villages on the way home. And that's just part of the disaster we inflicted there – poor people are being maimed every day, kids mainly, picking up fist-sized cluster bombs thinking they're toys.'

'What did Bloom do there?'

'He was like most Agency assets there,' Walker said. 'Running the Hmong guerrilla units. They were allied local fighters, feeding us intel on the Viet Cong. It was a damned dirty war.'

'Some would say all wars are dirty. That they're all crimes.'

'Yeah, well, that's probably right. But there're degrees of it. Of brutality.'

'War has rules. Espionage, not so much.'

'Right. Well, what we did in Laos created a civil war afterwards. The place is still a one-party Communist regime. Those who fought with us way back then are still being persecuted. All that crap we dropped on that place continues to kill people every day.' Walker was silent for a full minute, listening to the sound of the water lapping against the hull. 'So, that was Bloom's start. He's since been posted all over the wold. Seen it all. East and West Germany. Was there when they overthrew the Shah in Iran. You name it, he was there. Panama. Grenada. Gulf War. Libya. Syria. Beirut. Kosovo.'

'Yeah, that was a great move by the way, what you Agency guys did in Iran, it's really paid dividends.'

'Hey, it was you Brits who created all those lines on the map in the Mid East.'

'Are you saying we started all that mess?'

'No, but you messed around in that sandbox way before we did. Afghanistan too.'

'And what of all the oil and drugs that fuel it?'

'Fair call. Marty is one of those guys who has been like a magnet for wars to break out. And a good friend. Always dependable. Always there if I need him.'

Steph said, 'Where's he stationed now?'

'National Security Council,' Walker said. 'He's posted to the White House as an advisor and CIA liaison. And he hates it.'

'Too political?'

'Marty's a field guy, through and through. But he's had some health issues lately, so he's doing a few months stateside. He's a big guy.'

'You said that.'

'Big like three-hundred-and-fifty-plus-pounds big, about my height. Just had both his knees replaced, so he's been in a wheelchair and has crutches and rehab ahead of him. He's then hoping to get the all-clear from the Agency medicos so he can see out his last years back in Eastern Europe. I believe he misses the Cold War. Simpler times.'

'It's still around.'

'You think?'

'This War on Terror thing will wash over and be a blip on history. A distraction from the main game. Russia's the real threat, then, now, and for the immediate future. They're the ones propping up all these radical Islamist groups wanting to harm the West. And it will be so, as long as the current regime is in power in Russia. It's going to take a generation, maybe two, for real change to happen there. Democracy. Until then, it's us against them, and nothing's changed but how we fight and who's on the front lines.'

They fell into silence, with just the sound of the water on the hull. Eventually Walker stood, then put a kettle on the gas burner. Found the coffee they'd brought.

'Bloom told me to bug out,' Walker said, getting dressed.

'What are you going to do with that advice?' Steph asked, sitting up on the bed.

'I'm not going anywhere. I'm getting answers, for all of us.'

'Even if it kills you?'

Walker looked at her as he swallowed more pain and inflammation meds. 'It won't kill me.'

'Those Russians might. Or the GreyStone crew. Or another handful or two of those pills.'

Walker was silent.

Steph said, 'You sure you don't need my help to plant that tracker?'

'It's a one-man gig.'

'One lonely man out there to save us all? How grand. How romantic.'

'Should I have said "one person"?' Walker field stripped the SOCOM pistol and checked it over before reassembling it. He loaded the extra .45 rounds that he had from the pocketed clip of the Colt 1911 pistol from the crackheads' house.

'A small improvement.'

'I'll be fine.' He screwed in the suppressor. 'And I'll be quick.' He bent down and kissed her. 'You sleep. I'll be back before you know it.'

Steph nodded, then settled into the bed and rolled to her side. He took a couple more of the painkillers, and five minutes later he had made his coffee, put his boots on, and could hear that Steph was asleep. He made sure that her revolver was within easy reach, then took his coffee and closed the door, locking it behind him. He sat in the fishing chair topside, steaming mug of coffee in hand, and looked through the binoculars. He could just make out the top of the yacht by a running light upon its tallest radio mast. He would give it another hour, then make his move.

28

Walker swam the two miles to the yacht. The night was dark, with clouds blotting out half the sky, the moon hidden. He had secured the SOCOM in a watertight zip-lock bag, and put that into a plastic shopping bag that he then tied tightly to the front of his belt on his jeans. The SOCOM was rated as an all-weather weapon, but he preferred to know that it wasn't fully waterlogged on his insertion, just to be cautious.

The swim was slow going; breaststroke wasn't as efficient as freestyle but it gave him the least discomfort and it suited his covert approach, allowing him to watch the boat as he neared.

Up close, and from the waterline, the yacht was enormous. There were no lights on in the cabin. As he reached the end of the pier, he stopped and trod water then checked his watch. Almost three am. The coffee and pumping adrenaline and the thought of the task ahead kept him buzzed. He resumed a gentle sidestroke, in the lane between the timber uprights of the pier and the moored vessel. It was completely dark in that void, and the space was big enough to park several cars end to end. He found a spot around the midsection of the yacht where a wooden ladder was set alongside one of the pier's timber posts, and climbed up and out of the water, concealed between the boat and the pier. He unwrapped the pistol and tucked it into

his waistband at the front. He tied the bag to a rung on the ladder, and then he climbed.

The yacht's deck was several feet above the pier, so Walker reached out and grabbed a mooring line and shimmied hand over hand, his legs wrapped around the rope. His back flared up with a new level of pain, and he let himself hang there for a moment, using different degrees of pressure, stretching and pulling, to try to relieve some of the intense sensation coursing through his ribs and back. After what felt like a couple of minutes, as his hands started to cramp up, he hauled himself up and over the gunwale.

He crouched down, letting his back settle. He was dripping all over the yacht's timber deck, a puddle forming where he squatted. A tell-tale sign of an intruder, and an oversight on his part. Before he started to move, he kept very still, listening.

Nothing.

Nothing but the thrum of a generator far below deck. The craft did not move in the lapping sea for its immense bulk below the waterline. He quieted his heart-rate to its base rest rate, to the point where even his breath sounded loud.

All quiet aboard the yacht.

He moved along the deck, keeping close to the side-rail so that he didn't leave wet footprints in an obvious traffic area. He had no torch, so navigated by touch. The dull light from a greasy old vapour lamp at the start of the pier threw some long shadows over the aft deck. Walker paused at the pilot house, listening, watching.

There was a light at the stern of the boat. It took a while for Walker to make out exactly what it was. A man, on sentry, sitting on a deckchair, looking at a small hand-held lit-up screen and smoking a cigarette. Menthols, Walker thought. Terrible choices on both counts, but it suited Walker just fine. The guy's night vision would be shot for a long time looking up from a screen so bright. He probably had sound on the device too, watching a show or playing a game, not giving much thought to keeping an ear out to what went bump in the night.

Complacency, Walker figured. The guy was probably doing permanent night shift and never saw anything untoward beyond the occasional drunk tourists getting their gear off and rolling around on the pier.

Walker tried the main bridge area. Both doors were locked. He didn't want to go walking all over the deck, leaving wet footprints in easy view. Who knew when that sentry might do his rounds and check the yacht over. Maybe never. Maybe hourly, or between smokes. Maybe soon.

Walker climbed, his bare feet silent on the chrome ladder that ran up a side of the wheelhouse. The next level was another driving position, open to the elements towards the stern, which suited his needs just fine.

He put the GPS tracker under the cushion that was velcroed down to a fibreglass seat. The tracker was water-resistant, not waterproof. The box stated that the batteries would power it for four to five days.

Searching the yacht wasn't an option. There were an unknown number of well-armed hostiles below deck. He had the silenced SOCOM pistol and his knife. No small thing, but even in the dead of night a suppressed .45 going off inside the interior of a yacht would wake everyone. And killing someone with a knife wasn't an easy little slice like it was in the movies. Sometimes, sure, if you attacked with total surprise you could stifle your target's scream with a hand and use the other to draw the knife against the carotid artery. But Walker had seen and heard many well-practised Delta and SEAL operators caught out because they let the bad guy either get a noise out, counter-attack, or get their fingers to a trigger and light up the night and wake all their buddies.

So, no search of the boat today. No sabotage, either. This was an observe-and-track mission. As long as he and Steph knew where the boat was, they were okay.

Job done, Walker slipped into the water as silently as he could, causing only minor ripples to splay out. He lay on his back, floating, till he found the direction he needed to head via the constellation

above. Keeping his eyes towards the yacht, specifically at the dot of light from the sentry's hand-held electronic device, he kicked gently for the first hundred metres, his hands crossed on his chest, ready to reach for the SOCOM pistol in the front of his waistband. But the sentry was unmoving, but for flicking the butt of his cigarette into the sea, and then there was a flare of a match or lighter as another smoke was lit up.

Walker checked his bearings again, and started to put his arms into the backstroke.

29

Walker woke with the dawn. Steph wasn't there. Her side of the bed was cold – she'd been out of it for at least fifteen minutes. She wasn't anywhere below deck. The revolver was missing.

He took the SOCOM pistol and went topside, where he found her on the aft deck, sitting in the space between the outboards where a cut-out with a low gate gave access to the water. Her feet dangled in the green-coloured sea as she spoke on her phone. Walker couldn't make out the one-sided conversation.

He went below deck and set about making coffee, and bagels with cream cheese. According to the GPS tracker the Russians were still docked. By the time he got back topside with two steaming mugs, Steph was off the phone.

'Morning, sailor,' she said, taking the offered mug. She turned and sat with her back leaning against a fibreglass gate, looking up at him.

'I'll try not to be offended by that,' Walker said.

'Sorry? Oh, yes, airman, right?'

He smiled. 'Checking in with your superior?'

'And Luke.'

'I'm surprised he's an early riser.'

'Don't judge a book, and all that.'

'And checking in with your boss?'

'Bosses. Plural.'

'Sounds complicated,' Walker said, sitting on the game-fishing chair that was bolted to the deck. The sky was overcast today, and a light rain had started to fall. It was a refreshing mist, but the purple-tinged sky worried him. Bad weather was coming.

'You have no idea,' Steph replied, dipping the bagel in her coffee. 'What? It's a European thing. You should see me destroy a croissant.'

'I take it both your bosses are MI6?'

'What, you think one of them might be Russian, and that I'm a double?'

'Never crossed my mind.' Walker ate his bagel. Sipped his coffee. Watched Steph.

'Okay.' Steph settled cross-legged. 'It was a conference call. My local boss, from the Home Office, based in Washington DC. A real ball-breaker. And her boss, the Deputy Director General, back in HQ.'

'Sounds ominous.'

Walker caught the information and filed it away. *Home Office*. Which meant Steph was MI5, rather than MI6, which reported to the Foreign Secretary. That told him that she was here to mop up a counter-intel problem.

Steph sipped her coffee and nodded. 'They want me home, ASAP. I need to move on this yacht, find out what the Russians are buying.'

'They'll just give up if you can't finish things soon?'

'They'll conclude that the meet might have occurred already. That me being here is beginning to be a waste of time. And they're pissed, because I was the one who pressed this so hard. I made the connections. I insisted on being here.'

'So, you're not going to get the pomp and ceremony when you get home, and the pat on the head?'

'I must admit, tea with the Queen is looking unlikely at this stage. Certainly no statue of me atop a column in Trafalgar Square.'

'And your star power? How's that panning out? Still rising?'

Steph shrugged. 'Waning. Just a little. Not flickering, mind you. But I'm scrappy. And determined. We'll see what the next forty-eight hours bring.'

'That's your deadline?'

Steph nodded, resuming her breakfast as Walker's phone started to vibrate. He looked at the number, the DC area code.

'Marty?' he said.

'First thing,' Bloom began, 'you still in Louisiana?'

'Why wouldn't I be?'

'The place is an open-air lunatic asylum if you ask me. Keep your wits about you. Anyway, Richter . . .' Bloom said. 'He's working on an op that's coming directly from the Director of the FBI's Counter Intelligence office. I'm heading over there to see what I can find out. But it's weird, having it delegated like that – the FBI has no place giving out operational orders to CIA officers. Weirder still that he's allowing the CIA to operate on home soil.'

'Is Richter working alone?' Walker asked. He sipped his coffee as he watched a low-riding shrimp trawler returning from the Gulf.

'It's all compartmentalised, so as of right now you know all that I know.'

'It's the unknown unknowns that are going to bite us on the butt.'

'I thought it was funny when our Secretary of Defense said those words,' Bloom said. 'But now I have to be in a briefing with him every afternoon.'

Walker stood and started to pace the yacht, phone to his ear and coffee mug in his other hand. 'You think this FBI guy will be forthcoming? He might stonewall.'

'You doubt the power of the NSC, my boy.'

True, Walker thought. The National Security Council was the advisory body for the President on national security concerns. Through statutory power they could compel and coerce information paramount to national security from the intel community and law enforcement. And the FBI, while a law-enforcement agency, served as the nation's

counter-intelligence apparatus – the US version of MI5, hunting spies operating on US soil, and they were responsible for unmasking double agents and corrupt intelligence officers within America's own services. So, Walker figured, it would make sense that the FBI's Director of Counter Intelligence would comply with Bloom's request for the meet. But he could also tell him to butt out, citing some kind of internal hierarchy or jurisdiction.

'What about the two CIA assets I left behind in the car?' Walker asked.

'No news generated from that. It's not even on the New Orleans PD's radar. Like it never happened.'

'GreyStone operatives cleaned it up – for Richter?'

'Possible. They may have some cops at NOPD on the books.'

'Likely.' Walker looked across to Steph, who was awaiting news. 'And what of the boatload of Russians or Chechens? Any idea what they're selling or buying?'

'That, Walker my boy,' Bloom said, 'is the pickle in our milk.'

'How so?' Walker asked.

'They're definitely not here to sell,' Bloom replied.

'What do you mean?' Walker asked. He fought off the urge to look to Steph. He kept the phone tight to his ear, so that she wouldn't overhear.

'They're definitely not here to sell,' Bloom repeated. Then he said, 'They're here to buy.'

30

Walker's eyes were on Steph as he ended the call. Bloom hadn't elaborated, because he didn't know what it was that the Russians were buying. But he'd explained that the available intel suggested there was an ongoing joint Five Eyes operation – the intelligence alliance between the United States, the United Kingdom, Canada, Australia and New Zealand – focused on a Russian national, Peskov, who was in the market to buy something big. Something to give them 'power', according to intercepts. That the UK were quarterbacking an op and had sent a field officer to eyeball the transaction, meant that there had been intercepted communications – beyond a suggestion or suspicion – that the buy was legit.

So . . . Walker thought. *Was Steph lying about not knowing about the sell or buy? Or had she been told a lie?*

'News?' she asked.

'Not yet,' Walker replied. He started up the engine, went to the aft anchor and hauled it in, then pulled in the slip lines to the thick scrub of trees. 'Hopefully in a couple of hours we'll know more.'

'But whatever it is, it's enough to get you moving?' Steph asked, sitting next to him as he powered out of the sheltered inlet.

'The GPS tracker is up and running,' Walker replied. 'If the yacht moves, we'll know it. Meantime, I want to go and check out GreyStone.'

'You'll just swim out to Fort Lee? Straight to the people who want you dead.'

'Or alive.' Walker steered the craft out into the channel and headed for the deep water of the Gulf, where he would run parallel to the coast, all the way out to Fort Lee.

'That's the lion's den, Walker,' Steph said. 'What do you hope to get there? Answers? A nice warm welcome? You're a wanted man in their eyes. It's like you're just handing yourself over.'

'I can drop you off at the next stop if you like?' Walker said, looking across at her. 'Pick you up as soon as I see the Russians making a move? Or you drop me off and come back here and watch your boat.'

Steph shook her head. 'It's dangerous for you because they've moved on you already,' she said. 'I'll be fine – no-one knows me here.'

'Well, don't worry, I don't plan on dying today,' Walker replied. 'And I'll talk my way out, if it comes to it. I've got the NSC on speed-dial, remember? GreyStone's business is war, and they rely on US government contracts for the bulk of their income. Billions of dollars, annually, for all the contracts to guard our embassies and assets around the world. I'm sure I could come to some kind of understanding with these GreyStone guys, if it came to it. Maybe I could even get under their skin, see what all this fuss is about.'

Steph was silent for a while, then she said, 'You know why women make better intelligence officers?'

'You're able to charm your way with bellboys to get into hotel rooms?'

'That, sure, it's a part of it. But ultimately it's because we can combine sympathy and persuasiveness with a ruthless streak. Female agent runners who recruit targets from terrorist organisations or other intelligence services are often far more successful than their male counterparts.'

'I don't doubt it. Not sure it's strictly a gender-based thing, though. A man could apply those qualities.'

'Could. But it's not as likely. You'll see, one day. We of the fairer sex are often better at listening and instilling confidence in intelligence sources by keeping calm and putting them at ease. There's also a need for a degree of ruthlessness that I think is also a female skill, although perhaps it's not always wise to say that in polite company.'

'Present company, and all that.'

'Exactly.'

'So, you're saying women are better manipulators, therefore better spies.'

'Put it any way you like, America.' Steph drained her coffee. 'I'm saying that recruiting someone who is in a place to know what you want to know and persuading them to work for us in the first place – and then persuading them to *stay* where they are so you have a long-term source of information coming in – requires what I'd regard as *female* skills. It's about persuasion, sure, and it's about sympathy, it's about listening, it's about giving an air of confidence, a *calm* confidence.'

Walker looked across at her. 'You really don't think I can do all that?'

'You can probably be quite persuasive,' Steph said with a sly smile. 'But I also sense that your unique gift is the ability to blow things up.'

'Maybe I'm the Alpha *and* Omega.'

'You said it.'

'I'm just saying, I'm a terrific listener.'

'You may be good at hearing, but do you really listen?'

'I listened to what you liked last night, and adjusted accordingly,' Walker said, grinning at her. 'Three times, wasn't it?'

Steph punched him playfully in the arm.

'If you're going to be an intel operative, go all the way,' Walker said. 'That's how I see it. Otherwise, don't even start, right? It takes everything, I get that. That means losing your partner, relatives, and maybe even your mind.'

'So, you wouldn't have joined up if your marriage was still a thing?'

'Probably not.'

'Is that why you separated?'

'No,' Walker said. 'Love plus time minus distance equals hate.'

'It's that simple?'

'That's where things are presently at. All that distance was my fault. I like to think it wasn't by design, but who am I kidding? I just didn't prioritise things like a husband should.'

'And so now you have nothing to lose?'

'I didn't say that. We all have something to lose.' Walker upped the speed, kept an eye on the water ahead. The Gulf was choppy this morning, a storm was coming. 'This job could mean not eating for days. Being pursued by enemies you don't know exist. Being disavowed by your own government. It could mean freezing on a park bench. It could mean jail. It could mean derision. Lack of trust. It could mean mockery and isolation. I can deal with all that.'

'Isolation is a gift,' Steph said. 'And all those other things? They're just tests of your endurance, of how much you really want to do it. And you'll do it, despite rejection and the worst odds. And it will be better than anything else you can imagine. The job isn't about justice – but *getting to justice*. There is no other feeling like that.'

He looked across to her. 'Because we're fighting the good fight?'

She was looking at the sky when she answered. 'Time will tell, Walker, time will tell.'

It will, Walker thought. Soon enough we'll know if you lied to me, or were lied to by your bosses. Time will tell . . .

31

Fort Lee was originally a French port, built and run by the military as an overspill and ship-maintenance station from their main bases in the Americas. Then came the Louisiana Purchase. During the Civil War it was used as a port for outfitting and repairing ironclads, as well as running cotton to Europe to earn much-needed money for the Southern cause. After the war, it was renamed Fort Lee, part of the reconciliation process, to honour the Confederate General Robert E. Lee. It was taken over by the United States forces, and remained in the hands of the DoD until the early 1990s, when it was sold under the base realignment schemes that started in earnest with the end of the Cold War. It was touted as being converted into a museum, and there was real local support for it, but its dry-docks had been well maintained and improved over the decades and it still retained significant commercial viability, and therefore real market value, and three transactions later it was now owned by a shell company out of Panama, a distant subsidiary of GreyStone hidden from view for tax and privacy purposes.

From the edge of the east–west coast shipping channel, Fort Lee wasn't much to look at. It had a few miles of smooth rock levies and a pier that acted as a breakwater to a small harbour and the dry-docks. The buildings visible from the sea were low, long barracks, a mix of stone and timber, dating from the French Colonial times and later

the 1950s, when the US government used it briefly as a staging post for shore-assault training for the Army's infantry forces before they headed into the Korean War.

'You're just going to go straight in?' Steph asked. 'Honk the fog horn, see if someone emerges shouting out a greeting – or starts shooting at us?'

'Let's recon the area as much as we can,' Walker said. It was just after seven am, and Bloom's next update was two hours away. Walker wasn't in a rush. He throttled down and took the boat on a big winding arc, wrapping around the seaward side of the thirty-acre compound, taking it all in. There were no patrol boats, no warning signs, no watch towers. Walker looked through their small binoculars – they were crap, but they did the job. No activity ashore was visible, so Walker figured there would be newer buildings with mod cons nearer the road leading in, and that's where the GreyStone operatives would be based. There were no moored boats, but a small aluminium sheeted boat shed stood on a pier, big enough to house a couple of rigged inflatables for a security team. 'All clear.'

Steph shivered as a sudden wind change brought a strong gust of sea spray across the boat.

'Okay,' Walker said, looking at her. 'I'm gonna ask for a favour.'

He throttled right down, keeping the craft steady, and waiting until her gaze met his. 'Drop me off—'

'No,' she said. 'Walker, you're not up to full speed, physically, nor information wise – you've got no idea what you'll be headed into, let alone capable of dealing with it.'

'Pick me up at ten am, at the western edge, just over there, okay?' He pointed to a pebble beach overrun with a thicket of defiant weed and brambles, the dense scrub of twisted old limbs and branches that would tear at skin – as good as a razor-wire fence in keeping intruders out – going on for a couple of acres. 'I need to do this. I need – we need – more information. We need to even the odds a little, see what's what. Be more prepared for what's coming. While I do that, why don't

you spend the next couple of hours headed to the west and keeping an eye on your yacht? See if they're in a hurry, or seem like they're still waiting around for the transaction to take place.'

Steph was silent, but she didn't fight the idea, and she took over the controls of the boat. Walker drank a bottle of water, then made sure he had his cell phone pocketed, and the SOCOM pistol tucked into the back of his jeans, the suppressor in his front pocket. He put his flick-out combat knife in his sock, on the inside of his ankle at his left boot. Steph took the boat in front first, towards the pebbly beach, then threw the engine into reverse, making the impact soft, then kept a little forward power to keep them beached.

'Ten am,' she said. 'Right here, okay?'

'Okay,' Walker said, and before leaving he kissed her.

'See,' she said, pulling away, 'that's the shit I was talking about. We've entered business phase now, okay? Expert. Collegial. No more nooky.'

He pinched her butt and she smiled as he jumped overboard, the water knee-deep, and he was ashore by the time she put the boat into reverse and headed back out to sea. He stayed on the beach, hidden from view from the landward side by the thicket, and watched and listened until Steph was no longer visible. He sucked at the air, pain running up his back. All was quiet.

Walker checked his cell phone. No signal, which he knew could become a problem. He followed the tree line, keeping close for cover. Always listening, constantly stopping, being still, checking. When the thicket cleared, he reached wild grasses spread out over the old barracks encampment: at least two dozen buildings, uniform in size, the squat grey stone buildings of the French garrison in disrepair, grass growing in the eaves, windows long ago broken. The timber-clad barracks from the 1950s stood up pretty well, probably thanks to several layers of military-grade lead-based paint, but they too were clearly long unoccupied.

To the north he followed an unkempt black gravel path, pockmarked with age and neglect. He came to a clearing, and a sign that stated a warning about private property, and trespassers being shot. There was a tall water tower, a timber structure maybe five storeys high, the water tank made of tarred planks of timber. A flashing red light was set into its sides, no doubt a recent add-on for a nearby runway. He found the ladder, the steel rungs rusted and worn, and tested it. It held, but was loose at the fixings. It took him three minutes, occasionally skipping a step that seemed too worn out, and he gingerly put his weight on the two-foot timber platform that wrapped around the edge of the water tank.

Walker saw the new complex, two miles away, to the north-east. There were four double-storey concrete-and-glass buildings, and a large curved hangar big enough to accommodate a couple of private jets or a medium-sized cargo plane. The runway seemed new, the blacktop swept clean by the rain, gleaming in the small shafts of morning sun. There was a small control tower, and running lights, and a fire engine was parked up tight against the hangar.

His phone vibrated. He took it out of his pocket; it had two bars of reception up here, the highest point he could see. The text message was from Steph: *All okay?* He replied *Yes*, then added, *Silence until pick-up*. Then he pocketed the phone.

The sky today was greyed over, the storm clouds now too thick to identify, but despite the low visibility Walker could see a perimeter fence to the east, and beyond that what looked like swamp and brush, dotted with a few fishing shacks. He could hear movement on a busy road to the north, but not see it for thick, almost impenetrable scrub oak and pine. To the south the Gulf was clear, but he could imagine how battered this land would become when storms rolled in, evidenced by the bulk of the man-made harbour and pier, and the way the trees grew leaning to the north-west, as though the wind patterns over time pressed against them. Not much to be done against the tide of mother nature's persistence.

Walker began the slow descent, testing the rungs as he went, snapping clear through one that was made more of rust than steel. At ground level, he took an old path in the grass and headed to the newer complex of buildings. He walked, didn't run. He'd seen no-one, but he didn't want to attract attention. He figured he could explain himself out of a situation with a lax security guard, but if he was taken to a supervisor, and his image was known to them, then he'd be done. As he neared the hangar, he started to worry about guard dogs. That would be the smart security measure, on a compound of this size. They would be chained to their handlers, doing a perimeter, not roaming free, but still – a good guard dog on the front sentry gate could smell him from miles out with the strong wind at his back and raise the alarm.

Close to the hangar the grass cleared to loose gravel that crunched underfoot. There was the sound of a distant truck horn on the highway, and then a new noise. Gunfire. Deliberate, fast. The pitter-patter of small arms: 9-millimetre pistols, at least five of them, firing at targets at an open-air range, to the west, beyond the complex. It had to be at stationary targets, not a kill house, because the shots were rapid and in synch, and soon it stopped; a pause in which he imagined at least five armed people reloading. By the time his back was up against the wall of the hangar, the shooting had started up again. He hoped it was the base security detail, and that while they were doing their target practice, they wouldn't be doing any sentry rounds.

Walker followed the hangar to its end, away from the taxiway. There was an emergency-exit door set into it, and small windows. Rounding the corner, he saw new office buildings 400 yards away, their reflective glass giving no clue whether they were occupied. He couldn't risk it. Four hundred yards of exposed space.

He doubled back, to the other end of the hangar. There was noise inside, the sounds of people working. He edged around, squatted down, peeked through the open hangar doors. There was a Gulfstream inside, the gleaming white jet with its starboard engine cowling open,

two maintenance guys on a scaffold, their backs to him, working on it. No-one else in the hangar that he could see. He memorised the tail number to relay to Bloom so that it could be tracked if necessary. Beyond the jet were two helicopters, both painted matt black. One was an old Huey. The other a newer Bell. A couple of Humvees were parked inside, and a fuel truck.

Walker backtracked to the water tower, where he stopped and checked the time: 9.25. He considered climbing up again, checking his phone for messages from Bloom, but decided against it. Better to get to the water's edge early, wait for Steph's exfiltration, take the messages and calls from a safe distance. He took the worn path back to the old barracks, where he paused to make sure all was quiet and clear. He pressed on across the wild grass to the pebbly beach. Almost twenty minutes early. He found a place to hide, and he settled into a nook, shielded from all sides of view, his front covered with a few loose branches, and waited.

And waited.

32

Walker waited until eleven am. An hour beyond the agreed meet time. No sign of Steph, or any craft. He emerged and went as far along the edge of the waterline as he could get, in places having to dip into the water to get around rocks, constantly scanning the horizon. The day was hot now, and the water choppy. The sea lapped above his knees. He checked his phone, which had no service, and figured he'd have to go back to the top of the water tower. That journey took twenty minutes, the brambles cutting at his bare arms as he muscled his way through, and when he got to the top of the tower, to the seaward side and out of sight from the complex, he again checked his phone.

Two bars of reception. No missed calls.

But two text messages, both from Bloom.

He ignored them for a moment and first tried calling Steph. Aside from Bloom's number, it was the only number stored on the phone. He listened as it rang. And rang. And rang. No answer, and no message service. He sent her a text message, asking for an update. She could be trailing the yacht. She might have needed to stop for gas, or to help someone, been called away by something urgent – or been held up for any number of innocuous reasons. Or something sinister. All those possibilities had run through his mind over the past hour. The longer the time dragged on, the more he was leaning

towards something had gone wrong. It was the lack of contact that triggered his alarm bells.

He went to Bloom's messages. The first read simply: *Call me*. That was from 9.42. The next, from 10.24, read: *We've got problems. Call in. Be cautious.*

Walker dialled Bloom. It was answered on the second ring.

'You okay?' Bloom asked.

'Yeah,' Walker replied. 'What's news?'

'Okay, listen.' Bloom took a breath, and there was a noise, like the big man was shifting and settling in his chair to get comfortable in his upcoming sermon. 'I had the meeting at the FBI, about Richter. He's ostensibly posted stateside as a specialist trainer for Agency case officers to recruit and train and equip agents provocateurs.'

'I got that much from him.'

'Right. Thing is, he pulled a helluva lot of strings to stay in the Agency. The guy's jacket is heavily redacted, but from what I've seen, what I've heard, and what I've since found out, is that in his time in Afghanistan he was part of some . . . let's call it *obscure shit*. And there's an FBI flag on it. That's what made it classified there at Assistant Director level.'

'FBI? They're looking at him as a double agent?'

'That's all it could be. He's compromised, somehow.'

'Does he seem like the type to sell out?'

'Everyone has a price.'

'Everyone?'

'Everyone. You'll understand that one day.'

'You know I'm gonna need you to define *obscure* in this case.'

'Right.' Bloom paused, then said, 'Walker, you sure you're safe right now?'

Walker looked around. There wasn't anywhere he could go without a boat.

'Yeah,' Walker replied. 'I'm safe and sound, Uncle Marty. Continue.'

'Okay. Richter was a big part of our Mid-East Taskforce programs, hunting down HVTs throughout the country.'

'I was assigned to a couple of those.'

'Well, chances are he had his fingers in them, in the planning or logistics, in one way or another,' Bloom said. 'Ever hear of Taskforce 181?'

'Rumours. Hard nuts and specialist cases. Contractors only, so their missions couldn't come back to bite the US government in the ass when they smoked civilians or called in air support that took out hospitals.'

'That's them, and then some,' Bloom said. 'They mustered in late 2003, and are said to be still doing their work, albeit under a different codename, because things got too hot for them, even for an off-books team with no oversight.'

'How hot do things have to get for that to happen?'

'My thoughts exactly, and I'm hoping to have more on that soon.'

'I thought you said being part of the NSC gave you powers and clearance as close as possible to God.'

'It does. If there's files and intel available, I'll get eyes on it, it's just a matter of time.'

'Yeah, well, tick-tock my old friend, it's my ass dangling out here.'

'I told you to disappear, wait this one out.'

'I'm in it,' Walker said. 'Anything else?'

'Not verified yet, but some rumours that are fleshing out to seem legit,' Bloom said. 'Earlier this year, Taskforce 181 was the tip of a spear that went into Tora Bora. We'd intercepted chatter that the Taliban had an ace up their sleeve, some kind of big-ass weapon that the Soviets left behind, and that if they got it operational, shit could get real – real fast. Like turn-the-tide-in-the-war kind of big deal.'

'What kind of weapon could do that?'

'Nothing on that yet, but if you think about it, it's gotta be man-portable, to be in the caves and the mountains, so it's not like it's an Akula-class sub or a squadron of main battle tanks or Mig fighter jets.'

'But it could be something worth hundreds of millions?'

'Where'd you hear that figure?'

'My UK friend. That's the figure that GCHQ intercepted via the Five Eyes SIGINT program. That's what her Russian or Chechen goons were in town to buy.'

'Well, that ups the stakes. Makes it sound a lot more legit. Something game-changing was up in those mountains, ex-Soviet, and worth a helluva lot of money.'

'And could now be in play here, stateside, for sale to some arms buyers with their own little dirty war that they want to even up.'

Bloom was silent.

'But man-portable, for that money?' Walker said. 'It can't be Stinger missiles, because there'd be thousands of them. What else can a man carry into battle that's worth that much money?'

'What about a backpack nuke?' Bloom suggested, and his voice was grave.

'Did the Soviets have those?'

'We had them, they did too,' Bloom said. 'Man-portable. Low-yield tactical nukes, designed to be carried by an infantryman on his back, to blow up dams and critical infrastructure behind enemy lines. Ruskies even had nuclear artillery rounds.'

'Shit,' Walker said. 'You really think the Russians had a version they sent to Afghanistan – and they not only *didn't* use it, but they left it *behind*?'

'Maybe they lost it,' Bloom said. 'Or it was stolen. Or sold.'

'Lots of maybes.'

'The point is, they might have, and there might be a nuke out there,' Bloom replied. 'It makes sense, right? The Russians were bogged down in Stan for a decade. Lost tens of thousands of troops to combat and disease. Dirty-as-hell war, nothing as clean as ours in terms of all the air power and drones that we've brought to the fight. They had man-to-man, hand-to-hand stuff going on. They kept serious numbers of boots on the ground. A small nuke would have

been a helluva way to clear out the tunnel complexes up there in the Afghan mountains. And spook the shit out of the enemy nationwide.'

'And turn the tide of the war . . .' Walker shifted a little on the water tower, taking the pressure off his back. 'Okay, so what are we saying? Taskforce 181 find this missing nuke, and what – they keep it themselves? Sell it on the black market? And Richter's somehow in on it?'

'It's all a pile of maybes at this stage,' Bloom said. 'But I'm working on it.'

'But why did he want me delivered here?' Walker said. 'Alive, preferably. Dead, if necessary. What's that got to do with it?'

Bloom paused, then said, 'Jed, what do you mean, *here*?'

'GreyStone.'

'Tell me you're not at the compound.'

But Walker couldn't. Because at that moment, the red dot of a laser sight appeared on the centre of his chest.

33

Walker did as he was instructed. He kept his hands above his head, as the red laser dot remained steady on his centre mass. He breathed deeply and kept himself calm, hoping the man on the trigger was doing the same. He had a rule in situations like this: when someone has a gun on you, don't give them simple reasons to pull the trigger.

'Toss the cell phone down to the ground!'

Walker looked down at the guard. He was alone. Dressed in US Army fatigues, otherwise known as Battle Dress Uniform, in a forest pattern. He had a black baseball cap that had something written on it that Walker couldn't make out from this far away. He could make out the gun, though. An HK416, with custom scope, and the laser designator, and bulbous suppressor.

'I just came up here to make a call,' Walker said. 'There's no reception down there.'

The guy paused, then, he called out, 'What are you doing here?'

'My boat ran out of gas,' Walker replied. 'Just over there.'

Walker pointed in the vague direction of the pebble beach landing.

'Look,' Walker said, his hands still raised. 'I don't want any trouble. I've got a couple hundred bucks on me. It's yours, to look the other way. If you can let me get down, I'll get straight back to my boat, and the harbour master is sending out a skiff with emergency gas.'

The guard paused again, then yelled out: 'The harbour master's headed here?'

'Of course,' Walker said. He shook his phone. 'I was just speaking to them, on my cell.'

'Just get down here,' the guard ordered. 'And toss the phone first.'

'I just bought it.'

'You not see this gun?'

Walker nodded. He tossed the phone, and it landed in the tall grass about five metres to the guy's left. Well out of reach, and it would mean the guard would have to stay put and watch Walker's descent. He didn't want him checking the call log before he got down.

Walker sat on the edge of the water tank, and took the SOCOM pistol from the back of his jeans. He held it in his hands, behind his back, for a second, thinking of the possibilities and repercussions, then he put it behind him, against the water tank, out of sight, and he turned around. As he manoeuvred to get onto the ladder, he pulled the suppressor from his front pocket and put that next to the pistol, then descended. There was no way that he could have made his way down and not have the weapon seen. A tactical loss.

By the time Walker put his feet onto the gravel surface at the base of the water tower, the guard had a hand against his back and pushed him against the ladder. Walker didn't fight it. He put his hands to his head and kept them there as the guard patted him down, one handed. He did a half-thorough job. He went over Walker's waistband and pockets, but he didn't find the knife tucked inside his boot. And Walker could have stuffed the pistol down the front of his underpants, if he'd had the opportunity, because the guard avoided that area completely.

'Turn around,' the guy ordered.

Walker did, keeping his hands up.

The guard took a step back, which was smart, tactically. He was a pace away now and he held the assault rifle in a two-handed grip, the laser pointer directly finding home again at Walker's centre mass.

The guard's cap was embossed with the logo and name of GreyStone: the *Y* flourished to an infinity-like symbol, wrapping the name, so that one oval shape was around the Grey and the other around Stone. The guy was about six foot tall, maybe thirty years old, clean shaven and in good shape, and clearly an ex service member of some sort by the way he carried himself.

'Where's your wallet?' the guard asked.

'On my boat.'

'Why?'

'Why not?'

'It's your wallet, asshole. You carry your wallet.'

'Not me. I carry cash. My ID stays where it needs to – my car, or my boat, or my hotel room.'

'Why?'

'Why not?'

The guard paused, as if computing the logic, maybe figuring that it was a smart move if you didn't want to be identified, then he said, 'What are you doing here?'

'I told you, my boat ran out of gas. Faulty gauge. I managed to nudge it up to shore. Look at my arms – all cut up from your trees and brambles.'

'Ain't no brambles here.'

'Well, if they're not that, you've got yourselves some nasty-ass weeds along the waterline.'

'I'll tell the gardener to replace them with daisies.'

'That'd be nice. Improve the smell too.' Walker made a show of rubber-necking around. 'What is this place – military? Some kind of Big Easy version of Area 51?'

'Don't be a wiseass.'

'What is it with you and asses?' Walker asked, and instantly regretted it, as it went against his rule of not provoking a person with a gun pointed at him.

'Go retrieve your phone. Keep your hands where I can see them.'

Walker nodded and headed in the direction of his phone, his hands now down by his side. The guard was keeping his distance, and Walker knew he had no chance to take him like this. Can't outrun or outmanoeuvre a bullet, especially when the firearm is in the hands of a pro. He stomped around in the grass, using his feet to flatten it out rather than bending down. It took a couple of minutes, then he found it. The screen was lit up, with a new text message, but he didn't have time to check it, because the guard moved in close and snatched it up then shoved Walker onwards.

'Now, show me your boat,' the guard said. 'If it checks out, we can wait until your gas delivery arrives and you're on your way. If it's suspect, you'll have to come to the security HQ with me.'

Walker led on. A wise operator would have seen that the path through the wild grass had been taken more than once this morning, but the guard had his eyes fixed hard on Walker's back. Every now and then Walker paused and looked around, as though to get his bearings, and the guard kept gesturing south. The day was getting hotter; sweat ran down his back. The T-shirt was a cheap cotton blend, and it didn't breathe, and it was new and scratchy and irritating. Walker ran through possibilities and outcomes to various actions that he could take, but the fact was, the biggest unknown was what he would find at the beach. Likely nothing, in which case he would have to make his move against the guard. He figured he could feign exasperation, a real melt-down, as though his boat had drifted off, and he could spin a story about the boat being his employer's and he being in big trouble and losing his job and having to pay for the boat and maybe it was stolen and what was this place and he'd demand to talk to someone in charge – that they should be responsible, because if he'd not been held up at gunpoint he'd have made it back here in time to get to his boat. And then, in all that mayhem, Walker would make his move.

A hand to the danger end of the assault rifle. Get that out of play. His left hand. His right arm he would use as a weapon. First,

an elbow to the guard's face to send him back. Might even get the weapon out of his hands, use that on him, as a club, knock him out, no need to kill him. If he didn't let go, Walker would side-step, left hand still on the weapon, and use his right arm to choke the guy out. Hold him long enough until he closed the arteries that fed oxygen and blood to the brain, then let him drop. Not too long – too easy to kill someone, or leave them with an acquired brain injury. Then he'd tie him up, gag him, then swim for it. He couldn't wait for nightfall. This guy would be missed, at the very least by the end of his shift. Walker had to deal with him, and be gone.

It settled him, as he pushed his way through the last of the thicket and emerged at the edge of the pebbled beach, knowing that he had options. There were always options.

But then his best options went out the window.

A boat was there.

34

The boat in the tiny harbour up against the pebble beach was his boat. It was moored very close to where it had been earlier that morning. There was no engine sound, and there was no sign of Steph.

'Okay, well, maybe I owe you an apology, sir,' the guard said.

Walker glanced back at him. He'd lowered his assault rifle to a forty-five-degree tilt. Still action ready, but not pointed directly at him.

Walker didn't see it as good news. This was a problem. A big one – unless Steph was hiding in the scrub with the revolver pointed at the back of the guard's head. He glanced around, trying to be casual about it.

'What you doing?' the guard asked.

'I need to take a leak,' Walker replied.

'Do it in the water,' the guard said.

Walker went to the water's edge, where the waves gently lapped against the black and grey pebbles. He actually did need to go. He whistled as he went, loud enough to be heard. An English tune from Britten's *A Midsummer Night's Dream*, meant as a sign for Steph, if she heard it. He made his task last, hoping that Steph was either hidden away land-side, watching, or on the boat, now alerted to what was going on, looking out the port window, readying her revolver, waiting for a chance to act.

'Hey!' a voice called.

Steph.

Shit.

She emerged from below deck, saw the scene and froze. Walker zipped up.

The guard put the barrel of the assault rifle hard up against Walker's back, between his shoulderblades.

'Two-seven to base,' Walker heard the guard say into his coms. 'I need immediate support at south-east harbour, on the beach. Two possible hostiles, maybe more, in custody. Copy?'

Walker didn't hear the reply as he ran through the possibilities of taking the guard on, but none were good.

'You on the boat,' the guard called out. 'How many more are you?'

'Just – just me,' Steph replied. She was standing on the port side of the deck. Her hands on the rail. Concern on her face.

'Move an inch, either of you, and I shoot!' the guard yelled.

Steph nodded.

'Anything else you want to tell me?' the guard asked Walker quietly.

Walker remained silent.

Five minutes later, a ridged inflatable arrived from the water, with three GreyStone guards aboard. They boarded the larger boat, where one held Steph at gunpoint while the other two searched below deck. They called all-clear, then put Steph in flexicuffs and loaded her onto their craft. The whole while the barrel of the HK416 remained firmly planted against Walker's back. Two minutes after that, a squad of four GreyStone guards arrived on foot through a gap in the thicket. Walker was cuffed, his hands in front of him, and he was marched back towards the compound. His only glimmer of hope, as he was ducking and pushing his way through the gnarly branches that tore at his skin, was that on the east coast, his friend Marty Bloom might soon be worried enough about him to put a trace on his phone.

•

On the east coast of the United States, Marty Bloom was in his office. It was a small, nondescript room on the third floor of the Executive Office Building, opposite the White House. Perfect for a guy like Bloom to be on hand for NSC meetings for the few months he was assigned to the task. He was concerned that Jed Walker hadn't responded to his last message, but he figured that the boy was okay, that he could handle himself. Still, he had an uneasy feeling about it.

Because of GreyStone. And because of Richter.

He considered calling Richter directly to arrange a meeting. A little face to face in a downtown DC diner. Coffee, not drinks. Purely business. Get to the heart of the matter.

But he put the idea off for now. Better to find out more first, before poking the hornets' nest, if there was one where Richter was concerned. Because, Bloom was unconvinced that Richter was a double. He'd seen them before, plenty of times. He knew the MO. Women, money, glory, adulation. And from all he'd read, and those he'd now spoken to, Richter appeared to want none of that. He'd been married twice and divorced twice. One kid, a twenty-year-old daughter at college in Boston. He was considered something of a monk when it came to partying. Same went for money; Bloom had seen Richter's bank accounts and mortgage details on the small Bethesda apartment and his humble government $401k and the alimony payments and the support he sent his kid. All legitimate. And the guy was a patriot through and through. Started out a Marine, third in a line of family members to do so. CIA sent him to Vietnam and Laos. A respected intelligence officer ever since. Never considered politically motivated enough to rise up the ranks. Never got his hands dirty with any scandals, aside from agency-sanctioned missions, which was all par for the course.

Bloom looked out his single window, through the shutters.

His next lead was what he was waiting on. The boat of Russians.

His phone rang. The screen showed it was coming from the White House.

'Bloom,' he said.

'Mr Bloom, I have NSA McCorkell on the line,' the receptionist said.

'Put him through,' Bloom replied.

'Marty?' McCorkell said.

'Bill,' Bloom replied.

'I hear you're enquiring about a super-yacht stocked with high-grade vodka.'

It didn't surprise Bloom that the National Security Advisor to the President of the United States would be across his urgent calls and emails.

'You heard correct,' Bloom said. 'Anything you can tell me?'

'Think you can wheel yourself over here?'

'See you in ten.'

'Bud, don't flatter yourself, or have a coronary. Meet me in my office in twenty.'

35

Walker didn't get the chance to ask Steph why she'd missed the agreed extraction time, because the two of them were kept separate. They weren't half-bad, these GreyStone operators. Walker watched them closely, looking for anything he could exploit – a moment of lax concentration, where he could get a weapon, gain the upper hand – but it never materialised. Steph was taken ashore and marched ahead of them to a waiting Humvee, and was driven twenty metres ahead of the vehicle that Walker was bundled into. The ride was quick, the drivers urgent. One of the GreyStone operators, riding up front in the passenger seat, kept looking over his shoulder at Walker. It was clear that he knew who Walker was – and what Walker had done to the guy from the bar. Maybe they'd been friends.

But revenge would have to wait.

The vehicles pulled up to a hard stop by the tallest building of the new complex. A man waited outside. He wore a light-coloured linen suit, and a white cotton shirt undone at the neck. He was tanned and lean, and his eyes were hidden behind reflective shades. His shoes looked expensive.

The guards manhandled their two captives out of the vehicles, and the suited man told them to take Steph inside and seat her in an office. He headed over to Walker.

The guard who had originally taken Walker in passed his superior the cell phone. 'He had this on him.'

'That was all?' He looked it over.

'Yep.'

'Incinerate it. Now.'

The guard left, the phone in hand. The suited man turned to Walker.

'Jed Walker . . .' he said as he neared, then came to a stop a pace in front of his captive. He took off his sunglasses, his grey eyes searching Walker's. They were a similar vintage, but this guy looked like he'd lived a tough life and was now trying his hardest to reclaim some luxe time. He looked like he'd had some kind of makeover, with trimmed and neatened eyebrows and tinted lashes. His thinning hair was a shade of black not found in nature. 'Remember me, asshole?'

'Should I?' Walker said. He genuinely didn't. And it didn't go down well.

The guy's eyes watched Walker's intently, as though looking for a tell, or a sign that Walker was being tough or a wiseass. After about five seconds his eyes squinted and he called out: 'Johnson.'

Johnson stepped up to the plate, into position next to the suited man. Johnson turned out to be the operator who had been looking back at Walker in the Humvee. Johnson was a big guy. The suited man was a big guy, a hard guy. But Johnson was heavier. More a juiced-up powerlifter to the suited man's heavyweight boxer.

'Johnson, tell me,' the suited man began, 'what do you most want to do to Walker?'

'Kill him,' Johnson said, his eyes not leaving Walker's. 'Slowly. Make him feel it. All night long.'

'Well, we can't have that, not yet,' the suited guy said, the corners of his mouth crinkling into a smile, revealing Hollywood-white veneered teeth. 'It's a gift, having him here, with the woman. We're going to put him to work. But give him a little love pat or two, on the body,

let him know we mean business. And as a taste of what's to come. Make sure he can still function.'

Walker knew what was in his immediate future. Pain. He braced for impact, but he didn't bother evading or fighting it, and not just because a beefy hand held each of his biceps. Putting up a fight would just make it worse.

The first blow was an uppercut in the rib cage, and though he tensed for it, it knocked the air out of him and his knees gave out. The two guards holding his arms let him fall. The next blow was epic. Not just for the ferocity, nor the surprise, but for the injury he was carrying into the fight. Johnson dropped down onto Walker with an elbow that struck underneath Walker's right shoulderblade. The kinetic energy reverberated through him, lighting up pain sensors along his spine. Walker stifled a scream, and rolled to his side, where he met with Johnson's boot to the face. Walker's cuffed hands were up, an instinctive defensive move, and they took the brunt of the impact, but the force was enough to start up his nose bleed from the day before. Walker's world was one of stars and blackness, his body shook and he felt the dizzying pull of unconsciousness beckoning him, a whisper that said, *Tap out, you'll feel better . . .*

'Enough,' the suited guy said.

The shadow of Johnson moved away.

'He's in a bad way,' one of the guards said.

'Who cares,' Johnson replied. 'He's gonna be worse off soon enough.'

'Get him up,' the suited guy said.

Walker breathed hard through the pain as the two guards at his sides hauled him to his feet. His back felt contorted, as if his ribs and their tendons had popped out again, twisting him sideways.

The suited man passed Walker a handkerchief. 'My name's Spicer. Captain Spicer. 10th Mountain. We met in Kandahar. And again in Helmand Province. You were part of a recommendation that led to my termination.'

'Then I'm sure you deserved it,' Walker said, holding the cloth to his nose bleed. His hands were shaking.

'Well, I should be thankful, really,' Spicer said, looking around. 'I mean, shit, look at me now. Gone from a captain's salary in this nation's army, to running stateside operations for GreyStone. Hell, I'll be CEO of global ops one day. That's if I wanted to stick around. All thanks to you. But one never joins the dots going ahead for what they are when the chips are down, am I right? I mean, it's not like I could have imagined all this, leading up to this day, all that time ago.'

Walker was silent, and watched as Spicer paced around him. A full circle, appraising him, seeing if he was up to a task.

'Thing is, Walker . . .' Spicer said, stopping in front of him. 'Having you here was part happenstance, part planning. The cherry on top. But that's by the by. I'm a reasonable man. A business man. And I have a proposition. You do a job for me today, and we'll let your little lady go free. We'll keep her here, safe and sound, until we know the job is done. How about that?'

'I'd heard you didn't mind if I was delivered here dead or alive,' Walker replied.

'That's when there were two other newbie CIA assets we could have used in your stead, to draw out any other counter-intel operatives sniffing around,' Spicer replied. 'But those ex-SEALs are out of the picture, thanks to you. So, how about it? Feel up to it? Feel like you've got one last mission in that crippled-looking body of yours? Hmm? Not for me, but to save your little friend?'

Walker looked around at the GreyStone soldiers. Johnson had murder in his eyes, his right hand resting on the butt of a holstered sidearm. The others looked like they couldn't care less what Walker chose to do. But a choice was being presented, and Walker liked choices. Especially when they came with the chance to even things up a little, no matter how slim the chance of success; some glimmer of hope was better than none.

'And don't get any ideas,' Spicer said. 'You'll have a GPS tracker and microphone attached to you at all times, until you return. You stuff around, the woman bites the bullet – then I unleash the boys, and they will hunt you down, and they will kill you.'

'What kind of job?' Walker asked.

'I'll get to that.'

'Okay, I'll do it,' Walker said. 'But I need pain meds. And surely one of your goons here is trained as a field medic. I need some ribs fixed.'

'We'll fix what we can, and clean you up, and send you out,' Spicer said, smiling. 'I'm going to enjoy this, Walker. Far more than you are.'

36

'Marty, I'd say have a seat, but I see you've brought your own,' Bill McCorkell said looking up from his desk.

'I'd say respect your elders,' Bloom said, wheeling himself into McCorkell's office in the north-east White House, 'but judging by those bags under your eyes and those lines on your face, I'd say you're older than me.'

'Only in spirit.'

Bloom respected McCorkell. A career intelligence specialist, he was a year into serving this President in the position of National Security Advisor, just as he'd served the previous two, each POTUS from a different political party – a testament to the man's reputation as a bipartisan specialist with nothing but his country's security at heart. Word on the street was that the three consecutive Presidents had offered him his choice of job, and he'd chosen a position within the National Security Council each time.

'I see your Jets had a good year.'

'Don't, you'll open up old wounds,' McCorkell said. 'So, Marty, listen, this thing you're looking into? The Russian yacht? Last seen in New Orleans?'

'I thought it was Chechens?' Bloom said.

'Russians, Chechens – all one and the same in this instance,' McCorkell said. 'They're the Kremlin lackeys. And mark my words,

Marty: the Russians and their dictatorial puppet-master of a former KGB man in charge are going to be milking Islamic extremism for many years to come. They're developing and financing their own international bogeyman to mess with us. They're subversive and deceptive in ways we'll never manage to be.'

'Right. And?' Bloom asked, his hands in his lap. 'Why the call over here? You got something to share about this boatload of bogeymen?'

'Boatload? We need a better collective noun for Russian operators,' McCorkell said. 'A subversion? A deception?'

'A *problem*,' Bloom said. 'And I'm on the clock with a live one here, Bill, so get to it.'

McCorkell sat back in his chair. 'I called you over to let you know that the situation is covered.'

'What's that mean?'

'The Brits are all over this,' McCorkell said. 'It's their thing.'

'It's in our backyard.'

'All the more reason we don't have the CIA looking into it. You know how it works.'

'Well, there's a complication,' Bloom said. He went on to tell him about Richter. And Walker, though he left his name out of it, just said that it was a new CIA covert-operations officer, a family friend, who reached out and flagged it with him, and that's how he'd become involved.

'Shit.' McCorkell stood and went to his window. 'A shit storm of Russians.'

'I told you, it's our problem now,' Bloom said. 'So, what do we do about it? I can't just ignore it. This family friend – he's in harm's way. He's *in* it, Bill. And that's on us.'

'It's on Richter.'

'And Richter is on us too,' Bloom replied. 'He's bent. Gotta be. He had no reason to send this new recruit in there in the first place.'

'Then it's a counter-intelligence operation,' McCorkell said, turning around. 'You need to get the FBI involved. Have them move on it.'

'You want me just to call Mueller and put in a request?'

'No, I'll give you a name, a good guy, does a lot of NSC liaison,' McCorkell said, writing a name on a Post-It and passing it over. He sat on the edge of his desk, near Bloom. 'He's good, and can be trusted to move fast. We can't afford to blow up what the Brits have going on, with GCHQ and MI5 on the case. And then there's the time ticking for your new recruit.'

'He's a good kid.'

'I don't doubt it.'

'He's really gonna be something, mark my words.'

'Then make sure you have the FBI bring him back in one piece,' McCorkell replied. 'But talk to the Brits too, make sure their mission isn't fouled.'

'What was it? The Russian thing?'

'Something about a buy.'

'Right. An arms trade, right here in our backyard.'

'Could be. Sounds like you've gotta burn some rubber.'

'Hardy-ha.' Bloom stuck the Post-It in his inside jacket pocket, then wheeled himself around towards the door, and then paused. 'What about my guy? If he needs urgent assistance?'

'I'm afraid he's on his own until the Brits clear things,' McCorkell said. 'This op is bigger than any one man. Though I hear from Justice that there's a money-laundering angle to all this. Just contain the Richter thing. You said your man was a good operator. Let's see him prove you right.'

•

Walker was placed in a building adjacent to the tallest in the new complex. They were all of the same design and construction, all pre-cast reinforced concrete-slab walls with reflective window glazing. This building was double storey, and the ground level was a barracks of sorts, for the guard crew: twenty-four rooms, the doors to most open, each showing a private room and ensuite the equivalent of a

business-class hotel. The beds were made and the rooms squared away with military precision. Walker was led upstairs by the two guys who'd been holding his arms. Johnson was dispatched to some other task. Spicer maybe had an appointment with a tan bed or a teeth-bleaching kit. No sign of Steph.

Up stairs, each a mark of pain up his spine, and down a polished concrete hall, then shoved into a room that resembled a two-bed hospital suite. A minute later another uniformed GreyStone man attended, and Walker was let go by the two guards, who remained sentry by the door. After a brief line of questioning about his back injury, his binds were cut and he was helped face-first onto a gurney.

The medic applied pressure against the side of Walker's spine, and after ten minutes of manipulation, he was told to sit up, his legs to one side of the stretcher bed, and the medic started to twist and turn and pull at Walker's torso. After that there was more pressing and working at the problem area. It ended with the guy trying to stretch out Walker's back, but Walker had about eighty pounds on him, and there wasn't much satisfaction to it.

'Tape it up?' Walker asked as the medic applied some topical cream.

'Tape ain't gonna fix what you've got,' the guy replied, wiping his hands, then giving Walker a couple of packets of pain and inflammation meds from a cabinet. 'It's not broken bones, but they're dislocated, at least two each side. Stretched ligaments. You need time and therapy – but you're probably shit out of luck on both counts, right?'

Walker was silent.

One of the GreyStone guards spoke into his radio, nodded at the reply, then said, 'Okay, tough guy, we're dropping you back in New Orleans.'

'I want to talk to my friend first,' Walker said, standing up from the gurney.

'Not gonna happen,' the guard replied. His accent was Tennessee maybe. He'd probably be an okay country singer. But right now Walker just wanted to punch his teeth out. 'You've got less than two

hours until your first objective, Walker. I suggest you snap to it, or you'll never speak to your lady friend again.'

The medic put a small black transponder in Walker's front pocket. It had a thin wire attached, a tiny microphone at its end, which he secured with medical tape to Walker's chest.

'Testing, testing,' the medic said, and he put a transponder to his ear. He repeated the test, then nodded and told Walker to put his shirt back on.

'He's ready,' a guard at the door said into his radio. 'Copy that.' He looked to Walker. 'Go time.'

37

Marty Bloom picked up his office phone and held the number of the FBI Special Agent in his hand – and paused. He stuck the Post-It to his desk and dialled a different number.

'Yes sir?'

'I need the location of a cell phone,' Bloom said.

'Go ahead, sir,' replied the Navy lieutenant.

Bloom read out the number of Walker's burner cell phone.

'Sorry, sir, the cell must be off.'

'Last known location?'

'One moment.'

Bloom heard the tapping of fingers on a keyboard.

'Last known location, as of just over an hour ago, was Louisiana. Coastal region. Not far from New Orleans.'

'Email me GPS coordinates, will you?'

'Yes, sir.'

Bloom hung up. Then he dialled the FBI.

•

Walker was dropped off via boat at the edge of Woldenberg Park on the Mississippi River. He was given an envelope that felt like it contained cash.

'Tells you all you need to know,' the Greystoner from Tennessee said. 'And remember, we're going to hear everything you do, and track your every movement. Your success today reflects what happens to your friend.'

'And when I'm done?' Walker said.

'We'll come find you,' the guy replied, then they powered away in the ridged inflatable.

Walker watched them depart, then looked around. The paved walkway along the river's edge was busy with tourists and the occasional jogger and cyclist. He walked through the park, over the light-rail tracks before a rattling streetcar slipped by, and he stopped in at a Starbucks on Iberville Street. He ordered a tall iced coffee, added a little cream, then stood by a standing-only bench at the window and opened the envelope.

It contained two photos, each of a different man. The one labelled 'Target' showed a middle-aged man, average-looking, a little overweight, ruddy complexion and flabby in the cheeks and jowls like he'd had an office job his whole life. The other, labelled 'Watcher', was around the same age, but had lived a markedly different life. Definitely ex-military. Dark Slavic features. Square shoulders. Watchful eyes. The envelope also contained $200 in used twenties, and a note: *3pm, New Orleans Museum of Art. Follow the target. If you lose him, you lose everything.*

Walker drained his drink and considered the money; for cab fares and the museum entry fee, he assumed. He folded the envelope in half and put it in his front pocket, looking around the coffee shop until he decided on an elderly couple sitting and having lunch. Tourists, judging by the attire and the maps and the cameras. Walker headed over and politely asked if he could look at their map for a moment, which led to a discussion of where he was from, and ten minutes later he got himself out of the conversation and left with their copy of the hotel-supplied map.

Stepping outside the airconditioned cafe was like stepping into a sauna. It was near on a hundred degrees, with humidity to match.

Walker looked over the map, got his bearings. He also found the location of Luke's house, and memorised a couple of paths leading to there and the museum. He wanted to get to the museum fast, to get an idea of the layout, so he flagged the first cab he saw and passed over twenty bucks, asking the guy to ramp up the aircon.

He needed to contact Bloom, perhaps via Luke. Somehow get some cavalry in town and get Steph out of Fort Lee. But he couldn't call him on a phone, because of the GreyStone mic. By the time the cab pulled up to a stop on the museum's circular concourse, he had a pretty good idea of how he wanted to play things out.

Once inside he grabbed a tourist guide of the museum, and bought a disposable camera, a small pair of binoculars, a copy of an old map of New Orleans circa the turn of the last century, and a novelty pen. Sixteen-fifty. He found a bench seat and wrote out a note, then tore off the bottom corner, and wrote a smaller note. He folded the map and wrote Luke's address on it, then headed back outside, straight for the cab rank. He went up to a driver who was leaning on his cab, smoking, and he passed over the folded map with the address, and then a hundred bucks and the note.

Please deliver to this address.

Walker gave a thumbs up.

The driver felt the map, looked back at Walker and shrugged, then tossed his smoke, got in his car and gave a tilt of his hat to Walker as he drove off.

Back in the museum, Walker had half an hour until the meet. He paid the entry fee and passed security in the form of two uniformed guards. Neither would set any kind of quarter-mile record. Neither was armed with a firearm, though they had tasers and batons. There were cameras in the foyer, and in the corners of some of the halls that connected the gallery spaces. He swept the periphery first, taking in the patrons. He figured there were at least 500 people in there, maybe up to 700, some clearly coming into the airconditioned space to escape the worse of the early-afternoon August heat. He found the

landscapes hall, walked it twice, and checked the emergency exits. They were alarmed. There were two ways in, and a staircase that led up from a door set near the middle. In the centre of the room was a line of pre-Raphaelite statues. Between them and the walls adorned with paintings were leather bench seats, mostly occupied by tourists taking a load off. None of the patrons present seemed in any way a threat. None were military-aged males like himself. No sign of the Target, nor the Watcher.

Walker left the room via the stairs leading to a mezzanine level. The movement jabbed at his back, but he knew he would have the best vantage point up there, looking down over the railing. He assumed the Watcher was Steph's yacht guy. Had to be. There couldn't be too many deals going down with shady Eastern European types. He did a lap, looking down from the balcony as he moved, and then waited. He didn't have to wait long.

38

'What's Walker know about your mission?' Spicer asked.

'Nothing,' Steph replied.

'But you're working together?' he asked.

She shook her head.

Steph sat in a chair watching Spicer pace the room. She was not bound. She had a bottle of cold water in her hands. They were in Spicer's office, on the third floor, a corner suite with floor-to-ceiling windows, overlooking the airfield and looking back at the bayou and towards the Gulf. He turned to face her and leaned against the glass.

'When did you last see the Chechens?' Spicer asked her.

'In Florida, four days ago.'

'Bullshit.'

'That's the last time I saw them.'

'Ah, okay,' he said, his hands in his pockets, fidgeting a little. 'Right. Semantics. You've got *other* eyes on them, not your own. Who else have you got here? Hmm?'

'No-one. It's a solo mission. But you already know that.'

'Oh, I do, and I suppose you know how?'

'Because you've got someone back in the UK Home Office feeding you intel.'

'Something like that,' Spicer replied, then he went to his desk and sat down. 'Look, Steph. Companies like GreyStone are the future.

Governments won't be doing the spying or the killing for much longer. They're losing the stomach for it. The private sector is more efficient, and we get things done in a way that the squeamish politicians can look away from, and that allows them to keep getting themselves re-elected. They value us. They like us.'

'They just want to throw money at organisations like yours to get kickbacks and golden parachutes later on.'

'The future's here. You've got a chance here and now to be part of it. Just tell me everything you know. I'm not saying give up your life – you can go right on doing what you do, Queen and country and all that – but we can come to an arrangement. Name your price. And we will be powerful allies to have in your future.'

Steph looked out the windows. 'You really think you're the future, don't you? But you fail to see that your business model was archaic before you even set up shop. You're like a shitty version of the East India Company. Where are they now? And where's Britain?'

'In a truckload of debt, as is this nation,' Spicer replied. He paced the room. 'I think you're going to come around, and soon. You've got an opportunity here, and it won't be on the table for long. It's the best chance you have to move forward.'

'The only chance?'

Spicer paused a moment, stopping right in front of her, looking her close in the face. 'We'll see.'

'Walker will be back,' Steph said, a defiant look in her eyes. 'He'll come for me. And he'll come for you.'

•

Walker saw the Target. The middle-aged guy. He was alone. Wearing a pale-yellow short-sleeved shirt, the back soaked through with sweat. His suit pants seemed vintage, from the early 1990s. His shoes were scuffed, well-worn loafers. If he was another potential buyer for whatever the Russians were selling, he didn't look like he had much in the way of disposable income, but then, some of the richest people

on the planet looked like bums, so Walker reserved judgement on that. Maybe he was a seller. Or maybe he was Richter's middle-man, some washed-up contact, an old Agency friend or colleague from Vietnam or Laos days, here to settle whatever Richter was doing with GreyStone.

The Target was downstairs, ten minutes early, and he was sweating. And nervous. It was a public place, busy enough, broad daylight, a good place for a potentially dangerous meet. Walker watched as the Target scanned the room, then settled on a seat. Walker made a show of looking at his guide notes rather than directly down at the guy.

Then the Watcher entered. And he wasn't alone. The guy with him was big, probably the biggest guy Walker had ever seen in the flesh, and Walker had seen Shaq play a few games against the 76ers. They went straight for the Target. The Target stood, watching them come. He almost seemed relieved, as if he had expected a no-show.

Walker knew that the Watcher and his giant friend were not here to watch. It was clear in the way they moved. Like a couple of prison enforcers making a beeline for prey.

The Target started to say something, to complain about the Watcher not being alone, by the gesture he gave at the massive slab of beef. But it was a short-lived discussion. And very one-sided. The Watcher didn't stop to talk, nor listen. He walked right on by the Target, without so much as a second glance. The Target's eyes followed the Watcher, and his body turned too, to watch him depart, and his mouth was open, and his hands up and open in front of him, as if in wonder.

And that's when it happened. And the Target didn't see it coming, because he was looking at the man he'd come to meet who had just blown him off. The huge guy bumped into the Target, and the yellow-shirted man went down on the bench, as if he were lying down, and the big guy kept moving, walking across the gallery in the wake of the Watcher. It happened in two seconds, a choreographed dance move, full of savage grace – the huge guy, the bump, the assistance to the bench, and continuing on his way.

The Target was not moving. A spot on the front of his yellow shirt grew, fast. It was bright red, right in front of his heart. Arterial blood.

Walker's eyes scanned the gallery to get a bead on the killer – and then he stopped. Because in the middle of the gallery, the big guy, the killer, had stopped.

And he was looking directly up at Walker.

And a second later he was headed for the stairs to get to Walker.

And a second after that people downstairs started to scream.

39

Walker was no fool. He wasn't going to fight this man, not here, not like this. He was wounded and the guy was armed. Still, Walker reached down to his boot and drew his tactical knife, just in case. Then he turned and ran for the nearest exit. He hit the doors at the same instant the killer got to the top of the stairs, twenty yards behind him. He was impossibly fast and agile, for such a big specimen. Walker kept moving.

Down the stairs, three at a time, his back burning. He got to the gallery level and went another half-flight down, to a sign marked 'Emergency Exit', and he hit the bar hard, setting off a klaxon of warning throughout the building.

Outside was hot and humid, but Walker ran. He was at the western side of the museum and he headed south, to the drop-off area. As he neared the corner of the building he glanced back. The killer was chasing. He was fast. Faster than Walker.

Walker hit the road – and a throng of people streaming out of the museum. He parted a way through the mass, pushing and shoving. Most people didn't take much notice, too preoccupied with the news that was being spread about a man being murdered. Sirens sounded in the distance. EMTs, Walker thought, not police. He heard a shout behind him – at the edge of the throng, the killer had flattened out a couple of tourists and was momentarily held up by an angry gaggle. Walker made it to the road, where the crowd thinned, and he looked for a cab—

A car screeched to a halt in front of him. A cream-coloured Mini John Cooper Works, with Luke at the wheel. Walker got into the passenger seat, and without a word Luke took off in a tyre squeal.

Over his shoulder, Walker saw the first EMT roll in as the killer got to the edge of the crowd. He stood on the road and watched Walker until they were out of sight.

Walker turned to the front, then to Luke, who was working in third gear to weave through traffic to get them out of there in a fast-but-not-too-fast-to-attract-attention way. Luke looked his way, and they shared a knowing, silent nod. Then Luke passed over a note of his own: *Drop off tracker and mic to a third party, three miles.*

Walker nodded his thanks as he reached up and took his seatbelt and clicked it into place—

The impact was massive, and it came from the rear passenger side and sent their car spinning a full two turns across three lanes of traffic.

Out the windscreen, Walker saw their attackers: Johnson, and another GreyStone guard, in plain clothes, in a Crown Vic. Their cars were pointed at each other, like they were playing chicken.

The Mini came to a stop amid honking and jeers from other motorists. Luke kept his cool. The rear window had shattered. He restarted the stalled engine, put it into first. Then he reached under his seat and brought out an automatic pistol. A Glock. Small frame, twelve 9-millimetre rounds. He passed it to Walker, who wound down his window, then nodded.

Luke hit the gas.

Johnson hit the gas.

Fifty yards became thirty, then twenty.

A one-tonne Mini hatchback versus two tonnes of American sedan.

Walker held the Glock out his window and aimed it at Johnson's head, then squeezed off three rounds in two seconds.

Three things happened at once.

The bullets hit home. The first was a little low, hitting the Crown Vic's hood between the two occupants. The accelerating forces meant

that the Crown Vic was closer and the next 9-millimetre bullet hit the bottom of the windscreen and spiderwebbed it.

The second thing was Johnson's reaction, which kicked in before the third bullet hit. Johnson's reaction was to turn away from the threat, and he pulled his wheel to the left, unwittingly putting his partner in the firing line.

Then the third bullet found a target, in the top third of the Crown Vic's windscreen, right where the passenger was seated.

A car windscreen is made up of laminated glass. Two layers of glass, and a layer of plastic sandwiched in between to hold the glass together if it breaks. Usually around a quarter-inch thick, sometimes thicker. Sometimes with another layer of plastic tint or solar reflective coating. Designed to withstand rocks being kicked up on highways, and to keep the outside out. Developed over decades to protect occupants.

A 9-millimetre lead bullet, in this case a regular metal-jacketed round, had 115 grams of mass. Fired from the Glock at a velocity of over 1200 feet per second. The Crown Vic's forward momentum was immaterial to the equation. The bullet was designed to kill people, developed by arms companies for accuracy, reliability, and to inflict maximum damage.

In this case the windscreen was already weakened, and the bullet hit right on the mark, and while it deflected and deflagrated, enough of the sub-sonic mass found its way into the face of the GreyStone passenger. The result was a puff of red mist, and in the next second as the Crown Vic careened across the road, and the Mini flashed by it, Walker saw that the guy was down and out, his brain matter splattered against the side window. Johnson crashed the GreyStone vehicle into a storefront.

Luke drove them away from the scene. Not too fast. He wound several blocks north-east, then headed back in a north-west direction, and when they'd covered about three miles he pulled down a side street, and then down an alley, where he stopped the car and gave a brief honk of the horn. He held his hand out to Walker.

Walker passed over the Glock, but Luke shook his head.

This was the drop-off point for the microphone and GPS tracker.

A roller door opened, and a motorbike came out, a shiny sleek Japanese number. The rider, in black helmet and leathers, came up alongside the Mini and Luke buzzed his window down.

Walker ripped the tape off his chest, then took the box from its clip on his belt, and handed them to Luke. The rider took them in a gloved hand and zipped them into a pouch clipped at the waist, then, with a salute of sorts, they motored off.

'Shit!' Luke said, banging the steering wheel, relieved and overwhelmed at the same time. 'Shit!'

'Keep driving,' Walker replied. 'Get us away from here.'

As they merged onto the road, headed west, Walker asked, 'Who was the rider?'

'A good guy,' Luke said. 'He'll ride that tracker around all day and night, don't you worry.'

'They might catch up with him.'

'He was a motocross pro as a teenager, before some bad choices busted him out,' Luke replied. 'He can outride anyone. And his bike's faster than any car on the road.'

'He might not see them coming until it's too late.'

'He's a drug courier now,' Luke replied. 'He's got eyes in the back of his head. Relax about it.'

'Okay. Thanks. For everything.'

'We should ditch this car, right?' Luke glanced across to Walker.

'That would be a good idea.'

Luke nodded, glanced across again. 'What happened at the museum?'

'Someone got killed.'

'By you?'

Walker shook his head. 'No.'

'Where's Steph?'

'Let's just ditch the car and I'll fill you in.'

40

Four blocks from where they left the Mini, they found solace in a small double-storey bar. It was another twenty-four-hour joint, full of shift workers and professional alcoholics filling the afternoon with booze. The air smelled of all kinds of smoke, and the floor was sticky. It was in a timber building in the Fairgrounds district, and Walker used the GreyStone money to buy them iced teas and po-boys, then they sat on barstools by a big open window looking out to the street. Fans overhead worked hard to keep the air moving. It was hot, but bearable with the breeze. Walker had the Glock tucked into the front of his jeans, out of sight under his T-shirt. The safety on the Glock was part of the three-stage trigger mechanism, so it was one of just a few pistols he trusted stowed away in that position. His knife was folded away in the ankle of his boot. His hands were steady on his ice-cool glass.

'So, Steph's captive at GreyStone's base?'

'Yep,' Walker replied, draining his iced tea. He'd mentally run over a few ways to get into Fort Lee and extract her, and none of them was any good.

'What's their security like?' Luke asked.

'Too much for just us.'

'I could hack them,' Luke said. 'Turn off cameras and alarms and lighting systems. Report some hardcore nefarious activity, get the cavalry to turn up.'

'I know you could do all that,' Walker said. 'But they've got up to twenty guys, armed to the teeth. Maybe more. And a place like that, a company like theirs, they'd have money going to the local police and sheriff's department. They'd be tipped off and move Steph out via helicopter at the first sign of some kind of trouble with the law.'

'What do they do out there?'

'It's some kind of training and logistics station. Not too big, but not small either. I've heard their main training compound is in the Carolinas, spread over hundreds of acres, full of mock villages and houses to train their operators. Apparently puts our own military's infrastructure to shame, and that's saying something.'

'So, they're a full-on private army?'

'Yep.' Walker started on his sandwich.

'Great.' Luke looked across at him. 'How can you be hungry right now?'

'I need the fuel. For what I've expended, and for what's to come. You don't want yours?'

Luke shook his head and pushed his plastic basket to Walker.

They sat in silence for a while, the sound of drunks talking in the background, the Ramones playing low over the bar's sound system, the outside street full of the sights and sounds of cars and passers-by. An otherwise regular afternoon in this neighbourhood.

'So . . .' Luke said, using a straw to stir the ice around in his glass. 'What happens to Steph if you don't get her out?'

'Nothing good.'

'So, what are you going to do? What *can* you do?'

'I'm still thinking about that.' Walker crunched on some ice. 'I can reach out to my contact, have him get in touch with Steph's superiors. Hope for some sense to prevail. But I don't like my chances of getting far – nor her chances of having them help out. She's here on non-official cover – she'll be disavowed by her agency. Left to fend for herself. It's part of the job.'

'There must be someone out there who gives a damn about her wellbeing.'

Walker looked to him. 'You're lookin' at him.'

Luke was quiet for a minute, then put a hand on Walker's arm and said, his voice suddenly urgent. 'That big guy, at the museum?'

'He killed the guy that GreyStone sent me to follow. I need to find out who that dead guy was. I bet it leads back to the son of a bitch who sent me here and sold me out.'

'Right. Well, I don't know anything about that,' Luke said. 'But that big guy? Him I know something about. I've seen him before, Walker. Several times.'

Walker turned to Luke. 'Where?'

'He's from that big yacht Steph had me keep eyes on,' Luke replied. 'I mean, a guy like that, you don't soon forget, right?'

'Was he on the boat for a meet, or there as part of the permanent crew?'

'Crew, for sure,' Luke said. 'Every time we got images through, he'd be there, on deck, like some kind of big visible security for all to see.'

'I need to check the whereabouts of their yacht,' Walker said. 'I put a GPS tracker on it, I need to get to my boat to check it.'

'Let's get to my place,' Luke replied. 'It's closer.'

'Lead on,' Walker echoed, standing. 'If we can find it, maybe I can get some sort of leverage I can use to get Steph back.'

•

Johnson stood in a garden bed of ground-cover flowers at Fort Lee and hosed himself off until he felt clean. Until all the last bits of blood and brain matter and chips of skull were gone. As he threw down the hose he watched Spicer come out to the lot. He stood at the car, looking at it, then to Johnson, and walked over, double-time.

'What, the, actual—'

'It was Walker,' Johnson said. 'He got help, someone met him—'

'I've heard, it's all over the news, and the police network,' Spicer said. 'The Russians just up and killed Richter's guy at the museum. Reports are some kind of shanking, weapon was found ditched outside the museum, a long screwdriver ground down to a point.'

'I thought they were Chechens.'

'Whatever.'

'Well, that guy then went after Walker, who bugged out and then we hit him.'

'You were meant to be tracking him until you heard otherwise. What part of following orders don't you get?'

'You expect me to chase him in *that*?' Johnson pointed to the wrecked Crown Vic.

'Improvise. Ditch it, get a new car.'

'I wasn't leaving Mike's body and the vehicle behind like that. Besides, we're tracking Walker, we can see where he's at, and listen in.'

'I can't believe you drove back here like that,' Spicer said, shaking his head and pointing at the blood and gore painted inside the car. 'What if a state trooper pulled you over?'

'I thought you said we own guys in all the law enforcement around here.'

'Not the point. Some random trooper might have pulled you over, seen that shit, and shot you dead without thinking. Then where'd we be?'

'Well, I'd be dead, that's where I'd be.'

'A small relief,' Spicer said. 'Where's Walker?'

'Relax, we've got him. Walker's riding around on a motorbike. Doing circuits of greater New Orleans. Like he's looking for something, or someone. Or waiting to see who's gonna come after him.'

'A motorbike?'

'That's what it sounds like, over the mic.'

'Where'd he get a motorbike?'

'How the hell would I know?'

'He talk to anyone?'

'No-one.'

'Just hand the tracking receiver over so I can get another crew out to pick him up.' Spicer waited while Johnson trudged over in his saturated clothes and reached into the bloodied Crown Vic, emerging with the GPS tracking unit. 'Get rid of the car, then go get cleaned up. I'm gonna need you.'

'I think I need to take a personal day.'

Spicer looked at him.

'A joke,' Johnson said. 'I'll take care of the car, and Mike, then I'll go get ready. Be my pleasure to catch up with Walker.'

'With both the FBI agent and now Richter's guy out of the picture, Walker has outlived his usefulness.'

'So, gloves are off with Walker?'

Spicer nodded. Johnson smiled. On the tablet screen, the tiny dot continued to move around the city.

41

Walker and Luke stepped out of the cab two blocks from their destination, sticking to Luke's security protocol. The sun was baking behind the clouds, and the day was as hot and sticky as it would get. Walker bought cheap sunglasses from a street cart.

'I was caught once, by the law,' Luke said as he explained his cautious steps. 'FBI. I'd been doing some skimming work. I mean, banks deserve it, right? Bitches, ripping us all off at every turn. I'd put together an algorithm that sent a percentage of a cent of every internal bank transaction. Had it running three years. Then the bank got hit by a big proper hack, old-school and brute-force thing to steal IDs, and the Feds went in and found my little trail. I'd patched it through a bunch of servers, but they got to me. I learned a lot from that, and I'll never be caught out again.'

'Good to hear they didn't scare you onto a path of the straight and narrow.'

'Oh, hell with that, there's never going to be anything straight about me,' Luke replied as they crossed the street. 'And the government and the banks can eat my poop.'

'What happened when they caught you?'

'Offered me a deal. I took it. It was ten years in the Federal pen for stealing a couple hundred grand, or I could spend half that working for them. I chose the latter. They put me in a room full of

other misanthropes in Denver, and set me to work trying to locate internet bots that were attacking American interests. Mind-numbing.'

'Why Denver?'

'They had a big data centre there. The whole state of Colorado is weird, if you ask me. All kinds of secret government shit, and I'm not just talking about Cheyenne Mountain and all that. There's a lot of secret underground stuff in Colorado. It's a fall-back point, for the government, when the world falls apart. Millions can live there, underground, until the earth emerges from the ashes or nuclear winter or whatever. You know they've even got nukes stored there? Like, a lot of them. Hey – this way.'

They took an alley to the back of Luke's street, and he stopped at a big metal box bolted to a brick wall at the end of the lane. It was painted dark green, and looked like it had been there since the building was erected, painted over every other inauguration. Luke entered a code on the grimy locking mechanism, turned a big handle and the thick iron door opened to reveal a series of water and gas meters and pipes. He reached in and up, and pulled out a small case velcroed to the ceiling of the box. A power cable led from the case into the big box. He opened it to reveal a small laptop, and he punched in his login code and brought up a series of images.

'All my security cameras in and around my abode feed into this via wi-fi,' Luke explained. 'This is real-time. And I can access my remote hard-drives and watch up to forty-eight hours of history. Speaking of, wi-fi has an interesting history . . .'

Walker tuned out as Luke spoke about the Australian government inventing wi-fi. He looked up and down the alleyway, then back at the computer, to where Luke's fingers were blurring over the keyboard and entering commands and bringing up archived data from when he'd left his loft. Walker saw footage of Luke filmed from a camera's vantage from up high, going to the cab after the driver had buzzed his apartment, taking the note from the driver, reading it outside as the

cab drove off. Then he saw the reaction the note produced – Luke hustled into action, no hesitation.

'All clear,' Luke said, shutting the computer down and placing it back in the metal box. 'Can never be too careful.'

Walker followed Luke to the fire-escape out the back, and they ascended to the top floor, where Luke disabled a three-stage locking system on a window leading into the kitchen.

'Relax,' Luke said. 'We're alone. I'll go check in on the messages from the agents Steph's been running.'

'You got a clean phone?'

'Yep, here,' Luke said, producing a cell phone in new plastic packaging from his desk. 'You'll probably need to charge it up.'

'I'll make a call from the kitchen,' Walker said, tearing the package open. 'Yell out when you find the yacht.'

'On it,' Luke said, taking a seat.

Walker found an outlet on the kitchen bench and plugged the cell phone in then entered the number he'd memorised.

'Yeah?' the gruff voice said, wary of an unknown number.

'It's me,' Walker said.

'Thank Jesus,' Bloom replied.

'Your number might be compromised. My old phone was taken, supposedly destroyed, but who knows. And I'll have to ditch this phone after this call.'

'Okay. We can work out new numbers and communicate them via our usual channel.'

'Got it.' Walker looked out the window. 'Look. I've got a problem here. The British agent I've been working with: she's been taken. GreyStone have her at Fort Lee.'

'I'll tell the FBI,' Bloom said. 'It's the best we can do. I've just been speaking to a guy in counter-intel, about Richter.'

'And?'

'Nothing that he's heard,' Bloom replied, 'but he's working on it.'

'He needs to bring him in. Question him.'

'This is the US government,' Bloom said. 'She moves slow, my friend. And if Richter has some kind of Russian kompromat, then they'll want to build the case, not go in with guns drawn and risk sending their network of spies to the winds.'

'Time's ticking.'

'What are you thinking we can do?'

'Steph is priority number one.'

'I'll make sure her government knows.'

'Think they'll do anything?'

Bloom was silent a moment, then said, 'Want me to come down there to help out?'

'Thirty years ago, and with working knees, yes please.'

'Ha! Maybe a hundred pounds ago.'

'Look,' Walker said, 'I need to get into Fort Lee.'

'You know GreyStone's got a helluva lot of pull back here in DC. They own a lot of the Senators and Congress, especially those on the Armed Services and Intel committees.'

'I'm not asking for an armoured division,' Walker said. 'Just a distraction.'

'Hands tied, Jed,' Bloom said. 'CIA can't move on it, nor can the government. What I can get you is access to money. And money, as they say, makes the world go round – so you can use your imagination as to how to best use it.'

'How much?'

'This is the US government we're talking about,' Bloom said, a little levity in his voice. 'They throw money all over the place with little care or oversight.'

'Okay, better than nothing,' Walker said.

Then Luke called out. He'd found the yacht.

42

'See the yacht?' Luke said. 'That's only sixty miles from here.'

'It's there now?'

'Yep.'

'How can I access that money?' Walker asked Bloom over the phone.

Bloom relayed an account number and the name of the credit union that operated on weekends.

'Thanks,' Walker said. 'Next time we speak, new phones, and I just might be ahead of this.'

'Keep your head,' Bloom said and hung up.

Walker passed the phone to Luke. 'That burner's cooked.'

Luke pulled it apart, snapped the sim card, then put it in a metal rubbish bin under his desk.

'What are you going to do now?' Luke asked.

'Start a war,' Walker replied, checking the Glock. It still had nine rounds.

'I'll get you more ammo,' Luke replied. As he returned with a new box of a hundred 9-millimetre rounds, he stopped, mid-stride, and pointed at a computer screen. His security system. 'Friend of yours?'

Walker saw a face that took him by surprise.

Richter.

'Let's assume he's an enemy,' Walker said, loading three bullets into the mag to replace those he'd expended at the GreyStone car. 'Is he alone?'

'Looks it. He's about to buzz my apartment. What do you want me to do?'

'Let him up. But stall a bit before you do.' Walker went to the window, keeping back, out of sight, but just glancing enough to get a view across the street. 'Go back and check your cameras before you let him in – see where he came from, if anyone else is out there.'

'Right.' Luke started replaying various camera angles, then the apartment's call buzzer sounded. He left his computer and caught it before it stopped, had a brief conversation, then came back to the computer. 'Told him to come up, that I was in the shower, to give me a minute.'

'Good. How'd he ID himself?'

'Federal agent.'

'That old chestnut.'

'You watch his entry on that screen,' Luke said, pointing at a flat panel made up of nine different camera shots. 'I'll keep checking through his arrival, look back to see if I can make anyone else out there.'

Walker watched the screen as Richter took the stairs. There were security cameras at each floor, and Luke was tapped into all of them. Maybe they were his sole property, nothing to do with shared building security. He watched as the CIA man walked up the stairs, never pausing, never reaching for a weapon or a phone. He got to the top floor and found Luke's door, knocked, then crossed his arms and leaned against the wall and waited. He looked like he was dressed in the same dishevelled black suit from two nights earlier.

'Here,' Luke said, whispering and pointing at the screen in front of him. 'Look. He came via cab. Alone. Two minutes ago. Did a single lap of the street, then came up to my front door. And I've seen no other activity out there – no cars have parked in the past two hours,

and there's no vans or anything where a team of government agents could be hiding.'

'Doesn't mean he's here alone, not for sure,' Walker said. 'He might have a truckload of heavy-hitters waiting around the block. Or a helicopter hovering nearby.'

'What do you want to do?' Luke said. 'I can ditch this place. My computers are set with a magnesium destruction set. We can split, leave him hanging, get a head start.'

'You'd walk away from all your gear?'

'I can buy new. We can go back out the fire escape, or via the roof to the next-door building, and out their escape. I've got a car garaged there for bug-out purposes.'

Luke reached into a drawer and pulled out a set of keys. It was an old key, plain metal and worn to a bright shine, that suggested the car and its key were made in the 1970s.

Walker thought about it, but he knew he couldn't cut and run – even if it meant missing the yacht, again. He needed face-time with Richter, to get answers, and he might not get another chance. But he didn't want Luke put in any more danger.

'You can leave,' Walker said.

'Too late,' Luke said. 'Besides, they know where I live, so what's the point? Do what you gotta do. I'm already in this, so don't worry about me.'

'Okay. Let him in,' Walker whispered, taking off his boots so he could move quietly across the floor next to Luke, and Richter would only hear one person approach. He placed his knife in his back pocket.

Luke paused before the handle, looking at a small screen near the door, showing that Richter had not moved from his position against the wall. Luke looked to Walker, who held the Glock ready and waited on the other side of the doorway. He nodded, and Luke opened the door, then stepped back, allowing space for Richter to enter.

When Richter walked into the apartment, he did so slowly, and with his arms slightly raised.

Luke moved behind him and shut and locked the door, just as Walker moved into position and pressed the Glock's barrel hard up against the base of Richter's skull.

'You make a move, I shoot,' Walker said.

'Okay,' Richter said, his hands raised a little higher. 'I'm armed. Sig, right hip.'

'Luke,' Walker said.

Luke moved in, took the pistol, then moved away.

'You alone?' Walker asked.

'Yes.'

'How'd you find us?'

'We had a hit on Luke as a possible contact you or the British officer might use,' Richter said. 'He's the second guy I've visited this morning.'

'Who was the first?' Luke asked.

'Tom Wiley.'

'Pfft, he's a hack,' Luke said.

'What are you doing here?' Walker asked.

'I need to talk.'

'You sent me here as bait. To be handed over to GreyStone.'

Richter dropped his head. 'It's not like that.'

'What's it like?'

'Can we sit and talk?'

'Give me a reason to trust what you say.'

'Okay, I'm going to turn around, so you can see me while I tell you this,' Richter said, and he took a half-step forward, then slowly turned around to face Walker. 'They've got my daughter, Walker. They took her. I had no choice.'

43

'Steph,' Spicer said, sitting on a chair opposite her in a bland room that held just a desk and two chairs. Windows to one side, a view to the building opposite. Third storey up, toughened laminated glass, over half an inch thick; there was no way she was going to break out of there while she'd been left alone. The door had been locked until Spicer entered. 'I'm here to give you an update, and an option.'

He reached into his suit, pulled out a sheet of paper and put it on the table. 'Take a look.'

Steph looked at him. She wanted to hold out, but she knew there was no point – he would just hold it up and show her anyway. So, she leaned forward and looked at the colour picture. A photograph. The resolution was good, as was the reproduction of the printer.

It was a picture of her parents. They were seated at their local cafe. Steph knew the place well. She'd had many cups of tea and coffee there, and scones and toast and cakes. She'd met friends there. The owners and staff were friends. She'd been a bridesmaid for the owner's daughter, an old school friend. It was part of the fabric of her neighbourhood. And it was a recent photo. Her father was wearing a new shirt that Steph had bought him for his birthday a month earlier, and the man sitting directly behind her parents was clearly reading yesterday's *Guardian*.

'So, the deal is this,' Spicer said. 'I know you have someone watching out for the yacht. I need their whereabouts, and I need them now.'

'Why?'

'Because Walker has gone AWOL.'

Steph smiled.

Spicer banged a fist on the table, then used his other hand to take out his cell phone. 'The address. Now. Give it up, or I give the order to my guy watching your parents. He'll make it messy. He'll make your father watch your mother die. Then he'll tell him that you're dead too, before killing him. You have five seconds. Four. Three. Two—'

'Okay. Okay.' Steph refused to let the tears form in her eyes. 'My contact is in Algiers Point. Eliza Street.' She gave him the building and apartment number. It was mostly accurate.

•

Everyone has a price, Walker thought as he kept the Glock on Richter, after he'd patted him down. They sat on couches opposite each other, a big low coffee table between them. Luke was at his computer station, big headphones on, listening to music while he watched hacked CCTV footage in and around the area of the yacht.

'They took my daughter ten days ago,' Richter said. 'They've given me proof of life each day since.'

'GreyStone took her?'

Richter shook his head. 'They may be responsible, but the actual abductor was the big Russian guy from the museum. Not a mug you miss.' Richter paused. He looked like a man who had not slept more than a couple of hours a night for the past ten days. 'Truth is, I don't know. And believe me, I've tried every channel I can to find her. Their communications are encrypted and untraceable. And given what they know about me, they'd have her far, far off the grid someplace.'

'You know how these things usually end, right?'

'I . . .' Richter looked ill. 'I don't want to think about that.'

'Well, they've taken the British intelligence officer hostage, holding her here at Fort Lee,' Walker said. 'And the Russians on that yacht may have a federal agent undercover operative captive.'

'Says who?'

'Steph Mensch, the British officer. She suspects it. I trust her.'

'Well, they've got form,' Richter said. 'The MO matches their style: abductions in order to force people to do things.'

'What are they forcing you to do?'

Richter paused. 'A couple of things.'

'Like sending me here.'

'I'm sorry about that.'

'Why'd they want me here?'

'They wanted someone from the Agency sent in to flush out any other operatives that the FBI or British may have sent,' Richter said. 'Spicer specially asked for you. I assume there's history there.'

'That means that Spicer has someone inside CIA.'

'Don't act surprised.'

'Why the FBI?'

'They're running a counter-intel op here.'

'Against who?'

'I don't know. They don't share their CI operations with the CIA, for obvious reasons. Hell, it might have been because they got wind of my involvement – maybe they've been watching me. Saw something in my comms that led them here. Or they got wind of the British officer coming here and were keeping tabs on her.'

There was silence between them for a moment, then Walker said, 'You lied to me.'

'Welcome to the game, kid.'

'We're meant to be on the same team here.'

'You're in the big league now. This ain't the military,' Richter said. 'Besides, last I checked, you and I weren't friends. Co-workers, right? But we want the same outcome here, Walker. We both want to get someone returned, unharmed. And don't go blaming yourself, or me,

for what's happened, because that British operative would have come to a sticky situation whether you'd been here or not.'

'How'd they get your daughter?' Walker asked.

'From college,' Richter replied. 'They picked her up sometime in the night, from her apartment just near her college. Her roommates heard a noise, around three am, that in hindsight they think could have been a brief struggle. At any rate, they thought nothing of it, that she had her boyfriend over or something.'

'Any leads?'

Richter shook his head. 'Footage showed a van with two men on a camera in the area. Stolen plates, van burned out later that day. It could have been the vehicle. No usable prints. No witnesses. No decent IDs beyond two Caucasian males. That was, until I saw the footage from the museum hit. The big Russian from the museum was there, driving the van.'

'Then they contacted you?'

Richter nodded.

'And what was their demand?' Walker asked. 'What's the "couple of things" that dragged you here?'

'They wanted access,' Richter said. 'That was the first thing. They wanted access protocols to a DoD storage facility in Nebraska.'

Walker immediately thought of the tactical nukes. He swallowed. 'And?'

'And I managed to get it for them.'

'You *gave* it to them?'

'It's a mothballed site, there's not much of use there. It's been that way since Truman was in office. Stuff from World War Two was stockpiled there. Then Korea. And Vietnam. The Gulf War. We're now using it as a spill-over area for crap coming back from Iraq and Afghanistan that's not quite wrecked, but not quite useful, so it's sent there while the boffins in the military decide whether to scrap it or repurpose it. They've got some program for vets to work there,

fixing shit, stripping half-wrecked vehicles for anything of use or value before junking it, that kind of thing.'

'What could they want from there?'

'No idea.'

'Could there have been nukes stored there?'

'What?' Richter looked genuinely shocked. 'Hell no. That's a ridiculous question. We keep that sort of stuff very secure. Like in silos, and aboard submarines, and in hardened Air Force sites pre-positioned in Europe and Turkey and Guam and the-middle-of-nowhere Australia.'

'What about small nukes?'

'Nukes are nukes.'

'The small tactical nukes, portable and man-launched, for the battlefield.'

'I know what you mean,' Richter said. 'That program the army tested in front of Bobby Kennedy, who liked what he saw and recommended to his brother to have the Army in Europe and Korea field it, in case the Russians ever moved through the Fulda Gap or the North Koreans mobilised their armoured divisions south.'

'One might have gone missing?' Walker watched Richter's reactions but found nothing to suggest that this hypothesis meant anything to him. 'Maybe Russian in origin. Brought back from Afghanistan to be stored at that junkyard in Nebraska.'

'We also made thousands of small nuclear weapons, putting them into artillery shells, and tank rounds, mines, backpack nukes, missiles,' Richter said. 'But forget the nuke angle, this is not about that.'

'You don't know that, not for sure. The Russians are here to buy something worth a fortune.'

'I've been in and around non-proliferation work most of my career,' Richter said. 'Believe me when I tell you, Russians don't need to buy nukes from us, they've got nuclear weapons and materials all over the former Soviet Union that'd take little more than boltcutters and a

flashlight to get to. Hell, forget that even: spend the money on a bottle of vodka to give to the guard to look the other way, that might do it.'

Walker was silent a moment, then said, 'Could there be anything there worth hundreds of millions of dollars?'

'Nothing there's worth hundreds of millions of dollars,' Richter said. 'It's a junkyard. Where'd you get that figure?'

'That's what Steph was trailing the Russians for,' Walker replied. 'They're buying. But it's being transacted in cash, in exchange for something worth *hundreds* of millions.'

'Well, I'm telling you, it ain't a nuke.' Richter shook his head. 'No way it's a nuke.'

44

Steph sat up on her bed when Spicer entered her room. He turned to the GreyStone sentry outside her door. 'Leave us for a while, go get yourself a coffee until I call you back,' Spicer told him.

The guard looked from Spicer to Steph, smiled, then left.

Spicer closed the door, then sat next to Steph on the steel-framed single bed, the only furniture in the room. One window, high up, recessed neon light in the ceiling tiles.

'Steph . . .' he said, putting a hand on her leg. 'I want you to tell me what you know. About the Russians, and what you think they're after. I'm giving you this chance to make a good deal here, okay?'

Steph was silent as she looked at Spicer. He was taller and had maybe forty pounds on her. He was trained in US Army combat, some kind of special forces, no doubt. Steph hadn't had that training, but she had trained in jujitsu since she was a girl of six. Her father, a journalist, had enrolled her at a local dojo after a colleague had been raped and murdered while on assignment in Egypt. She kept that up long after ditching ballet.

'I'm going to make this easy on you,' Spicer said. He tried a smile, but it was unattractive, unnatural, more like a grimace. 'You tell me what you know, and you get to walk away from all this, once the transaction with the Russians is done. You don't tell me what I want

to know . . . Well, I've got to say, I won't make it easy on you. But you'll be leaving me with no choice, you understand?'

Spicer's eyes searched hers, and when they found something harder looking back at him, he looked away.

He stood and started to pace. 'I'm aware that you've had good training, no doubt the best the UK has to offer.'

He took off his suit jacket, and looked around the room.

'And I should say—'

Spicer didn't finish the sentence, let alone the thought.

Steph moved fast, up from the bed to grab his wrists and drive a knee into his head as she violently yanked his upper body down, then she used his momentum to spin around behind him, pulling him into a grapple hold, choking him out. Steph had never done the move with such anger and aggression. Never for keeps. Spicer's hands tugged at her forearm but she just kept constricting, and felt him go limp after about thirty seconds of putting up a fight. She dropped him forward to the floor, and his head hit the tiles with a satisfying crack.

She checked him over. He was unconscious, not dead. He didn't have a weapon, or a phone, or wallet or keys. Steph used his jacket to hogtie him as best as she could, then stuffed one of his socks in his mouth, and left the room. The hall was empty as she crept out warily.

•

'Steph said it was something left behind in Afghanistan,' Walker said.

'American?'

'No idea.'

'And you're sure the Russians are buying, not selling.'

'That's my understanding,' Walker said. 'Maybe we left something embarrassing there, and they're selling it to GreyStone, who will then either use it or on-sell it, or blackmail the US government with it.'

'But then the logic doesn't follow, because why would GreyStone blackmail their best cash cow?'

'Maybe they plan to gift it back to the Pentagon,' Walker said. 'Have the DoD owe them favours into eternity, make GreyStone the go-to for all future private contractor work. Or they could use it.'

'Use it?'

'False flag op. Get more work from the government in response.'

'It can't be a nuclear thing. Nukes can be tracked back after the fact to their point of origin, so a state actor wouldn't get away with using one of their own for a nefarious purpose.'

'The Russians were deeply entrenched in Afghanistan for a decade,' Walker said. 'As you said, the security of the Russian tactical nuclear weapons arsenal is a joke. I remember reading a report that bin Laden bought a suitcase bomb with thirty million in used US currency and two tonnes of Afghan heroin.'

'That report was debunked as false, by the CIA and others,' Richter said. 'Look, Walker, Russia's entire military arsenal from Afghanistan wouldn't amount to that value. And if they'd ever shipped a nuke there, we'd have heard about it – we had good intel all over that campaign. And even if you added up every conventional weapons platform that they deployed and left behind there, from wrecked tanks to downed helos and jets—'

'Near-on five hundred of them, thanks to our Stinger Missiles, right?'

'It's still not adding up,' Richter said. 'You could sell every single Kalashnikov and RPG and bullet on the black market to the highest bidder, and it'd amount to tens of millions of dollars, not hundreds of millions. And this isn't some Tom Clancy novel, where a jet was shot down carrying a secret nuke no-one ever knew about.'

'Okay.' Walker resumed his pace of the room. He stopped at the window looking down at the street out front. Nothing doing. 'But you can't tell me the Russian military were cataloguing everything going in and out. Hell, some grunt might have traded a nuclear artillery shell to the Mujahideen for a crate of heroin.'

'I'm telling you, Walker, nothing nuclear ever passed into the US via DoD stuff coming back from Afghanistan,' Richter said. 'The military may be a lot of things, but I tell you, since the Gulf War when we "lost" a lot of deleted uranium rounds rotating back, they check everything – they've got barcodes on everything, and it gets scanned going out and coming back. A nuke, even one that might have been left behind, would not slip through cataloguing.'

'Okay. So, let's rule out a nuke until we know better.' Walker let a moment of silence hang, and his mind filled it with all kinds of possibilities – but none was expansive. 'What's that leave us? What could they have wanted from the site in Nebraska so badly? And what could be worth that kind of money?'

'The hell I know.' Richter looked more tired with every minute that passed. 'I've thought long and hard about what they have and may have stored there, and I did look into it. Reclaimed gearboxes and drivetrains from wrecked Humvees? Switch-out barrels for M1 Abrams tanks? Redundant up-armour kits for fighting vehicles? Old reactive armour? But nothing worth what you say. And nothing that has been noticed as stolen, if they've already gone in and taken it.'

'Nothing secretive or proprietary?' Walker said. 'Nothing that might save Russia years of R and D to catch up?'

Richter shook his head. 'It's not that kind of place. The base guards there have the most basic DoD security clearance.'

'I'd heard rumours in Iraq of a squadron of tanks we sent over, with experimental cloaking armour. They were covered in hundreds of tiny cameras and projectors, so that they blended into the environment. I'd heard it worked pretty well, as a proof-of-concept, but they didn't see battle because they didn't want the tech falling into the hands of the Iranians, or Chinese – or maybe the Russians.'

'Well, I don't know anything about that,' Richter said. 'But you know what? It could be just about any damned thing. And we could speculate like this for days, and never figure it out. The only way

you get to the correct answer is to get face to face with these sons of bitches and beat it out of them.'

Walker was silent a moment, then said, 'And the other thing they asked of you?'

'To send a CIA asset to New Orleans, to flush out the British element,' Richter said. 'They knew the Brits were on their tail. They wanted that to stop. This is where the GreyStone connection is obvious. Because they're inside our system, all the way into the halls of power in Capitol Hill. You were selected, specifically.'

'Two birds with one stone,' Walker said. 'The GreyStone guy running the shop here, Spicer. Apparently I had a hand in getting him booted out of the Army, but I've written up quite a few such reports. He said he's king of the contractor world now, but he's still got a grudge against me.'

'That name again?'

'Spicer.'

'First name?'

'Didn't catch it.'

'Army? You know what unit?'

'No. But you could probably find out, right? Have the Agency look into all GreyStone employees?'

'Unfortunately the access isn't a two-way street,' Richter said. 'But Spicer . . . I ran HVT hunter teams in Stan and Iraq. There were a few Spicers.'

'You've had contact with GreyStone about me being here.'

'A burner phone, a voice, never a name.'

'This Spicer was an officer. Terminal at captain. About six foot, medium build, grey eyes.'

'I think I know the guy, maybe. From a group in Stan in the opening weeks of that war,' Richter said, shaking his head. 'Son of a bitch . . . If it's who I think it is, he didn't just hand-pick you – he also hand-picked *me*.'

'Any chance he came across something of immense value in Afghanistan?'

Richter shrugged.

They fell silent, and after a while Richter said, 'What happened in the museum this morning? How'd it go down?'

'Spicer told me to go to the meet. Gave me a target to follow. Didn't say why. And I can't figure out why, unless it was to flush out anyone else watching, and he figured that if I was killed in the exchange, all the better for him. But the Target was killed, by the Russian crew from the yacht.'

'I saw images from the museum. Like I said, the killer matches the big guy in the car who snatched my daughter.'

'Then she might be captive on their yacht,' Walker said. 'Because that big guy's from the yacht – Luke here has taped footage and surveillance.'

Luke still had his back to them, headphones on, oblivious to their discussion.

Richter nodded. 'Was it quick, the guy at the museum?'

'Instant.'

That news seemed to put Richter at ease a little.

Walker said, 'That guy was a friend of yours?'

Richter nodded. 'An old military bud. I sent him to do the in-person meet, because yesterday's proof of life seemed weird, and when I demanded more, a spoken question and answer that only my daughter would know the answer to, we arranged the meet at the museum.'

'We can go after their yacht.'

'Maybe. As a back-up. I still think getting them to a meet is key.' Richter shook his head. 'Smart move by Spicer. Get the Russians to do the dirty work, the snatch and grab, and the hit on my guy. While he makes the demands. Keeping us occupied, getting the Brits off the scent, while the deal goes down.'

That made Walker pause, and he said, 'Your deal with them should be done now, right?'

'Yesterday they asked me for a third thing,' Richter said. 'A third thing, and my daughter goes free.'

'What's that?'

'I have to give myself up. To the Russians.'

45

The sniper found position to the north of his target. He set up his Finnish-made Sako TRG rifle. With the suppressor attached, it would sound no louder than the backfire of a distant car. He called in to Johnson, reported the scene, and was instructed to wait until the team on the ground was in position, then take the shot.

•

'That's why you're here,' Walker said. It was the response of a weary man who knew his time was nearly up. 'You're gonna hand yourself over to the guys who took your daughter so that they can, what, bleed you for intel?'

'I'm giving myself over so that my daughter can live,' Richter said.

Walker said, 'You trust them to honour that deal?'

'It's the deal I got dealt.'

'You know how this will go down.' Walker watched for his reaction, for some defiance, some inkling of Richter being a step ahead of the game, of holding an ace up his sleeve. But he saw none of that. Nothing but resolve.

'They won't get shit out of me, Walker. I'm a street fighter from way back. They can beat me, shock me, deprive me, but I'll be fighting and scrapping and I'll be dead before I reveal anything that might put my country in jeopardy.'

'You're choosing to die for your country?'

'And my daughter.'

'There's gotta be another way.'

'If there is, I'm far too tired and concerned to hear it. And believe me, I've kicked this around every which way. This isn't the wild west. I can't mortgage my house and bring in contract killers to shoot it out in the streets with these guys, killing bystanders and probably my daughter in the process. And this isn't a movie, where I can bring in black-clad CIA paramilitary operators to wage war on the streets of America. This is life-and-death for the thing I hold dearest. I'm going to toe the line.'

'But you were happy to send me here.'

Richter was silent.

Walker asked, 'So, how's it going down?'

'I'm calling a number, at five pm. They answer. We arrange a handover place for ten pm. I'll choose it. It'll be public. I see my daughter go free. It was meant to be into the hands of my friend, from the museum. I was going to have him there to take her away, ensure her safety. That may now have to be you, if you'll do it. After all I've done to you, I don't expect it. Then I turn myself over to them.'

'You've got no chance of getting FBI back-up?' Walker said. 'No government agencies to help out?'

Richter shook his head. 'GreyStone are too connected. If they get wind I'm up to something, my daughter's gone.'

'No more old friends you can rely on?'

'My daughter's life is the number-one priority here, Walker,' Richter said. 'They've made it very clear that any sign of outside forces will end that. One intermediary on my part, my friend Tom, and now he's gone. That was it. Anything more is not a risk I'm willing to take.'

Walker was silent for a moment, then he stood and paced the room. 'It's really that easy? To get to a high-ranking CIA source like you? To just up and snatch your daughter from her college dorm?'

'She's never known the potential for danger that could come her way,' Richter said. 'I thought I was helping her, by letting her live free and away from everything I did abroad. I can see now that's been a mistake.'

'A mistake?'

'You hold anything dear, it's a point of exploitation,' Richter said. 'Pretty sure they told you that in week one at The Farm, just like they taught you how to shoot straight in week one at The Point.'

Everyone has a price.

'And they mentioned that there were unwritten rules of that game,' Walker said, remembering back to those early days at the CIA's training facility. And he remembered Eve, his estranged wife. He'd always said to her that his Air Force career would only be so long. When deadline after extended deadline passed, she up and left. He didn't blame her. It killed him a little, knowing that the choices he made wrecked something so special. But the more days he spent on the front lines, the more he felt he'd found where he most needed to be. 'I know they said to us that families of intel officers were off limits. That if that line was crossed, all kinds of international fire and brimstone would result.'

'Rules have changed, kid,' Richter said. 'These might be Russians we're dealing with – and this may even lead straight back to the FSB and SVR and the Kremlin, an officially sanctioned op – but the days of mutually assured destruction and detente are over. Now there's a global power vacuum. China's rapidly filling it. Russia is on the rise – their former spy turned autocratic leader wants nothing more than to restore some of the glory of the old USSR days. He trusts no-one. He's a life-long intelligence specialist – as long as he's in power, he's going to subvert and attack and undermine at every opportunity. And the old world order that we've known since the end of World War Two is out the window. Ten years, twenty years from now, America's gonna lose its relevance. Lose our place as the world's sheriff. Our influence abroad is already being eroded. We're gonna go back to

Jacksonian foreign policy, putting America first. Looking more inward. At war with ourselves. And that means our global allies will be out in the cold. The world will have to sort itself out. And there's probably a hell of a lot of people in middle America who are gonna welcome that change.'

'Okay . . .' Walker said, stopping by the door. He looked at a large print on the wall, a Picasso, *Guernica*. 'How about *you* take an eye for an eye? Not here, abroad. Get a black-ops snatch crew in Moscow or a Russian Embassy to pick up the kids of some Russian minister or spy. Demand the release of your own. Send a message that this won't stand.'

'You're talking like this is the CIA of Jack Ryan and Jason Bourne,' Richter said.

'I'm just saying it's an option. Take the fight to them, play how they play.'

'It's starting a war, Walker. Maybe not with armies, but with back-room reprisals and actions and black-ops hits against our embassy staff and their families. It would escalate real fast, real far, before diplomacy managed to catch it. No. This is me, and them, and ensuring my daughter's freedom.'

'Whoever they are.'

Richter nodded.

Walker examined the print. It was about three feet tall and seven feet long, decorating the entry wall. Black and grey and white. He wondered why Luke had chosen it, what it meant to him; if it meant the same for everyone, representing a slaughter on the people by their own government and sanctioned allies.

Walker said, 'Ten pm handover?'

'Correct.' Richter paused, then asked, 'Can you help me? Be there for the handover? Get Alice to safety?' Richter paused. His eyes searched Walker's. Walker was silent. 'After all I did to you, I know it's a big ask.' Richter stood. He looked deflated. 'You can tell Langley everything. They'll understand what I've done. What I did

to you. I've written things down, here, so there's no confusion about your involvement, or how things went down.'

He reached into his inside pocket and pulled out an envelope, not unlike the one Walker had been given by Johnson.

Walker checked his watch. Only hours to the handover. He wondered how the guy on the motorbike was going spreading the chase around the city. He worried about Steph. About losing the yacht. About not having enough time to achieve half of what he needed to. And now this.

Walker sighed. 'Where are we thinking this meet should take place?'

'I thought Jackson Square,' Richter said and bent down to place the envelope on the coffee table. As he stood back up, there was a little hope in his eyes, as he sensed that Walker would help him out, that his daughter would be okay. 'It's a public space, busy, and it's safe—'

The sound of breaking glass punctuated Richter's speech. He fell. Not straight down, but across the room, as though an invisible force violently shoved him, from the north to the south.

Walker's brain registered: *Sniper. Suppressed weapon. Fired from a rooftop to the north.*

Walker ducked and kept close to the wall. He yelled out to Richter, but got no reply. He yelled to Luke, but the guy was bopping away to loud music through headphones and had his back to the scene, oblivious to what was unfolding. Walker took a paperback from a shelf by the door and threw it across the room. It hit a screen near Luke's head and he turned around, looking pissed. Walker mimed for him to take off the headphones. Luke did, and then he saw that things were unravelling, fast.

'Richter's down,' Walker said to him. 'Sniper on the roof out back.'

'Shit!' Luke went into what Walker assumed was his self-destruct mode, getting under his desk and pulling at tabs and connecting wires. 'The button near the door – press the one that says "Down".'

Walker considered their situation as he looked up at the control panel near the security screen by the door. Sniper covering the rear fire-escape. A team would soon be headed up the stairs towards the only door in or out. The Glock in his hand. No shoes on his feet. A dead or dying man a few yards away.

They were trapped.

46

'Richter's down,' the sniper said into Johnson's tactical mic. 'Walker's found cover near the front door, and I've got him pinned there. No sign of the computer geek, it might just be Walker in there. Copy.'

'Copy that,' Johnson said as the van pulled up out the front of the building and he and three other GreyStone employees piled out. They were in civilian clothing, innocuous but for their silenced sub-machine-guns as they rushed the front door. One operator carried a heavy steel ram. He was through on his second swing. 'You see anyone else move in there, you drop them.'

'Keeping eyes on target.'

'We're entering the building now.'

'Copy that.'

•

Walker reached up and hit the button next to a bank of light switches. He pressed 'Down' as instructed, and immediately an electric hum sounded. Black-out roller blinds whirred, shutting out the light and the view on all the windows, north and south facing. Walker stood as they were nearly closing, his back to the brick wall in the entryway. He saw on the security screen the guys rush the front door downstairs; he counted four, Johnson among them. He looked out to the rooftops

to the north but there was too much glare, and then the scene went dark as the blinds shut out all view.

'Two-minute delay on the charges,' Luke said. 'How's your guy?'

Walker tipped the bookcase across the door, figuring he might buy an additional minute against their attacking force, then ran across the room and checked Richer. He'd taken a high-calibre bullet to the left side of his chest; he was alive but bleeding out fast. Walker took his hands, tried to get him to focus, bent down close and said, 'I'll get your daughter. You hear me? I'll get Alice.'

There was no response. Richter had checked out.

'He's gone,' Walker said. 'We need another way out.'

'Upstairs, out my bedroom window to the roof,' Luke said. 'It'll get us to the building next door, and we can go down the internal stairs to the car park.'

'Lead on,' Walker said, grabbing the letter from Richter. They were up the spiral staircase and in Luke's bedroom when he heard battering on the door downstairs and then—

WHACK! WHACK!

The automatic blinds here were clearly on a different control, and a bedroom window facing north was shot out by the sniper. Again, no sound of the gunshot, just the sound of jagged holes being punched through the glass.

Walker pushed Luke onwards, and they kept low, below the window level, as three more rounds followed them, taking chunks out of the brick wall opposite, debris and dust filling the air. Serious battering was going on, on the door downstairs. They had a minute before the front door was breached, best case. Luke undid the latches on the bedroom window, which faced south, to the front of the building, and pushed it up. He looked out and then ducked down again.

'Seems clear,' Luke said. 'But the shooter might see us climb out.'

'You go first,' Walker said. 'I'll distract the sniper.'

'How will you get out?'

'I'll be right behind you.'

Luke nodded.

'On three,' Walker said. They counted it out, and as Luke got up Walker laid down cover fire. He shot out the bedroom window casing near where the sniper had first hit, making the shooter aim away from them, to the eastern side of the room, for a couple of seconds. He imagined the sniper on a roof to the north, his silenced rifle resting on a bipod or improvised stand, tracking the movement of the glass and timber being blasted out, looking for a target who might be foolish enough to use a pistol in a gunfight with a scoped rifle. Meanwhile, three windows across to the west, he could have sighted Luke through the apartment, climbing out the window. Walker stood and shot out the next window, then backed out where Luke had gone, and within three seconds he too was outside the building.

They were on a small parapet just wide enough to walk along. The pitched roof sloped upwards behind them. The building next door was a full storey lower and butted up against its western neighbour. It had a flat roof, about the size of a tennis court, and it had a box-like structure in the centre with a door set into it. Luke descended first, turning around and hanging onto the leading edge with his hands and lowering himself down as far as he could reach, so that the drop was just a few feet to the other roof level. Normally, Walker would have jumped down and rolled through the move to carry the inertia out of the fall, but with his back all messed up he followed Luke's manoeuvre, the Glock tucked into his belt, his socked feet padding down onto the roof.

'You didn't bring your boots?' Luke asked.

'Least of my worries,' Walker said. He looked at the boxed room, the size of a van, the door facing their way. It was a clear run straight at it. Maybe twelve yards. All of it in the open, potentially watched the whole way in by the sniper. A killing field. 'Is that door unlocked?'

'Last time I checked.'

'When was that?'

'A month ago.'

'Okay. We don't have a choice. We run for it, close together. I hit the door first. If it's locked I try to bash it in, worst case I shoot the lock out – but the sniper will be onto us as soon as he sees our movement. It'll take him a couple of seconds to track our movement. He'll have an aim about the same time as we hit the door. It'll be close.'

Luke looked north, to where the sniper was poised in an unknown location. He was worried. Rightly so. 'It'll take him two seconds to acquire us?'

'Another to get a good aim,' Walker said, though he hardly believed himself. 'Another for the shot to happen.'

'Four seconds.'

'Best case.' Walker tried a smile. 'He might be distracted, take him a couple of seconds longer. He may be reloading. He may be less than competent. But if we wait here any longer, those guys will be through your front door, up the stairs and onto us. There's four of them, all armed. This is our only chance. Ready?'

'Okay. Okay.' Luke was breathing fast. 'Now or never, right?'

'Right. Ready? Let's—'

There was a cacophonous blast and the sounds of windows shattering. Fireballs licked out the sides of Luke's building, the roar of the sudden fire sucking the oxygen from the air.

'My charges!' Luke shouted.

'Run!' Walker pushed him.

They ran. Walker hit the door with a crash and it flew inwards. A shot pinged off the metal frame and ricocheted into the concrete block wall. Inside four seconds, beginning to end. The shooter was good. Or lucky – maybe he'd been scoping the roof at the time. Maybe there was more than one shooter. Whatever. Walker was surprised that the blast in Luke's apartment hadn't put him off, which meant he was better than good. With the money that private security contractors had thrown at them, little wonder. The guy was probably an ex-Marine or Ranger sniper, and had spent thousands of hours

and tens of thousands of rounds on the government's dime getting good at killing people from a long way out.

Walker took the stairs as fast as he could, and Luke was close behind him. In twenty seconds they were heaving and puffing and inside the ground level, which was a car park facing the laneway. Walker scanned the scene with the Glock held out double-handed. No threats.

'Car?' Walker said.

'Back row, your left,' Luke said. 'Black.'

Walker found the car, the last in a row of eight. All the others were modern machines, more plastic than metal, made mainly in Asia or Mexico. Not this. This was an all-metal, all-American beast.

A triple-Black 1970 Chevrolet Chevelle SS LS6 coupe.

'Original Tuxedo Black paint,' Luke said.

'I drive, you navigate,' Walker said, catching the keys over the car's vinyl rooftop.

Inside was all black. The bucket seats were wide and deep, the tank full of gas. It took a few turns of the flywheel before the 454 HP big block V8 thrummed to life. Walker pulled the big centre console floor-shifted 400 Turbo automatic lever into drive and eased out of the parking space, then made for the exit gate, which Luke had started to open via remote.

'Careful,' Luke said. 'There are a couple of slight tweaks under the hood. She slings off the line like a bitch.'

Walker didn't doubt it. He liked muscle cars. He knew this was rated at somewhere nearing 500 brake horsepower, giving the LS6 the highest horsepower rating of all muscle cars. The giant Holley 780 CFM carb spooled up as he took the exit and made a hard right turn, headed east, and floored it up the laneway, the back tyres, fatter than the standard originals, leaving trails of rubber. He half-expected the sniper to take pot shots through the thin roof, but no bullets came. He dreaded some kind of back-up team that GreyStone might have brought along and pre-deployed, a couple of

guys waiting at each end of the laneway as a cordon, but there was none. They were out and he was onto the road headed towards town. No-one behind them in his rear-view mirror, or in front of them. No threats. Just the two of them, in the car, the wind from the Gulf at their backs. Walker wound the window down. Luke too.

Walker felt the vibration of the massive engine through his socked feet as he kept on the gas where he could, slowing for intersections.

Eight blocks and a few nervous checks over his shoulder later, Luke said, 'Sorry about that guy back there.'

'He knew the game,' Walker said. 'He had a good run.'

'What are you going to do?'

'Start a war.'

'With what?'

'I'll improvise.'

'I don't think I can be much help, in the physical sense.' Luke looked out his window. 'I don't wanna kill anyone.'

'You can help me and Steph out, without killing anyone, don't you worry.' Walker drove in silence for the next fifteen minutes, then as they approached the Louis Armstrong airport he pulled into the drop-off lane and handed over the letter from Richter. 'Take this. Get yourself a flight to DC, then a cab straight to the EEOB.'

'Which what?'

'Eisenhower Executive Office Building, across from the White House,' Walker said. 'Get through to a man named Marty Bloom on the National Security Council. He's a good guy, like a father to me. Tell him I'm seeing this through for the next forty-eight hours. That if he can help out with the yacht, I'd be grateful. Some bullshit search warrant executed by the Coast Guard or something.'

'You sure?' Luke took the envelope. 'I can be an asset for you here. Get a new computer, log into the camera feeds and network that Steph set up. Get us a couple of burner phones. Handle the logistics.'

'I'm sure,' Walker said. 'It's time for me to get into this, elbow deep.'

'Here,' Luke said, reaching into his backpack and retrieving a USB from a small zip pocket. 'It's a back-up database of the crew that Steph recruited. Short bio on each, last known location, their burner cell numbers.'

'Thanks.' Walker took the memory stick.

Luke stepped out of the car, and closed the door then leaned inside the open window. 'Marty Bloom, of the Security Council, office at the EEOB.'

'Yep. Mention my name.'

Luke nodded. 'Good luck.'

'Thanks.'

'And Walker? Tell Steph I'm sorry. Sorry I couldn't be there to help her get out.'

'What you're doing is helping,' Walker said, checking his mirror. 'Besides, none of this is your fault. Like Richter, Steph knew the score.'

•

Steph was atop the water tower, lying flat on her back on the three-foot-wide platform that skirted its diameter, hidden out of sight. She'd found the H&K SOCOM pistol, and the suppressor, which she'd screwed into place. She knew it must have been left there by Walker, because no-one else would have done so with such an expensive piece of hardware. Plus, it had only been in the elements a short time, the gun oil in the mechanism still gleaming and slick. It felt good, to have the firearm. It gave her options. And it gave her a connection to Walker, which reassured her, because she was sure he was coming. The hell he'd wreaked on the GreyStone team was evident. They were spooked. And down on numbers.

She edged around the tower, to the seaward side, so she would be out of view from the complex of buildings. She worried about a helicopter search of the ground, but none came. She knew she could hold out to nightfall, if needed, then descend and make her way to the water, where she could swim out to the channel and let the tide take

her out, then come ashore somewhere friendly. She kept her head to the side, listening intently for someone coming up the rusted ladder of the water tower. She had counted the rounds in the SOCOM. A full clip. She would make each one count, if it came to that, and she would be sure to keep one in reserve, if it came to *that*.

47

The big block V8 rumbled a soundtrack to Walker's thoughts as he watched Luke head into the airport. Several years at the pointy end of the nation's special-operations forces had led to this very moment. On his own. Three hostages – Steph, Alice, and the unidentified federal agent – likely at different locations. GreyStone operators on the loose, hunting for him. And a boatload of Russians here to buy something for hundreds of millions of dollars.

You couldn't make this stuff up.

First up, he needed to get his Tom Archer ID. With that, he could access the money Bloom had deposited in the credit union under that name.

He shifted the car into drive and pulled away from the kerb.

•

Steph lay face-up on the water tower, the heat now unbearable. She had her shirt pulled up over her face and felt her bare stomach baking, but she dared not move.

At some point, she felt vibrations and heard movement. Someone was coming up the ladder. Her body was rigid, the SOCOM pistol in her hands. Silencer screwed in. Waiting to see someone emerge on the rotted-out timber platform, shimmy around the tower. If they came around headed towards the south of the water tank, the water-side,

she would see them through her feet. An easy shot – *whack whack*. Chest and head. They would probably fall off the tower. Which would alert anyone down there. Which wouldn't end well, for her.

Or they might come around the tower the other way, clockwise, the direction that her head was pointed. In which case she'd have to bring the weapon up and aim and fire, two-handed, straight up, and she'd be looking at her target upside down.

Then the guy would fall to ground level, and the same result.

She tucked the SOCOM underneath her thigh. Out of sight. Waited. Listened. If the guard found her, she'd make a show of getting up, slowly. Needing help. Wait for the guy to lean down to her. Then – pop. Have him fall on her. Get his weapons. Buy time. If he had any buddies waiting at the base of the tower, they might hesitate shooting blind for the sake of their friend.

Steph tilted her head, listening hard. The vibrations were growing in intensity as the GreyStone guy was getting closer to the top of the old metal ladder. Nearing.

•

At the cheap hotel, Walker used a coat hanger to retrieve his Tom Archer ID from the gap between the wall and the airconditioning unit. The room was as he'd left it. He washed his face and hands, and changed into his spare clothes. His cropped hair had no need for maintenance. He looked as neat and tidy as he could muster. He took the last of the tablets he'd been given from GreyStone, secured his knife, then pocketed the thumb drive and his ID, and drove to the credit union.

•

Steph was rock-still. And so was whoever was making their way up the ladder. For a moment she had a delicious thought – what if it was Walker, coming back? She waited. Waited to see who would appear

around the edge of the water tank. Friend, or foe. More likely a foe. But she was prepared for that.

But it never came. No-one came. The person had paused, waited, maybe looked around, then started to descend.

Was it Walker? Had he come back for the pistol?

Or was it a GreyStone guard, looking at the scene, seeing the deteriorated platform, figuring that a quick check was enough to clear the water tower without having to chance the decaying platform on the top of the tank?

She had to see, to know. She rolled to her side, carefully got to her knees, the SOCOM in hand, and crawled to the edge. She kept low to the platform, moving clockwise around the water tank. She pressed herself closer to the timber under her and looked over the edge.

Not Walker. A GreyStone uniformed guard. Almost at the bottom of the ladder, looking down at his feet as he navigated his way to the ground.

Steph went to hide.

Too late.

He looked up.

48

The GreyStone guard reacted, but so did Steph – and she was faster. She got to one knee and leaned out, aiming, tracking him down the pistol's sight as he dropped away from the ladder and landed on his back on the grass and reached for the silenced MP5 strapped across his chest. He brought it around, trying to get an aim. The MP5 was a fearsome weapon: 9-millimetre, rapid rate of fire, compact and accurate in close quarters; known affectionately as the 'room broom' among special operators. The GreyStone guard didn't get to use it that day.

Steph fired, double-handed, three times. At least two of the shots found their mark, the guard's chest and head turned to ragged gore. She scanned the scene through the sight of the weapon, a wide arc, ready to shoot at anything that moved. She couldn't see any other threats, but it was clear that she had to move from here, fast, and she descended the ladder as quickly as she dared.

The only real option was to swim for it, in open water, broad daylight. Make it to friendly territory. Avoid being spotted by the GreyStone boats.

The wind had picked up, fierce off the Gulf, and Steph worried about the sound of the silenced weapon being carried back towards the GreyStone compound.

•

Walker looked up and down Canal Street. New Orleans was quiet, much quieter than he'd seen the streets over the past two days. It was like everything was coming into sharper focus. Too quiet.

The credit union was closed. It shouldn't have been, according to the opening hours posted on the window. He rapped on the glass door. The staff looked like they were packing up. Hurrying, but not harried. One of them looked his way, then waved in a dismissive fashion, so he knocked again, louder this time, big knuckles on thick laminated glass. This time all three staff members looked up, clearly annoyed. He tapped his watch, then the opening hours stencilled on the window by the door.

A woman came around from the counter and shuffled to the door. She slid it open half a foot and said: 'Honey, we're closing for the hurricane warning. You should be getting outta here with all the others.'

'I just need to access some cash. It's an emergency.'

'Sweetie pie, you been living under a rock? The only emergency here is the big old hurricane bearing down on us. You need to get your skinny butt outta town, while the going's good. If you need a ride out, the government's got all kinds of buses leaving from the Superdome, which I hear is pretty filled up. But you best hurry now, or you're gonna get stuck behind.'

Walker let out a breath. 'Look, I really need to access my money.'

'And I can't give you squat,' she replied. 'Even if I wanted to. The coms systems are overwhelmed – we've not had access to our servers for over three hours. You need to just get going, while you can.'

'But—'

'Why don't you try Baton Rouge?' she suggested. 'If you leave now and hustle, you'll make it before they close. They've got outlets there, on different coms lines. Sorry. Gotta go pack, get myself out while the going's good. Best you do the same.'

She locked the door and walked back to her colleagues, and Walker walked back to his car.

As he headed north-west to circuit the block back to the car, he noticed that all the stores were closed or, like the credit union, closing. Most had big chains on and locks, some were boarded up, almost all had tape over the windows. The hurricane explained the cloud systems he'd seen. He got inside the car and turned on the radio, and news of the storm was everywhere – every channel was playing the same emergency broadcast and update.

The huge storm, packing 160-mile-per-hour winds, is expected to hit the northern Gulf Coast in the next nine hours and make landfall as a category four or five hurricane. New Orleans will be hit early tomorrow morning. The time to act is now. Those exempt from the mandatory evacuation are essential federal, state, and local personnel; emergency and utility workers; transit workers; media; and hotel workers. Those left behind not on that list are advised to head to the Superdome. Loiterers by nightfall will be rounded up by police and emergency personnel. City officials advise stranded tourists to stay on third-floor levels or higher and away from windows. The storm surge could reach twenty-eight feet; the highest levees around New Orleans are only eighteen feet high . . .

Walker had heard enough.

The streets were near empty. Some of the lights were out, flashing amber. He saw a fire crew evacuating a medical centre, putting staff and patients on buses.

He kept heading north-west, thinking as he drove. No access to the money from Bloom. Not that it would be useful now, with this storm.

He held little hope now for Richter's daughter, Alice. There would be no ten pm meeting at the park. Like the rest of the city, that would be empty. The only thing he could do was go after that yacht while it was still there. Then figure out how to help Steph. But he needed weapons.

Walker was nearing the interstate feeder road when he slowed and then stopped the car. He reversed, looking left, down a side street. There was a pick-up truck with at least three, maybe four, guys – young twenty-something-year-old gangbangers – going in and out of

an electronics store, loading up the back of the pick-up with boxed goods. Stereos and television sets, mainly.

And they were better value than buying guns – why go to all that trouble of finding money and buying black market weapons, when he could just take them? Walker pulled over and turned off the ignition. With his eyes on his targets he pocketed the keys as he got out at the end of the street. The guys were intently going about their task, little head for being caught out in a city where self-preservation was well and truly kicking in for those left behind.

He popped the trunk, found the tyre iron, and headed towards the looters. They might learn a lesson today, these young men. And while Walker was on most days a good teacher, usually patient, able to impart all kinds of knowledge, today was not that day. His lesson would be simple.

49

Three of the looters headed into the shop. The fourth was at the open tailgate, loading the stolen goods onto the truck's tray. His back was to Walker, who saw the grip of a big automatic pistol tucked into the kid's jeans. He wore a red bandana and a black singlet. He was tall and muscled, like a power-forward basketballer. Not a junkie. Probably traded in drugs but didn't touch the hard stuff himself. Probably ran guns and girls and whatever enterprise was paying well at any given time.

Walker didn't give him a chance to fight; why waste the time and energy when surprise was on his side. He went in fast, closing out the last ten yards at a run, his socked feet silent on the blacktop, and as he neared he stooped down and pulled the tyre iron back one-handed and swung. Hard. The impact was spectacular. The back of the guy's right knee bore the full force of the blow, slightly off centre, and he went down, hard and fast, like a puppeteer had cut the strings.

The kid screamed out in pain and shock.

Walker was already past him, and on the way by he pulled the guy's pistol out of his jeans and he kept going, forwards, to the store, dropping the tyre iron and holding the pistol in a two-handed grip, staring down the sight, waiting.

Two guys emerged, one with a big flat-screen TV, the other with a boxed deep-fryer under each arm.

'Don't move!' Walker screamed at them.

They didn't move. He closed the distance. The guy behind him was screaming at them to *smoke* Walker. *Cap* him. *End* him. Furious and pain-filled variations of the same.

'Your buddy in there,' Walker said, pressing the barrel of the automatic hard into the forehead of the one holding the TV. 'Tell him to come out with his hands held high.'

'Fuck you, man,' the guy with the TV said. 'He's the danger here, not you. You messing with some hard—'

'I'm counting to three,' Walker said. 'You need to decide if you want to die for a Korean-made TV. If so, go for it. And don't think I won't do this, because I'm mad as hell, and I've been killing people left and right when I wasn't even half-mad. One . . . Two . . .'

'Tyrone!' the TV guy yelled out. 'Get out here. Let this cracker see what you got.'

Tyrone came out. He was a short guy, overweight. In his hands was a weird-looking firearm, unlike anything Walker had seen on the battlefield. Black, boxy, like it had been stamped out of sheet metal. The ammo clip was longer than the barrel, at least thirty stacked rounds. High rate of fire and full automatic, Walker figured, seeing the barrel pointed his way. Maybe a generic Mac 10 or some kind of homemade version. A drive-by special, made in a backyard factory for bangers like these. Useless at any kind of range. But up close, as deadly as any other machine-pistol.

Walker said, 'Put that pop-gun on the ground, Tyrone.'

Tyrone was silent. Still. Unmoving.

Walker pushed the pistol harder into the TV guy's head, forcing him back and a little to the left, so that he became a human shield between Walker and Tyrone's weapon.

'What you want, fool?' the guy holding the fryers asked Walker.

'Your weapons,' Walker said.

The guy gave a chuckle.

'What's it to you guys,' Walker said. 'These pieces of shit you're packing are probably worth less than that TV. You can keep all the stolen goods. I just need these pieces. All of them. You can buy more later. You've probably got a crib full of weapons. Or a little factory of your own, making ugly stuff like what Tyrone's holding.'

'It'd end you good enough,' Tyrone said.

'It'd probably blow your own hand off,' Walker said. 'I'm on the clock, guys. Need me to start counting again? What were we at?'

The guy with the TV looked as if he was going to comply, but the one holding the fryers had other ideas. He muttered something as he dropped his loot then went for a weapon concealed at the front of his pants. Walker's reaction was faster. He had trained hard for a decade to be proficient at killing. These guys were amateurs at the task. Walker pointed his pistol at the guy and fired, blind, then brought it back to the TV guy and pressed the hot barrel against his forehead. It smoked a little against the skin, and TV guy started to shake.

'He got me!' the fryer guy said. 'This bitch got me!'

Walker chanced a glance. He'd clipped the guy in the meat of the arm, his left triceps, not life-threatening.

'Next one will be in your brain pan,' Walker said to the TV guy. 'The twenty-two calibre doesn't pack much, but it's a small and quick round, so it'll either go right in and rattle around for a while and whip up whatever's in that big head of yours, or it'll pop right out the back, sucking your grey matter with it. What's it gonna be?'

'Okay, okay,' the TV guy replied. 'Pieces on the ground. Slow, Tyrone. Let this crazy cracker be on his way.'

Walker watched the guy he'd shot pull a big revolver from the front of his pants and place it on the ground, then he went back to holding his arm. Tyrone put the backyard machine-pistol down.

'Now you,' Walker said. 'Slowly.'

The TV guy nodded, put his TV down, then produced a sawn-off shotgun that had been on a strap on his back. Pump action, pistol grip, near new.

'All of you, by your truck, now,' Walker said, scooping up the weapons, his automatic covering their movements. 'Ammo?'

Tyrone tossed two spare mags from his low-riding pants pockets.

'That's it?' Walker asked. They all nodded. Walker neared the guy he'd winged, looked at the wound. 'Through and through. Keep pressure on it, keep it clean, you'll be fine.'

'Fuck you.'

'You,' Walker said to the guy whose knee he'd blown out. 'Gimme your shoes.'

'You can't take a man's kicks,' the TV guy said in protest. 'That's next-level shit.'

'It's happening,' Walker said. 'Help him out of them, now.'

'My Jordans?' the guy said. 'Hell no, man, come on . . .'

'You pay for them?' Walker said. 'No? Thought not. Besides, you're not walking anywhere for a while.'

Five minutes later Walker was in his car, the guns on the seat next to him, the Jordans on his feet, and the looters disappearing in his rear-view mirror. Ten minutes after that he was headed west. There were police on the highway, and they didn't look friendly. The roads into New Orleans were closed to all but essential personnel, which was fine with him. He was headed out of town, and on to the water, and the hurricane was ticking away at his countdown.

50

'No sign of her,' Johnson told Spicer.

'She's around,' Spicer said, holding a cold pack to the side of his head. 'No perimeter alarms have been tripped?'

'No.'

'And you say the sea's too rough to swim?'

'Our boats can't even go out,' Johnson said, then added, 'Maybe we should get the hell outta here. This hurricane's gonna be a big 'un.'

'We get out when we get the deal done,' Spicer said. 'I've arranged for the meet to happen tonight.'

'You're not waiting for the other buyers?' Johnson looked disappointed. 'I thought we were going to wait and see what the market would force these Russians to pay.'

'Let's not push this any more than we have,' Spicer said. 'A couple hundred mil from these Ruskies is plenty enough to go around.'

'You're sure head office won't cotton on?'

'They probably will, when we all retire rich,' Spicer said. 'That's why we have to be systematic about how our guys leave, and when they leave.'

'Right.' Johnson paused, hesitant, then he said, 'You know that they think the deal's for thirty mil?'

'And they're getting two mil a pop. That's life changing, for all of them. They earned it. You and I split the remainder.'

'Most of them earned it.'

'What?' Spicer got up, moved closer to Johnson. 'What's up?'

'Three of the guys we have here weren't even in Afghanistan, on that op.'

'We needed more bodies on this. You agreed to that since day dot. You hand-picked those extra guys, brought them in. And you've already lost two good soldiers from our platoon.'

'Two fine men,' Johnson said. 'Both were up there in those mountains with us, hunting the Tali. They were there when we found it.'

'What are you saying you want to do?'

'Let me choose the guys to take to the meet,' Johnson said. 'We'll take the helo. Send the rest on the jet to meet us outside Houston, after we've landed in the field to pick up the money. Then we regroup and celebrate and stick to the plan about how we all depart the company with our cash.'

'And after the meet tonight?' Spicer said. 'You're just going to off them? They've made firm friends with our team. Couple of them are like brothers, they'd served together several times on tours all over. If it's just you and me turning up with the cash, it's going to be suspect. And they won't be fooled.'

'You let me worry about that.'

Spicer stared at Johnson, hard, looking for a reason to object to this new part of the plan, last minute. But he'd always trusted Johnson's instincts, from when he'd been his platoon sergeant, and he knew the men and their temperaments and their relationships better than Spicer.

'Okay,' Spicer said. 'Your call.'

'What about the Brit?'

'Get your teams to check all the old barracks again,' Spicer said. 'And the boat shed, and the boat that she and Walker came in on. If you can't find her, forget it, she can't do anything.'

'And Walker?'

'If we see him again, you can't miss. Not again. You get me?'

'Believe me,' Johnson said. 'I won't.'

•

Walker got onto a busy I-10 and headed west, towards the Gulf. He needed a private marina, where out-of-towners would have their boats moored to weather out the storm. He'd been in a hurricane once before. Hugo. 1989. He'd been on a family trip to Orlando's theme parks and Cape Canaveral and the Kennedy Space Center. He'd been to Johnson Space Center in Houston a bunch of times, being a Texas boy. But this was to see his first launch. Not to be.

Hugo had hit, and hit hard. At the time Hurricane Hugo was the most damaging tropical hurricane to strike the United States since records began. Many lives were lost. The Carolinas bore the brunt particularly hard. For the Walkers, their trip was cut short, and they headed back west, following the exodus. He missed the space launch, and he'd still not seen one in the flesh. He remembered staying in a hotel in Tennessee, by a river tributary, and waking up the next morning to find the water had swelled over ten feet and was starting to flood the streets. He remembered his mother's worry, his dad's stern determination at the wheel of the family car, the wipers on full whack, the streets full of people fleeing.

The highway that Walker was on now was quieter than those roads that day, because he was late to heed the federal warning. He had no doubt that this was going to be a Big One; he knew that the government didn't order the evacuation of a city like New Orleans for kicks.

He passed a small convoy of slow-moving evacuees. Kept his eyes on the road. Planned what was ahead. He couldn't help thinking back to Richter's words. What could be worth hundreds of millions of dollars to the Russians, be man-portable, and give them power? Nothing made any sense.

51

Steph turned back after ten minutes of fighting a current. It seemed to be whipping into the coast from both directions, which in her mind seemed bonkers. She then figured it was the storm surge fighting the natural tide and current, and when she found herself in what felt like a rip, she stopped fighting and let the water take her where it wanted. Ten minutes later the water calmed, at least from one direction, and she'd been swept into the small natural cove at the tip of Fort Lee. She smiled as she side-stroked to the one object there – the boat that she and Walker had brought.

On deck, she huffed and heaved. Then she panicked, feeling herself all over at the band of her shorts. The SOCOM pistol was no more, lost to the bottom of the Gulf. It was raining, and visibility was poor, but she kept low in case there were GreyStone guards on the land. The keys were gone from the control panel, but when she went below deck and felt under the mattress at the foot of the bed she and Walker had shared, she found the revolver. A small victory. She shivered and wrapped a towel around her shoulders, then set a pot of water on the gas for a cup of tea. Some things just worked to soothe the nerves.

She then went topside, peeking out before fully emerging, and used a knife to unscrew the assembly housing around the ignition switch, then found the wires and cut them and spliced them, completing the circuit as a turning key would. But the engine didn't turn over. She

rechecked her wires, then made sure the fuel gauge was fine, then checked the fuel switch on the outboard engines, and the fuel lines going in. Frustration was building – and then she saw that a cowling was loose on the side of the boat near the wheelhouse.

Steph shimmied over the rail, holding on and edging across, and opened the panel. It was the stow area for the batteries, which were two racks where a pair of car batteries would be. The racks were there. The wires were there. But the batteries were gone.

Stranded.

•

The I-10 feeding into Baton Rouge was a car park, then Walker peeled off on a B-Road and headed south, where he thundered through Gramercy and Thibodaux, and met up with Highway 90, which would take him to Lafayette if he stayed on it. He had no intention of that. Some eighty miles in, winding the engine out to near on 110 miles per hour where he could, he slowed as he entered Morgan City. Signs flashed on stationary generators by the side of the road, with red 'Hurricane Warning' placards attached to signs along the road, and others stating 'Evacuations in order'.

Walker turned south, towards the water, following the sign for a marina. He'd seen it on a map while on the boat with Steph, where it had showed up as a refuelling station, to the south of Morgan City. He crossed the rail lines to the less-developed side of the town that faced a waterway, with a view beyond of scrubby islands and further yonder the Gulf of Mexico. He had always been good with maps, a skill that had served him well in the Air Force, particularly in Afghanistan at night, on long-term patrols with mixed special-operations forces deep in the mountains, where sometimes GPS wasn't reliable.

He turned down Dead Water Road and pulled the car to a stop in a car park that was empty but for one big pick-up. Helicopters buzzed overhead, coming in from the Gulf. Evacuating the oil platforms and refineries, Walker figured. There were several hundred such

installations out there. Thousands of workers. The thought of being on a structure tenuously tethered to the sea floor in a category-five hurricane wouldn't be anyone's idea of fun.

The sky was grey, and the winds were kicking up sea spray to add to the rains.

The marina at Avoca Island Cutoff didn't disappoint. Down at the level of the docks and jetties, the sea was ferocious. No little tin dinghy for him; he needed something that could handle rough seas. A long, slender hull was going to have a softer ride, as long as the designer got the roll time right, which was mostly about the length-to-beam ratio, generating a steeper dead-rise and a sharp, steep entry. A wide, shallow hull wouldn't perform anywhere near as well. He needed a boat with a length-to-beam ratio of at least 3:1. A true deep-V hull with a dead-rise at the transom of over twenty degrees. Stout stringers, hulls and decks bolted together and bonded, a heavy boat – a hull's dry weight would help soften the ride. Minimal superstructure, or there would be increased roll and handling problems. From his vantage, he saw maybe six good possibilities.

He checked over his weapons before exiting the car. First up was the shotgun. He checked the rounds, pumped them out into his hand. Five shells, black plastic casings marked '00'. Buckshot. Designed for hunting large game, like deer, as well as self-defence. The gun itself was a Remington twelve gauge, variants of which had been used by military and law enforcement for decades. Good for close quarters. He pulled off his T-shirt then slung the shotgun over his chest by its strap, then pulled his T-shirt back over it, slid and turned the strap around so that the weapon was on his back, concealed.

The automatic pistol was an unfamiliar, generic-sounding brand. It held ten .22 rounds, nine remained. The slide seemed a little gritty, but the spring in the magazine seemed okay, and the firing pin action worked, so he figured he could rely on it. He thumbed the safety on, checked it did the job, and thumbed it off and on again until he was satisfied he could draw it and unsafe it and fire it with speed.

The third weapon was the unmarked, backyard machine-pistol. A simple thing. The barrel looked like it had been repurposed from another firearm. The mags held forty 9-millimetre rounds apiece, and they appeared to be reloads. Tyrone didn't strike him as the type to spend countless hours machining his own guns and loading his own bullets, so Walker figured he'd bought or scored the piece from a backyard professional. It was more than the work of a carpenter or hobbyist. The spot welds and seams and joins were tight and aligned. The pistol grip and receiver looked like they were repurposed from an Uzi. There was a selector on the side from safety, to single shot, to full auto. He figured forty rounds of unknown provenance at full auto would probably head the thing to breaking point, but if it came to that kind of action, then it would be a life-and-death situation anyway.

He stepped out of the car and tucked the pistol in his front jeans pocket, where his right hand could rest on the grip and conceal it. He then put the machine-pistol into the back of his belt. The spare mags went into his back pockets, where they stuck out a couple of inches but it would have to do.

At the marina, there were a few people in hi-vis yellow jackets tying extra lines. There must have been 200 craft before him. Some of the jetties had barbed-wire-topped gates to stop transients entering, and the boats berthed in those were big day cruisers. Half the slots were empty. He headed for those, because they were what he needed and were away from the marina custodians. As he neared, his list of six possibles was whittled down to five, when he saw the cabin lights glaring on one.

He walked into the wind, a hand up to shield his face from fast-blowing rain and sea water and sandy grit. So much for calm before the storm. Maybe that would come later, a brief lull. He hoped so. Using the weather as cover for a surprise attack was one thing; being able to get to the attack site intact was another. The first doubts about being out on the water in anything short of a battleship began to creep in.

He walked along the marina and stopped at the second jetty, specifically in front of a grey-hulled forty footer named *Mistral*. It had accented running strakes that ran lengthwise from the prow and down along the hull bottom. They were intended to help the deep-V hull reach planing speed, since each strake has enough horizontal area to act like a tiny flat-bottom for lift, and when the boat was pounding in rough seas or chop, the strakes would act as shock absorbers to cushion the motion of the hull. The superstructure was sleek and squat. It looked to Walker like a lot of the *Mistral*'s bulk was under the waterline, which suited him for tonight's mission.

He looked eastward, made sure that the hi-vis crew were occupied and not looking his way, then he made his move. He vaulted over the fence, the barbed wire nicking at his hands and forearms and tearing the bottom hem of his jeans. The impact of landing sent pain shooting through his ribs and back, and he took a moment to compose himself. He kept in a low crouch as he ran, using the cover of the other craft that bobbed in the sea swell.

At the stern of the *Mistral*, which was tied up tightly against the rubber pontoons of the jetty, Walker used his knife to cut the lines. Once aboard, he took the .22 pistol and did a quick search. He had to kick the door in on the cabin below decks, but the boat was empty. He went to the wheelhouse and used his knife to pull the control panel apart, found the ignition and a fuel-line kill switch, and a minute later he heard the deep thrum of twin inboard turbo diesel engines starting up. He wasted no time, because he knew that the marina crew would be alerted, and after a couple of false throttle spurts – the craft had small port and starboard thrusters in the bow for tight steering – he was out of the berth. He eased the engines as he made the turn, the propellers biting and *Mistral*'s bow rising a little, and when he was out into open water, he opened the throttle.

52

The two FBI agents, Chavez and Oberman, were at the New Orleans airport, as ordered by the FBI's Director of Counter Intelligence. They were there to look for Walker, and to expatriate their colleague back to DC once the hurricane had passed. Their government-leased twin-prop had already bugged out, turning on a dime after refuelling and heading north in a hurry. The place was packed. Last flights were scheduled at two am.

'Looks worse than I thought,' Chavez said, looking out the window.

'It's a hurricane, not a sun shower.'

'Right.'

'What do we do?' Oberman asked.

'I'm thinking . . .' Chavez replied.

'If Walker's out there, and Richter, they're hunkered down someplace good and tight. So, we're off the hook for now, right? We wait this out, then see what's what.'

'Well, we can't wait here overnight.'

'We could. It's as good a place as any.'

'We'll get a hotel,' Chavez said. 'Get a bottle of whiskey and some Chinese. Put CNN on and wait for this thing to blow over.'

'You're lead agent, your call.'

'Boss will be pissed.'

'This is becoming a category-five hurricane,' Oberman said. 'No-one's doing anything out there tonight or tomorrow. He'll understand. Especially if the city floods.'

'It's got levees.'

'Built by the Army, a long time ago. They're saying this storm is hitting NOLA head on. Big storm surge. Higher than the levees.'

'Pfft, this is god's own country,' scoffed Chavez, 'and this city's a right old dame, she'll pull through. Have a little faith.'

'I'm from tornado country. I've seen shit dealt out by God that you wouldn't believe.'

'Did your house ever get picked up and dropped on a witch in a magical land?'

'Hardy-ha,' replied Oberman. 'Fine. You wanna stay, we get a decent hotel. Up high, like the fifth floor plus. And whiskey and Chinese. Your idea, your shout.'

'The Chinese restaurants will all be shut, I bet,' Chavez said as they walked towards the exit and the signage for the hire cars.

'They won't want to lose the business. Plenty of cops and emergency personnel sticking around, someone's got to feed 'em. They'll be open, making a killing.'

'Right. Well, if not, it's jerky and Doritos from the gas station.'

'Your idea, your shout, you know the rules of the road,' Chavez said. As they stepped outside, the wind was picking up litter and rain and sending it every-way sideways. 'Shit. Come on, quick now, we need to get somewhere high and dry. This is insane.'

•

Walker was just sane enough to keep the craft at half-power. He wanted to rush, but this was one of those times where slow and steady won the race. Too fast and he'd start jumping the waves instead of slicing through them, then he'd lose control and be in real trouble. He was headed south-east, though more easterly than southward. He kept the sharp hull pointed into the worst of the

seas. The strakes were doing their job, keeping the craft planted in the rises and falls, the hull planted as well as any could be. He kept the throttle constant, only adjusting when he or the waves altered course.

As he came around the tip of Port Fourchon, the swell coming at him from the side almost made him lose control; he'd turned too far against it and was now running perpendicular to the rising crests. He powered harder and took a wide arc back out to sea, directly into the worst of it, slicing the waves again, and when he felt he'd covered enough sea, he throttled back and let the boat drift, the power right down, and soon, without all that forward momentum, the boat was rising and falling like a cork, up and down, and it was making him sick in the stomach, but soon the waves worked against the long creased lines of steel and fibreglass that striped along the hull and the vessel was turned, an almost complete 180, pointed landwards, and he throttled back up to the point where he was again slicing waves – this time in exactly the direction he was after.

He shot through the shipping channel by Grand Isle and into Barataria Bay. The sun was setting now, and it shone through the grey sky to the west, giving the world a golden hue, and sending ribbons of light onto the tops of the subdued waters in the bay. He powered further down as he entered the waterways of the islands shielding Little Lake. The treetops bent with the wind. The world was getting darker. He kept his running lights off as he neared his target.

Fort Lee was dark. No lights on at the jetty or boathouse. No torch beams of search parties. No visible craft on the water or in the air. No sounds to be heard over the deep resonance of the diesel engines of the *Mistral* and the howl of the wind over the water. He was headed to the cove, towards where they'd left their boat. He could moor the *Mistral* and make an assault on the compound to try to find Steph, but nothing about that equation stacked up in his or her favour.

Overwhelming odds, a defending force in good positions and better armed, Walker trapped outside in the elements with what equated to a rag-tag armament of pop-guns, and Steph in an unknown location among all those buildings.

None of it worked. His best bet – and Steph's – of securing her safe release was to get to the Russians, and thereby gain some bargaining power with Spicer. If the buy had yet to be completed, the Russians held value to Spicer and his GreyStone cronies.

Walker trimmed the engines right back as he neared the small sandy bay. He made out the white hulled craft amid the gloom: it looked just as they'd left it, which gave him hope.

His target now was the GPS, which he had hidden in a pot in the galley. Find the GPS tracker, find the Russian yacht.

He let the *Mistral* get in close but not too close – it was a bigger craft, and he didn't want to risk running it aground. He found the settings for the thrust vectors at the bow to work in tandem with the engines to keep the boat in situ, then he went to the edge of the stern deck. He watched and listened but could discern no threats. He left the machine-pistol and .22 behind, but he still had the pump-action, now strapped across his chest, ready for action.

He jumped feet first into the water: grey, foamy and slick from what he imagined was industrial run-off and oil spills being all churned up in the Gulf by the approaching hurricane. He trod water, found his bearings, and swam to the white boat. He used the swing gate between the two outboards to climb aboard. His back screamed out in pain, reminding him he was the walking wounded, but also that he had left his meds in the cabin, by the bed.

Walker led with the sawn-off shotgun. He swept the scene at the beach but it was too dark to make much out. He went for the door to below deck, seeing that a cowling cover had been removed from the side of the bridge, and the control panel too. Someone had done a good job of disabling the craft. As he moved, his Nike Jordans

squeaked on the wet deck. Not the ideal choice for a covert operation, but they fitted well, and felt better than being in socks. He reached for the handle of the door, turned it slowly.

It was locked. From the inside.

53

Walker knocked hard on the cabin door and then quickly backtracked on the deck and lay down. He kept the shotgun pointed at the door as he waited. Rain fell, hard, but he was in a good position.

Possibilities ran through his mind. *Could Steph be in there? Hiding? Scared? Armed? Ready to shoot whoever tried to get in?*

After a few minutes of getting saturated by the driving rain, Walker chanced another knock, this time with a fishing rod. He kept low on the deck, reached out with his hand on the end of the stick, and used it to rap on the door. A single gunshot rang out. Not through the door. He couldn't see where the shot was fired, but it came from inside the cabin. A warning shot.

And Walker knew the calibre. The .357. Either Steph, or someone using her weapon.

He commando-crawled forward across the deck, and when he was closer he yelled out: 'Steph!'

He inched back, gun aimed just in case. Waited.

Not for long.

The door opened. Walker knew the wide eyes behind the iron sight of the revolver. He got up on his knees as her eyes softened in recognition, then she stood and the door fully opened and Steph came running out and crashed into him with a bear hug.

'I knew you'd come back,' she said.

'Hence the shooting.'

'Sorry.'

'Bad guys tend not to knock,' Walker said, getting to his feet. 'What happened?'

'I took Spicer down and ran,' Steph said, still holding onto him.

Walker looked out at the dark shoreline, wondering if the gunshot had been heard by any close-by GreyStone employees.

Walker asked, 'Is Spicer dead?'

'No.'

'Okay, let's get out of here,' Walker said. 'I just gotta grab—'

'This?' Steph said. She took the GPS from her pocket and passed it over, along with the .357 revolver. 'They're moving, but westwards, away from the storm; they're about a hundred nautical miles from here. I think they're going to wait it out then head out across the Gulf and on to Cuba.'

'Any indication that the meet has gone down?' Walker asked, looking at the blinking dot on the GPS tracker.

'No,' Steph replied. 'But I heard Spicer say they were moving at dawn.'

'So, they're gonna meet up, away from here.'

As if on cue, the noise of a helicopter split the sky. It was faint, headed away. Walker looked for it but it was out of sight, going with the wind, in a north-west direction.

'Okay, I'll grab some pain meds and whatever else we left here that's handy, then let's go find this yacht.'

•

Marty Bloom watched the news from his apartment in DC. There was nothing he could do to stop the hurricane bearing down on New Orleans, but he felt he had to do something. Anything. Just being on hand, present for Walker, might do. It was better than sitting around, waiting.

If the storm was as bad as they were saying, the levees would fail. FEMA would be out in force. He would stay in some out-of-the-way hotel, cut off from the flooded city, ready to roll with a 4x4 or a tin boat to do what he could to assist Walker.

Then, his phone rang.

54

'Marty Bloom,' he said into his phone. It was his government cell, encrypted. The number was from the UK. London prefix.

'Mr Bloom, please hold,' a crisp English voice said, then a new voice came onto the line.

'Mr Bloom, this is Margaret Fuller. I take it that you know who I am.'

'Yes, ma'am,' Bloom replied. Dame Margaret Fuller, head of MI5. Career intel specialist, just as he was. He recognised her voice from a conference he'd attended at NATO two years back, where she'd presented a masterclass in catching Russian double agents operating in Europe. Clearly she'd got word of his calls into her agency.

'I understand that you have an interest in a situation off the coast of Louisiana,' Fuller said.

'Louisiana is a long way from London, Dame Margaret.'

'Indeed. And please, call me Fuller.'

'Okay,' Bloom said. 'Louisiana. I take it you're not talking about the hurricane.'

'Quite,' Fuller said. 'And as bad as I hear that looks, the outcome of this, if it comes to it, will be much, much worse.'

'How so?'

'I'll get to that. But most pressing is the fact that I have an officer on assignment there, which I understand you're aware of. My section

chief in Washington has worked back up the chain to me, because we're in a bit of a pickle.'

'How bad?' Bloom asked.

'We've lost contact and fear the worst.'

'This line is encrypted, so speak freely.'

'She was looking into an MI6 agent they had running within the incoming Chechen regime.'

'The Kremlin puppets.'

'The same. Six managed to recruit a well-placed agent, some years ago, and it seemed to be a big pay-off headed their way. But since power has come to this group, we took a close look, and suspected that agent was a double – and I'd say my officer's work, and her missing three check-ins, confirms this.'

'Is the nil-contact the only indication that something has gone wrong?'

'Yes. She knows not to break protocol, and never has. She was nearing the end of things, we believe. Closing in. She may have taken too big a risk in an attempt to pull off the operation. Or the double agent made her. And then today's attack on an ex-CIA man in the museum in New Orleans. And an FBI agent the day before. These things add up, Bloom, beyond happenstance, wouldn't you say?'

'Basic arithmetic suggests so.'

'This has all dragged on longer than we'd expected. So, we're of the belief that our officer recruited one of yours to expedite things. And that things then got out of hand.'

'If your officer is nearing the end of her mandated op, she may have gone dark for operational security.'

'I very much doubt that, but I admit that there is some hope among the ranks here that that is indeed the case.'

Bloom paused, then asked, 'What do you propose I can do?'

'I'm reaching out to you, Mr Bloom, because McCorkell just passed the buck to your door,' Fuller said. 'Nothing personal on his part, nor disrespectful, he wanted me to say. We spoke just a moment

ago – he's at the Mid-East summit with POTUS at Camp David. He explained to me that you would be the most across the situation, as you're aware of a CIA asset in the area who may have been in contact with my officer. That you may have a way of contacting him. So, here I am, calling you late at night my time, with what may or may not be an emergency. But it's a gut feeling I cannot shake.'

'I do know of an Agency officer there,' Bloom said. 'A new recruit. Though I suspect you already know that, and probably a lot more. I'm sure that your officer on the ground reported contact with him, just as he did with me. Stephanie Mensch, right? And I'm sure the fact that I've been looking into her raised a flag somewhere at Five, which is why you're reaching out to me now, not to McCorkell. He didn't give you my name. You came to me yourself, because you're trying to cover your butt. Ma'am.'

'Mr Bloom, I don't think—'

'You're panicked, Director General Fuller. You're running an op on US soil that you didn't tell us about, and now it's gone to shit and you're freaking out. And it's MI5, counter-intel, and you've got a rogue agent you're looking into – a mess, that maybe your MI6 started, and you sent Stephanie Mensch in to clean it up. Am I close? Or should I contact McCorkell and see what's what?'

There was a pause, then Fuller said, 'That won't be necessary, but it's your prerogative. I've been reading all about you this past hour. You're as astute as your file notes make out. So, I'm asking, one career spy to another, for a – how would you chaps put it – a solid?'

'So, what do you want from me?'

'I need your help. And I will cooperate fully in return. You're right, we never should have gone down this road in this way, and I assure you that in the wash-up of this, I will ensure that it won't happen again. But right now there's far too much at stake to mess around. And for the record, I couldn't give a damn about my career in the face of what might soon play out.'

'And what's that?'

'We're a couple of old war horses, you and I,' Fuller said, then there was a slight creaking noise, and Bloom imagined her leaning back in a big leather office chair and putting her feet up on the desk. 'What do you know of the joint US–UK Cold War program codenamed Brilliant Pebbles?'

•

Walker had the GPS system in a nook by the controls in the *Mistral*'s wheelhouse and was headed south-west. Cutting through the chop, as before, as fast as he dared push the craft. The engines were terrific. Volvo turbo diesels, he now knew, having glanced in the engine bay. Below deck he had shown Steph the stainless-steel galley and the king-sized suite with a wardrobe full of clothes. The men's clothes were a few sizes too wide for Walker, but the women's items were close to Steph's size. She selected jeans and a top and was making good use of the fully appointed bathroom. He took a big plastic windbreaker and put it over his T-shirt, then used a belt to tighten it closer to his body so that the high winds didn't buffet it every which way. The lounge and seating area would comfortably accommodate twelve, but for now the dining table only held the machine-pistol and shotgun and Steph's revolver.

Walker steered one-handed and checked a chart, planning the spot he might start a big arc and come at the Russian yacht from the south-east. They seemed to be doing about ten knots. Walker was doing closer to seventeen, so he figured they would meet up in around two-and-a-half hours.

Steph came up twenty minutes later, in new clothes, smelling of soap and linen. She passed him a large travel mug of coffee, which he sipped through the small slit in the lid in-between every second clip of the waves as the *Mistral* cut through the water.

'What are you thinking?' Steph asked him.

He looked from the view ahead, which was dark but for their powerful navigation lights that sliced a brilliant beam through a few hundred yards of inky black.

'There's likely two captives on the yacht,' Walker said.

'The cop, and Richter's daughter?'

'Yep. So, we can't just storm the thing. We might have to ghost them for a while. Wait until they berth. Use any advantage we can exploit.'

'Say we do that,' Steph replied, 'then what are our options?'

'Then,' Walker said, sipping his coffee and checking the course ahead, 'I do what I do best.'

'Kicking down doors . . .' Steph wrapped her arms around him from the back. Over the rain on the windscreen and the rough water on the hull she stood on tip-toes and said into his ear, 'Though, I think you're good at quite a few things.'

'Yeah, well, you ain't seen nothin'.'

55

Chavez and Oberman were in a La Quinta near the Louis Armstrong airport. Just far enough from the coast for them to feel comfortable. The place was packed with government workers hunkering down before the storm, ready to launch when they got the all-clear. They were predominantly state officials. About ten New Orleans PD. Some state troopers. A bunch of firefighters. Some medical staff. A couple of Wildlife and Fisheries guys. The atmosphere was a subdued slumber party; jovial but wary. They all congregated in the lobby and the breakfast room, spread across couches and chairs and around tables. There was pizza and Chinese food and plenty of beer and pop. No sign of FEMA but for the officials appearing on the big TV sets.

'Hey,' Chavez said to Oberman, pointing at a coffee table.

'What is it?' Oberman asked.

'Your phone's ringing.'

'Shit.' He sat up and shuffled around the empty food containers and beer bottles. 'Probably the wife, worried she's gonna lose this fine—'

'What?'

'It's DC.'

'Well, answer it, man!'

'Oberman,' he said into his phone. He listened for a full minute, then replied, 'Sir, yes, sir. I've got it. Won't let you down.'

'What?' Chavez asked after he'd ended the call.

'That was our boss.'

Chavez sat straighter. 'And?'

Oberman leaned forward, looked around to check he wouldn't be overheard. 'We're to meet a Marty Bloom of the CIA, on the—'

'CIA!'

'Not so loud, man,' Oberman said as a nearby trooper looked their way. 'We're to meet him on the tarmac, he touches down in an hour. We're to set him up with a room here, take him around where he wants, keep an eye on him and report back. He'll likely lead us to Richter.'

'What's the CIA doing here?' Chavez, in a hushed tone, asked. 'First Richter, now this guy?'

'What the hell do I know?' Oberman replied. 'Probably started this damned hurricane with some experimental weather weapon.'

'You need to drink more water, less beer,' Chavez said, and Oberman did as instructed, filling a glass from a water jug on the table and downing it. 'This was always a counter-intelligence op of Richter, right?'

'I know.'

'Maybe this Bloom guy is bent?'

'Maybe.'

'This could be it.'

'What?'

'*It.* This is gonna get us noticed by the big brass. We're moving up in the world!'

•

Walker checked the GPS tracker and their course, and calculated forty minutes to target. The Russian yacht had been stationary for almost two hours. He planned to cruise by to see what was what but would then await the dead of night for any assault. But before anything else, he needed more intel. He had already figured out a

couple of ways to get all those on board off the boat. Much better out in the open to deal with hostiles, rather than going below deck, cabin to cabin.

So, it was time to settle something that had been nagging at him.

'Steph,' he said. 'I need to know more about this Russian and Chechen thing.'

'Like what?' Steph leaned against the wall of the pilothouse.

'Are they buying, or selling?'

'I told you before.'

'Tell me again.'

'Does it really matter?'

'See,' Walker glanced out at sea, where he saw the distant lights of a big fishing trawler or freighter, headed west. 'I've heard through my friend Bloom that they were *buying*.'

'Where'd he hear that?'

'Does it matter?'

Steph paused, bit her lip. 'I'd trust my intel over his. I've been on this for almost two years.'

'Okay, tell me about that.'

'About what?'

'Your target on the boat, that's the agent you've been running, correct?'

'That's right.'

'Who is he?'

'He's the security advisor to the incoming president of Chechnya,' Steph replied.

'So, what is he, SVR, FSB?'

'Something like that.'

'Except you're not running him as an agent, are you?'

'What do you mean?'

'You're MI5, Steph. Not MI6. This is all about counter-intelligence.'

Steph paused, sipped her coffee, looked out to sea. 'I never told you I was MI6. You made that assumption.'

'True,' Walker said. 'But, Steph? If you want to work together on this, you've gotta let me in. Tell me everything you know about what's going on here.'

'It's complicated,' she said, staring down into her coffee. 'It's really messed up, actually.'

Steph looked up to Walker. There was something about her look that Walker hadn't seen before. Sadness, he thought. He gave her the room, the time, to get her story out. The silence lasted about thirty seconds.

'I'm with Five,' Steph said. 'The agent in question is a Six asset, who they've cultivated for close on a decade. I was brought in to see if he was a triple – if he's our agent, but then passing our info *back* into the Kremlin. This is a counter-intelligence operation, first and foremost. The buy, or sell, is incidental. Not that it should be, but it is.'

'They could be selling or buying an arms system worth hundreds of millions of dollars and that's incidental?'

'This agent has provided huge dividends,' Steph said. 'But, two years ago, the MI6 officer running him was found dead in Moscow. Stabbed to death, stuffed into a gym bag, dumped outside the British Embassy. *Natural causes*, Russian state media reported as his cause of death.'

'It might not be related to the agent you're looking into,' Walker said. 'Your MI6 officer was probably running dozens of assets.'

'We're not complete idiots, Walker.'

'I'm not saying you are.'

'We looked closely at this. Lots of eyes. From Five and Six and GCHQ. And our allies. When things brought our asset into focus, they sent me in as his new handler.'

'So, he thinks you're now running him as an agent?'

Steph nodded.

'What's his name?'

'Igor Peskov.'

'So the Russian buyer is a highly valued asset?'

She nodded.

'Right. And you're telling me you have no way to reach out to him?'

'He'd gone silent, for three months, since being named the Chechen Republic's incoming security chief.'

'What's he know about us, or British intel, that could be so important to you? More important than what they're buying?'

'For one thing, he knows how we communicate with our agents in Russia.'

'Change the methods.'

'It is *so* not that simple.'

'And what else?'

When Steph next spoke there was tension in her jaw, like she was fighting against a rising anger. 'We're looking into him as the sell-out of our man in Moscow. And the way that our MI6 officer died, they may have bled him for intel first. They may have got his whole network of agents and turned them against us. I think Peskov knows. Either because he was involved in the interrogation, or if he wasn't he's high enough up the chain of Russian intelligence to know who did it. Either way, I want to find out. We've been dancing around it all this time. But I need to know. I have to know. This trip to the US may be our last chance to pick him up, before he's surrounded by Chechnya's security apparatus.'

'Surely you'd know if your whole network is compromised by now, two years on?' Walker said. 'This is Russian intelligence we're talking about. They kill their own on a daily basis, at the merest suggestion of betrayal. Surely a bunch of them would have turned up in gym bags?'

'That's the scary thing, there's been no more deaths in the network,' Steph said. 'This is a long game, and they're playing it well. Too well, which has us worried. They could move at any moment. Think about it. That—' Steph paused, fought back a tear. 'That MI6 officer they killed? He ran some eighty agents that we know of. And we're still running most of them, though we're aware that they might be

compromised. As far as we know, they're all still alive. But that could change at any second. Overnight. Simultaneous hits.'

'Or they all could have been turned by Igor Peskov, or whoever got to your man.'

'Possible.'

'Do *you* think he sold your MI6 officer out?'

'I didn't. Not for the longest time. But now, I'm not so sure. Peskov is patriotic, he's ambitious, he's a real mover. He's basically Putin's eyes and ears in the Chechen Republic. His next position will be back in Moscow. Head of FSB, or Deputy Prime Minister. And from there, ten years on, who knows?'

'You're saying that if Peskov *isn't* a triple, that if he is still a legitimate agent working for MI6, and he had nothing to do with the death of your MI6 officer, then you could one day have a President of Russia who is an *agent of Britain*.'

Steph nodded.

'No wonder this multi-hundred-million-dollar transaction is superfluous to your mission,' Walker said. 'This is huge. It's world-changing, if it comes off.'

Steph was silent.

'You need to be sure,' Walker said. 'What are we doing here with him? Following him? Making contact? Getting a confession? Killing him?'

Steph looked out over the dark water. When she spoke, her voice was barely a whisper. 'I still don't know. But I need to know the truth, from his mouth.'

56

Bloom exited the government jet, alone. He held onto the rail of the stairs, a walking stick in his other hand. The rain was near-on horizontal, and as he set foot onto the tarmac he used his free hand to hold out his carry-on as a shield against the gale. As he shuffled towards the terminal, two men approached. FBI in bright yellow lettering was visible on their front left jacket pockets.

'Mr Bloom?' the shorter of the two said.

'Yes,' Bloom replied, still moving to get out of the rain.

'I'm Special Agent Chavez, this is Oberman,' he said, falling into step with the older man. 'AD Webster of the FBI asked us to meet you here and arrange accommodation and assist in any way we can.'

They entered the terminal and the howl of the wind and rain was shut out. Inside was the hum and hubbub of an overcrowded airport with stragglers desperate to get out. He eyed the two FBI agents. They seemed earnest enough. Typical-looking G-men of the modern era. Diverse. Dependable. While Bloom's default position was to be wary, he allowed these two to carry on with their directive.

'Okay, boys,' Bloom said. 'Lead on.'

'Anything you need?' Oberman asked as they headed for the car park.

'Dinner. Wine. Best you can muster, under the circumstances.'

'Right,' Oberman said. 'Can do.'

'And I don't know what kind of set-up you have here,' Bloom said, leaning on his cane, 'but I need you to have on-hand communications that will hold up against this storm. I've got a CIA officer out there who will need assistance. You boys help me at every turn, and the Agency, and the National Security Council, will be grateful. That's a gold star in your jackets, you understand me?'

'Sir, yes, sir.'

•

When Walker found the yacht, right where the blinking GPS tracker said it would be, a tiny voice at the back of his mind quieted. It had been giving him cause for doubt, saying that maybe they'd done an electronic sweep of the yacht, found the tracker and placed it onto a decoy vessel. But they hadn't. The rain had let up. The lights of the yacht were all on. It was five minutes to midnight. He headed for the far pier, where he saw there was room to tie the *Mistral*. The weather had cleared to a light drizzle. The calm before the storm.

Walker looked across to Steph as he powered down and turned the craft. 'Do you have a picture of your agent?'

Steph just looked at him, one eyebrow raised.

'Right. Any defining features?' Walker said. 'I'd hate to kill him, and piss you off.'

'He's not much taller than me. Wiry build. Cropped dark hair, silvering at the sides. Brown eyes.'

'Right. Narrows it down.'

'If we see him, I'll point him out, how about that?'

'Probably best, given the circumstances.' Walker trimmed all power after a spurt of reverse, then turned the wheel tight and feathered the forward thrusters, turning the boat on a dime and docking aft-first.

'Hold the controls while I tie us ashore?'

'Right.' Steph took over, keeping a little thrust going.

Walker went aft, then forward, looping ropes to the tie points on the pier. He then went to the pilothouse and killed the engines. The

lights on their craft kept on battery power, until a small generator below deck automatically kicked in to top up the batteries.

'So, you're going to get them off the yacht?' Steph said, looking across the pier. The Russian boat was by far the largest craft in view. 'How, pray tell?'

'I'm gonna smoke 'em out.'

57

'The guys are pissed,' Johnson said to Spicer. They were sitting in the helo at an airfield to the east of Baton Rouge. A small private airstrip, used for student flights and charters. It was busy tonight. Refuelling for those bugging out. Stowing away in hangars for those weathering the storm. The rest of their GreyStone crew, down to seven men, were aboard the jet, awaiting orders. 'They think leaving Bruce behind at Fort Lee was some cold shit.'

'What do they expect – that we put all our plans on hold until he showed up? Tell them to deal with it.'

'You know, there's now just two of the outsiders left,' Johnson said. The rain pattered on the windscreen. The engine was off, the pilot sitting in his chair, headphones on, looking over maps. 'I don't think I can take them out as I wanted to.'

'Send the two of them on an errand. We'll leave them behind, like Bruce.'

'They know too much.'

'Like what? Only you and I know what's really in that case.'

The two of them looked at the dull green metal box between them, strapped to the floor of the helicopter. A two-foot cube. Steel grab handles at each end. About forty-five pounds in weight. Black painted Cyrillic writing stencilled on the sides.

'They know enough,' Johnson said. 'And they'll be pissed for being cut out. As our originals will be if we leave those two behind after the transaction.'

'Our guys are gonna be rich, they'll turn the other cheek,' Spicer replied. 'In fact, announce to them all that we'll divvy up the crew money of those fallen to all those remaining. Go make that statement to them all, then send the two outsiders to keep an eye on the yacht – tell them it's so that when we meet the Ruskies we're not going into an ambush.'

'You really want me to do all that? I mean, offer them that extra money?'

'Of course. It'll ensure they're onside when it comes to leaving two more men behind. Money motivates, buddy. Or are you forgetting why we're doing this?'

Johnson smiled, and he looked pained at the plaster over his nose and black eyes from the car crash. 'You and I are going to be very rich.'

'You better believe it. Now, go get things moving with the crew. Leave the rest to me.'

•

Steph put the revolver in a pocket of her coat. Walker had the .22 pistol, nine rounds, and the shotgun, with five slugs loaded, which he slung over his back. He gave Steph a quick rundown in how the backyard machine-pistol worked, and passed that and the spare mags to her.

From the galley, he'd emptied three jars of condiments from the refrigerator, gave them a quick wash out and dried them. In the engine room, he'd filled the jars near full with gasoline from the spare jerry cans for the gas generator. There was plenty of diesel on board, over 200 gallons, but diesel didn't burn anywhere near as well as gasoline. But when lit, it did smoke, and he added some to each jar. The heavier fuel swirled and slowly settled to the bottom. He'd used his combat knife to make slits in the top of the metal lids of the jars, where he stuffed torn strips from a tea towel.

'Right,' Walker said, putting his improvised Molotov cocktails and a gas lighter in a small wicker basket, covering them with the plastic sleeves he had cut off his jacket. 'I'll take the inflatable to the waterside of the yacht. Once in position, I'm going to start three fires, at the stern, their skiff, and in the upper pilothouse. They'll congregate on the forward deck, then, if they're smart, they'll get off and move onto the dock while the crew try to suppress the fires. Depends how quickly they find enough extinguishers, because water ain't gonna do the job.'

'You look like Red Riding Hood with that basket of goodies.'

Walker smiled. 'I'm the Big Bad Wolf.'

As they went topside, Steph asked, 'What if they stay on the yacht and don't get off?'

'If it comes to that, I'll improvise.' Walker looked out at the yacht. Some of the lights had gone off, but he could see the main bridge was lit up, and through their glasses he spotted the big guy and a crew member.

'You don't want me to come with you?'

'If it comes down to shooting, I need you to be in a better cover position than aboard the inflatable,' Walker replied, pointing at a small trawler on a dock between them. 'If you get on that, it's got good protective cover for you, and it's also got good sight lines towards the yacht. Take the machine-pistol and spray the bridge, a full sweep or two across the window-line, empty a whole clip in maybe three bursts, then take cover. That'll scatter those who aren't fighting the fires, buy us both time. I'll be back to pick you up then, or if that doesn't need to happen, I'll pick you up then anyway.'

Steph nodded, but she didn't look sold.

'For what it's worth,' Walker said, 'I'll try not to shoot your Russian agent.'

'Please don't. After all the time we put into cultivating him, it would be a shame, to put it mildly.'

'If I get the chance, I'll try to bring him off the boat.'

'What? No.' Steph shook her head. 'He won't come. And you can't just blurt out something to him that might jeopardise everything British Intelligence has worked for.'

'You still hold hope that he might not be a triple agent?'

'There's a chance. So, tonight's not the night to blow his cover. If you get him off the boat, make him look like a legitimate hostage. I need to talk to him.'

'If I can get him off that boat, you can talk to him all you like.'

Steph looked uneasy. 'I'm telling you, he won't come.'

'I won't give him a choice.'

Steph shook her head and looked over at the yacht.

'Right,' Walker said, making his final prep to take out the inflatable dinghy. 'Well, we need intel. At least, I do. On what they're selling to GreyStone at dawn.' Walker put a hand on her shoulder. 'Are you ready for this? I'm relying on you to act, fast, if it comes to it.'

'Yes. Of course. Let's move.'

58

Walker dropped Steph off at their side of the trawler, hidden from view from the yacht. He gave her a boost, then she hauled herself up and over the edge of the gunwale. She looked back and gave Walker a thumbs up. He powered away, slowly, careful to keep the small Honda outboard as quiet as possible, the high winds helping disguise the engine noise. Once he had good bearing towards his target, he would cut the engine and drift to position, using the outboard as a rudder to keep the track true, then go from bow to stern along the seaward side, tossing his lit petrol bombs up onto the decks. Then he would start up the engine, go around the stern of the yacht and berth the small craft inside the void between the yacht and the pier.

All good in theory, though in practice it would be something else entirely. Military service had taught Walker that anything could happen, at any time. The yacht might suddenly start up and power out of the marina. The gas-soaked strips of towel might not light or burn as he wanted. One or more of the gas-filled jars might not break upon impact, and just roll across the deck and burn as harmlessly as an overturned tiki torch. He needed all three Molotov cocktails to have maximum impact. He wanted the fires to spread across the decks wherever the spilled gas ran, and catch alight secondary and tertiary incendiary materials, like the teak decking or the plastics in the pilothouse, the foam padding in seat cushions and the rubber coatings

on wires. He wanted the distraction to last as long as possible, to soak up as much manpower as possible, and to spook those aboard to clamber out from below deck.

Walker motored towards the mouth of the small harbour, then did a big arc and headed towards the yacht. He kept the throttle low, and the inflatable dinghy bobbed along in the swell. He looked forward and to his left, towards the trawler. He couldn't see Steph, which was a good thing. She knew well what she had to do. As he entered the final fifty yards of his approach towards his target, he killed the little outboard motor. The engine sputtered as the fuel was switched off, leaving him in silence but for the wind and rain. As he drifted towards the tall, sharp bow of the yacht he uncovered the Molotov cocktails. He lit the first up with the butane lighter, the gas-soaked towel flaming instantly. He held it in his right hand, and as his boat neared the bridge of the yacht, he tossed.

It was a good pitch, strong and direct. He watched the flame flicker in the night like a slow-moving tracer round homing in on target. The Molotov cocktail hit the ceiling of the open-air upper pilothouse, the same small space he had compromised a night earlier to place the GPS tracker. The jar, which held about sixteen ounces of the gasoline-and-diesel mix, shattered on impact, and the lit towel ignited the splattered fuel. The flames spread wherever that fuel had spilled and splashed, an area of about ten square feet, and the fire grew in intensity as secondary materials lit up. Fingers of orange and red blazed in the night. A good first strike.

Walker lit the second. He waited until the towel caught and the fire burned well, then he launched it. He tossed it up, underarm, as high as he could, and as he was lighting the third he heard the impact on the stern's teak deck – breaking glass, then a whispered whoosh and the flare of orange flames in the night. Strike two.

The third jar he tossed like a football, and it hit the big tender of the yacht, itself a thirty-foot cruiser at the stern, hooked up to a gantry. The gasoline–diesel bomb had spun through the air, dripping fire as

it went, as if he had thrown a handful of fire that had splattered on impact and engulfed the yacht's tender. That third fire took hold fast, the canvas cover of the cruiser clearly not flame-retardant, and the length of the boat blossomed and bloomed into a spectacular bonfire that sparked and crackled in the night sky. Strike three.

Walker switched on the fuel line of the outboard and pulled the cord, the little Honda engine coughing to life. He then powered around the stern of the yacht, the fire raging above him as he turned hard and entered the cave-like space between the huge yacht and the pier. He made it about halfway then put the outboard into reverse and came to a stop by a tall concrete column, which he tied the inflatable to.

Waiting time. It didn't take long. First came the shouts. Then, sounds from inside the yacht. Calls to action, and frantic movement of doors slamming and feet clamouring. He saw a couple of lights come on in cabins, the portholes a few feet above his head glowing from within and spilling out shafts of stark light. He looked up. The sheer wall of the side of the yacht was too steep and smooth and raked outwards to climb, so he dropped over the side and swam back towards the stern and hauled himself up a chrome-plated ladder on the diving deck.

He drew the .22 pistol as he stood. The fire-engulfed tender between him and the big stern deck acted like a partially translucent wall that changed with every flicker and movement of the flames and smoke. Two guys rushed the scene, each with a dry chemical extinguisher, which they started to deploy. They would need more than just two, but they were making some headway in beating the fire back. A smarter move would have been to use the gantry crane to drop the tender overboard, and tend to the other fires, but neither of these guys would get that chance.

Walker squinted through the wall of flames. One guy was tall and bald, dressed only in underpants. The other was short and rotund, wearing a dressing gown. Each used the extinguishers in

sweeping motions against the fire. They stood shoulder to shoulder, and advanced as they fought back the flames. They'd had training. They were either the ship's crew, or security who'd been taught how to fight a fire. Whatever their involvement, they were in cahoots with the abduction of two women, and were part of something nefarious on a national-security level, and they were in Walker's way, and the sum of that equated to them being fair targets.

Through the flickering sheet of orange and red fire, Walker sighted the tall guy's shiny bald head. They were ten feet away. They might as well have been a foot away; while this was not the SOCOM pistol, the .22 round was small, quick and accurate.

Walker squeezed the trigger, twice. The sound of the .22 round cracked in the night against the crackle of fires and whoosh of the extinguishers and the roar of driving rain. The tall man's head jerked back and he fell to the deck. His shorter comrade stopped applying his fire extinguisher to the task at hand and he looked across, incredulous at the sudden disappearance of his buddy. Then he looked back towards the fire-engulfed tender, his synapses firing and telling him that gunshots had come from that direction, Walker fired. One shot. It hit the guy in his upper lip, and though Walker couldn't see it from this angle, he knew that the back of the guy's head, where it met the spine, was no more. He dropped, almost straight down.

Not a bad start.

Walker moved, fast. Around the fire, to the port side, he saw a crew member rushing up the stairs to the top pilothouse, extinguisher in hand. Without pausing, Walker sighted and fired two shots. The guy was hit in the chest, twice, then he fell backwards and hit the railing on the way down and cartwheeled into the sea.

Four shots remained in the pistol. Then he would have to bring the shotgun into play.

Walker entered the open doors to the main cabin then headed below deck. His movement was cautious, the pistol leading the way. The stairs were wide and carpeted. Where he ended up in the hallway

at the bottom was roughly amidships, like a spine running through the yacht, and there were doors leading off fore and aft, port and starboard. Walker headed towards the back of the boat first. A man emerged from a room ahead, buttoning his pants as he did. He eyeballed Walker – then he was shot in the eye. The right eye. It spun him violently around, twisting to the floor, where he lay in a squirming heap, and Walker put another shot into the back of his head so that he was now as lifeless as a stack of dirty laundry. Walker paused and checked his six – no-one behind him. He pressed on.

He checked the first door to his right: a mess room, large enough to seat twenty-four people at four tables. All tables had place settings. The thought of around twenty possible targets on board gave him pause, but he kept moving. The door behind him was a sitting room. Empty. Further along the hall a doorway opened up to a big galley, where a guy had his back to Walker, wearing headphones, scrubbing pots and pans. Walker stepped over the body in the hall and continued his search, the .22 still in a double-handed grip. He peered around doorjambs and checked each room. Five more staterooms cleared in ten seconds. All were the same configuration, one of them containing a guy who was sleeping, oblivious to the chaos going on aboard the yacht. He had a bandage wrapped around his face and head, covering at least one eye. Walker let him be. In the hall, Walker checked his six again – no-one there.

Four doors remained ahead of him, two to each side. Stairs at the end, a set leading topside to the stern deck, another spiralling down to the service level of engine and storage compartments.

The first door to his right was locked. The door to his left was open, and empty. A large bed, unmade. Down the hall he tried the door to his right. Empty. Large bed. Made. A lamp on. These rooms were larger, and had their own ensuite. He paused and listened, heard the crackle of the fire above, saw the glow of the flames out the port window.

The final door was also locked. He looked up and down the hallway. He knew he didn't have much time. Maybe not enough to break down the locked doors and head towards the bow and check the remainder of the rooms. But he had to be sure. And this door was right in front of him, so he would deal with this first.

59

Walker wished he still had his boots – the Nike Jordans did not make a good battering ram, but there was 240 pounds of mass behind the kick, plus a whole lot of leverage and aim. It took four hard kicks, by which time his heel hurt and his back screamed out in pain, but then the door flew open and a figure flew out. It emerged from the darkness and launched with speed, hands out at Walker's face. He dropped his pistol and grabbed the figure's wrists. The wrists were small. In one hand was a shard of mirror, which he caught just shy of slicing his neck. He looked at the woman, who was intent to get him.

'I'm a friend,' Walker said. 'I'm here to get you out.'

Her expression changed as she looked at Walker, heard his American accent. Then she looked up and down the hall, and saw the body. She dropped the mirror shard and hugged onto him, hard.

'What's your name?' he asked.

'Alice Richter,' she said.

'I – I know your father,' Walker said, catching himself and using the present tense. Now wasn't the time for a full catch-up. 'Quick. There's another woman on board, from Florida. She might be a cop or a federal agent.'

'She's dead. She was undercover Homeland Security looking into people-trafficking.'

Walker scooped up his pistol, looked at Alice Richter. There were dark bags under her eyes, like she'd had even less sleep than her father had. She was dressed in gym clothes, maybe what she wore to sleep in, perhaps what she'd been abducted in days ago. Her hair was matted and messy. There was no trace of make-up on her. She looked gaunt, like she'd been on a hunger strike, or they'd not fed her.

'You're sure?' Walker asked, already leading Alice towards the stern, to the stairs.

'Yes,' Alice replied. 'I saw them do it. Three days ago. They were putting her through hell. She managed to attack one of the Russians – put a butter knife through his cheek, and his eye. The big guy dragged her topside and cut her throat. She fell overboard, her hands to her neck. She didn't even make a sound. I don't know if she drowned or bled to death. I don't know . . .'

'You're okay,' Walker said, a hand on her shoulder. 'Keep moving, stick close behind me. I'll get you out of here.'

Part of Walker was relieved. The guilt he'd carried since he'd first been on the yacht to plant the tracker, when he'd failed to search for the woman, was now gone. She was as dead then as she was now; there was nothing he could have done about it. But his emotions changed. The guilt was gone, but a rage brewed, a sensation that arrived as a heat that flared up his neck and his face. *The big guy dragged her topside and cut her throat.* He wanted to kill more of these men, especially that big guy who seemed so fond of knives. At the stairs that led to the stern deck he stopped as he spotted a guy down the hall, thirty yards away. He was wearing pyjamas but held an AK-47, which he was lifting up to bear at them.

Walker brought the .22 up, one-handed, aimed and fired twice. The weapon was now empty, so he dropped it like Michael Corleone. Ahead, the guy jerked back like he'd been punched in the gut. He stayed on his feet, but dropped his assault rifle and put his hands to his stomach, where a red flood spread over his pyjama shirt. Walker smiled.

'Quick, keep close behind me,' Walker said to Alice, taking the shotgun and leading the way up. At the top of the stairs the door opened out to the side of the dive deck, a half-level below the main deck. The fires were raging, but not as badly as when he'd last seen it. The nearest blaze, aboard the ship's tender, was shifting as he watched. Finally someone had decided to use the crane to put the boat into the water, away from the yacht, ditching it at sea. Walker looked up and across the flames. The deck was level with his chest, so he was looking up at the figure at the controls of the gantry. There was no mistaking who it was.

'That's him,' Alice said, standing next to Walker and peering up on tiptoes. 'That's the son of a bitch who abducted me. He's the one who killed the Homeland agent.'

Then, the big guy looked their way.

60

'Get overboard,' Walker said to Alice. He kept his eyes on the Russian, who pressed the release on the crane and the brightly burning ship's tender hit the sea on the port side with a splash. Spot fires remained on the deck where it had been. 'Swim between this yacht and the pylons, head towards the end of the pier. You'll find a small inflatable. Yank the cord to start the engine, untie it, travel to the west – that way.' Walker pointed. 'Stop at a light blue fishing trawler and pick up a woman named Steph. Got it?'

'Blue fishing trawler, Steph,' Alice said. 'You sure about this?'

'I'm sure,' Walker said. 'I'll get my own way out.'

The Russian was a big guy, that was well established. He was the man from the museum. The shanker. His shoulders were about a foot wider than Walker's. Tucked in the front of his belt was the butt of a huge automatic pistol, maybe a Desert Eagle. Walker headed up the steps to the teak deck, stepping out to where the fire was clear. There was now just five yards between them, and a wall of fire behind the big guy. Another guy was positioned to Walker's right, busy with an extinguisher at the deck fire. Walker made out another two guys above, trying in vain to combat the upper pilothouse fire, which was by far the most pressing.

'Think you shoot before me?' the guy asked Walker. His accent was thick, his voice a deep baritone.

Walker's hands tensed on the shotgun: his right hand on the pistol grip, and his left on the pump action. He would need to move slightly to fire it, either his left leg forward or his right foot back, to turn a little sideways as he aimed and fired and reloaded to fire again. Could this guy draw and fire within that time? Probably. Walker had seen how quickly the guy had moved in the museum. Fast. Practised.

'Okay,' Walker said. 'Guns down?'

The Russian smiled. He was missing a couple of teeth. Maybe through fighting, or maybe he hailed from an Eastern Bloc town untouched by modern dentistry. Whatever. He was grinning and clearly happy with the prospect of getting to use a blade or bare hands against someone half his bulk. He kept his movements slow and deliberate as he drew an IMI Desert Eagle from his belt.

Predictable, Walker thought. Give a guy like this props and he'd jump at the chance to prove how violent he could be. In synch, the two men bent to the deck and placed their firearms down. The giant put his Desert Eagle near his feet and slid it across to his right, a pace away, so that his path forward to Walker was clear. So, he was right-handed. Important to know such things, in a fight.

At the same time, Walker put the shotgun down and pushed it forward and slightly to his right, mimicking the giant's movements.

As the giant stood from his crouch, so did Walker.

The Russian reached behind his right hip and drew a long blade. More a filleting blade than a combat knife.

As Walker stood, he'd pulled the folded tactical knife from inside his back pocket. The sight of it seemed to delight the giant. More teeth flashed in his head, shining in the firelight like lonely tombstones on a desert plain. He took a pace forward, the knife in a forehand grip in his right hand. Walker had seen how fast this guy could move. He would close the gap between them in a few strides.

There was a sound to Walker's right, up ahead, almost in line with the Russian. Down at the waterline. It was the sound of the outboard starting up and Alice giving it too much throttle.

The giant didn't much react. Walker made his attack.

It was an attack in three movements. Walker was a skilled and practised operator. On a good day, able bodied and well prepared, he might have been able to beat this guy in a knife fight. But he had no intention of finding that out. He had a lot of life ahead of him, and throwing it away for no good reason just didn't add up – certainly not when there were options in front of him.

First up was his tactical knife. *Know your knife*, a Delta sergeant used to say back in Afghanistan. He and Walker had been firm friends. Still were. He'd instructed Walker in ways that the DoD didn't teach new recruits. He'd helped Walker select a knife that he liked, and Walker had stuck to the make and brand his whole career and never regretted it. He'd taught Walker how to use it, how to hold it, if it ever came to hand-to-hand combat with an edged weapon.

And how to throw it.

For countless hours, damaging and losing a few good knives along the way, the Delta sergeant and the then Captain Walker had thrown their knives at makeshift targets stuck onto plywood boards. They threw and tossed until Walker was nearly as proficient as his Army buddy. They'd talked those hours away with all kinds of bullshit about home, from missing their spouses to victorious moments on the football field and hypothetical basketball trades and the food they missed most. Glory days.

The first movement of Walker's attack was to throw his knife. It spanned the remaining four yards and thudded into the Russian's left pectoral, sticking deep against the hilt, the full four inches of anodised razor-sharp blade puncturing internal organs.

As the giant reacted, looking down at the offending projectile, as if in wonder, Walker was into his second movement, which was to scoop up the shotgun.

The first action with the gun was to aim and fire, which he did while still in a crouch, because his aching back was restricting his moves. Ordinarily he'd have rolled through the move and got to a

knee and fired, but he had to adapt. The first shot got the big guy in the right hand, the one holding the blade, because he had that out and up, in front of his body. The deer slug was designed to take down buck weighing about as much as this guy. The lead shot reduced the hand to a pulpy stump at the wrist.

Walker's third movement began with pumping the shotgun and standing.

The big guy dragged her topside and cut her throat.

Walker approached the giant, who backed back. His mouth was opening and closing like a fish out of water.

She didn't even make a sound. I don't know if she drowned or bled to death.

Walker kept moving, one pace, then another, closing the distance, as his opponent walked backwards, towards the railing behind him. When he was close enough, Walker fired. He was holding the shotgun two-handed, down low, but the distance was only two yards and his target a big, beefy wall, so the aim was dead-on. The shot got him high, in the top of the chest and throat, and the giant toppled backwards and hit the sea with a splash.

He didn't know if the Russian was dead from the gunshot, or drowned or bled to death. He didn't care.

61

Bloom answered the knock on his hotel-room door. It was Agents Oberman and Chavez, both looking like they'd fallen overboard in the middle of the ocean, water pooling at their feet. They held out two plastic bags.

'Best wine we could find,' Oberman said. 'A Syrah, and a Pinot Grigio, both Californian.'

'Both over twenty bucks,' Chavez added. 'Each, I mean.'

'Cheap wine is a false commodity,' Bloom said, taking the bag. 'Don't ever forget that.'

'And some fresh-baked calzones,' Oberman said, passing over the other bag. 'You wouldn't believe what we had to do to get those.'

'Right,' Bloom said, taking the second bag. 'And the communications link? My landline is out, and the cell reception is spotty at best – it's clearly overwhelmed.'

'Working on it, sir,' Oberman said. 'Both counts.'

'You didn't think about splitting up?' Bloom replied. 'Doubling your work output?'

'We're, ah . . .' Oberman looked to Chavez. 'We're partners?'

The senior FBI man then appeared to have a thought breakthrough, and said, 'Sir, we had an update just a moment ago from the NOPD. GreyStone's property at Fort Lee is deserted. No-one there.'

'Hence, deserted,' Bloom said. 'Any sign of Walker or Richter?'

'The site was completely empty, sir,' Oberman said. Chavez elbowed him. 'I mean, no, no reported sighting, as yet. Him or Richter.'

Bloom continued, 'What about that Russian yacht?'

'Coast Guard have the name and ID, but the yacht's transponder is still off,' Chavez replied. 'Which is kinda good news if you think about it.'

'How's that?' Bloom asked, when it became clear that he had to prompt the FBI man to continue

Chavez smiled. 'It gives our guys, whether police or Coast Guard, probable cause to stop and search—'

'Probable cause?' Bloom echoed. 'You have the National Security Council of the United States government to give authority, via the Constitution, and the Patriot Act, and a bunch of other statutes – the Espionage Act springs to mind – to search the . . . what is it?'

While Bloom was berating them, Oberman had pulled out his cell phone to check it. The screen was lit up with a message. He looked up from the phone, and his face broke into a smile.

'The Russian yacht – it just popped up on the grid near Morgan City. EMT arrived on scene to put out a fire, along with local police, in response to reported gunfire. It appears that they've made some arrests, and found several deceased on board, dead from gunshot wounds . . . And fished one body out of the water.'

Bloom put the bags of food and wine on the floor of his room and picked up his coat. 'Morgan City? How far is that?'

'From here?' Oberman asked.

Bloom flushed red.

'About eighty miles by road,' Chavez said quickly. 'But the roads will be a mess.'

'Get us a big, heavy vehicle,' Bloom ordered. 'Be ready to roll in fifteen minutes.'

'You want to go out in this storm?' Oberman asked.

'It's a hurricane,' Chavez chimed in.

'Unless you boys want to spend the rest of your careers cleaning the staff quarters at Quantico, the two of you better sharpen the hell up, stat. Get a good all-weather vehicle from the local PD or state troopers – commandeer it by threat of obstructing a federal investigation if you have to – along with body armour and firepower.'

Oberman paused, gave a just-perceptible glance at Bloom's massive girth, then said, 'Body armour?'

Bloom smiled. 'Not for me, don't worry. You two will be between me and any shooting.'

•

Walker looked back at the marina, about two hundred yards away. Within twenty minutes of the first fire, two fire engines and six squad cars were in attendance, the car park at the dock awash with enough blue-and-red strobing lights to make a Michael Mann movie seem like it had limited production values.

Steph stood next to him on the deck of an empty houseboat, one in a row of empty houseboats. She looked through the binoculars at each face of the handcuffed Russian and Chechen crew as they were led off the pier to the waiting police cars. All the lights along the pier had come on, spilling stark beams of bright white light over the scene. The fires were almost out but for the yacht's tender, which was left to burn down to the waterline where it had drifted out to harbour.

'He's not there,' Steph said, taking the binoculars down and looking from the scene to Walker. 'I can see that the police have just given the yacht the all-clear below decks. And I counted twelve suspects taken into custody.'

'Plus the six I took out,' Walker said.

Alice shivered, her arms wrapped around her body. She and Steph had picked Walker out of the water and headed west in the inflatable, away from their big cabin cruiser, away from the fire-engulfed yacht,

away from the flashing sirens of a local squad car that was first to arrive on scene. A couple of small craft bobbed in the harbour, their occupants rubbernecking at the fire.

Alice had told Steph about the fate of the Homeland Security agent. Walker told them both about the fate of the giant Russian thug. The two bits of information did not cancel each other out, but there was a semblance of justice to it.

'Who were you looking for on the yacht?' Alice asked Steph.

'Someone among the passengers,' Steph said, 'who might have been able to help us.'

Walker turned around, then busted the lock on the sliding glass door of the houseboat and went inside. He was fast getting used to breaking and entering. He felt like he'd been drenched a long time, and he wanted to get dry. He also needed coffee, hot and strong. And to take a moment to sit down, to take stock, to think. Inside the houseboat it was empty, dark and quiet. It was furnished as a holiday house, a nautical feel with shells and driftwood artworks and blue-and-white decor. There were framed photos of an old couple, and some showing the next two generations. All the pictures were of people in the sun, smiling at the camera, tanned and creased faces locked in good times. Suddenly Walker started to feel queasy about the prospect of failing to find whatever was being sold for hundreds of millions of dollars. That failure might well bring harm to the nation. To people he'd sworn to protect, like the family looking back at him.

'I know that four of the Russians left the yacht to go to some meeting,' Alice said, following Walker inside.

Walker looked back to Alice, and then to Steph, who then looked to Alice.

'Do you know who?' Steph asked, joining them in a dark living room and kitchen. She stood close to Alice, watching her, as though if she listened intently enough the news would help them all out.

'I didn't catch their names,' Alice replied. 'No-one really used names on board. It seemed like what my father would call an operational thing. Or maybe it's just cultural, among Russians. And I guess people who know each other rarely slip each other's names into conversation, right?'

'Peskov?' Steph made for a light switch.

'Maybe,' Alice said, 'I don't know.'

'Leave the light off,' Walker said, as he emerged from a bathroom and passed around some towels. He'd also found a pill container in the drug cabinet. Opioids. Powerful painkillers, prescription only. Someone had had surgery at some point, and Walker was the thankful beneficiary. 'We don't need attention.'

Steph nodded.

'How do you know that they were going to a meet?' Walker asked.

'I heard them talking,' Alice said. 'I had my ear to the door most of the time. They kept me locked up. I was drugged, back in my dorm, when they took me. When I woke, I was on the yacht, in that room you found me in, on the bed. I couldn't move my body the first day – I thought I was tied up, but it must have been whatever they drugged me with. They visited me once a day, dropped off a meal and bottled water. Let me above deck for about ten minutes each night. I don't think they knew what to do with me. But I'm here because this is about my father, right?'

She was looking directly at Walker. He moved to the kitchen, found the coffee pot and filled it from the faucet, sighing as he fought the desire to just come clean about her father. Not yet, not here, hiding like this.

'Yes. I'm CIA too,' Walker said. 'Steph here is British intelligence.'

'Sure, tell everybody,' Steph said to Walker, sitting at a stool at the bench. 'Alice, what time did they head out?'

'Maybe a couple of hours back?' Alice answered while watching Walker, who had his back to her. 'Did my father send you to rescue me?'

'In a sense, yeah, he did,' Walker replied. In the head-height cupboards he found an empty coffee container, which turned out to contain three hundred bucks in cash, which he pocketed. He found a fresh can of ground coffee and some filter papers. He set it up and plugged it in and switched it on. A little orange light glowed. He turned to face her. 'What else did you hear?'

'They're pissed,' Alice said. 'Being played, they were saying. They're here to buy something.'

'Buy?' Walker said. 'You definitely heard them say *buy*?'

'Yes,' Alice replied. 'At *bolotnyy*. They referred to it as that a couple of times. And I'm sure something about a playing field. Near Lafayette.'

'And they left a couple of hours ago?' Steph asked.

Alice nodded.

'Shit,' Steph said, looking to Walker. 'They're moving early. We spooked them, made them bring their plans forward.'

'But the meeting isn't until dawn,' Alice said. 'I heard one of them say that they were leaving early to get a van, which they needed for a transfer, and to set up.'

'You're sure about that?' Steph asked.

Alice nodded.

'Four guys?' Walker said.

'Yes.' Alice looked from Walker to Steph. 'I mean, at least four. Four voices that I could differentiate. But they might have taken another one or two, right? If it's a van?'

Walker was silent.

'Any idea of their roles?' Steph asked. 'Did one sound like he was giving all the orders?'

Alice nodded. 'One seemed a leader, because he was directing things. Another was a logistics-type person, offering solutions, like the van. And maybe two, what would we call them, heavies? Security? Redshirts?'

'How can you know all this?' Steph asked. 'From just eavesdropping through a door.'

'The leader's room was opposite mine in the yacht,' Alice replied. 'He'd sometimes talk to others in there, leave his door open. He'd be like, "We need this," and "You two need to be ready to do this . . ."'

'They were speaking in English?' Steph pressed.

'In snippets here and there,' Alice replied. 'But it was mostly in Russian.'

'You speak Russian?' Steph asked.

'Passable Russian,' Alice replied. 'But much better French. I guess the former has now paid off a little, right?'

'Handy,' Steph said, eyeing her, then she looked to Walker.

Walker looked at Alice. She'd been drugged, abducted, malnourished, held captive. And she had the wherewithal to do what she could to stay alive, to look for an escape. Her father would have been proud.

'Believe me, if you have *my* father,' Alice said, 'you don't have a choice, whether it's studying languages or jujitsu.' She stripped off her soaking wet T-shirt and wrung it out in the kitchen sink. There were bruises on her torso, ranging from deep purple to yellow-brown. She wrapped the towel around herself.

Walker gave Steph a look, and he could see that any wariness the British intelligence officer held about Alice was now dispelled.

'I'm studying classics at college,' Alice said. 'But Dad always insisted I do languages. Lucky I went through school when I did – if it was nowadays, he'd make me learn Chinese, and I know from friends at college that it's a bitch to learn.'

'Did those guys on the yacht . . . hurt you?' Steph asked, motioning to Alice's body.

'When they abducted me,' Alice said, letting the towel go a little slack and looking down at the purple marks. 'I managed to bust one guy's nose. And kicked the big one in the nuts.'

'I don't suppose you heard where they were going to the meeting?' Walker asked. The coffee started to drip, and the smell filled the room.

Alice paused for a while, like she was straining to recall any relevant part of a conversation. 'The *bolotnyy*, they'd said, like it had specific meaning. It isn't a common word. It means marsh, in Russian.'

'*Bolotnyy . . .*' Steph said. 'Maybe *mud*?'

'Could be somewhere along the coast?' Walker suggested. Steph shrugged.

'I'm going to see if the shower works,' Alice said, getting up from her stool.

'I'll snoop around for a change of clothes for you,' Steph said.

'I'll yell when the coffee's ready,' Walker said. He looked through the refrigerator, found a frozen pizza and held it up.

'Rescuing me was one thing,' Alice said with a small smile. 'But that's something else. You're my one true hero, Walker. I'm going to make sure my father puts in for a commendation for you. Have you posted to Italy so there's more pizza than bad guys.'

Alice disappeared into the bathroom. They heard the door shut, and a moment later they heard the water run.

Steph walked around to Walker's side of the kitchen as he put the pizza in the oven and set the temperature.

Steph spoke to him in a hushed voice. 'When are you going to tell her about her father?'

'After,' Walker said. 'Let's get this done first.'

'You think we can catch up with Peskov?'

'They're going to need a new way to get out of here once they make the buy,' Walker said. 'Whatever it is, it's big enough to need a van, but they're not going to drive over the Mexican border with it and risk being searched. Same with airports. And they won't head into the hurricane, or what's left of New Orleans come tomorrow.'

'They might look for another boat,' Steph said, 'and head back to Cuba.'

'They could head anywhere – touch down on Mexico's eastern coast then skip transiting the Gulf altogether, head overland across Mexico, hit the Pacific coast, then sail south till they can go ashore

someplace and meet up with a private aircraft to get their package home.'

'So . . .' Steph said, looking around the cabin. 'We're in the dark as to where to head them off.'

'That's all plan B anyway, if we miss the buy,' Walker said. The coffee machine stopped and he found three large mugs and poured out three serves, then changed the filter and refilled it, figuring they would need the caffeine. 'We make sure we find this *bolotnyy*, the playing fields near Lafayette. Be there for the meet at dawn.'

MONDAY 29 AUGUST

62

Spicer looked around the dark stadium on the outskirts of Lafayette. It was as good a place to meet as any. A big open field. His best sniper was up high atop the bleachers, keeping an eye on things. Another two operators were out on the road leading in, in a car hidden behind an outbuilding, ready to act. They had an AT-4 rocket-launcher to take out the Russians, if it came to it, along with a squad machine-gun. All the team were former Army, who had served under him in Afghanistan. Each was about to be made very rich.

A light rain was falling, but he didn't care. He hadn't slept in over twenty-four hours, but he didn't feel tired, thanks to medication that had been passed around the team. He had his whole life ahead of him to sleep. With the coming of dawn, he would have more money than he could ever spend. And the Russians would have what was in his helicopter, currently motored down and waiting a mile to the north, ready to make the delivery as soon as he gave the all-clear.

A figure emerged from the players' race near the dugout. Spicer knew the gait. Johnson. His former senior sergeant walked double-time then stopped close by and looked around.

'Good spot,' he said.

'How'd it go?' Spicer replied.

'Perfect. Just sent our two outsiders to the dock where the Russians' boat is at. They're under orders to wait and watch until the Russians bug out, then to call it in and meet us at the safe house.'

'And that's it?'

'Not quite,' Johnson said. 'They're going to call me again when they're in transit, after half an hour of being on the road.'

'And?'

'The call will be diverted to a phone in their trunk. Wired to a switch and detonator in the spare tyre, which I packed with C4.'

'Jesus.'

'I know.'

'That's Kandahar all over again.'

'I know,' Johnson repeated.

'I thought you didn't want to get your hands dirty with them.'

'Only in regards to how it would look to the others,' Johnson said. 'But this'll look like the Russians did it.'

'Speaking of, do a final call-in to our team,' Spicer said, heading to the cover of a dugout. 'Make sure they're all perky and ready to roll. Those Russians might turn up early.'

'They might do a lot of things, but we own this night.'

•

Walker found a road atlas of Louisiana in the second vehicle he broke into. He'd targeted older cars, a Lincoln sedan, and then an F150, figuring they wouldn't have alarm systems or GPS, so a road map or two would be stowed somewhere. He didn't steal either car, because he'd already done that nearer the dock.

Steph and Alice were waiting around the block when Walker returned. They were in the regular working-class town of Baldwin, on the I-90 headed for Lafayette. The yards were well kept, and the windows were all blacked out and some were shuttered and others were taped over with thick crosses of duct tape. The weather had turned for the worse, mainly the wind, which buffeted Walker head-on as he got back to their vehicle.

It was an early 1990s Toyota 4x4, a big high-riding thing with a diesel engine, easy to hot-wire. Steph was at the wheel, and Alice sat

in the second row. Walker climbed into the front passenger seat along with a gust of wind and rain. He had tried to persuade Alice to stay on the houseboat until the weather cleared, then make her way to the nearest police station and explain the situation of her abduction, but she was having none of it. Her father would clear everything up, she'd said. Walker didn't reply, other than to say that if she tagged along, she needed to keep out of the way.

'Okay,' Walker said, flicking through the road atlas by the interior light above him. 'We've got ten playing fields. No. A dozen. At least.'

'It won't be any that are marked as being evacuation points in case of emergency,' Steph said.

'Good point,' Walker replied. 'Okay. Hit the gas and get back on the I-90 for Lafayette. I'll see about narrowing down the options as we approach, try to work out a good way to hit them all before dawn.'

Steph kept the vehicle steady in the worsening conditions, the wipers at full whack. The suspension had been heightened, and the ride on what must have been a two-and-a-half-tonne vehicle was as smooth as any would have been on the road that night. Walker found a pen in the glove compartment and scanned the map, circling the possibilities.

'So,' Alice began from the back seat, 'you two an item, or what?'

Walker looked to Steph, who gave a tired shake of the head and tried her best to hide a smile.

'You could say that we've been . . .' Walker said, 'working to improve US–British relations over the past couple of days.'

'No wonder my dad's hung around the Agency his whole life,' Alice said, her tone finding some humour in the situation. 'And no wonder my mother dumped his butt.'

63

Bloom sat in the back of a commandeered state police Chevy Suburban. Chavez drove. Oberman navigated. It took them forty minutes to cover four miles out of the outskirts of New Orleans. Once further out on the I-90, things hardly improved, with B-Road detours around a low-lying section of the highway that was already washed over. Bloom had drunk half a bottle of the Syrah before leaving the hotel, and it had lifted his spirits. It was a halfway agreeable drop. He preferred the old-world wines of Europe, with a more pronounced sense of terroir on the palate. But, it turned out, as the world is blowing apart around you, a Californian red would suffice.

'When we arrive, and make arrests,' Bloom said, 'we need to get the Russians' leader in a room with me. Got it?'

'You got it, sir,' Chavez replied.

Bloom said, 'It's imperative we find out what's at stake here.'

'And what do we do with the rest of the Russians?' Chavez asked.

'You act with extreme prejudice,' Bloom replied.

Chavez and Oberman shared a sideways glance.

'We need to know what they know,' Bloom said. 'At any cost, you got that?'

Chavez glanced in the rear-view mirror. 'Serious?'

Bloom looked out his window as the Chevy Suburban's red-and-blue lights in the dash pierced the night around them. 'Always.'

•

Walker at that moment was getting back into the car. Fourth sports field, fourth with nothing showing. Two full hours eaten up. Dawn two hours away.

'We've gotta change things,' Walker said. 'This map shows another twelve sites. And there's bound to be plenty of others that aren't on here.'

'You said to start with the big playing fields,' Steph said. 'Closed-off spaces, where the GreyStone crew could break in and remain undetected while they're doing their transaction?'

'The Russians need to arrive and leave in a van, GreyStone in their helo,' Walker said. 'Tall bleachers where shooters might be stationed. Light towers even.'

'And there's at least another eight possibilities, scattered all around Lafayette,' Steph replied.

They looked over the map. There was not enough time to search them all.

'Give me a direction, so I can keep moving,' Steph said.

'Get back on the main road, head towards town,' Walker replied.

Steph stood on the accelerator, pulled out of the car park and headed back towards the I-90. 'We're going to need diesel,' she added, pointing at the brightly lit gas station signs before the entry ramp to the interstate.

'You two handle the gas,' Walker said. 'I'll go in and pay and see if there's any more local maps.'

Steph pulled in and came to a stop at a pump. Alice got out to keep her company as she filled up, and Walker went inside the big truck stop. It had a 24/7 diner attached, and the smells of grilled burgers and onions and bacon filled the air. He checked out the road maps and found one that showed the city in greater detail – and it made his stomach lurch. There were indeed many more sports stadiums. At least another dozen, on top of the eight he had circled on the road atlas.

He stood behind a couple of people waiting to pay for gas and snacks. When it was his turn, he craned his neck to check the pump number, and relayed it.

'Nice night for a drive,' the cashier said as Walker paid for the gas and the map with the GreyStone cash. He was late twenties, had thinning greasy hair, looked like he spent most of his shifts eating hot pockets and jerky that had gone past their use-by date.

'I know, right?' Walker replied. 'And charge me for three coffees to go.'

'You got it,' the guy replied, ringing up the charges. 'Help yourself over there. Cream and sugar no charge, but don't let that be a green light to go loadin' your pockets.'

'Thanks,' Walker said, getting his change, and he paused. There was no-one waiting behind him, and the cashier seemed talkative, so he said, 'Hey, if you ranked the sports complexes in town, what'd they be?'

'Huh?'

'Stadiums,' Walker said. 'Got any big ones in town?'

'Nothing on at the moment, man,' the guy said.

'But if you'd recommend someone caught a game at one or two, where'd they be at?'

'Right. Well, you've got the University of Louisiana's grounds, that'd be Cajun Field for football, and their baseball field right next door.'

'They're big?'

'Sure. Off the 167, can't miss 'em, not a few miles from here.'

'How many do they seat?'

'Gee, I don't know, mister. Never been there myself.' He scratched at his hair. 'Not my thing.'

Walker nodded. 'Thousands?' he prompted.

'Gotta be. Big bleachers. Light towers and all that. Especially The Swamp. Tailgaters seem to head there in their thousands.'

'The Swamp?'

'Yeah. That's what they call Cajun Field. Pretty funny, huh?'

Dirt. Mud. Bolotnyy . . . Swamp?

Walker said, 'You got any cell phones for sale here?'

'Huh?'

'Does this store sell cell phones?'

'This ain't no Walmart, man.'

Walker nodded, saw that the cashier had a cell phone plugged into a socket behind him.

'What about that there?' he asked.

The guy looked around, then back at Walker. 'That's mine.'

'Pay phone here?'

'Nope.' He thumbed a sign above the smokes cabinet, which read: *Management reserves the right to refuse service. Toilets for staff only. No pay phone.*

Walker pulled the remainder of the GreyStone and houseboat cash from his pocket and as he counted it onto the countertop, he said, 'That phone of yours, it's all charged up?'

'Probably,' the cashier said, watching the cash stack up.

'Three hundred and forty-two dollars,' Walker said, then dumped a few coins on top. 'And change.'

'For what?' the guy said. 'To make a call?'

'For that money, I figure I can hire that phone of yours for a few hours. I'll drop it back here first thing in the morning. How about it?'

'You're serious?'

'Yes.'

'Something illegal?'

'Nope. I just gotta make a call and leave a message for a friend, and I need to be contactable by that person.'

'Geez, mister,' the guy said, looking at the cash, then his phone, then up at Walker. 'I mean, for three hundred and forty-two dollars and change, this phone is yours, man. It's pre-paid. Got about thirty bucks' credit on it. Keep it.'

'I'll need you to write down the phone's number for me,' Walker said, and a moment later he took the phone and the scrap of paper.

It was an old model, felt greasy to the touch, cracked screen, but it was fully charged, and had credit on it, and currently displayed full bars of reception. 'My thanks.'

'Sir – your coffees?'

'Next time,' Walker said.

As he headed for the waiting car he dialled operator assistance, then asked to be connected to the number for the EEOB in Washington DC. After a few rings a night officer answered. Walker left an urgent message for Bloom, informing him that he was headed to Cajun Field to head off the transaction at dawn, to contact him on the pre-paid cell number, then hung up.

He hustled into the car, told the women about the stadium and then found them on the map. 'Four miles from here. Take the I-90 and peel off onto the 167.'

'Baseball?' Steph said.

'Like cricket, but awesome,' Walker said. 'But we're headed for the football stadium, which it says here seats about forty thousand. Home of the Louisiana Lafayette Ragin' Cajuns. And you want the kicker?' He looked to them both as Steph drove. 'It's nicknamed The Swamp, and reading this, it's probably because it's a couple of feet below sea level, and had irrigation and pumps to—'

'The swamp!' Alice said from the back seat. 'That's it! Not marsh, or mud. *Bolotnyy* – swamp!'

'It's it,' Walker said. 'So, we approach with caution.'

64

'That's it,' Walker said, peering out the windscreen. 'Keep driving, take the next right.'

Steph followed Walker's instructions, keeping on Highway 167. Walker looked out his window and saw that the road leading to the Cajun Field, Cajundome Boulevard, was tree-lined along one side, and he knew from his map that side roads spilled off all along it. A perfect place to park a vehicle, or have sentries hidden in the tree-line. A kill zone. Steph took the next right, North College Road. It was deserted at almost five am. A little over an hour-and-a-half to sunrise.

'As we get close to the turn-off to the sports fields, I want you to slow and I'll jump out,' Walker said, looking across at Steph. 'Do a big circle, go back to the 167, park opposite the first turn-off, here.'

He passed the street map over his shoulder to Alice. He'd circled the spot. 'Twin Oaks Boulevard,' she read aloud.

'Yep,' Walker said. 'You'll see the Russians arrive, and all going well, you won't see them depart. But if they do, you can follow them and call it in. Either the FBI, or the last number I dialled, ask to be put through to Bloom, or leave a message for him. He'll get back to you ASAP.'

'He hasn't got back to *you* yet,' Steph replied.

'He'll call, as soon as he gets my message,' Walker said, putting the cell phone in the centre console.

'You think you're going to take on Spicer's GreyStone guys and the Russian outfit all on your own?' Steph asked as she slowed the car near Reinhardt Drive.

'If I have to,' Walker said. He looked down at the shotgun in his hands.

'Here,' Steph said as she pulled over and came to a stop. She passed the revolver, but Walker waved it off and was already half out of his door.

'You might need it,' he said.

'But Walker—'

'Steph, I'll be fine. You two keep out of view. When Bloom calls, tell him to send the cavalry. No doubt he's moving heaven and earth to get forces here as we speak.'

Walker closed the door. He looked through the window at Steph, who stared back at him, bit her bottom lip then looked ahead and drove off with a spin of the truck's tyres on the loose gravel at the shoulder of the road.

•

Ping.

'Cell service is back,' Oberman said from the passenger seat, looking down at the lit-up screen of his government-issue Blackberry. 'Must have moved far enough out of New Orleans to hop onto the other towers.'

Bloom looked at his own government phone – as three messages came through. The most recent one, relayed from Walker, made him sit up. He played it back to make sure he had it right, then started to punch in a number, calling out to the two FBI agents sitting up front, 'How far away is Lafayette?'

Oberman entered it into the SatNav. 'About fifty minutes if we get back on the I-10 and it's not too clogged up.'

'Lafayette is a smart move,' Chavez said. 'They're making the Russians go inland by road, when GreyStone can go in by air.'

'Make it there as fast as you can,' Bloom said. 'We've got to head them off.'

'We'll merge with the I-90,' Chavez said, glancing at the SatNav screen. 'It'll be clearer.'

'Head straight for Cajun Stadium,' Bloom ordered. 'Call it in, all the hands we can bring to bear by dawn. Have them set up, with caution. We don't want to spook these guys to move the meet someplace else.'

Oberman turned around in his seat. 'What about the Russians arrested at their yacht?'

'No need to talk to them just now,' Bloom said, hearing the phone start to dial in his ear. 'The exchange is happening at the stadium. Call Lafayette PD, have a SWAT unit readied, and have their air wing requisitioned to us. See what FBI assets you've got who can be there in the next hour and a half. We've got until dawn. Walker's there – make sure you get an image of him from his service jacket at the DoD sent to the local cops; can't have him being taken down by some trigger-happy police sniper.'

'Got it,' Oberman said, already on his call to Lafayette PD, and Chavez gave the Suburban more gas as he headed for their new objective.

Bloom was listening to the cell phone ring in his ear, having dialled the number that Walker had left in the message, and then it was answered.

'Walker?' Bloom said.

'No,' the female voice replied in a British accent. 'But I know where he is . . .'

65

Walker ran in the shadows. Past the athletics track, by the baseball field, to which he gave a cursory look and ruled out – too open at the two end fields. He kept up his jog towards the tallest structure – Cajun Stadium. The Swamp. With every passing minute the sky turned just that little bit brighter. It was still nightfall, the cloud cover blotting out any moonlight, but there were yellow vapour lights at irregular intervals along the street that serviced the sports facilities of the University of Louisiana.

He stopped at the base of a big oak that sat in the middle of a traffic island, and looked at the football stadium. Closest to him was a tall stand of bleachers with a concrete building atop, perhaps viewing boxes for dignitaries and coaching staff, the total height equivalent of maybe ten storeys. That seemed the highest point. Banks of lights were atop the stand, facing the field. All was dark but for a couple of old lamps at each end of the 360-foot football field, for security. To his right, in the end zone, shorter bleachers spanned the 160-foot width. He couldn't see the other end or side from here, which meant that they were smaller in stature, certainly not taller.

Walker was still as he listened and watched and waited. At least ten minutes. All was quiet as the deadline neared. The darkness was fading. Conclusion lay ahead. Time to move.

The main entrance had a large gate hanging open, its chain cut – the welcome sign to the Russians – and he ran past that. He found an exit at the far end of the main bleachers that was ajar. It had been chained up, as with the exit at the closer end, but this one was in darkness – and this chain too had been cut. Walker pictured a GreyStone guy headed up there, having cut his way in, little heed for operational security because this was a get-in-and-get-out operation, over in a flash. Walker looked the gate up and down, and spotted it: about two feet off the ground was a thin cord of nylon fishing wire. He stepped over it and squeezed through the doorway, then stopped to watch and listen. Nothing doing.

He bent down and traced the line. It was tied off to the metal gatepost to his left. To his right, it was tied to the release pin of a grenade, which was taped to a steel handrail of the stairs leading up. The grenade was a flash-bang – designed for special-operations and paramilitary forces to make an incredibly loud bang and blinding flash of burning magnesium, used to breach buildings and small spaces as a way of disorientating occupants. A good warning for the sniper, who would be lying prone on the roof far above, that someone was sneaking up. Walker held the pin in, and tore the tape off, then the flash-bang was free and he looped the fishing wire around it all the way to the other end, where he used all his weight and snapped the line off where it was tied to the gatepost. He put the weapon in his pocket, picked up his shotgun, and moved on.

The Nike Jordans were good for this role – they were well worn, and the rubber soles were silent on the concrete underfoot as he ascended the stairs. He moved carefully, always checking for another trip line, in this case waist-high as the steel handrails were the only things in the concrete staircase to tie to. But there was nothing. Not on the first flight of stairs, nor the second, and it went like that, all the way up to the door that led to the roof. There, he paused. If he were Spicer, he would have sent a sharp shooter to the roof, to watch over the meet, and then pick up that shooter on the way out with

the helo. One sniper could cover the whole field, including the entry point out front.

There had been a lock on the door, but it had been shot out, from the inside.

Would the sniper have a spotter, Walker wondered, a guy with a scope to find targets, and a decent secondary weapon on hand to protect the prone, preoccupied sniper?

Maybe. Maybe not. Only one way to find out.

Walker opened the door. Just an inch. He ran his fingers up and down the full height of the open doorway, the space just wide enough to fit them. He was quick – but not too quick. He wanted to check for a trap, not set one off. And he didn't like the idea that at that very moment on the other side of the door a GreyStone operative might kick it shut and sever his fingers at the second knuckles.

But nothing happened as he pushed the door open a little more. He could see only darkness beyond, and some distant illumination of street lamps and the vague night-time glow of the city of half a million people. Brighter than the dark stairwell, lit only by the secondary light that spilled through the small slits in the concrete walls to allow for ventilation of air and noise as thousands of people left the stadium in a disappointed hubbub or a raucous celebration.

Walker opened the door to the roof just enough to squeeze himself through. He exited, then twisted the handle gently to silently shut the door behind him. The strong wind was blowing over his right shoulder, from the Gulf, pushed ahead of the storm. Ahead of Walker was the roof, and beyond that the yawning dark of the drop down to the football field. Maybe twenty yards worth of stark expanse stood before him, and it was a good fifty yards across to the small concrete pillbox in the far corner, with a door set into it that would lead to another set of stairs. The roof was flat, concrete. Smooth and wet under foot, which wasn't great for his worn-smooth rubber-soled shoes.

So, Walker lay on his stomach and inched away from the doorway as he waited for his eyes to adjust. He thought he saw a shape ahead, and he used his elbows to haul himself along, then his knees and toes to push, the shotgun out front, his back flaring with pain with every motion. As he moved closer, he made out the form of a man, lying prone. Alone. The sniper. His boots were facing Walker. He would have his eye to a scope, watching the field, checking the scene, looking to see if the Russians tried to get here early and set up an ambush. Why pay over 200 million dollars for something when you could get the something *and* keep the cash? If they never planned to deal with GreyStone again, if this was indeed a one-off transaction, why not take it all and burn that bridge?

Walker got to within six feet without being noticed. Less than his body length. He stopped. The shotgun was not a weapon to covertly take out a person. Nor was the backyard machine-pistol strapped on his back. He put the shotgun quietly on the roof as the rain started up again. He could see the sniper lying rock-still. He was good. Maybe he'd been a sniper in the Rangers, serving under Spicer. They were damned fine shooters, and experts at lying prone for hours, sometimes days at a time, waiting for targets to present. This guy was leaning slightly to his left, which meant he was right-handed, and therefore his right shoulder was back and slightly elevated to snuggle into the butt of the rifle, while his left hand was forward, maybe just before the trigger guard, or maybe on the stock. He would be using a bipod, or something else to lean the forward stock of the rifle on. He was clearly concentrating on his task. A professional.

Walker moved forward, inch by inch, and slightly to his left, so he could surprise the shooter from his non-dominant side. As Walker moved, he took the flash-bang from his jacket pocket. He held it out in front of him, still inching forward and slightly left, unwinding the nylon fishing wire as he went. He unspooled about five feet of line, keeping the rest twisted around the flash-bang, and wrapping the other end tightly around his left hand. He wasn't going to use the

grenade against the guy, which would only serve to disorient them both, wreck their night-vision and hearing, and warn all those within a couple of miles that something sinister was up.

No. Walker had another plan, but as he passed the guy's boots, then his knees, then his waist, Walker ran through the motions in his mind – get as close as he dared to the sniper's neck, then sit up and get to his knees and slip the wire over the guy's head and pull it against his neck, twisting his arms over to get maximum leverage. With all the exertion that the sniper would be expending to fight the constricting wire, he'd likely be choked out in under thirty seconds. Walker figured that he'd soon enough find out.

But he didn't. Because as Walker neared, he inhaled a familiar smell. Death. Sometime in the last thirty minutes, because the guy's sphincters had opened up and released bodily fluids where he lay. Walker knew that the sniper was dead before he saw the blood, which was plentiful. He'd been cut with a blade, across the neck, almost from ear to ear. GreyStone was not the only one on scene.

66

'Walker told us to wait,' Alice said from the back seat of the truck.

'I can't leave him to do this alone,' Steph replied as she put the revolver in the pocket of her raincoat and stepped out of the car. 'He's got no idea what he's up against, and Bloom and the others are too far away to help. Come here into the front seat. You might need to leave in a hurry. If you're scared, head for the police station – here on the map, see?'

'I can see,' Alice said, climbing through to the front seats. 'I can also come help you?'

'This isn't a job for a civilian,' Steph said, pulling the hood over her head. 'Do you want the cell phone?'

'No,' Alice said. 'You might need it. How far off are the police?'

'Probably forty minutes,' Steph replied, checking the time on the cell phone's screen, then tucking it into the back pocket of her jeans. 'Though you may see some local units turn up sooner. If you do, make sure they're observing Bloom's instruction to keep quiet and wait until he's here to give them the go-ahead. If they move early, it may put Walker in danger. Got it?'

'And they'll listen to a *civilian*?' Alice said, then looked immediately remorseful. 'Sorry, I didn't mean to sound like a wise-ass.'

'Tell them – tell them who your father is, if you have to,' Steph said, then shut the door and ran in the rain towards the sports complex.

She didn't like being part of the lie of omission, of not filling Alice in on the fate of her father, but now wasn't the time to play nice. She took the revolver in her hand. She was on the main boulevard leading to the stadium, and she kept to the side of the road closest to the trees. The wind was strong, and every few paces she checked over her shoulder to make sure she wasn't being followed.

•

Walker knew that the Russians were here. Four of them. Two heavies, Peskov and a logistics guy, presumably waiting somewhere with their transport, the van, engine running, ready for extraction. Turning on the American crew without taking a bigger force with them surprised Walker, but then he figured they must have done so on the fly. They had adapted their plan – clearly assuming that GreyStone was responsible for the attack on their yacht – and so were not fully prepared for this assault. But they were now taking no chances, and were going to get out of this meeting with everything that they could get – their purchase, the money, and maybe even a new way out of the country via the GreyStone helicopter or jet.

Walker moved as slowly as he could, reaching forward for the sniper's rifle, his hands under the left arm of the dead man, in case there was someone watching. He stopped the second he heard a noise. It was coming from the man. A voice . . . from his ear. Walker reached out and retrieved the small earpiece.

'Ryan, come in!' Walker heard Johnson's voice. 'Ryan, copy? If you can hear us, you've lost your voice coms. I can see you now – I'm at the south-west corner of the opposite bleachers, ten rows back. I'll flash my light. If you see me, give me a signal, I'll watch with my scope.'

Walker saw the flash of light, two deliberate strobes from a small Maglight.

Walker reached forward to the dead sniper's left hand, held it at the wrist and carefully raised it in a wave then put it down again.

'Great, copy that, Ryan, your mic's out,' Johnson said. 'You had us worried. Hang tight, we'll be outta here soon enough. Helo's coming in twenty-five minutes, we'll do the transfer and bug the hell outta here – pick you up soon, buddy.'

Walker saw movement in the bleachers, a dark shape amid the dark space, and he reached across and pulled the rifle from the man's grasp then scoped the area – it took him just a few seconds to find Johnson, and then he tracked him. The scope was good, and it had an infra-red setting, Johnson lighting up in a man-shaped flare of red and white as he jumped over the fence and onto the grassed playing surface, and then ran towards the ramp that led to the dressing rooms. Out of sight.

Walker scanned the bleachers and field through the rifle scope. He couldn't make out any other heat signatures. He inched back, and used the cover of the body to check his roof. Empty but for residual heat marks on the door through which he had emerged minutes earlier. He then scanned the other two rooftops of the stadiums. Nothing. Nothing at the grassy mound at the end of the field. No heat blobs anywhere.

He found it odd that the sniper's killer had left this vantage point and weapon. It was a perfect perch to control the high ground. Unless they figured that they had surprise on their side. But to kill him so early before the scheduled meeting – with dawn still twenty minutes off – meant that the Russians were ready to jump the gun and act now.

Before leaving the sniper, Walker took the man's sidearm – a Glock pistol that had been just near his right hand, ready for use. Walker put that in his right-hand coat pocket, the flash-bang in his left pocket, and the machine-pistol on his back, then rose to his feet, the rifle in his hands. It was a Swiss-made Brügger & Thomet Advanced Precision Rifle, with APR308S stamped on the side, the shortest of the barrels made for that firearm, chambered for .308 Winchester ammunition. The suppressor was almost as long as the barrel. Much better than the shotgun, which Walker left behind. He quickly made his way to

the farthest of the roof's edges, then dropped again to his stomach and set up to scope the scene to the front of the stadium. Nothing on the road. Nothing in the tree-line, nor the car park, nor in the—

He stopped. A figure emerged in his field of view, running through the tree-line on the main boulevard towards the stadium. It was a small figure, light on its feet, in a good rhythm except when it broke every few strides to check over its shoulder. He changed the setting on the scope as the figure neared the yellow cone of light thrown down by a street light.

Steph. Running his way. Then, she stopped. Still on the road. Just inside the beam of a vapour light overhead. And she slowly turned around, looking back at the way she'd come from.

Another figure emerged, this one from the cover of the trees, where he had been hiding in wait. He was carrying a big machine-gun – a Squad Automatic Weapon. Massive rate of fire, 200-round belt-fed magazine. The holder was saying something to Steph, who had her hands raised, twenty yards ahead of him.

Walker settled the rifle on the edge of the rooftop and sighted the man threatening Steph. He zoomed in tight, recognising his target from the GreyStone compound. The guy was standing still, getting Steph to walk slowly towards him, her hands high above her head, and her revolver tossed to her side. Walker made the distance at 400 metres. An easy shot but for the strong wind, which was blowing head-on, which from his elevated position would exert extra downward force onto the bullet, along with gravity. Walker could see that the sniper had already zeroed-in the rifle to fire from this elevation. He gave it an extra click on the scope, so that he was aiming a little higher, to allow for the extra drop over the distance. His finger slowly squeezed the trigger, his right eye tight up to the scope, until it fired.

He missed.

67

'It's okay,' Johnson said to Spicer, who was seated in the canopied dugout near the ramp that led down to the players' change rooms in the basement of the main building. 'Ryan's mic is out, is all. This weather, right?'

'And Garry?'

'He's got the in-road locked down, don't worry. And Steve's inside to greet the Russians. We've got this.'

There was a vibrating noise, and Johnson took a hand from the fore-grip of his M4 and pulled out a cell phone.

'Speak of the three devils,' he said, then answered the call. He listened for a while, then said, 'You're sure about all that?'

Spicer watched as Johnson listened.

'Right,' Johnson said into the phone. 'Okay, you three hang tight on scene and await further instructions.'

He clicked off and looked to his commander.

'What is it?' Spicer asked.

'That was our two newbies with the C4 in their trunk. The Russian yacht was attacked,' Johnson said. 'The dock's a crime scene; fire crews, dozens of cops, total lockdown, bodies going out on stretchers. No sign of our buyer though.'

'Shit,' Spicer said, and he could see that Johnson was having the same realisation. He started to dial the cell phone that would detonate

the explosives in the car of the GreyStone operatives who'd just called in the news. 'The Russians are gonna think it was us.'

•

Walker missed with his first shot. It was just a little too high; he saw the bullet take a chunk out of a tree behind the GreyStone guard's head. Neither Steph nor the guard heard the shot, but they did hear the nearby impact, for they both looked in the direction of it. Walker fired twice more, in quick succession. The first shot clipped the target's right shoulder, and the guy's arm came away from his body, the massive force of the .308 Winchester dislocating the joint and sheering off the muscle and skin. The dismembered arm dropped to the ground, taking the M249 SAW with it. The second shot from the sniper's rifle connected with the top of the guy's head, and through the scope it looked as if his hair was blown off in a gust of wind. The GreyStone guard fell to the ground.

Steph looked around, then scooped up her revolver and continued her run towards the building that Walker was atop of.

Then two things happened.

An engine started up, headlights came on and a van emerged from the cover of an outbuilding at the other end of the road, to Walker's left.

And at the same moment, gunfire rang out.

68

Walker used the advantage he had, while he had it. He couldn't see where the gunfire came from, but it sounded like it was inside the building below him. He hoped it wasn't directed at Steph, but there was nothing he could do about that. There was something he could do about the van speeding towards the entrance.

He sighted the front end of the van. It was a boxy design, basically had a flat nose, no hood. Walker loosed three shots, each tracked in front of it where they found home in the grille. Steam hissed out and the driver veered hard to his left, either a survival reaction against the attack, or one of Walker's shots had blown out a front tyre or severed the steering assembly.

Walker kept aim on the van, watching until it hit the big oak on the traffic island head-on. The crash was spectacular, the cabin of the van concertinaed in on itself from the impact. Glass and steam and bits of plastic and metal exploded into the air. The driver spilled out his door and staggered out of Walker's view behind the side of the wrecked van. Walker stayed on target. Waiting. Watching.

Not for long. The driver appeared at the rear end of the van, his head, and then his torso, eyeballing the stadium. He looked shell-shocked, and he held a pistol in his hand.

The Russians' logistics guy, Walker figured.

Walker shot him in the head. He'd been aiming for the torso, but the shot went high because of the scope's settings.

Walker dropped the rifle and ran. By the time he was through the door leading down the stairs, he had the backyard machine-pistol in his hands. He stopped at each landing to check the way down was clear, and to listen. He got halfway down when more shooting started up. The familiar and unmistakable *crack-crack-crack* of an M4 assault rifle. GreyStone guys, maybe shooting at the Russians. Then he heard another sound. Also unmistakable. The boom of Steph's snub-nosed .357

•

When the first salvo of shots fired her way ended, Steph stepped around the ticketing booth and acquired her target.

She shot the Russian in the back. She'd thought against it, but he was starting to turn around and she knew that he would shoot her without hesitation, so she pulled the trigger. The recoil of the revolver was ferocious, and threw her arm back and up. The Russian slumped forward, his face hitting the brickwork he had been hiding behind. He was alive, but clearly out of the fight, labouring for breath as he bled out. Just as soon as she'd put her revolver back into a two-handed grip out front, the edges of the brick wall just inside the entrance area started to crumble away.

The *crack-crack-crack* of an assault rifle came from further inside the stadium, a different place from before, so she knew that there were either two shooters, or the shooter was moving to a new position. It was certainly a GreyStone guard, firing at the Russian. Now firing at her.

Steph backtracked to the ticketing booth. She kept in a ground-close run, and as she neared, the windows above her head were shot out. She changed tack and made a beeline for the stairs that led up into the bleachers.

69

Walker stopped his descent as he heard footfalls approaching from below. He was three flights from ground level. He reached into his pocket and pulled out the flash-bang. He flipped out the pin, counted to two and then dropped it down the void between the handrails. He crouched down, bit down on the strap of the machine-pistol, put both his hands over his ears, and closed his eyes.

In the confines of the concrete stairwell, even with the small slits designed to allow for ventilation of air and noise, the sound of the flash-bang concussed and reverberated through his body. His ears rang with bells. The light, even though his eyes were closed and he was not in the direct sight line, was a flash that made him see stars.

He got up and moved, the machine-pistol in a double-handed grip, going down two stairs at a time, and as he got to the first flight he saw a target.

Another GreyStone guard. The flash-bang had gone off right in front of his face, and his hands hovered over his burned flesh as he screamed in pain. He would be blind forever. Certainly out of this fight. Walker kicked the guy's M4 away, and went to the door leading out to the ground floor.

•

Johnson and Spicer called in to their three-man team and got nothing in reply. They were on the leading edge of the concrete race that headed to the change rooms below the main bleachers.

'Call in the helo, now!' Spicer yelled to Johnson, who did as instructed.

Spicer was on one knee, scanning over the sights of his M4, covering the race, as well as the bleachers above it. The confidence of having his sniper providing overwatch had vanished. The crackle of his team's M4s inside the stadium's main building had ceased. There had been a single pistol shot, at least a .357.

'They're inbound,' Johnson said. 'ETA four—'

Johnson started to gurgle. Spicer looked across at him. He was still to Spicer's left, where he'd been crouched covering the other end of the bleachers. He'd dropped his rifle. Both hands clutched his throat. His eyes were wide. Even in the darkness, Spicer could make out the blood running over his fingers.

Then there was movement, behind Johnson. A man got to his feet. He was dressed in black, mud rubbed over his face like camouflage paint. The whites of his eyes shone in the gloom. In one hand he held a short curved blade. In the other was a Russian-made pistol, levelled at Spicer. He shook his head at Spicer, and the GreyStone man put his M4 on the ground and slowly got to his feet.

70

Steph emerged onto the first level of the bleachers and stopped still. The wind pounded against the front of the stadium, but she was sheltered here. It whistled and howled against the metal sidings and the structure's edges. The sun was minutes away from breaking dawn. Already the clouds in the sky were being lit by an orange tinge.

She kept crouched down, headed for the centre of the space, and stopped. She was behind some seats in the centre of the bleachers. She couldn't make out any movement on the playing field, nor in the stadium seating. But she figured she just had to wait. Wait until she heard something, or saw something. The sun would bring answers.

Steph shifted a little, putting one knee on the ground for stability, resting her gun hand on the back of a chair and her chin on the back of that hand. She sat still like that for about five seconds, then she moved.

She moved, because something pressed against the back of her head.

Then, a voice behind her said, 'Hello, Steph.'

•

Walker moved quietly through the entrance area of the stadium. It was dark and quiet as he headed for the nearest ticketing booth, where he could peer around a brick wall to the open entry gate leading out. Now he heard faint breathing. Laboured. Pained. He went around the

booth, the opposite way to the sound, and came across the sprawled body of a Russian, face-down, a gunshot wound to his back. Walker got close, reached down to the guy's face and smothered him with a hand. The Russian put up no fight, and went limp. A small mercy, and better for Walker too. It was quiet now. Completely silent but for the wind.

Then came the sound of a helicopter.

•

'This is it,' Oberman said, and Chavez pulled up close to two squad cars parked nose-to-nose across the 167, blocking it off. There were another two stationary vehicles a half-mile down, blocking the road coming in from the other direction. No sooner had they stopped than a police officer walked up to them and Chavez buzzed down his window.

Bloom got out of the car, leaned on his stick and waited for the officer to approach him. Wind and rain buffeted.

'You in charge here?' Bloom asked.

'Yes, sir,' the officer replied. Bloom's presence had that effect on people – in his presence, everyone knew who was ultimately in charge.

'You got SWAT here?' Bloom asked.

'No, sir, we've got—'

'Why not?'

'They've been called into New Orleans sir, Governor's orders. State of Emergency and all that,' the cop replied. 'All state police too. What you see here is what we've got – eight members, another two on the northern road leading in and out.'

'What about air?'

'In this weather?' the officer replied, then regretted it. 'Sorry, sir. Again, our air wing is—'

Bloom cut in, 'Anything to report?'

'Well, one of my guys thought he heard a gunshot, but it's hard to tell in this—'

'Thought he heard a—'

'Hey! Stop there!' the officer pulled his pistol and pointed it at Bloom – who showed mild surprise, but then he saw that the officer was looking just past him.

Bloom turned around, to see a young woman standing by the end of the Chevy Suburban.

'I'm a friend,' she said. 'Alice Richter. Jed Walker and Steph Mensch are in there.'

Bloom turned to the officer and motioned to him to lower his weapon, and then he turned around and closed the distance to Alice.

'You're Marty Bloom, right?' Alice said. 'Walker described you.'

'You're Robert Richter's kid,' Bloom said.

'That's right.'

'I'm sorry, for what it's worth,' Bloom said.

'Huh?' Alice said.

Bloom quickly picked up on his mistake. 'Tell me, what's happening with Walker and Steph?'

Alice paused a beat, then told him.

71

Steph and Spicer kneeled side by side, both with their hands behind their head. They were in the middle of the field. Peskov had a pistol to Spicer's head. The driving rain was washing the mud from the Russian's face. He'd tossed Steph's revolver, and made her strip off her raincoat to check for other weapons. He had his last guy go back to the darkness of the ramp that led down to the players' change rooms, to watch over the scene with an assault rifle. The helicopter was coming in to land. It was clear that the pilot, once he'd spotted them with his landing light, had hesitated at seeing the scene of a gun being held on his boss. But then he was ordered by Spicer, via the tactical radio link, to come in and land.

'You double-crossed me, Spicer,' Peskov said.

'No,' Spicer shook his head. 'It must have bee—'

'Shut up!' Peskov said. He looked to Steph. 'And of all the people . . . but then, I should have expected it, right?'

Steph looked up at Peskov. He was smiling at her.

'Oh,' he said to her. 'Where to from here for us?'

Steph was silent. The helicopter touched in the middle of the field. The rotors stayed spinning at full.

'Get aboard, both of you,' Peskov ordered, then he followed them. He had them sit with their backs to the pilot, and he took the seat opposite, his gun trained on Spicer. Between them, strapped down

to tie points on the floor, was a dull-green metal case, a two-foot cube. Peskov stared at it a moment, lost in it. Then he looked up to Spicer. 'It's in there?'

'Yes,' Spicer said.

'You swear on your life?'

'Yes. Take it.'

'Oh, believe me, I will,' Peskov said, grinning. 'This will change the world.'

•

Walker went down, not up. He went through the players' change-rooms, moving fast through the dark. He could hear through the open doors to the ramp that led up to the playing field that the helicopter had come in to land. He started to run. Up the ramp—

Crack-crack-crack.

An M4, firing at him. The bullets pinged off the concrete walls, sending bits of debris all over the place as he dropped to the ground. The gunfire stopped, and he brought his machine-pistol up in front of him, a two-handed grip, the bottom of the extended magazine resting on the concrete, and he pulled the trigger.

Give them something to chew on.

Nothing happened.

The trigger didn't move. He felt around in the dark for the safety switch, flicked it, and pulled the trigger.

Nothing. The trigger moved but just clicked.

He heard the helo powering back up, the revs growing as the rotor bit at the air and started to lift.

Walker pulled back on the cocking mechanism, and a bullet spat out the ejection port, showing him that a round had already been chambered. He pulled the trigger. Nothing.

As he saw movement ahead, Walker tossed the backyard machine-pistol ahead of him and reached down for the sniper's Glock in his pocket—

When the machine-pistol hit the concrete floor of the ramp, it fired. Full auto. Pointed ahead, slightly to the right. Firing well above the head of whoever had been shooting at him. The noise in the enclosed concrete ramp was intense, as near-on thirty 9-millimetre rounds blasted out in rapid-fire.

Walker used it as cover, getting to one knee then looking down the sights of the Glock and acquiring a target.

A tall figure, running back for cover.

Walker shot him twice in the back. He went down as the machine-pistol stopped. Walker got to his feet and ran towards the playing field. Past the dead Russian. Past the lifeless form of Johnson. Towards the helicopter, which was taking off, ten yards above the field, fifteen, twenty . . .

At thirty yards, its nose started to dip and it banked to the north-west and picked up speed and altitude. As it left the ground, a figure was pushed out the open doorway, falling to the ground with arms flailing. In the light of the rising sun, Walker saw Steph inside the helicopter, and Peskov at the open door.

72

By the time Walker got to the crumpled form of Spicer, the stadium was lit with the headlights and flashing lights of three squad cars and a big Chevy Suburban. Police fanned out, weapons drawn. Two suited FBI men, also with firearms in hand, stood by Bloom.

'Talk,' Walker said to Spicer's face. 'Did they get it?'

Spicer was silent. His arms and legs were bent at angles not designed for.

'Did they get it?!' Walker yelled at him.

'Yes . . .' Spicer said. Red foam came out of his mouth. Shattered ribs had punctured his lungs and added to all kinds of internal injuries.

'What was it?' Walker asked. 'What'd they get?'

'Weapon . . .' Spicer said. 'Russian weapon . . .'

Spicer fell silent. And remained still.

Walker looked up from the dead man, and then headed over to Bloom.

'We have to intercept that helo,' Walker said. 'Fast.'

'No-one is going up in this,' Bloom replied. 'And all available resources are being put to the hurricane – it's hitting New Orleans as we speak. A category five is making landfall. The city's levees weren't made to fend that off. It's going to be an epic disaster.'

'Then track the helo,' Walker said. 'Steph's on board.'

Chavez shook his head, his cell phone to his ear. 'Air traffic control doesn't have it. No transponder, and they're not on any radar; the system's out between here and the Gulf coast – it's a dead zone right now, all power's out, everything.'

Walker looked at the dawn sky. 'They're headed for the Gulf. They'll be headed south-west. Mexico. A set-down, then transfer to a vehicle, maybe then overland to the Pacific Coast.'

'Lot of maybes.'

'That's why we need to intercept them in the air,' Walker said. 'What can we bring to bear?'

He looked to Bloom for the answer.

'Jed,' Bloom said. 'Do you know what was aboard that helicopter? What the Russians were buying for the Chechen regime?'

Walker shook his head. The wind and rain buffeted them.

'It's part of a weapons system,' Bloom said, standing in close, the end of his walking stick sinking deep into the muddy grass at their feet. 'A space-based weapons system, like an orbital cannon. And in the case were guidance chips for a mobile control panel. If they get those chips into a control centre rumoured to be recently found in Chechnya, they can launch a strike anywhere on the globe. With no warning. This isn't a missile-launch thing. We can't defend against it. They could take out DC, or New York, with one press of a button. They can ransom the world. Change the order.' Bloom leaned in. 'This is it, Jed. This is what we're working for – to stop stuff like this.'

'What are you saying?'

'There's an Arleigh Burke–class guided missile destroyer in the Gulf. I can have them vector in on the helo, and if their Aegis system can acquire it, we can end this with a phone call.'

'With a missile?'

Bloom nodded.

'Steph deserves a chance,' Walker said. 'If that navy ship can find the helo, then we can intercept it with—'

'If it shows up, we might have the smallest window to strike,' Bloom said. 'They might hightail it to Mexican airspace, where we can't touch them. If we get the shot before that happens, *we have to take it*. You know that. You know how this works.'

Walker looked at his friend. 'You've already given the order.'

Bloom nodded.

Walker looked around the field. The police were doing a sweep of the bleachers by flashlight, moving in pairs. Spicer lay dead on the sodden grass. The lights of the police cars strobed. Radios squawked and bleeped with emergency calls.

Radios. Emergency calls . . .

Walker looked to Chavez, who still had his cell phone to his ear.

Cell phone . . .

Then he looked to Alice, sitting in the back seat of the Chevy Suburban. He ran over to her.

'The phone,' Walker said. 'Did Steph take the phone?'

Alice nodded, then said, 'They killed my father, didn't they?'

Walker looked at her face, the sadness in her eyes. 'Yes. I'm sorry.'

'Get them,' Alice said. 'All of them.' She buzzed her window back up and then cupped her face in her hands.

Walker picked up Steph's discarded raincoat and checked it over. Nothing. He turned to the others. Rain whipped at all of them.

'Steph has a cell phone on her,' Walker said to Bloom and the FBI men. 'Get a location on that. The number that we left for you. We find that phone's location, we can track the helo.'

Bloom nodded, and both Oberman and Chavez started making calls.

'It's a long shot, Jed,' Bloom said. 'Many towers are out, just like the power.'

'It's worth a try,' Walker replied. 'And, if they thought that you might plan to have a Navy presence on hand, maybe they planned for that eventuality too. They might be sticking *inside* US airspace, flying over Texas, headed due west all the way to the coast, figuring

then that you won't shoot them out of the air from a Naval destroyer in the Gulf over the US mainland.'

'We got the phone!' Chavez called out. 'They're headed due west!'

'Texas,' Walker said, looking at Bloom. 'Get me the Navy helo from the destroyer. They'll fly in this. Give it a chance. We can run them down. I'll sort this out.'

Bloom nodded, relayed orders to the FBI men to follow through on, then said, 'I'm going with you.'

73

'We got them touching down on a small airstrip thirty clicks ahead,' the pilot called over the intercom headsets of the Sikorsky SH-60 Seahawk from the USS *Farragut* out of Mayport, Florida, currently on station off the coast of the Texas–Louisiana border after steaming at Bloom's orders from a port visit to Galveston. 'Must be fuelling up for their next hop.'

They'd made good time, the pilots under Bloom's instruction to pull out all the stops, engine damage be damned, and they'd been cruising at over sixty miles an hour faster than their quarry. Bloom sat opposite Walker. Chavez was next to Bloom. Oberman had stayed behind with Alice.

'Set me down,' Walker replied to the pilots. 'You guys stay in the air and keep them covered.' He turned to the crew chief. 'Have your door gunners keep the 240s ready to lay some tracers down range. We gotta keep that helo grounded – take out their tail rotor if you've got to.'

The crew chief gave a thumbs up.

'Four minutes,' the pilot called.

'Jed,' Bloom said. 'Let the Navy guys take them out at range.'

Walker shook his head. 'There's Steph, and the GreyStone pilot, an American. You want our Navy killing a British and US citizen on US soil this morning, when there's another option staring you in the face?'

Bloom was quiet for a moment, then said, 'Officer Mensch would well know the score, Walker. If this is all for her, putting yourself into harm's way, don't do it.'

Walker was silent as he took out the sniper's pistol from the pocket of his raincoat on the floor of the helicopter. It wasn't raining here. The pistol was a Glock 17. Full size, loaded with 9-millimetre hollow-points.

'If it comes to it,' Walker asked Bloom, 'do you want Peskov alive?'

Bloom paused a while, then said, 'Nope. But Steph Mensch probably will.'

'Drop me off down field,' Walker called to the pilots over the intercom. 'Then you guys circle out and approach them head-on as a show of force.'

The helicopter dipped lower, just skirting the tops of trees and houses. The sun was up and it was already heating up. They were just south of San Antonio. *Richter was right,* Walker thought as the Navy helo flashed by a windsock at the end of the airport, his hand tight around the grip of the pistol. *This wasn't about nukes . . .*

•

Peskov made Steph pee on the grass near where they'd touched down, at gunpoint, rather than letting her go inside the fuelling depot. After landing, an airport official had run out, Peskov had the pilot order the gas, then a small gas truck came out and the rotors stopped turning. As they were refuelling, the pump guy came to get credit-card payment, and instead got a bullet between the eyes. Also at gunpoint, the pilot finished the refuelling process.

'What's in the case?' Steph asked Peskov, standing a pace from him, looking him in the eye.

'Something that will see my homeland thrive,' Peskov replied.

'*Your* homeland?' Steph said. 'Russia? Or Chechnya?'

Peskov glanced at the pilot, who had switched off the pump and was starting to unscrew the fuel hose.

'You never were good at uncovering the truth on your own,' Peskov said.

'Why take me hostage, after all that we've done and been through?'

'All that *we* have been through? You did it all for *you*, and your Queen, surely,' Peskov said. 'Sleeping with me wouldn't have happened by chance. Nor mutual attraction, I'm sure.'

Steph's fists clenched.

'Tell me,' he began, 'did you ever get any closer to figuring out who killed your husband? I must say, I never bought that it was a suicide, what with his body being stuffed into a sports bag. That's very FSB, wouldn't you say?'

Steph's eyes searched his, frantically, and she then knew, and it was like her stomach screwed up into a knot. *After two years of trying to coerce him, it had all come down to this: Peskov didn't just have information that would lead to the killer of her MI6 agent – her husband – Peskov was the killer . . .*

'I needed you, Steph,' Peskov said. 'I needed someone to follow me, someone I could get onside, so that I knew what British and US intelligence knew.'

'No,' Steph said, her voice shaking. 'I never told you anything!'

'And I knew, the whole time, that you needed me. It was perfect.'

'I – I never . . .'

'That's right,' Peskov said 'But it's what you asked me, in the quiet moments, alone at night, in bed. That's what you told me. And it was all I needed to know. Your silence said it all. You knew nothing. You needed me. To watch me. To work me.' He smiled, took a step closer, and said, 'And look where that has got you, my little—'

Steph punched him, hard, an uppercut to the jaw. He composed himself and looked back at her, enraged.

Then came a noise. A vibrating sound. Coming from her back pocket. A cell phone.

74

'Hello?' Peskov said into the cell phone.

'Hey, man,' a voice replied. 'Sorry for the call, but I just realised – I, like, totally need all the numbers that were in my phone.'

'Who is this?' Peskov said.

'It's me, man! From the gas station? Three-forty-two and change?'

Peskov looked at the phone. And then he heard the noise. A helicopter. Then he looked back down at the phone – and he dropped it to the ground and stamped on it with the heel of his boot, again and again until it was obliterated on the grass-covered landing pad.

Steph heard the helicopter too. It was a far different sound from their commercial craft. This was a deeper sound. Louder. More powerful. More urgent.

'Get us in the air!' Peskov yelled to the pilot, who was already moving towards his open door.

The pilot didn't make it. Two bullets from Agent Chavez's service pistol made sure of that. He slumped into the cockpit. Peskov turned around, saw the threat homing in.

Walker was rushing him, fast. His shoulder was low – he was going for a brutal tackle.

Peskov brought his pistol up, and two things happened before either Peskov or Walker could act.

Twin tongues of fire from above ripped into the ground either side of the helo, tearing up tufts of dirt and grass. The inbound US Navy Seahawk stood on station, hovering maybe fifty yards above and out from the stationary helicopter.

The second thing was Steph's move. She kicked down hard on the back of Peskov's right knee, and he went down, careening around while reaching for his wrecked right knee, and as his body turned Steph paid a brutal left elbow, all her weight behind it, into his right eye. There was the sound of bone fracturing in multiple places, the full orbital socket destroyed with the savage blow.

But Peskov wasn't out. He was bringing his pistol up to fire, slightly back, over his shoulder, at Steph.

Then a third thing happened.

Walker hit Peskov, hard. A full shoulder, now at head height. The meanest tackle he'd ever executed, because he'd never wanted to kill a person with a tackle before. Have them stretchered off the ground, sure, that was part of the game. All good fun. But this was for keeps.

Peskov landed backwards, in an awkward position because of his hyperextended right knee, plus he had 240 pounds of Walker land on top of him. The Russian was knocked unconscious, either from the blow to the head or the whiplash, or both. He would probably never regain full cognitive ability – this impact was the sum of twenty or more severe concussions in one. And then there was his right leg, where it had refused to bend in its designed way because of torn ligaments and cartridge. His right hip dislocated, but not before his femur snapped in half, and that only happened because his tibia and fibula had been first to fracture, like circuit breakers that did their job but failed against the tidal wave of assault.

Peskov was out of the picture. All kinds of future pain was headed his way – and that was just from the people who would line up to question him from the US and British intelligence services after being rendered to some faraway black site in Egypt or Afghanistan.

Walker rolled to his feet, put a hand to his back and breathed through the pain as he stood. Steph came to his side.

'You okay?' she asked.

'I was gonna ask you the same thing,' Walker replied. He looked down at her. She tried to smile, then hugged him tight, and started to cry, and he rested his chin on her head and wrapped his arms around her.

Chavez holstered his sidearm and signalled an all-clear to the Navy helicopter, which pivoted in the sky and came to a gentle touchdown. The crew chief and a door gunner, M4s ready, escorted Bloom across the grassed field. The grass here was nothing like the swamp at Cajun Stadium. Here it was dry and burned in places, well worn and yellow. The ground hard underfoot. Texas. Walker felt like he was home.

'It's gonna be okay,' he said to Steph before the others arrived. 'You're gonna get all kinds of medals and promotions that you can never tell anyone about. Probably even have tea with the Queen.'

She held him tight. 'I don't want any of that.'

'What do you want?' Walker asked. 'Maybe I can help. So long as I don't have to move much.'

Steph closed her eyes and relaxed her grip on Walker. 'I got what I wanted.'

FRIDAY 2 SEPTEMBER

EPILOGUE

Jed Walker and Marty Bloom sat in a booth of a southern-style diner in downtown Washington DC. News played on both the TVs above the counter. One showed the aftermath of the hurricane, the other the war in Iraq. Walker's plate was loaded with soul-food favourites: ham hock, black-eyed peas, collard greens, fried chicken, corn bread. Bloom's was similar, though he had ditched the ham and had double all the rest.

'What exactly was in that Russian box?' Walker asked.

'It's about switches. Arming codes or circuit boards for a space-based weapons system the Soviets called The Dragon. But it's long been considered all old hokey stuff, Cold War–era crap, not a viable threat, let alone a big deal . . . Guess we were wrong.'

'Have we got something like that?'

'We worked on a thing called Brilliant Pebbles, a system of satellite-based interceptors designed to use high-velocity, watermelon-sized, teardrop-shaped projectiles made of tungsten as kinetic warheads. Basically heavy metals dropped from sub-orbital heights. "Tungsten thunderbolts," *The New York Times* called them, and the idea was that they could impact enemy strongholds below with the power of a meteor strike, obliterating highly fortified targets – like, say, Iranian centrifuges, or a North Korean dictator's bunkers – all without the mess of nuclear fallout.'

'And you can't protect against it with missile defence, like a nuke launched from Siberia or someplace.'

'That's right. No warning at all. Just – boom.'

'Did we deploy them?'

'Hmm? Oh, I don't know. Probably. If the Ruskies have got it, chances are we've spent more on it, so we're bound to have it and then some. Railguns in space and all that. The Strategic Defense Initiative, the current administration calls it, ostensibly developed to shoot down enemy missiles, but just as useful to turn against enemy targets. SDI, Star Wars . . . same shit, different name, right? The weaponisation of space, that's all it is. Dangerous. Scary. We've got enough problems with weapons on the streets, let alone up there hiding among the stars.'

Walker thought of Steph. *A star in the making.* He missed her.

'So . . .' he said. 'We secured the guidance chips, and Peskov is detained, so it's over?'

'Maybe.' Bloom wiped his hands with a napkin. 'Maybe not. The incoming Chechen regime put a lot of time and effort and money into this operation. If they've got the controls of this space weapon based somewhere in Chechnya, which could well be why the Russians want to hold onto the region so badly, they'll find another way to get it up and running, now that the easy way – handing over cash for the old original guidance chips – is out of the picture.'

'Why would they have been in Afghanistan?'

'A portable strike panel, I'd say,' Bloom said. 'So that front-line troops could literally steer the weapons in on the target. Like a rain from god. It would have won them the war, if they'd used it. I guess the Mujahideen got the better of them that day, and it was lost or captured, until Spicer's team found it and shipped it back stateside with a bunch of other junk to the storage facility in Nebraska.'

'Will we hear about it, before they get that close again?' Walker asked. 'Have we got other intel assets there? Or our European allies?'

'Hell,' Bloom said, stripping meat from a chicken bone. 'The European intel community's got more leaks than a Soviet-era Albanian-made condom, so the whole world will probably hear about it.'

'But we've got Peskov. That must make some noise in the Kremlin. Surely we'll see who fills that void.' Walker looked at Bloom. 'You know they're not gonna stop. Failure to a terrorist is a rehearsal to a success. They'll find another way.'

'Battling bad guys is asymmetric, sure,' Bloom said. He sucked his iced tea dry through the straw, then held the glass up and rattled the ice around to get attention for a refill. 'We have to secure a billion things. They have to succeed just once. Honestly, the only thing that scares me more than some all-out nuclear war, is the terror of one person, a lone wolf, acting alone, undetectable, unstoppable.'

'So, what happens next with this?'

'We're going to go after what's left of things in Grozny. Chip away at it. See what's what.'

'We?'

'The Agency. DoD. Not your concern. Or mine. It's been passed up the chain. It'll be handled, believe me.'

Walker nodded. He looked at the Iraq news on TV.

'You miss it?' Bloom asked.

'Hell no.' Walker absently picked at his food. 'I'm hoping that as part of the Agency, in helping gather intel that'll lead to policy decisions, I can play a part in having us avoid the next one of these. These wars are gonna drag. "Mission Accomplished" in '03, the guerrilla warfare in Iraq is going to go on for ten years, maybe more, until we get sick of it and bug out. Failed from the get-go.'

'No planning for the power vacuum worth a damn, I can tell you that.'

'People are deluded if they think we can make them into some version of us,' Walker said. 'We gain no wisdom by imposing our ways on others. Sure, I didn't want to go to that war, but then no-one wants to go to war, no matter what it is or how just the cause seems.'

'I think that's at the root of all our problems right now,' Bloom said. 'Until Iraq, the West was not seen as the aggressor. We do disagreeable things, but it's been defensive. Korea. Vietnam. The Gulf War.'

'What about Panama?' Walker asked.

'Panama was a picnic,' Bloom said. 'We've had plenty like it. This, my boy, is war for war's sake. It's more than a policy or ideological shift. It has changed who we are. We're *The* United States – not *These* United States. Get it? During its first hundred years, this nation was divided on multiple levels. The myriad differences between the North and the South, city and rural, the fight over slavery. The way Americans settled these differences was, by and large, by admitting that there was more than one "America". There were separate states, separate identities, and even separate loyalties – they were the times of "these" United States. The Civil War proved a turning point in all that. "Before the war, it was said 'the United States are,'" the late historian Shelby Foote said. "After the war, it was always 'the United States is,'" as we say today without being self-conscious at all.'

'And that sums up what the Civil War accomplished,' Walker said. 'It made us an "is". We've got to get back to doing what we do best.'

'Our policies might be peaceful, but if we're fighting asymmetric threats like in Iraq, our methods can't be less ruthless than the opposition. But when the driving force is war and war alone . . . Shit, you served over there, Jed, you know all this to be true.' Bloom sighed, then smiled. 'What's next, for you?'

'I guess I wait for my first real posting.' Walker looked at the TV. 'They've given me two weeks off. I might go say hi to Alice, make sure she's okay. Then head back to Texas. See Eve.'

'Not Steph?'

'Maybe. Not sure.'

'You should catch up with your folks too. Tell them I said hi. To Eve too. Keep them all in your life, Jed. Don't make my mistakes. If anyone in the Agency ever tells you that you can't hold anything

dear in this line of work, that there shouldn't be anyone back home that you couldn't walk away from, don't believe them.'

Walker thought of Richter and his daughter. He looked back at the TV. The news out of New Orleans was brutal. It was like the government abandoned the city, like they did with Detroit, because it became too black for America to love. And now it was happening in real-time. *America*. He heard Steph's voice say it in his mind. *America* . . .

'Man,' Bloom said, still shovelling food from his plate into his mouth. 'These greens, with plenty of pot liquor – it's nectar of the gods, my boy. The greens alone are worth the price of admission.'

Walker was still watching the TV. The news showed a convoy of US National Guard troops and supply trucks arriving in New Orleans and distributing food and water to residents stranded at the Superdome and convention centre. The work of repairing the city's levees, pumping out the floodwaters, and finding homes for tens of thousands of displaced residents was underway.

'New Orleans will never be the same,' Walker said.

'Yeah, you're right, but she'll survive,' Bloom said, wiping his mouth with a napkin. 'I've been in similar places, fine places, overrun by war or disaster. Coffee shops and bars and drugstores are always the first to reopen. New Orleans may be broken, and she may take some time to heal, but the old dame will come back. Can't break soul, nor spirit. Same-same, but different.'

'None of us will ever be the same,' Walker said. 'We'll be forever damned for our lack of preparation, and ashamed of our response to this disaster.' He pointed at the TV. 'Our reaction to Hurricane Katrina is going to be synonymous with the worst of our failures. I've just got to make sure that America is around long enough that we learn from it.'

ACKNOWLEDGEMENTS

Big thanks to the awesome crew at Hachette worldwide. My editors Vanessa Radnidge, Claire de Medici, Tom Bailey-Smith make me a better writer. My publishing team of Fiona Hazard, Louise Sherwin-Stark, Justin Ractliffe, Jason Bartholomew, Nathaniel Marunas and Krystyna Green get my books out there to the world and into the hands of readers. Thanks to all the sales, marketing, publicity and design staff involved.

My family and friends have put up with me writing thriller number ten with grace and acceptance. Special shout-outs to: my awesome beta-reader Emily McDonald, editing maestro Melissa O'Donovan, and cheers to all my literary friends for helping me laugh while on deadline.

Thanks to my agent Pippa Masson and the A-team at Curtis Brown.

Nicole Wallace, thanks again for giving me a reason to put my pen down at the end of the day.

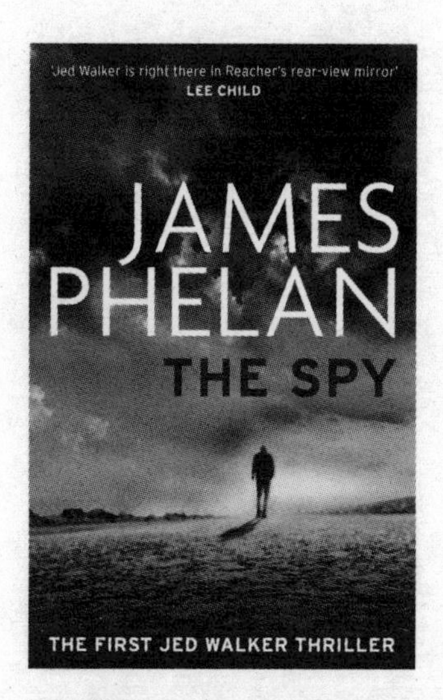

Jed Walker is the man you want watching your back.

A sinister group – code-named Zodiac - has launched devastating global attacks. Twelve targets across the world, twelve code-named missions.

Operating distinct sleeper cells, they are the ultimate terrorist organisation, watching and waiting for a precise attack to activate the next group. It is a frightening and deadly efficient way to stay one step ahead. And cause the most chaos. For ex-CIA operative Jed Walker, chaos is his profession. On the outer, burned by his former agency, he is determined to clear his name. Stopping Zodiac is the only way. Desperate to catch the killers and find the mastermind, he can't afford to lose the next lead, but that means that sometimes the terrorists have to win.

Ultimately, it all comes down to Walker: he's the only one who can break the chain and put the group to sleep . . . permanently. It's exactly eighty-one hours until deadline.

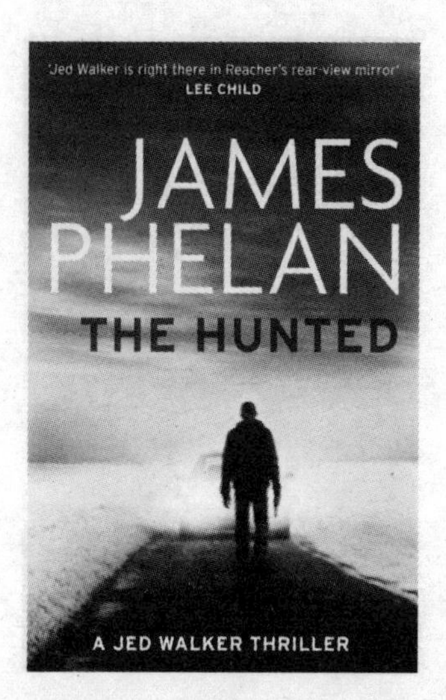

When the hunters become the hunted,
ex-CIA agent Jed Walker is the man you need.

In 2011, Seal Team Six killed Osama Bin Laden. Now, four years later, someone is eliminating Team Six – one by one they are turning up dead.

Jed Walker, ex-CIA, is an outsider back in the game. He's been chasing down a sinister group code-named Zodiac that the big guns – MI5, CIA, the Pentagon – have failed to eradicate. But as Walker follows the trail of bodies, uncovering secrets and making connections he's not supposed to make, he finds the answers are closer to home than he ever imagined.

Revenge is the obvious motive, but nothing is ever that simple in love or in war.

Can Walker find who's responsible before the body count grows higher? Can he stop another terror attack before more innocent bystanders suffer?

When the line between the good and the bad become blurred, when the hunters become the hunted, only one man can save us all.

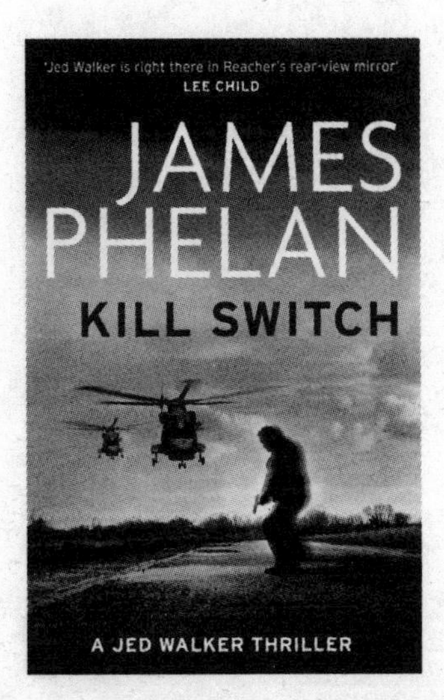

Jed Walker has 48 hours to save the world.

The countdown has begun . . .

The world is under cyber attack. The secretive terror outfit, known as Zodiac, are preparing to unleash chaos. The options for the hackers are endless.

From massive data breaches, take-downs of critical infrastructure, and commandeering military hardware, nothing networked is safe. Knowing where they will strike is half the battle. The only thing certain is their intent to create a devastating global catastrophe.

The US President has the power to enact the Internet Freedom Act – the 'Kill Switch'. Turning off the Net will stop the attacks. But it's not that simple. The US will plummet into pandemonium if electronic communications cease. The rest of the world will follow.

One man, ex-CIA operative Jed Walker, has two days to stop the terrorists. But for Jed, Zodiac isn't the only thing he has to worry about. To protect the future he must reconnect with a woman from his past. No matter which way he turns, he has tough choices to make. Not everyone will get out alive. For Walker the countdown starts now . . .

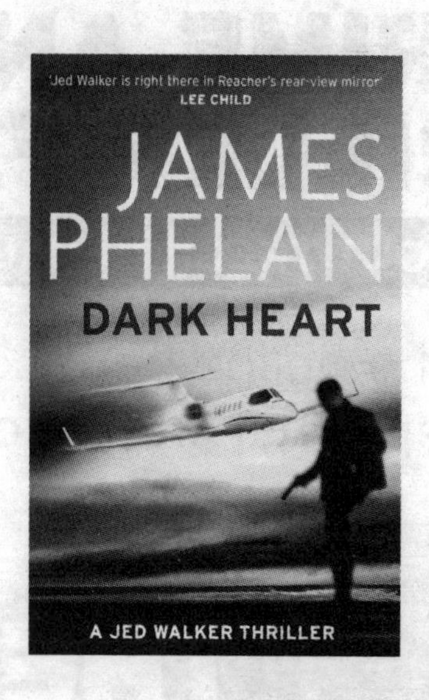

In war-torn Syria, a massacre survivor is pulled from beneath a pile of bodies. She is given one instruction: 'Find Jed Walker.'

Walker is ex-CIA - a man who thought he was long out of the game. Discovering a terror outfit is running people-smuggling from the Middle East and into the United States, he is drawn back in to fight their evil trade. At first Walker thinks these human traffickers are driven purely by profit and greed. But it is much worse than that – and it has ties to the highest levels of power.

As the body count rises, and deadly enemies stalk from the shadows, Walker uncovers the shocking truth behind an operation intended to bring America to its knees. He must work against time and powerful adversaries to uncover the truth behind the operation and prevent a global catastrophe being unleashed. If he lives, Jed Walker will learn the true cost of life . . . and the knowledge will change him forever.

Praise for James Phelan

'James Phelan has produced a big, juicy, rollicking tale in the spirit of Robert Ludlum. We haven't seen an international thriller like this for a long time'

Jeffery Deaver

'James Phelan is one of the hottest thriller writers to arrive on the scene in years'

Vince Flynn

'Must-read'

Amazon reader

'James Phelan has earned a new avid fan'

Steve Berry

'Vivid and suspenseful . . . an espionage novel with grunt'

Sydney Morning Herald

'Walker's so tough he's got muscles in his spit'

West Australian

wo

five years

The ex-CIA character of Jed

which was followed by *The Hunted*, *Kill Switch*,

The Agency.

James has also written five titles

and the Alone trilogy of young adu

time novelist since the age of twen

thrilling stories and travelling the

To find out more about James and his books, visit
www.jamesphelan.com

Follow and interact with James
www.facebook.com/realjamesphelan
www.twitter.com/realjamesphelan
www.instagram.com/realjamesphelan
www.whosay.com/jamesphelan